DANCE OF DESIRE

Last night they had danced for the first time in so many years. Last night Lily had felt feelings she had not felt since she had been an innocent girl, torn between fear of the unknown and hunger for fulfillment.

Tonight she was in Sash's arms again, as he suddenly lifted her from her feet to set her on the bed. Her hands were flat against his chest, and she felt the blood surge to her face as his muscles rippled beneath her palms and fingertips. Still she didn't take them away, even when he covered them with his own and stepped nearer. She let her eyes roam the perfectly chiseled planes of his face. There was something frightening about his beauty. Something pagan and savage.

He's like a powerful, sleek cat, Lily thought.

A cat about to spring on his willing prey ... in this place where both desire and danger refused to die....

Slow Dance

SLOW DANCE

by
Donna Julian

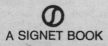

A SIGNET BOOK

SIGNET
Published by the Penguin Group
Penguin Books USA Inc., 375 Hudson Street,
New York, New York 10014, U.S.A.
Penguin Books Ltd, 27 Wrights Lane, London W8 5TZ, England
Penguin Books Australia Ltd, Ringwood, Victoria, Australia
Penguin Books Canada Ltd, 10 Alcorn Avenue,
Toronto, Ontario, Canada M4V 3B2
Penguin Books (N.Z.) Ltd, 182–190 Wairau Road,
Auckland 10, New Zealand

Penguin Books Ltd, Registered Offices:
Harmondsworth, Middlesex, England

First published by Signet, an imprint of Dutton Signet,
a division of Penguin Books USA Inc.

First Printing, December, 1995
10   9   8   7   6   5   4   3   2   1

This is for the eight wonders of the world.
Lacee, Jonathan, Jerry, Ila,
Morgan, Zachary, Gabriel . . . ,
and welcoming Anabelle.
You're each precious, and you
all keep me dancing!

Acknowledgments

Slow Dance was a work of love, but if it works well, it's because of the generosity of expertise, time, and caring from you:

Diana Burkholder—dance instructor extraordinaire. Thanks for bringing Lily's talent to life.

Michael Kahn—attorney and fellow Dutton Signet author, who disproves the theory that nice guys finish last. Thanks for always turning up the answers to my questions on legalese!

Eileen Dreyer—reigning queen of medical thrillers. Thanks for keeping me straight on all the nurse/doctor/forensic stuff.

Audrey LaFehr—*prima* editor. If your gift for dance was even half as brilliant as your editorial talent, then you were surely remarkable. Your guidance and faith are so appreciated.

Mureen Walters—super agent. Your efforts on my behalf have definitely been Wonder Woman impressive. Thank you, ma'am.

Anna Eberhardt—creator of the romantic sensual comedy genre. Despite what our Capricorns believe, your over-the-phone hand holding helped this one happen.

Prologue

Midsummer, 1980

It was a miserably hot night in the city of Rosehill, which is located on the far north-by-northeast border of the county of Cotton, in the state of South Carolina.

A faint breeze stirred the petals and leaves on the flowering plants and trees, yet offered only a breath of relief to an otherwise steamy July heat wave.

Even so, in most ways and on the face of things, folks who resided in Rosehill would agree that it was the "beau ideal" of southern-small-town-USA. Gentility, softly uttered drawls, and good manners were as indigenous as the multi-columned, deep-porched antebellum houses that dotted the hillsides. Intricately crafted wrought-iron, Spanish moss, and hand-woven sweet grass baskets, marshes, live oaks, palmettos, fiddler crabs, and oyster banks—all this was Rosehill, too.

Though its name implied a single knoll sprinkled with velvety blossoms, Rosehill was in actuality a valley edged to the south and east by water—St. Helena Sound and the Atlantic Ocean, respectively—and a trio of hills that crowned the city to the north.

It was on this exquisite and enviable acreage that the

founding fathers had settled. Today, more than two hundred years later, their progeny still owned the deeds, and the hillside estates now number twelve.

It was past the dinner hour, yet not fully dark, and most of the privileged who lived on the hills sat within the comfort of air-conditioned homes. The torrid temperatures had unintentionally accomplished an eerie quiet. Even the birds that usually occupied the waning hours of daylight in noisy chatter seemed to have retired into sulking silence.

From the valley floor below to the west, and from the fishermen's cottages and boats to the east and south, the dozen estate homes appeared palatial in size and in the twilight glittered like jewels. The residents of the hills were well aware of the majestic image. After all, their ancestry had claimed the land in order to establish dominance. Nothing had changed in the two hundred years since. The oligarchy that had ruled then, governed today.

Nevertheless, few were thinking about the business of running Rosehill that evening. Most were occupied with more commonplace cares. Oliver and Dixon Price, twin teens, argued about what Sunday night movie they were going to watch. Charlotte Forsythe, a perpetually weary mother of four, curled up with a new novel. Mae St. Charles and Jenny Lynn Afton chatted amicably on the telephone. Dan Lucas sat in front of his computer, getting a jump on his pharmaceutical sales orders for the coming week. Alison Hutton was upstairs, well on his way to getting drunk, and his wife, Sara, was in the ground-floor, converted dance studio at the back of the house.

She heard the grandfather clock chime eight in the living room as she raised her foot to the bar and began the exercise of loosening up before practicing the dance steps she would show her daughter, Lily Dawn, the following morning. A year ago, the family of three would have been sitting together in the den discussing plans for the upcoming week, or popping popcorn and pouring sodas as they prepared for their favorite television night, or lingering in a favorite restaurant, content to sit there and talk long after the last of their dinner dishes had been cleared.

Sara sighed. So much had changed.

She met her reflection in the mirror that covered the length of one entire wall. At thirty-two, she was a beautiful woman. Her long, black hair gleamed with youthful luster, her eyes, as dark as her thick mane, sparkled with vigor though perhaps with less wonder, and her honey-golden skin was soft and unlined. Yet there was subtle evidence of the ravages being claimed by time and unhappiness. Her lips, now, tilted into a smile less and less frequently, and rarely did her cheeks glow with passion as they had in the early years of her marriage. It wasn't Ali's fault, though. No, he was a victim as surely as she.

She glanced at the ceiling, wincing as she heard what she knew was her husband knocking into something in their bedroom. She loved him every bit as much as she had the day she'd exchanged wedding vows with him. But for the first time in her life, she was beginning to understand the old saw, "sometimes love isn't enough."

Ali loved her, too. Of that she was as certain as she was that others hated her.

A frown marred her smooth brow as she lowered her leg from the exercise bar and crossed the room to insert a tape in the stereo. Her hand trembled as she rifled through the cassette case.

Hate. That was the problem. Hatred as raw and mean as an open wound. And from whom? From his own, that's who! From his neighbors and kin. The pillars of society, the crème de la crème. The perfect, old money, blue bloods. Those who spoke in hushed drawls, wielded power with wolflike craftiness behind lambs' masks, and raised their harmonizing soprano and baritone voices for the hymns at Sunday services.

Damned lying hypocrites. Bigots, every one of them.

She'd sworn she wouldn't let them destroy what she and Ali had together. But she'd been wrong. They had not been able to break *her*. At least she had that. She raised her chin a notch as she took pride in the empty victory. For they'd started to work on Ali.

A noise near the kitchen door stopped her just as she was about to insert the cassette she'd chosen for Lily Dawn's practice session. Sara glanced at the watch on her wrist. Only ten minutes after eight. Too early for her brother to be bringing Lily Dawn home from the ballet they'd attended in Charleston.

Canting her head slightly to the side, she listened. Nothing. And then she heard the door from her bedroom to the veranda creak. A half-smile tilted one corner of her lips as she put the tape in. Ali was going out onto the terrace. It was like a sauna out there, but maybe the fresh air would sober him, calm the war raging inside.

As the music came to life, filling the room, Sara began to dance. She swayed gently with the first strains of the haunting music, her Osage Indian heritage incarnate in the grace and elegance of her movements. Her long, straight raven tresses seemed almost to dance with a life of their own as her supple, lithe form interpreted the music as a sensuous, seductive rite.

Forgotten at once was her husband, her neighbors, even her daughter. Forgotten, too, was the noise she'd heard coming from the kitchen at the far end of the house. Forgotten as always was the world that existed outside her dance.

*   *   *

There were three hidden witnesses to the beautiful solo being performed by Sara Hutton in the ground-floor sunroom the doctor had converted to a studio for his wife and daughter. Not that any of the voyeurs had intended to spy.

Sixteen-year-old Sash Rivers, for instance, had come to visit with Sara. He was at her house often. He loved it there with her. She made him feel good about himself, made him forget the way his stepmother caused him to feel.

He'd planned to knock on the kitchen door and ask if she and Lily minded some company. Even though it was Sunday, Sash knew that Sara's husband was often at the hospital. But as he'd approached the Hutton house from the back, he'd caught sight of her standing at the entertainment center in the dance studio. She was dressed in a form-fitting black unitard, and as she started to dance, Sash was mesmerized. Despite his discomfort at watching her covertly, he was unable to move as he reveled in her incredible beauty. Then he saw Dr. Alison come out onto the veranda above, and he knew his visit would have to be postponed. As much as he wanted to be with her, to hear her voice, see her smile, or feel her casual touch when she passed him by, it would have to wait. But he could watch her for another minute or two. What would that hurt? Nothing. Then why did it piss him off?

Hugging his knees, he jabbed his kneecaps with the sharp edge of his chin as he glared at the man above him on the veranda. Why the hell wasn't he at the hospital like he was supposed to be?

Well, suppose Sash didn't care if he was home. Suppose he went ahead up to the house and visited Sara anyway? He could surprise her. Probably Dr. Hutton wouldn't even know he was there.

Sash crept along the hedge that rimmed the west side of the property.

And what if he did come downstairs and find Sash with Sara? No big deal. Doc Hutton wasn't a bad guy. Not really. He was just married to the woman Sash loved.

Sash's eleven-year-old half-sister, Imogene, had followed him, knowing he was probably on his way to see Ms. Sara. She'd hoped to catch him going into the Hutton house so she could tell her mother. Sash was forbidden from spending time with their neighbor. Not that he paid any attention to what Imogene's mother said.

When Sash stopped in the shadow of a small copse of mimosa trees, Imogene was disappointed. Maybe he wasn't going to see her after all.

Sweat trickled from her pale hairline. Genie swiped at it with the back of her forearm. Geez, it was hot. If Sash didn't do nothing but watch Lily's mom dance, she was going back home.

Glancing over her shoulder at the road that wound up the hillside to make sure her mother wasn't returning from her meeting at the church, Genie chewed uncertainly on the inside of her cheek. Maybe she should go home anyway. Even if she got to tell on Sash for going inside Ms. Sara's, it would hardly be worth it if she got grounded for sneaking out after being told specifically to stay inside.

She caught sight of Sash's profile in that instant and stubbornly opted for her original plan of watching him. It wasn't that she didn't love her half-brother. She did. Who wouldn't love him? Sash was gorgeous! Tall, dark, and handsome . . . and sometimes dangerous.

Maybe that was why as much as she loved Sash, she hated him, too. Genie frowned. He could be really scary when he was angry. Even when he was only sulking.

He did that a lot. Her mama said it was the dark blood he'd inherited from his mother; said she'd been a Russian gypsy and that even though it was their Christian duty to love Sash, they needed to be careful as well.

He didn't look dangerous right now, Genie thought. He looked kind of sad actually, and she knew why. He loved Ms. Sara. He loved her a lot. It was a sin because she was married and a mother and much, much older than Sash. But sometimes Genie wondered if it wouldn't be better if Sara Hutton would just love him back. Then maybe the two of them could run away, and everyone else in Rosehill would be happy again.

Her mother would be happier. That was for sure! Mama hated anyone who wasn't pure white Christian like herself. Ms. Sara might be beautiful, but she was still a stinkin' Indian. All her, money, education, and pretty ways couldn't change that!

Imogene sighed. It was miserably hot and getting dark. She should go home. Forget all about Sash for right now. But what if he heard her when she tried to sneak away? A shiver scurried the length of her spine with the thought. She could just imagine the fire that would flash in those weird dark blue eyes of his!

She decided to stay right where she was. Besides, the music had suddenly stopped inside the Hutton house. She was too far away to see much, but it looked like Ms. Sara had left the sunroom. She raised up so that she half-stood, searching for the woman. Nowhere to be seen.

Good. Maybe Sash would give up and go home now. Sitting back on her haunches, Genie propped her elbows on her thighs and cupped her chin in her hands. Turning her attention to the mimosa trees again, she searched the gloom for her brother, but he was gone as well. Panic streaked up her spine only to race down her arms to her fingertips. Where was he?

It was then that she heard the scream from the terrace above, and then Genie was screaming, too.

Old Joe Joseph—nicknamed Joe Joe by the children at the elementary school where he'd been a janitor for more than thirty years before retiring ten years ago—often did odd jobs for Doctor Hutton's missus. She'd arrived at his front door on Friday to ask if he could check out the lawn sprinkler system which had quit working the day before. Joe Joe knew she could have called the company that had installed it for her husband, but he knew, too, that she wouldn't. She never did. She always called on him. Had given him work for more than eight years now. Made his life considerably easier with the extra money. Even recommended him to some of the other fine folks who lived up on the hills. A few had called him a time or two. Joe didn't forget kindnesses. That was why he'd come up the hill today after Sunday services. He'd promised to get it fixed before the weekend was over, and he'd kept his word.

Soon as he'd satisfied himself that the system was working good as new again, he'd eased onto the bench inside the Hutton's gazebo behind the house, intending on resting some before making the long walk back down to his own little house. He'd closed his eyes thinking it was just about hot enough to thaw Ms. Eudora Rivers's frigid little titties. Then with a deep rumbling laugh, he'd fallen asleep.

He awakened now, sitting up quickly and not too awkwardly considering his advanced age. His old heart was pounding out a real drumbeat and for just a second or two he wasn't sure what it was that had awakened him with such a start. The same deep, rolling laughter that had rocked him to sleep more than two hours before, shook him into complete wakefulness now. He'd been dreaming about his wife, dead more than twenty years already. He shook his head and scratched at his scalp beneath the cap of silvery wire hair. Amazing how real a man's mind could make a dream seem. Why, he wouldn't be surprised to look up and see—

His eyes widened as he forgot the dream and watched the nightmare unfolding above him on the veranda.

The doctor was stumbling backward onto the terrace from one of the rooms. He was screaming, and lord if it wasn't the wail of a mortally wounded animal. And there was Ms. Sara, too, her arms outstretched as she rushed after him.

From the gazebo more than thirty feet from the house, he thought he heard her scream as well. Was it possible for a human to make a sound like that? Like the shrill screech of a crazed falcon?

The old black man felt his lips stretch taut as they drew back away from his teeth in protest against the horror unfolding before him. Good lord, this couldn't be happening! But it was an empty, useless prayer, and even as he silently uttered it, he saw Dr. Hutton pitch backward and topple over the edge of the wrought-iron railing. Even in the shadow of dusk, Joe Joe saw the blood as Alison Hutton's body tumbled through the sky, recognized it despite his failing eyesight. And though it was impossible to see what Ms. Sara held up in front of her, he knew instinctively it was the weapon she'd just killed her man with.

He heard the child's screams begin behind him then, saw her dash from the trees toward the house, and knew she'd just witnessed it all the same as he.

His old muscles protesting, Joe Joe leaped from the gazebo's platform floor. He grabbed the girl, wrapping his arms around her thin shoulders and knocking her to the ground.

Genie wrestled with him, punching and scratching, and begging for release. "Let go! *Please!*" she cried, her child's voice breaking with emotion. "I've got to find Sash! Please, Joe Joe, let me go!"

But the old man held on, shaking his head. "*No, missy!*"

He was on top now, the girl pinned beneath him, though Joe Joe had no doubt his body would remind him of the cost of victory later. He spit blood from his mouth into the grass, then jerked his head in the direction of the house. "Honey chile, we find your brother soon enough. Right now, we gotta go help Miss Sara. Look up there, missy! That poor lady be needin' our help jes' now. You calm down and git yerself up there. I gonna go call the police, tell 'em there's been an accident over at Doc Alison's house. I gonna get an ambulanz sent over, then ol' Joe Joe'll come help you take care of Ms. Sara. Okay?" he asked. With her answering nod, he fell off the girl onto the lush grass, rolling onto his back and drawing in a painfully ragged breath. "Go on now, missy. See to Miss Sara."

Genie sat up, then crawled onto her knees, but she stopped there still torn between the need to look for Sash and follow the old man's instructions. She didn't want to go to Ms. Sara. What if she was crazy and tried to kill her, too?

Reading her indecision and fear, Joe Joe said, "Ain't nothin' for you to worry about." Then he closed his eyes as if he'd used up the last measure of strength he'd possessed.

Imogene scampered to her feet, hiccupping on the last of her sobs. "I'm going, Joe Joe, but you call my mama, too, you hear? You tell her to come get me."

Joe Joe nodded, but he didn't hurry to get up. There wasn't any need. He knew that somehow. Felt it in his soul. Maybe that's what happened when a body and mind got old enough, he thought. The soul just started doing the thinking. Maybe so, but the heart still did the feeling. He knew that was right, and his old heart was hurting mighty bad for young Doc Hutton, his pretty wife, and that sweet child of theirs who was gonna be an orphan now. A tear slipped from the corner of his eye and trickled into the grass beneath his head.

"He's already dead, isn't he?" Imogene suddenly asked in a strangled whisper, startling the old man.

"Ain't you gone yet?"

"He is, isn't he?" the girl persisted.

He nodded. "Ain't no doubt."

"She killed him. *Why?*"

Joe Joe flinched at the charge, but there weren't no sense denying it was true. They'd both seen what they'd seen. "I don't know *why*, missy. I jes' knows she had a good reason. I jes' knows it."

Chapter One

Late winter, 1995

There's no business like show business! The clichéd phrase played itself over and over in Lily's mind as she wandered the streets of the magical city of New York.

She stopped abruptly, laughter erupting. Magical? *New York?* Yes, today New York *was* magical. Today there was beauty and wonder even in the thick, hazy smog that wound itself around buildings and corners like a smoke-breathing dragon. Yesterday she'd hated the dismal city that had been her home for the last six years. She laughed again. Hell, yesterday she'd hated everything!

She hugged herself as she spun in a graceful circle then tossed her head back and flung her arms wide. "I'm going to dance on Broadway, New York! Lily Dawn Hutton is going to be a star!" With that, she leaped through the air, back arched, head tilted heavenward, and legs outstretched.

New Yorkers were inured to harebrained antics, even by delirious dancing girls such as this one who had just shouted the gleeful pronouncement for all of Rockefeller Center to hear before executing a flawless *grand jeté*.

After all, New York City was famous for its eccentrics. What was one more screwball?

So the only reaction to the beautiful girl's display of ecstasy was a muttered oath by a fellow intent on watching the ice skating below, and a roll of the eyes by an elderly woman who had been within inches of the dancer's light-footed landing.

Flopping down onto a bench, Lily was amazed to see her breath billow in front of her face in a vaporous cloud. She laughed again, this time at herself, but with no less delight. Hadn't Willard Scott announced that the high today would be only thirty degrees? Yet, she was warm, glowing. And all because of a conversation she'd shared an hour earlier; a conversation that hadn't lasted ten minutes.

"I've watched you work, Lily, and you're a very fine dancer, indeed."

"Thank you," Lily said softly, uncertainly, from the edge of the stage floor where she'd stood since being beckoned from the chorus line by the director of the off-Broadway production she was currently performing in. Was it possible that the man standing below and paying her such a compliment was really *the* Gerald Geldman as he'd been introduced? He certainly looked like the famous producer/songwriter she'd seen pictures of in the trade magazines. Same graying hair and neatly trimmed Vandyke. Same snapping, energetic eyes. But could the great composer have truly noticed her performance in such an insignificant part? Lily blinked, half expecting herself to wake up and find him only a figment of her imagination who had disappeared. Then he spoke again, convincing her he was real; that the entire glorious moment was real.

"I've had a vision, Lily. I've seen you on stage. Not in the small part you have now. In a starring role on Broadway, dancing to music written expressly for you.

I've come to watch you several times now in rehearsal, and I'm convinced that I'm right. You can act and sing, but your passion, your gift is your dance. You are another Maria Tallchief, and I want you to help me bring her story to life again on the stage. I can write the music that would showcase the talent you share with her, Lily. Think about it. This will be the vehicle that pays tribute to her while it's your name we would put in lights." He began to slowly spread his arms, his fingers moving as if unfurling a banner. " 'Lily Dawn starring in *The Maria Tallchief Story*.' How does that sound?"

"Unbelievable," Lily whispered to herself as she captured a snowflake in one of her gloved palms before standing once again and retracing her steps to Forty-ninth Street where she would catch the subway that would return her to the Village and the converted loft she shared with Errol Mills.

With the thought of her roommate, the corners of her lips dipped downward as if weighted strings were attached to the name. But they were, weren't they?

Lily gave herself a good mental shake that was almost physical. Nothing was going to blemish the day. Not Errol, not the weather, nothing! She was going to be a star!

Errol Mills was flying. The acid he'd dropped was some powerful stuff, and the virtual reality of the trip he was taking as good as the real thing. Better! Hell, he didn't have to pack! He giggled at his cleverness and closed his eyes.

Jesus, he felt good. Relaxed. Loose. Loose as a goose, and that was pretty fuckin' loose. Errol giggled again.

Colors swirled around his head, prisms of light dancing on air. Dancing. Just like the prima donna he lived with. Miss Goody Two-shoes. She'd wet her pristine panties if she came home and found him tripping.

The front door opened, and Errol squinted his eyes. A visage in black. One of those shadowy things like in the movies. Come to take him writhing and screaming into the bowels of hell? Errol put a hand over his mouth to stifle his laughter. He knew who it was. Lily Dawn. The great mistress of the manor. Better for him if it'd been one of those creatures.

From his place on the floor, he saluted her, then closed his eyes once again. Eric Clapton's voice filled the room from the stereo speakers as he sang the words he'd penned to his little boy. Bummer, Errol thought. Sad damn song. Make a guy cry like a baby. Shit, life was sad. Look at him. An actor without an act. Was there anything sadder than that? And then he looked up into Lily's angry face. Fuckin' A, there was! Losing the woman you loved was a lot worse. And then he was laughing again.

Lily let herself into the apartment again eight hours later. This time Errol was seated at the table in the kitchen area, head in hands.

He spoke first. "Hi, babe. How'd the show go?"

Lily dropped her dance bag, then her gloves and coat onto the chair next to him. Tossing her head and shaking her long hair loose, she went to the refrigerator without answering and grabbed a bottle of Evian water.

"So, this is how it's gonna be, huh? You gonna give me the silent treatment all night."

Lily sighed and rested her forehead against the refrigerator door. "I'm tired, Errol. Give it a rest, okay?"

"What? I just asked how the show went."

Lily straightened, twisted the cap off the bottle and in a neat little *fouetté*, spun around and kicked the fridge door shut, then crossed the room to flop down onto the sofa. "Fine. It went fine."

Errol pushed himself from his chair, following her. He sat beside her and laid a hand on her knee. "Don't be sore, baby. Please. I'm sorry about the stuff. I know how you feel about dope. I just had a bad case of the blues. Was feeling sorry for myself, and when Todd said he had some, I went for it. I won't do it again. Swear to God."

"It doesn't matter, Errol. As long as you don't hurt anyone else while you're stoned, I don't care what you do anymore."

Errol started to make a joke, thought better of it. Besides, the truth of her indifference hurt. "Yeah, guess I knew you felt that way. Maybe that's why—"

"Don't!" she snapped. "Don't you dare blame your weaknesses on me. I've been too damned good to you for you to try and lay your sins at my feet."

"Oh, yeah. You've been a virtual saint, baby! Why, if it wasn't for you, I'd probably be lying in some gutter somewhere. I'm thirty-eight years old, sweetheart. You're what? Twenty-five? God, how did I survive before you came along?"

Lily had jumped to her feet with her anger, but she sank down to the sofa once again. "I didn't mean that," she conceded wearily. "I only meant that I've been patient while you looked for another place to live. I haven't pressed you."

Errol rubbed his face with the heels of his hands, then let loose a long sigh of defeat and regret. "No, you haven't pressed me. You haven't needed to. I've seen the look of disappointment in your eyes every time you come home from rehearsal and see me still here."

Lily opened her mouth to object to the unfairness of his statement, then closed it again. It was true. Once, forever ago it seemed, she'd thought herself in love with him. Looking at him now, it wasn't hard to remember why. He was beautiful; a tall, blond Adonis. His hands were those of an artist, his green eyes those of a dreamer. He was a poet and a scholar. He'd once told her that the theater was as much a part of him as his soul. He hadn't lied. Lily simply hadn't understood how greedy and self-centered both could be.

Relenting as she always did, she granted him a slight smile. "Let's not argue anymore. I have some exciting news."

Errol grinned. "You've been discovered!"

Lily laughed. That was the standard line used by all of their friends whenever one of them announced good news. "Actually, that's exactly what's happened," she told him. "I still can hardly believe it. I keep pinching myself to make sure I'm not dreaming."

"So tell," he said, turning sideways on the sofa so that he faced her fully.

The trill of the telephone checked her answer. Scooting to the edge of the couch, Lily picked up the receiver. "Hello?"

"Lily," the hushed voice entreated. "Listen to me. You have to know. I didn't kill him. I *remember!* I loved him. They killed—"

The dial tone buzzed in Lily's ear. Her hand began to tremble so violently the telephone receiver slammed painfully against her ear. "Oh, my God," she said in a strangled whisper.

"Lily!"

She looked up. Errol was standing over her, his gaze locked onto hers as his hands worked to free the phone from her grip. "Lily, my God, who was that?"

Tears washed over her lashes, spilling down her cheeks. "I . . . I think it . . . I think it was my mother."

"Your mother? Sara? But that's impossible, Lil. She hasn't spoken in fifteen years."

Chapter Two

The Striped Tuna was a dive, and Charlie Wesmeier, the owner/bartender, would be the first to admit it. But it suited him. Upkeep was minimal. Customers were usually regulars who didn't expect anything but cheap domestic beer and rotgut hard stuff. And times being bad or good didn't affect the pub's business. Guys who patronized his place would always come around for a drink—sometimes to celebrate their victories, other times to drown their sorrows. Charlie suspected that Sash was here today to do the latter.

He slid a whiskey across the bar along with an unsolicited comment. "Must've heard about Doc Hutton's squaw dying up'n that funny-house where they been keepin' her since she murdered him."

Sash downed the whiskey in one gulp, then ignored the remark as he pushed the glass back to the bartender. Looking up for the first time, he grinned, though if the room hadn't been so poorly lit, Charlie might have noticed that it was a smile that didn't reach the dark blue eyes. "A little quicker on the service and a lot slower on the conversation, huh?"

Charlie's laughter rattled around in his throat for a long moment as he refilled the glass, then leaned forward to ask, "Hear she's gonna be buried next to the doc. That true?"

"How would I know?" Sash asked.

"How would he know?" Charlie asked two fishermen seated at the far end of the counter. "Like just because he lives down here with the rest of us, goes out on one of them trawlers every day, and comes in here to drink, we're all just gonna up and forget his daddy owns the company and the real estate our houses is built on."

"Too bad he doesn't own your mouth, Wesmeier," Sash said in an ominously quiet voice. "Maybe then I could persuade you to shut it."

Charlie was a big man, standing well over six feet. In his younger years, he'd been proud of his hulking frame that was pure sinew and muscle, but that was then. Now, he owed his bulk to fat, pure and simple, and though he might razz his customers, he knew when to back off. "Hey, don't go gettin' your skivvies in a bunch, Rivers. I was just making conversation."

This time Sash's smile was friendlier. "No problem, Charlie. I just don't want to talk about Sara Hutton."

"Hey, Rivers, didn't you have a thing for her when we was back in high school?" Tony Pfeiffer, one of the fishermen, asked.

"Yeah, I heard you was there when she stabbed her old man and pushed him off that balcony. Saw the whole thing, didn't ya, buddy? You and your kid sister both."

Sash pushed himself off the bar stool, laid a couple of bills on the counter, and turned his back on the three men. "Later, Charlie," he said as he strode toward the door.

"Guess he don't wanna talk about it," Jake Miller, the other man, said.

"Shit, neither would I," Tony said. "Took me a good

long while to get used to the sight of fish blood. Don't reckon I'd like to see what she done either."

"It wasn't Sash who saw it," Charlie explained. "The way I remember, it was his kid sister—"

Sash let the door slam on the rest of the man's statement. He stopped outside, jamming his hands into the back pockets of his jeans. His gaze was on the horizon of fishing boats rocking restlessly on a choppy, gray ocean. The gloomy winter day complemented his black mood. His thoughts on the cemetery in the opposite direction where he'd learned Sara Hutton would be laid to rest the following afternoon, he pulled his hands from his pockets and yanked up the zipper on his windbreaker. Tears blurred his vision, the result of his hard stare at the roiling water and not of the ache in his heart.

Turning away from the wharf, he ambled along the boardwalk. Since learning about her suicide three days before, he'd fought the memories of the beautiful woman he'd once believed he loved. But it was no use. He'd never forgotten her, never even stopped thinking about her for long. So why had he abandoned her? That was the question that kept him awake at night and governed his moods by day.

Oh, he'd found excuses.

He was young. Only sixteen years old when it all came down.

If only he hadn't gone into the house that night. If he'd just stayed where he was, it might've all played out differently.

He ran his hands through his thick black hair. *Jesus Christ. Stop thinking about it.* But how could he stop remembering? Especially now after what had happened at Tremont?

For years he'd avoided visiting her there. It wasn't difficult in the beginning. Hell, he hadn't even been in the States. And after he came back to face the music, he'd stayed away because he couldn't bear to see her as *they* said she was after the . . . accident. He'd asked. A mistake. They'd been only too happy to supply the gory details. His father, his stepmother, their friends. Said her beautiful dark eyes were empty as black glass. Talked about how thin and wasted her once strong, supple body had become. Even her thick sable mane had lost its luster, they said. Claimed it was streaked with white.

That was the truth of why he hadn't gone. That and the fact that he couldn't bear to face her after what he'd done. And then he'd changed his mind. Had to go see her and play fucking Truth or Consequences. Now, she was dead, and he was the one who'd killed her.

The winter wind was cold, biting, but Sash barely noticed its sting as he continued his desultory progress along the boardwalk, then through the meadow grasses that edged the bluffs, and on to the trailway that snaked upward through the hills to his childhood home.

He saw her then and stopped dead still with the shock. Sara. She was approaching from above, disappearing from time to time at a bend in the lane or behind a bush that was in his line of sight. More than a hundred yards separated them, but he knew her, would have recognized her anywhere.

But that was crazy. Sara was dead. Even if he didn't know that for a certainty, this young woman walking toward him could not be Sara Hutton. She was too young, her gait too agile and quick. He'd seen Sara. He knew how frail she'd been.

No, it was impossible. He shut his eyes, pinching the bridge of his nose with his thumb and forefinger as he willed the apparition to disappear. It was the combination of missed sleep and too much alcohol imbibed since his visit to that hellhole mental institution that was causing the hallucination. This wasn't real. *She* wasn't real!

Even with his eyes closed he could hear her footsteps as they crunched dead leaves, twigs, and gravel. He opened his eyes just as she rounded a bend. She was much nearer now, this Sara lookalike, and he could discern the subtle differences between this woman and the young woman of his boyhood memory. This girl was taller, though only slightly, and thinner—her figure not as mature. And her face was not quite as long; more oval, and the cheekbones not so pronounced. The hair, though, was almost exactly the same true black—almost blue in its darkness—and nearly as long. She wore it parted down the middle just as Sara had, only he couldn't remember if Sara had ever curled the ends this way.

She was dressed in black from head to toe. A heavy cable-knit sweater hugged her hips above long legs clad with a second skin of leggings that disappeared into black calf-high boots. Black had been Sara's color of choice, and Sash realized the dark attire had influenced his initial impression.

Her eyes were downcast, her attention focused on the path. She hadn't seen him yet, and Sash opened his mouth to call out to her before she could be startled by suddenly noticing him standing in her path. Too late, he realized, as she looked up abruptly, yelping with surprise and sharply breaking her stride.

There was the great difference, he thought, meeting her gaze. Her eyes. Rounder than Sara's, surely, but the real dissimilarity was the color. Sara's had been as black as ink. This woman's were the color of sherry. He remembered them in the face of a young girl. Sara's daughter.

"Hello, Lily," he said quietly.

She didn't answer at once, and he watched the exotic

eyes that had given away her identity narrow and darken. She opened her mouth to say something, then appeared to reconsider. Turning quickly, she started away from him, back in the direction from which she'd come. Sash grabbed her arm, stopping her.

"Lily, wait. I didn't mean to frighten you. I only want to talk to you, tell you how sorry I am about your mother." He felt her stiffen, though otherwise there was no sign that she had heard him. "Lily, please. Don't you remember me? I was your mother's friend. I'm—"

She turned them, spinning on her heel. "Sasha Rivers. I know who you are."

He smiled slightly at the use of his given name. "She was the only person besides my own mother who ever called me that." He continued, "Sasha. Everyone else—well, it was too ethnic.

"Anyway, I didn't mean to intrude on your privacy. You must have come out here to be alone with thoughts of your mother, the same as I. I won't keep you, but I wanted to convey my sympathy."

He started past her, but she turned the tables on him, sidestepping quickly, and blocking his path. "Will you be at the services tomorrow?"

Sash blinked, surprised, then nodded. "Of course."

Lily exhaled, and only then did Sash realize she'd been holding her breath as she waited for his answer. "Good," she said. "She loved you very much. I know she'll be glad you're there."

Sash knew how to cloak his feelings. He'd learned at a very young age the importance of masking his emotions. His heart slammed in his chest, but he allowed only the slightest lift of the corners of his mouth in response to the odd statement. "Yes, well, I loved her a lot, too."

Lily stared at him for a long moment, her eyes locked onto his as she seemed to take measure. Then she smiled, and his breath caught at the beauty of the simple gesture. Was it possible for Sara's shadow to eclipse Lily's radiance? He wouldn't have believed it two minutes ago.

She lifted her hand in the barest signal of farewell, turned to leave, then hesitated once more. "I'm sorry I was rude when I first saw you. You caught me unaware. It's such a cold, dreary day, I didn't expect to run into anyone. Especially not someone I knew." The wonderful smile flashed into place once again, and then she was hurrying back up the lane the way she'd come.

Sash fell in beside her after only a couple of long strides. "I'll walk with you. It's getting dark."

He thought she shrugged, and when she didn't protest, accepted her silence as acquiescence. Neither of them spoke as they climbed the hill. When they reached the edge of the manicured lawns that separated their childhood homes, Sash stopped. "I'll watch until you get to the house."

As if sensing the sudden tension in him, Lily followed his gaze to the upper gallery. She laid a hand on his forearm, smiling gently. "It's not my father's ghost, Sash. That's Errol, my friend from New York."

Sash managed a tight grin. "You gotta admit he looks sort of like your dad. Blond, thin . . ."

"The likeness ends there," she said, her tone sharp, and then she was laughing, causing him to wonder if he'd only imagined the jagged edge in her voice. She was pointing and he followed her raised arm to a red Chevy pulling to a stop in the driveway. "But here comes a face from the past you'll recognize right away." She cupped her mouth with both hands as she shouted a greeting. "Uncle Jesse! Back here!"

She was right. Even from this distance, Sash would have known the Native American. The long onyx-black hair and barn-brown skin were telltale, but it was the man's fluid grace as he approached that distinguished him from other men.

Sash stood back as Jesse and Lily exchanged greetings. Obviously uncle and niece were close though it was apparent from the smiles and eager hugs and kisses that it had been a while since the two had seen one another.

When Jesse looked his way, Sash extended his hand, grinning as Sara's brother accepted it without hesitation. "It's good to see you, Dr. Two Moons."

The man grinned. "Just Jesse, please. I know your mama insisted you call me by my last name, but you're a man now."

"I want you to know how sorry I am—"

"Thank you," Jesse said, his deep voice not raised in the slightest, yet somehow colder, more remote.

"Well, I'd better be getting back down to the docks. Got some business to attend to before it gets dark."

"Will your family be attending the services with you tomorrow?" Lily asked.

Sash looked over his shoulder at the house he'd grown up in, then shook his head as he met her gaze once again. "I suppose they'll be there, just not with me. I keep my own schedule these days. Why do you ask?"

The wind had picked up, and Lily captured her long hair in one of her hands as she answered, a gesture that reminded Sash painfully of her mother. He barely recorded her response. In fact he was more than halfway home before he registered it. Then he stopped to look back up at the hill as if by doing so he could make sense out of the enigmatic statement.

"Just curious," she'd said. "It's always easier to follow the dance if all the dancers are in step."

Chapter Three

As Lily and Jesse watched Sash walk away, she hugged her uncle's arm and rested her head on his shoulder. Both of them stared after the departing man until he disappeared from sight. Then it was as if Lily had been delivered from a spell. She shook herself and gave her uncle's arm a tight squeeze. "I'm so glad you're finally here," she said truthfully, the passion in her voice revealing more than she'd intended. Jesse's brows drew together, but for now he did not question her.

"Come help me carry my bags inside," he suggested.

Lily didn't move at once. Instead, her gaze went back to the place where Sash had disappeared from sight. "For a few minutes I actually forgot she was really dead, Uncle Jesse. She was my mother! How could I forget even for a second?"

"Your head was turned by your handsome visitor, I think. When the view before us is so full, we often lose sight of what is behind us. Your mother would forgive your momentary lapse." Gently extracting himself from her grasp, he circled her shoulders with his arm and led her toward the rental car parked in the driveway. "She often remarked on that boy's rare beauty. I'm certain she wouldn't criticize you for appreciating his good looks now, which maturity has only enhanced."

Lily felt her face catch flame, but she laughed in spite of herself. "Can I ask you a question?" Then, not waiting for permission to continue, she rushed on. "Do you practice up on your shaman wise-man routine before your visits with me?"

Laughter rumbled almost silently from the man beside her, but his tone was decidedly sober when he replied. "I fear I did you a great injustice when I took you to live with me. I failed to teach you respect. Perhaps if I had left you with your father's people . . ."

He felt her stiffen beneath his arm and knew the time for levity was past. "Let's go inside. We can come back for my luggage later. I think it is time for you to tell me what you left unsaid on the telephone."

"I'm looking forward to seeing Rebecca again," she said, speaking of the Osage Indian woman only three years her senior, whom he'd married less than a year before. "But not just yet."

He smiled. "That'll work out then, because she didn't come with me. It's too near her delivery date to chance traveling."

At mention of the baby cousin who would be arriving within the next six weeks or so, the lines in Lily's face disappeared for an instant. They returned with her next thought. "Errol is here," she said.

"And you prefer that we speak in private," he interpreted for her.

Lily shrugged her shoulders. "I don't think there's anything he doesn't know about." Her uncle didn't approve of her relationship with Errol even though she'd assured him that they were no longer romantically involved. She stopped to turn and stand in front of Jesse. "Look, I didn't want him to come with me, but he insisted. Errol has a lot of faults, but he's a friend, and he's been there for me. It's just that I've been waiting to talk to you, tell you some things I didn't go into on the phone, and I don't want his opinions to influence your impressions."

Jesse stared into her eyes for a long moment before nodding. "Let's go for a drive. We'll go to the beach. I've missed the ocean."

Neither of them spoke until Jesse had pulled into the cordoned parking lot that overlooked a long section of deserted coastline. Even then, they shared the drama nature was acting out for them in silence.

Waves rolled lazily, almost seeming to stretch and reach out as they broke into frothy whitecaps before languidly receding once again.

Lily hugged herself as her cognac-brown eyes scanned the bleak horizon, her hands rubbing her upper arms briskly though Jesse hadn't cut the engine and it was warm inside the car. "As a child I loved coming to the beach in the summer," she said. "I think I like this winter ocean even better now. It's so gloomy and lonesome. It suits my dark side."

"Or perhaps it sanctions your grief."

"Maybe," she agreed as tears burned behind her eyes. "I don't think her heart just stopped," she said abruptly.

Jesse didn't reply, and Lily knew he would wait for her to explain the surprising comment. Choking back the threat of tears, she continued.

"She called me, Uncle Jesse. On the telephone. It was a week ago today. She was whispering so I didn't recognize her voice at first, but she sounded desperate. She said, 'I didn't kill him.' No names. Just *I didn't kill him.* She made a reference to 'they' and before I could question her, we were disconnected." Lily had been staring straight ahead, but she looked at her uncle now. "Errol was with me. I told him what she'd said. Of course he thought it was someone's idea of a joke. I wanted to leave right then and there and catch a plane to Charleston, but he convinced me to call Tremont and ask how Mother was before I went flying off on a wild-goose chase."

At mention of the institution where his sister had been remanded for the past fifteen years, a muscle rippled in Jesse's jaw. Instead of answering, he stalled for a moment by reaching forward to switch the lever on the heat control panel to defrost. "Crack your window," he said. "We're steaming up."

Lily did as he'd instructed, then inhaled deeply of the frigid salty air. Almost immediately the windshield began to clear and the pair in the rental car discerned a lone jogger crossing their path. They watched in silence until he disappeared from view, then Jesse brought the subject back to Lily's phone call to the Tremont State Mental Hospital which facilitated the criminally insane. "Did you speak with Dr. Teggs?"

She shook her head. "No, he's on vacation in Europe. But one of the nurses assured me that Mother was asleep in her room. I told her about the telephone call and insisted she go check on her. She was pleasant and offered to call me back in a few minutes. I said I'd hold on."

"And was your mother asleep in her room as this nurse claimed?"

"No, but I didn't find that out then. I stayed on the line for almost forty-five minutes. Finally, I hung up and called back. The lines were all busy. I must have dialed that number two dozen times. I was just about to give up and go back to my original plan of flying to Charleston when the phone rang.

"It was a lady who identified herself as Dr. Lepstein. She was very—what's the word I'm looking for? Crisp. Almost brusque, yet not really rude. Efficient. I don't know."

"And she told you Sara was not in bed as the nurse had believed?"

Lily nodded. "She said there was a small fire, nothing to worry about. Apparently someone had dumped an ashtray in one of the trash bins on Mother's ward and it caught on fire. She said no one was hurt but that they'd taken all of the patients to another wing for the night. She explained that many of the inmates had become agitated by the upset in routine and it had been necessary to sedate them."

"Sara included," Jesse suggested.

Again Lily nodded her head in agreement. "Yes, but when I asked if it was possible that in the confusion Mother had gotten to a telephone, she insisted it was not. For one thing, she said, the patients hadn't been left alone for even a minute. And for another, she reminded me that Mother hadn't spoken a single word since Daddy's death."

"What happened next?" Jesse prodded gently.

Lily shrugged. "I don't know," she said, beginning to run her fingers through her hair over and over again, a gesture Jesse recognized from her childhood. "Let's see. I think I pressed Dr. Lepstein about the phone call and she got mad. Said I was perfectly welcome to come to Tremont and talk with the staff, find out for myself whether or not she was telling the truth, but that she certainly didn't appreciate having her integrity impugned."

"So you backed down."

"Sure. What else could I do? If Mother's condition hadn't changed, then Errol was right. Someone had played a sick joke. I decided to forget it."

"But when your Mother died suddenly your suspicions resurfaced."

In spite of the grim topic and the very real pain which had not eased for a second since her mother's death,

Lily smiled. "Wrong, old wise one," she said with a teasing grin.

Jesse smiled with her, relieved that she could rise above her grief if only for a moment. Though many of his patients teased him as relentlessly as his niece about his "medicine man" sapience, the truth was he was a licensed psychiatrist who specialized in traumatic stress syndrome. If they ascribed inherent mystical insights to his Native-American heritage, he wasn't going to protest too stringently. Besides, he'd discovered a reverence for many of the ancient Indian tenets that was compatible with his respect for modern science. He winked at Lily and played along, letting her set the pace with which they proceeded. "All right, impertinent youthful one, you tell me."

"I'd learned some exciting news about my career—which I'll tell you about later—so I forgot all about the strange phone call and focused on that for the next couple of days. And then Uncle Sander called me." She held up her hands, emphasizing her surprise at the unexpected call. "He's called me before, of course, but always with a purpose. A birthday, an upcoming visit to New York, something, but this time he didn't seem to have anything to say. I finally asked him if he was all right, you know? He said no, he wasn't. Not really. He told me he'd had a call from Tremont. Dr. Teggs had returned from Europe and telephoned him with a complaint from Dr. Lepstein."

Jesse sat forward a bit with this. "Don't tell me. The good Dr. Lepstein was still perturbed with you because of your phone calls and questions about Sara."

"Yeah. I thought it was all water under the bridge. I explained about the prank someone had played, but I assured him I'd accepted the fact that it was just someone's idea of a sick joke. We talked a few minutes more. He was solicitous. Really sorry someone had played such a sick joke. Then we sort of switched roles. He was upset, and I was comforting him." She hunched her shoulders, blew out a gust of air. "All of a sudden he was promising to drop everything and make the two-hundred mile drive to Tremont."

"But why, after you'd told him—"

"I don't know, Uncle Jesse," she said pounding her thighs with closed fists. "I argued with him. Told him it was silly. But he insisted."

"When was this? His phone call, I mean," Jesse asked.

"Thursday. The same day Mother died."

Jesse rubbed his deeply furrowed brow, his mouth compressed in a thin straight line as he digested everything his niece had told him. "One more thing. Did he get to Tremont before she died?"

"He says not. Says something came up before he could go."

"But you don't believe him."

Lily shook her head firmly. "Nope."

"My God, Lily Dawn, are you accusing Sander of murdering your mother?"

"Of course not! But I am accusing someone. Dr. Lepstein or Dr. Teggs, maybe even one of the nurses. I think Sander went to see her and someone got worried. What if she spoke again? Would she name names this time? Tell exactly what happened when Daddy died?"

"This is pretty farfetched, sweetheart."

"I know. It sounds fantastic. That's why I didn't get into any of this when I called you to tell you about her death. It doesn't make sense, and her doctors are adamant in their insistence that she would not have suddenly started talking no matter what the stimulus. But I know I'm right. When Uncle Sander went to see her, someone panicked."

Jesse gripped the steering wheel and stared out to sea until the swiftly falling darkness obscured it. "Let's go back to the phone call. I'm not going to agree with the doctors that she couldn't have spoken. Mental illness is almost as great a mystery today as it was a century ago. But let's use some logic here. How would Sara have gotten your number? Surely she still thought of you as her little girl. If she had called anyone, it would have been me, and she probably would have dialed the number to my parents' home in Broken Arrow."

Lily shook her head, her conviction unchanged by his reason. "Not necessarily. Like you said, we don't know what's been going on in her head. I've gone to see her three or four times a year since I moved to New York six years ago. I've sat and talked to her for hours; told her everything I was doing. It wouldn't have been too difficult to get my number from information. Or she could have sneaked a peek into the patient files and found my number that way." At her uncle's doubtful expression, she clenched her fists with frustration. "It's *possible*, isn't it? Won't you at least concede that much?"

Jesse rubbed his jaw and Lily cut to the crux of it. "I think she was murdered, Uncle Jesse. I think whoever killed Daddy killed her as well."

"You know how this sounds, don't you?" he asked with avuncular patience.

"Like I'm crazy, too, I know. Why do you think Errol insisted on coming with me?"

"Well, I have my own theories there, but we'll hold off on that discussion," Jesse said, only partially jesting. "Let's get back to Sara. Let's assume that something set off a memory; that somehow she was able to escape the catatonia, get your phone number, and then call you. Let's go so far as to assume she started the fire in the trash bin as a diversionary tactic so she could sneak to the telephone and talk to you without being caught.

Then someone found her anyway and hung up the phone. I'll go along with every bit of it, sweetheart, but I'm not going to buy a conspiracy to shut her up by killing her just so she wouldn't reveal the true identity of Alison's murderer. There were two witnesses, Lily Dawn. The Rivers girl was too young to be a part of some conspiracy. We both agree on that, don't we?"

Lily focused on an amber mercury light at the end of the parking lot. It began to shimmer in the tears that filled her eyes, and she struggled with her grief, gulping convulsively. At last, anguish and defeat won the battle, spilling over her lashes as she nodded.

"And that old black fellow, Joe Joe"—Jesse continued relentlessly though he was aware of her distress—"certainly admired her. Why all she had to do was wag a finger and there he was at her beck and call. I can't conceive of any circumstances that would have induced him to lie about what he saw."

"He never said he saw anything. In fact, he always insisted he couldn't tell exactly what happened. But okay"—she swiped at her tears and sniffled noisily—"forget about Daddy's murder for a minute. The autopsy report on Mother was inconclusive, Uncle Jesse. I read it. The pathologist wrote that there was no apparent infarction or other evidence of disease, et cetera, et cetera. I didn't understand all the medical jargon, only enough to know the doctors couldn't find a logical reason for a forty-seven-year-old woman with no prior history of heart problems to suddenly die."

"Other than enough long-term drug therapy to weaken the strongest heart," Jesse countered.

Lily ignored that. She didn't want to dwell on what her mother had endured over the past fifteen years. "What about injections that can induce a heart attack without leaving any trace?"

"I think you've seen too many Perry Mason mysteries."

"Don't! Don't make fun of me, of this. I'm completely serious. I know it sounds wild, even impossible, but I was convinced that she called me, and I'm not backing down again. It was her and I know what she said."

"And you know it's impossible that someone else killed Alison." He rubbed his broad face with his thick hands, then exhaled sharply. "We're not getting anywhere, and we're only going to keep moving in circles here. For now we'll agree not to disagree. I'll keep an open mind if you'll do the same, okay?"

Lily nodded, then segued from the subject long enough to ask him to turn on the dome light. "It's gotten so dark, I can't even see your face anymore."

"Let's go on back to the house," Jesse suggested instead. "We can talk as we drive. Your friend will be worried about you, and if Sander has returned from the office he'll be wondering where you've gone as well."

As he started the engine, Lily pulled on her seat belt absently. "That's another thing that bothers me, Uncle Jesse. Why has Daddy's brother lived in our house all these years? I mean, I know all about that stupid proviso that the house and land stay in the family, but what does that have to do with Uncle Sander living there? Couldn't the housekeeper look after it without anyone living there?"

Jesse shrugged as he backed out of the parking space, then pulled out onto the deserted coastal highway. "What difference does it make? When he called me shortly after we arrived in Oklahoma, he explained his marital troubles and asked if he could move into the house until you were either old enough to return or agreed to sell it to him. I didn't see any harm in the arrangement. However, if you want him out while you're here, I'll tell him."

Laying her head back against the seat, Lily sighed. "No, you're right. It doesn't matter." Then turning her head so that she faced her uncle, she added, "But I'm not giving up on this. You might want to warn Uncle Sander."

"Uh-uh," Jesse grunted. "Not me. He works out with a trainer every day. All my brawn has turned to blubber. Besides, you're forgetting that I have a very feisty young bride and a baby on the way. I have a duty to them to conserve my strength."

Lily was suddenly tired, drained from her reeling emotions, but she rewarded his attempt at levity with a soft chuckle. "Coward."

"Absolutely," he agreed as he turned the sedan up the hill toward his niece's house. Neither of them said anything more until Jesse pulled to a stop behind Sander's hunter-green Lincoln. When she reached for the door handle, Jesse stopped her. "I know it would be easier to find an alternative to the terrible circumstances surrounding Alison's death. Unfortunately the truth is not always what it's cracked up to be."

"I know what Imogene and Joe Joe think happened, Uncle Jesse," Lily said, "but I can't help hoping they were wrong. They had to be! Have you forgotten how much Mama and Daddy loved each other? They were crazy in love even after almost a dozen years."

"Yes, they were, Lily Dawn, but it wasn't Camelot. There were grave problems in their marriage." That said, he opened his door, blinking in response to the sudden bright car light. A hoot owl called out in the night. "Ah, another wise one adding his two cents' worth."

Lily wrinkled her nose at him.

"Okay, so I've lost my touch. Let's be serious then. Can I offer one more bit of counsel?"

"Sure," she said with another slight shrug of her shoulders. "Shoot."

"Look into your heart and find the memories that are stored there. Not just the happy ones, Lily Dawn. Search until you find them all. The sad and ugly as well as those you treasure."

"Why don't you just tell me," she said wearily.

Jesse shook his head. "Memories are only convincing if they are your own."

"You can quit playing shrink-shaman with me, Uncle Jesse. It won't work. I know their marriage wasn't perfect, but I also know she didn't kill him. I think I've always known it. I just couldn't accept it until I heard it from her last week."

Chapter Four

"It's supposed to warm up considerably tomorrow," Sander Hutton observed midway through dinner, disrupting the awkward quiet.

Lily looked up, acknowledging the statement with a slight nod as she searched her mind for an appropriate response. Coming up empty, she lowered her gaze to her plate once again. She pushed her fork around for another minute or so before laying it aside with a sigh. She granted each man what she hoped was a cheery smile as she stood. "I'm sorry, I really don't have an appetite for this. If you gentlemen will excuse me . . ."

All three men were on their feet at once, though Sander had risen as a matter of etiquette while the other two were expressing concern.

Lily brushed away their worries. "I'm fine, really. Just tired and in need of solitude. Finish your dinner. I'll see you all at breakfast in the morning."

She sat on the edge of her bed for a while, eventually scooting up to the pillow and lying down in a tight curl. Closing her eyes, she began a game from her childhood. Listening for night sounds. At first she heard nothing. Only the hush that belonged to winter alone. Spring, summer, and autumn were different. Noisy, alive, vibrant. But there were sounds that belonged to nights of winter. One need only be attuned. Her mother had taught her how to find and identify them.

The barn owl that had greeted her and Jesse a few hours earlier called out again, and she wondered if, like she did, the bird talked to himself.

She heard a dog's baleful howl in the distance.

A tree limb grated against a downstairs window.

A whistling wind rose and quieted, then rose again.

The sounds were lonely, too closely reflecting her own loneliness. Lily abandoned the game, reaching inside her memory for happier noises.

Almost at once, she heard stifled giggles in the hallway outside her door. Her lips responded with a smile as she recognized her mother's lilting laughter, then her whispered entreaty for her father to stop tickling her before he woke the baby. Even now, Lily wrinkled her nose. She'd been seven or eight then. Hardly a baby.

"But that's exactly what I intend to do, love," her father had declared. "I'm going to wake her up and carry her into our bed where the three of us will stay up all night watching movies and munching popcorn."

Sara had giggled again, still protesting between her gales of hilarity. "You're crazy, Alison Hutton. Lily Dawn needs her sleep, and you have early morning rounds at the hospital. Or have you forgotten that you have patients who depend on you?"

"Certainly not, madam!" Her father had fairly shouted, making Lily giggle beneath her heavy comforter. "But everyone knows a happy doctor is an effective doctor. And I'm happiest when surrounded by the two most beautiful women in the Carolinas."

Then she heard her door open and with her mind's eye saw her father's handsome face as he peeked around the corner. She'd pretended to be sleeping, of course, not even giving herself away when he'd lifted her into his arms and plied her face with kisses.

Tears leaked from her eyes, spilling onto the bedspread until it was damp beneath her cheek. Sitting up, she licked one from the corner of her lip, then dashed the rest away with her fingers. Scooting from the edge of the bed, she almost groaned with longing for that happier time.

She'd told Sash that her loss had been suffered fifteen years before. That was true, but her mother's death had reopened the painful wounds in her heart, inflicted all those years ago. Now they lay exposed and raw and further chafed by the memory of what had been lost. Still, it was a hurt that was bittersweet and impossible to leave alone, like blood sucked from a split lip.

Lily slipped from her room into the hall that was bathed in semidarkness, its only source of light a full moon dimmed by the lacy branches of a fir tree.

As she tiptoed along the hallway, she heard Errol, then Uncle Sander's voice on the landing below and knew the three men must be preparing to retire for the night. Quickening her steps, yet maintaining her stealth as ably as an accomplished burglar, Lily reached her parents' bedroom, and stole inside, shutting the door behind her almost soundlessly.

Then she stood still as she searched the blackness for a recognizable silhouette. After a moment, her eyes accustoming themselves to the darkness, she made out the four-poster bed and crossed the room tentatively until she captured one of the heavy mahogany posts in her hand. She'd visited the room earlier that day and knew that most of her parents' possessions—their clothing and such—had been removed at some earlier date. Probably within days or weeks of the . . . accident. But a few things remained and even in the darkness, she could see them as she had earlier.

Sterling silver framed photographs of the pair as well as one of herself still sat atop her father's armoire. His collection of vintage model cars was grouped just as he had left it on an oblong table in the far corner of the room. Her mother's needlepoint basket rested there as well, and Lily wondered nonsensically if the inanimate objects had awaited her return all these years.

The room began to come into focus, and Lily pivoted in a slow circle, taking in all the familiar, yet almost forgotten images as she willed more memories to come. Her gaze fell on Sara's vanity table, and Lily crossed the room to sit on the stool before it just as she'd seen her mother do countless times.

Picking up a gilded hand mirror, she looked into the shadowy reflection. For an instant she was as startled as Sash had been at the eerie likeness to her mother that stared back at her. Her fingers trembled, and she quickly set the mirror aside, reaching instead for one of her mother's cut glass perfume bottles.

Even before she squeezed the bulb on the atomizer, Lily caught a whiff of Sara's fragrance. Immediately dizzy with the sense of her mother's presence, she grasped the edge of the table, inhaling in quick, deep breaths.

She squeezed her eyes shut, fighting the yearning that throbbed in her chest and twisted in her stomach. With her eyes closed, she began to calm, and then she heard her father's voice calling to her mother.

Not opening her eyes, Lily spun on the stool so that she faced the terrace doors.

"Sara! Come out here! It's glorious after the rain," her father said.

And then, with haunting clarity, Lily heard her mother's answering laughter and teasing reply. "I think maybe we should move to Seattle. It rains there almost every day. You'd be in your element."

"Move? Are you crazy, woman? How could I leave my loving relatives and friends behind just to satisfy my craving for wet, misty weather year-round?"

He'd spoken in jest, but Lily felt Sara's sudden sadness as tangibly tonight as she had all those long years ago when she'd sat right here toying with the perfume bottles and listening to this very conversation. And even in the gloom of night, she saw her mother's beautiful face and remembered how sweet her smile had seemed as she answered him in kind. "Well, of course. How silly of me. Besides, if we moved away our life would simply be too perfect, and we'd have nothing to argue about."

With a sigh, Lily stood up and crossed the room, wondering at how heavy her legs felt. She wasn't ready to give up her visits with the past though. Not yet. Tomorrow she would bury her mother beside her father. But tonight she was going to spend a few hours with memories of them.

Outside in the hall once again, she stood still, listening for noises that would tell her whether or not everyone else was already asleep.

Silence greeted her and she moved toward the stairs and then down them. Once in the foyer below, she groped for a wall switch. Blinking a couple of times against the sudden brightness, Lily went into the living room. This time she didn't bother with the light. Somehow it seemed to her that it was easier to conjure her ghosts in the dark. This thought brought a smile to her lips. Imagine her preferring the dark. She thought her parents might share a laugh over that one. Hadn't her father always called her Fraidy Cat?

She sat cross-legged on the sofa. She thought of Jesse's challenge to recapture memories and promised herself to share some of her happier ones with him the next morning.

Relaxed for the first time since news of her mother's death had been communicated to her, Lily turned a lamp on beside her. This time she was prepared and kept her eyes closed until the ache that the strong light caused dulled. Then she looked around her. So many memories, she thought as she stood up and circled the large room. As she walked, she let her hands trail over the furniture.

She remembered the day her mother had invited all the ladies to her house for a baby shower for . . . someone. Lily had forgotten whom. Not that it mattered.

Lily recalled it was her father who had pushed Sara into hosting the party, if for no other reason than to show off how exquisite the living room looked since she'd decorated it. Sara had reupholstered the twin sofas, sewn the matching drapes, and hung the silk wall fabric herself. Ali was proud and eager to share it with their friends.

Lily had been standing at Sara's side when Imogene's mother had admired the new look. "Why, it's simply beautiful, Sara. But I must confess, I'm a bit surprised by your choice of color as well as some of your other selections. I'd have thought you'd prefer simpler lines, and more neutral tones; more of a southwestern, Native-American look."

Lily felt her teeth clench with remembered anger.

She went into her father's den, hitting the switch on the light, and leaned against the doorjamb as she stared at his big leather chair behind his desk. She could almost imagine him sitting there, prescribing meds on the telephone for an ailing patient, or . . .

Lily frowned as she doused the light once again and turned from the room.

Her imagination was becoming too keen, for she'd been able to see him sitting there drinking himself into a stupor as he had too many times in the last few years of his life.

She walked from room to room, turning on lights and pausing to recapture a lost moment before moving on.

In the family room, she recalled a favorite Christmas, heard packages being shaken before the wrappings were shredded, then the oohs and ahs of pleasure as gifts were revealed. But the picture was marred by the unbidden memory of a large box left beneath the Christmas tree after all the other gifts had been exchanged. Even now after all these years she resented the fact that her mother had taken time to shop for Sash Rivers.

In the kitchen, she could find no memories that didn't include the dark-haired boy sitting at the counter watching Sara as she cooked or seated at the table with them for lunch.

He appeared again in the library, his long, jeans-clad legs draped too comfortably over one of the oversized easy chairs. She snapped her eyes shut and willed the image away, but only managed to conjure a more recent picture of him.

"Damn it!" she said, protesting this unbidden image. Yet no matter how she tried, she couldn't dispel the chiseled perfection of his strong jaw which was no longer smooth, but shadowed with a two- or three-day growth of beard. His dark hair, too, was longer, testifying better than words to the freedom he enjoyed now; freedom he hadn't known as a boy except when he'd visited Sara.

Lily frowned as she leaned against the wall just outside the dance studio. This was the room she'd dreaded going into more than any other. She knew she'd feel her mother here more forcibly than she had anywhere else, and she wasn't sure she could stand the bittersweetness of it.

Yet now as she hesitated, it was Sash she thought of.

He had never known the love, and security, and happiness she had. It was obvious to everyone who knew the Rivers family that his stepmother, Eudora, hated him almost as much as she detested Sara Hutton. Perhaps that was why her mother had reached out to the taciturn boy, offering him friendship and a mother's nurturing love.

Lily had been jealous, unwilling to share what should have been hers alone. Even when Sash, his incredible midnight-blue eyes turned on Lily, and his full lips parted in a teasing smile, had suggested a game of Parcheesi or Chinese checkers, she'd silently accused him of trying to impress her mother.

Today on the hillside she'd seen the joy in those heavily lashed dark eyes when, for an instant, he'd recognized her as Sara. She'd witnessed the ensuing pain when he'd realized it was Lily and not her mother who approached him. Her jealousy had been replaced fifteen years ago by hatred when he disappeared before Sara's hearing. Today, for the first time, confusion took precedence over both emotions. How could he have deserted Sara when he'd claimed to love her so much?

With a ragged sigh, Lily pushed herself from the wall, turning away from the dance studio toward the stairs. It was getting late. She should be going to bed, beginning her struggle for sleep. But a yawn surprised her as she stepped onto the first stair. Perhaps her trek down memory lane had tired her enough to drop off without the customary battle.

Five minutes later, she was taking off her leggings and pulling her sweater over her head when her bedroom door opened. Choking back a cry of surprise, she dropped to a crouch, covering herself with her sweater. When Errol stepped through the door, she shrieked with anger, grabbing one of her boots and slinging it at his head.

Errol deftly dodged the flying shoe, then held up both hands. "Hey! I'm sorry." He turned his back to her, rushing on with an explanation. "I didn't mean to scare you, Lil. I've been sitting in my room worrying about you since you left the dinner table. I even came in here to check on you after your uncles went to bed. I've been waiting ever since. I heard you walk past my room and I came over to make sure you're all right. Just say the word, and I'll disappear back to my own room. But if you want company, need someone to talk to, I can do that, too."

"Have you ever heard of knocking?" she asked.

Errol glanced at her over his shoulder, then turned around and leaned against the door. Folding his hands over his chest, and crossing his feet, his expression was clearly devil-may-care. A smile twitched across his lips. "You gotta admit, that wouldn't have been as much fun."

"I don't gotta admit anything," she said, but she was suddenly laughing under her breath. "So stay and watch, and get your cookies off."

Dropping the sweater onto the chair beside her bed, she walked away from him. She even treated him to a provocative wiggle before stopping at her dresser to pose for him in her bikini briefs and bra. "You know, Mills, you're a piece of work. But I'm glad you pulled your little stunt. It was predictable and I needed that. I needed to be reminded that in this crazy, fucked-up world there are still a few constants."

She opened a drawer and pulled out a set of sweats, then modestly turned her back to him as she unsnapped her bra and shrugged it off. In seconds, she'd wriggled into the sweat pants and drawn the oversized shirt over her head. She tugged her long hair free of the collar and looked his way once again. "I'm going into the bathroom to brush my teeth and wash my face." She stopped at the door to peer at him over her shoulder. "When I finish I'm going to bed. I suggest you do the same."

His blond hair tousled, and his green eyes glinting with roguish delight, he started for her bed. "You got it. I'll be waiting right here for you when you come out."

Lily laughed in spite of her initial pique and though she would never admit it, for just an instant considered taking him up on it. What would it hurt to find release in his arms? To forget for a little while in mindless sex? To push away the ghosts she'd conjured too well? And then she sighed. "Your bed is in the room next door, Mr. Mills."

He shrugged in good-natured defeat. "That's always been our trouble, you know," he complained en route to the door. "Beautiful and talented, I can live with. It's the smart part that's always doing us in, sweetheart. If I was in love with a dummy, chances are pretty good I could convince her *this* was my room."

Lily laughed again and even went so far as to hurry after him and stop him before he could close the door behind him. She laid a hand on his shoulder and when he turned, wrapped her arms around his neck and kissed him softly on the lips. "Thank you."

"For what?" he asked, all flippancy gone.

"For being here. For making me mad and then making me laugh. For being such a good friend even when I don't deserve it."

He almost went for the joking response that came to mind, decided against it, and grabbed her up into a bear hug. "We'll get through this, babe. We'll find out what happened to your mom, then I'll take you home, and you can start thinking about seeing your name in lights once Gerald Geldman gets that play written for you."

Lily slipped from his embrace and stepped back inside her room, closing the door behind her gently. Maybe she should forget all about the mysterious phone call, put all the tragedy and questions behind her, and go back to New York as soon as the funeral was over. Uncle Jesse had offered to stay on until her affairs were settled. Uncle Sander, too, for that matter. And maybe once she was back in the Village, she and Errol could start again.

All of this was thought out as she brushed her teeth, plaited her hair in a loose braid, and slipped beneath the covers.

But in sleep, her dreams directed another scenario, and she found herself in the arms of a dark-haired stranger with brooding, deep-set cerulean-blue eyes, a strong, aquiline nose, and lips that were full and sulking when they weren't drawn back in a sensuous grin. He looked vaguely familiar, a handsome visage from her past, yet wrong, somehow.

In her dream state, Lily struggled against the desire that his touch evoked in her until she suddenly realized who the man was.

It was Sasha, of course, all grown up. Handsomer, yes, and a man instead of the boy she'd last known. This was the Sasha her mother had loved and nurtured. But her mother was gone now, and Lily was here to take her place. She understood then that it was all right to want him as she did, and she let him kiss her as his hands began to fondle her bare skin.

The dream-Lily writhed with passion and need as the man Sasha made love to her with deliberate and artful care.

"Ah, Sara," he whispered against her hair. "I've waited so long to hold you like this."

The jolt of his confession awakened Lily. She was breathing heavily and as she laid an arm over her eyes, she realized that her skin was damp with perspiration.

Shame washed through her, confusing her. Sasha Rivers hadn't been Sara's lover, only the boy next door who had loved her like a surrogate mother. So, why the strange dream and ensuing guilt?

Crawling from the bed, she went into the bathroom and rinsed her face with cool water, blotting it dry with a towel, and all the while refusing to meet her gaze in the mirrored shower door.

When she returned to the bedroom, she crossed to the window seat she'd curled up in numerous times as a child. She tossed the assortment of rag dolls and stuffed animals to the floor, holding onto only a mangy-looking brown-and-white rabbit she'd once inexplicably named George. She climbed into the alcove and hugged the bunny to her as her cheek rested on her knees. Outside, the night was as black as her mood. Still, she imagined she could see Sash out there, standing as he had so often in his youth, looking up at her house with that beautiful sad face. The face was still as handsome, she thought, recalling their earlier meeting in the woods. But no longer sad. Instead, she'd seen something else, something dangerous and seductive. A feral hunger that had caused her to back away from him, yet dream of him in her sleep. "You might seduce me in my sleep, Rivers," she said in a husky whisper. "It doesn't matter. I won't forget that when she needed you most, you ran out on my mother."

Chapter Five

It's raining on your parade, Mama, Lily thought as the drizzle that had begun at daybreak continued throughout the graveside funeral service.

Her eyes scanned the meager gathering for the umpteenth time as the Reverend Garrett recited the prayers and Psalms she had personally selected.

Most of them are here, Mama. Your and Daddy's loving family and neighbors.

How odd to realize they were *all* related, in one way or the other through her father.

Charlotte Forsythe, older, graying, yet without those deep caverns beneath her eyes that Lily remembered so well. Maybe now that her kids were grown, she wasn't so harried.

Mae St. Charles. Still frumpy and haphazardly put together as if every article of clothing were an afterthought she'd tossed on with the rest. Her husband, Stuart, a police officer if memory served correctly, was one of only four men in attendance. Lily supposed, bitterly, that for most, the death of a crazy Indian woman hardly warranted missing a day at the office.

Lily's lips parted in the slightest of smiles as her gaze met Jenny Lynn Afton's. *Moon Face.* Lily felt her cheeks heat with the memory of the cruel nickname assigned to the homely woman by the neighborhood children. Though certainly odd, Jenny Lynn had always been kind and friendly to both Sara and Lily and even now, she returned Lily's smile of recognition without hesitation. A moment later, she looked away as confusion clouded her simple features.

Lily's brows drew together in a perplexed frown. What had happened to the receptive smile? Had someone signaled disapproval for the open, unguarded sign of welcome? Lily sighed. What did it matter? One day soon, she would be saying good-bye to Rosehill and everyone in it forever.

Her gaze moved on to her Uncle Sander who stood behind his wife's wheelchair, and a twinge of pity twisted in her heart for her father's older brother. He looked so tired today.

Lily's gaze fell to the woman sitting in front of him. Marla Hutton. Her aunt by marriage, though Lily had never really thought of her as a relative. In fact, she barely remembered her uncle's wife except as "that poor, brave woman" who had survived cancer. Sara had talked often the last year before Alison's death about Marla's courage, especially in the face of the tragic result of surgery to remove the malignant tumor from her spinal column, which had left her paralyzed from the waist down.

Lily had thought her mother was too generous. Marla might appear quiet and withdrawn, but that did not mean stoic and silently suffering. Rather, Lily believed, covertly surveying the turned-down mouth and pale, cold eyes, it was a case of vitriolic bigotry and festering hatred.

Lily looked at Marla's two daughters. Caroline and Belinda. Lily's cousins. She almost laughed as she wondered what they would say to that reminder. Probably swoon with horror just like any well-bred southern belles.

Her gaze drifted to Marla's younger sister, Eudora. What a difference there. Though both women were nearing the passage from middle age into senior citizenship, Eudora had retained a good deal of her youthful beauty and vitality.

Her Uncle Jesse slipped an arm around her waist, and Lily leaned her head on his shoulder with an appreciative smile. Had he known, somehow, how alone she'd felt in this gathering of family?

Had he noticed as she had, that not a single tear had been shed? Oh, faces were properly grim, eyes downcast, hands reverently clasped. Still, Lily knew the tribute being paid her mother was one of duty. None of the fewer than one dozen residents of Rosehill in attendance had come to mourn her passing. Only Lily and Jesse hurt for her loss. Only they would miss her as they had for the past fifteen years.

Almost as if he'd whispered her name, Lily felt her gaze being drawn to Sash who stood slightly apart from the rest of the assemblage. Their eyes locked for an instant of pain shared, and Lily reluctantly admitted to herself that perhaps, he too cared that Sara was dead.

Keeping her head bowed so that the brim of the wide hat she wore concealed her eyes, she cast another furtive glance his way. There was no denying the anguish he was suffering. It was evidenced by the stormy darkness of his blue eyes, the lines in his forehead, the ticking muscle in his jaw, and his fisted hands at his sides. She should have been grateful for his caring. Here was the only other living being besides her Uncle Jesse who had loved Sara and would keep a memory of the person she had been. Still, his grief angered Lily. How dare he stand beside her casket and mourn her so openly! Didn't he know that Lily remembered the way he'd looked at her mother? The way he'd glared at her father when he thought no one was watching?

Someone was suddenly holding her arm and murmuring in her ear. Lily jumped at the intrusion on her thoughts. Errol was calling her attention to the reverend who was staring at her expectantly.

"He asked you to scatter the first shovel of dirt on the casket," Errol said, and only then did she notice the tiny silver scoop the minister held out to her.

A sob caught in her throat as she bent to do the clergyman's bidding, and escaped in a ragged wail of anguish that mingled with the thud of dirt against wood.

Errol wrapped an arm around her shoulder and though she was grateful, Lily turned away from him and into the circle of Jesse's arms for comfort.

She had vowed not to give in to the pain, not publicly at least. But the finality of that single gesture had penetrated the protective shield she'd erected over her heart.

Several minutes must have passed while she wept, for when she could at last step out of Jesse's comforting embrace, everyone was walking across the wet lawn toward their cars. Only Eudora Rivers, Sander Hutton, and his wife remained where they'd been throughout the service, apparently waiting for her attention. Lily ignored them as she looked around for Errol. She knew she'd hurt him and wanted to apologize.

"Your friend said he'd wait for you in the limo," Sander supplied.

Lily managed a thin smile as she looped her arm through Jesse's. "Thank you," she said. Then to Marla and Eudora because she couldn't ignore them any longer, "Mother would have appreciated you being here." It wasn't a lie. Sara had tried so hard to fit in. Lily believed she would have been grateful for the tiny morsel tossed her way even if it was too late in coming.

Eudora smiled and stepped forward to take one of

Lily's hands in hers. "I've asked everyone in attendance to my house. I've arranged for a meal to be served. Nothing extravagant. Just a light repast we can share as we remember our neighbor and friend."

Jesse must have felt Lily tense for he squeezed her arm gently in a gesture that was clearly a warning and took a step forward so that he was standing almost between the two women. "That was very kind of you, Mrs. Rivers. Lily and I will join the rest of you as soon as we've said our private good-byes to my sister."

Lily's personality was fiery and impetuous. Still, as a dancer she'd long ago learned the importance of discipline. She was jolted by the intensity of her anger at his mild-mannered acceptance. She loved her mother's brother more than anyone on earth. He was the only relative she truly considered family. But, how dare he?

She opened her mouth to protest even as Eudora turned away and Sander followed, struggling awkwardly with Marla's wheelchair over the uneven terrain. Almost at once she could hear her mother's voice chiding her. *Silly, darling girl. You are so beautiful, so talented. But what does all the beauty, all the talent in the world matter if you don't have charity? If you don't understand tolerance? And if you haven't mastered your temper?*

At the remembered lecture fresh tears burned behind Lily's eyes and in her throat. Swallowing hard against them, she lowered her cheek to Jesse's shoulder and hugged him. "We don't have to stay long, do we?"

She sensed rather than saw his smile and heard approval in his tone when he answered. "Of course not. The generosity you're exhibiting by making an appearance is enough. Your mother and father would be very proud of you."

Together they stood looking down on the handsome mahogany casket for another long moment in silence, then by unspoken agreement, turned away in unison.

They were almost to the cars when Lily caught sight of a stooped old black man standing alone in the rain, head bowed, hat in hand. Without a word to her uncle, she changed course. "Joe Joe?" she asked.

The man flinched but brought his head up to meet her gaze. "Yes ma'am. It's ol' Joe Joe. I don't mean no disrespect. It ain't my intention to bother any of you folk. I jes' wanted to say my good-byes to Ms. Sara." He hung his head again, this time shaking it from side to side. "She was a fine lady. It ain't right what happened to her. No sir. It ain't right at all."

"But—" Lily began but quickly stopped herself. Was the old man senile? Didn't he remember that he had testified against Sara at the inquest and later at her insanity hearing? "You probably don't remember me," Lily said. "I'm Sara's daughter, Lily."

He didn't look at her, but he nodded. "I know who you are, missy. Who wouldn't know? You look enough like her to test an ol' man's heart . . . 'specially with her being buried today and all."

Lily frowned at the man. He certainly sounded coherent. She laid a hand on his, stilling his fingers which had been nervously turning his hat. "I didn't mean to shock you," she said gently. "I'm glad you came. Mother was always very fond of you."

"Yes, ma'am," he said, nodding fiercely again. "I know that's true. She was good to ol' Joe Joe. I've missed her and Dr. Alison these past long years."

Lily's frown deepened as her confusion intensified. "But you do remember why—"

"Please excuse him, Ms. Hutton," a voice said from behind. Lily turned slightly just as the man who'd spoken stepped to Joe Joe's side. He, too, was African-American, though much younger. Only a few years older than herself, she guessed. Too young to be Joe Joe's son. His grandson?

"He didn't mean any harm," the stranger continued. "It's my fault. I'm afraid I'm the one who read the obituary in the paper yesterday. I told him about the service today, and he insisted that I drive him out here. He waited until the service was over, but he was adamant about paying his respects."

Lily smiled. Oddly, she'd never blamed the old man for the testimony he'd uttered against Sara. Perhaps it was because he hadn't claimed to actually see her kill Alison, or maybe it was because instead of seeing him at the courthouse as a witness against her mother, Lily had always pictured him at work on some project Sara had come up with to provide him a few extra dollars of income. "Certainly I don't mind. My mother would be touched that you remembered her, Joe Joe." She looked from the frail, bent man to the younger one, and suddenly she remembered. "Abraham?"

The man's dark face split in two with the breadth of his grin. "Yes, ma'am, though these days folks just call me Abe. I'm Joe Joe's grandson. I didn't think you'd remember me. No reason why you should."

"Of course I remember. I didn't at first, but I suppose that's because I'm not thinking too clearly today."

She lifted her hand, her fingers fluttering in the direction of the funeral bier in the distance to her left, and the smile that had crossed Abe Joseph's face was replaced by an expression so tragic, Lily had the urge to wrap her arms around him and offer comfort.

"She was a beautiful lady," Abe said. "I told her once that I was going to be a lawyer, and then I got all defensive-like 'cause I knew she was going to scoff at such lofty goals in someone . . . well, in a black man. I'd been sitting in my grandpa's truck, and she'd come out to say hello and talk a while. I was feeling kind of belligerent waiting for him to do the handy work for an uppity white woman, so I kind of tossed my dream out there like a challenge, a gauntlet, you know?"

"But she didn't laugh," Lily said, remembering her mother's pride in the young boy's ambition which she'd related to her father and her at the dinner table later that night.

Abe grinned as he shook his head from side to side, and a tear slipped from the corner of his coffee-brown eyes. "No, she didn't. She reached right inside the cab of that truck and hugged me. Embarrassed me something terrible." A sound that was part laugh, mostly sob erupted from him as he dashed away the tear running along his nose. He cleared his throat, then bowed his head quickly. "Well, it was good seein' you, Ms. Hutton. If you don't mind, I'll just walk my grandfather over to the grave so he can say some words over your mama. Then we'll be on our way."

Lily fought the urge to hug both men, instead merely stepping aside and thanking them once again for coming. But as she turned toward the limo where Errol and Jesse waited, she noticed that everyone was still standing by their cars. Every face was turned in her direction, and though she was too far away to make out their faces, it seemed to her that they stood very still. Too still. Their attention held rapt by curiosity about her conversation with one of her mother's accusers?

As she sloshed through the soggy grass, she admitted that in all probability she was being fanciful. The crowd of mourners had merely awaited her return to the limo out of respect.

But as she sat in the backseat with Errol and Jesse and Sander on the journey back to the city of Rosehill and the Rivers home, it occurred to her that Sash Rivers had not stayed with the others. She recalled the way he'd stood apart from everyone, his father and stepmother included. And what of Imogene Rivers, Sash's half-sister? She hadn't come at all unless Lily had failed to recognize her. Giving her head a shake to clear her thoughts, she knew that was impossible. Though the young girl of her memory would be a woman now, two years older than herself, Lily was confident she'd recognize her anywhere. If there was one face time would never manage to alter enough to escape her notice, it was that of Genie Rivers. Lily squeezed her fists in her lap until her nails bit into the flesh of her palms. Even a decade and a half later, she could still remember the crocodile tears that had poured from Genie's eyes, distorting her pretty Kewpie-doll features as she sat on the witness stand and identified Sara Two Moons-Hutton as a murderess.

Turning her gaze out the tinted windows, she realized for the first time that the rain had stopped. The day was still dismal and gray, missing the light and warmth of sunshine. Closing her eyes on the sigh that escaped her lips, she empathized with the dreary winter day. Like the rain, her tears had stopped. The darkness in her soul would linger on.

Chapter Six

"Nothing changes," Lily said, though she was alone and speaking only to herself. She'd been trapped at the Rivers home for three hours, almost smothered by the cloying, stifling crush of sympathetic neighbors and friends.

"Friends, my foot," she muttered, kicking a fallen twig with the toe of her shoe. "Busybodies, bigots, and hypocrites, more like it."

She sat alone on a wooden bench on the boardwalk overlooking the Sound. Dusk bathed the choppy water and listing boats in varying shades of pinks and purples, and the winter cold was quickly permeating even the thickness of her down coat. Still, neither the threat of approaching dark nor impending frostbite was as intimidating as Miss Eudora Rivers and her ilk, who were probably still gathered in her living room reliving the disastrous events that led to the ultimate destruction of the Alison Hutton–Sara Two Moons union.

Craning her neck, Lily looked up at the hill, trying to discern the moonlit pink house with its silly gingerbread white trim. The density of the fir trees obscured it from her vision, but she could still see it in her mind and hear snatches of conversation from her earlier visit.

". . . So tragic. She was so young, though I suppose living without a mind isn't really living at all, is it?"

"Ah, but weren't they spectacular in the beginning? I can still remember the first time I saw them together, Ali so tall and blond and handsome, Sara so fragile and darkly beautiful. They didn't have a chance. Mixed unions are always destined to failure. Nature is such a stern mistress. If only they'd understood that."

"Well, I certainly wasn't surprised by what happened. And I don't believe for a moment that she lost her mind. She inherited her ancestors' penchant for blood, pure and simple."

"Alison owned a considerable share of Rosehill industry stock, not to mention property. Has the girl said anything about her intentions . . ."

Lily exhaled, her breath shuddering with anger remembered and recaptured. Her hands uncurling from tight fists, she flexed her long fingers and indulged herself a thin smile. It hadn't all been terrible. There had been those few sweet moments of victory.

Like watching Errol work the room, making the old bats titter with confusion as he kissed their hands or granted one of his famous lethal smiles. They didn't approve of him. He didn't belong. Not dressed as he was in a brown sports jacket, black T-shirt, faded jeans, and Nikes. His dishwater-blond hair was too long and the small silver earring dancing in his ear inappropriate, even if it had been a cross. But they couldn't resist his charm. Not even Eudora. At least not until she asked him if he were related to the great actor, John Mills. "No," he'd told her with an apologetic shrug. "More's the pity. But I'm glad you asked. I was just wondering if your husband's family was related to the comedienne, Joan Rivers. I've been a fan of hers since she first guested on Carson."

Lily had been almost certain Eudora would faint

dead away with the insult, but the angry mottling of
her delicate fair skin had been telltale enough even
without her frantic denial. "Of course not. The woman
is a Jewess. Rivers is a stage name, nothing more. Everyone knows that."

Lily had almost kissed Errol then and there.

And there'd been the moment when she'd told Uncle
Jesse that she had to get out of there, away from all the
wicked-tongued vipers. Without so much as a hint of
what he intended, he'd turned to Eudora, capturing one
of her hands in his. "I'm sure I speak for both Lily
Dawn and myself when I thank you for opening your
home to us in our time of bereavement. But as Lily has
just pointed out, it's time for us to return to my sister's
home. After all, now that we have seen to the Christian
formalities of burial, and the ensuing customs of Alison's people, it is time to see to our own passages and
rites. Only then can we be certain that Sara's spirit is
free to soar to the heavens as it must."

Lily could see some of the ladies trying to decide
whether or not he was pulling their legs. A couple of
them even giggled, but as she followed their gazes, she
knew they were seeing a savage in designer togs who
might at any moment decide to pounce on their scalps.

Putting a hand over her mouth, Lily stifled a chuckle
of her own as she looked at her uncle and saw him
through the eyes of ignorance.

He wore a handsomely stitched black Armani suit
that was tailored to fit his massive physique. That, along
with the expensive ostrich boots on his feet and the
Rolex watch on his wrist, were his only concessions to
the dictates of modern fashion. His long gray hair was
parted in the middle and wrapped with rawhide and
feathers at his jawline. Intricately crafted silver and turquoise adorned his neck as well as his fingers. But it was
the beaded bag that hung from his waist that seemed to

fascinate the gathering down to the last when he moved his coat jacket aside and gave it a little shake. Lily had almost choked, and Eudora's face had turned as pale as her platinum blond hair. But the crowning blow to the woman's well-orchestrated afternoon had been delivered when she'd taken Lily in her arms. "I know you'll be returning to New York and the stage and your life with your handsome actor, but I beg you to come by one last time to tell me good-bye before you leave."

"Oh, but Miss Eudora, I thought you knew. I'm not returning to New York for some time. As a matter of fact, Errol and I plan to stay at least through spring. Maybe longer."

"Oh—" Eudora began, and then unable to recover her equilibrium, a second breathy, "oh."

Sash hadn't intended to follow Lily. One minute he'd been alone, cutting a path through the grasslands toward his destination on the wharf. The next, she'd appeared a dozen or so yards in the distance, head bent, shoulders bowed forward.

The encounter had been pure chance. Not that it was an encounter exactly. He'd seen her, she hadn't noticed him.

Sash stopped, hesitating in the shadows until she'd put some distance between them. He didn't want to talk to her. Not tonight. Not in his present mood.

He hadn't gone to Eudora's along with the others following the graveside service for Sara. He hadn't been invited. Hunching his shoulders and burying his neck deeper into the warmth of his jacket, he jogged in place as the cold began a more determined crawl under his jacket. Hell, he wouldn't have walked through those doors if the big man himself had asked.

Not that Jason Rivers would ever ask. Sash doubted

he and the old man had exchanged fifteen words in the past five years.

Pivoting on his heel, Sash could just make out the metallic shimmer of Rosehill's newest building situated in the most advantageous location in the central downtown business district. Headquarters of Rivers Enterprises. Lights shone here and there creating an eerie impression of a looming, glowing monster. But the monster wasn't there in the office building. The monster was up above on the hill in a pink house, draped in silk and dripping diamonds.

Dismissing Lily entirely with thoughts of his stepmother, he moved out of the penumbrae of the trees, avoiding the boardwalk where he'd last seen the girl. He jogged briskly, inhaling the biting air. By the time he pulled open the door of the Striped Tuna, his lungs were on fire. But he welcomed the pain. In a few minutes, he would begin to ease it with a bottle of Johnny Walker. In the meantime, the burning in his lungs helped him forget the other ache.

Work on the fishing boats was the best medicine to numb the terrible hurt that never fully went away. Today he'd taken off to pay tribute to Sara's memory. That had been a mistake. Now guilt mingled with the hurt. And memories he'd been able to suppress had crept to the surface once again.

Without a word, he motioned to a bottle on the shelf behind the bartender. A minute later, he was seated in a dark corner, already filling the first glass.

It had all come back today. His boyish love for Sara. His jealousy of her husband. The guilt that had refused to be buried since the night Alison Hutton had been murdered. And today when he should have grieved for Sara and all that had gone wrong, he'd lusted for her daughter. Jesus! What kind of sick bastard was he?

*   *   *

Lily blinked rapidly against the immediate darkness that folded around her as soon as the tavern door closed behind her. Her eyes adjusted quickly and in only a matter of seconds, she could make out the long narrow bar, shiny glasses and bottles, the rude silhouettes of men seated here and there. Taking a couple of tentative steps, she approached an empty stool. In the dimness she could see her reflection staring back at her from a large mirror behind the bar.

Music blared from a jukebox somewhere in the back of the room. Garth Brooks arrived at the chorus of "Friends in Low Places," and a lone slurred voice joined in. In spite of her ill humor, Lily allowed herself a small smile.

Lily shrugged off her coat, laying it on the stool next to her just as a man appeared across the bar from her.

"What you drinking?" he asked, his deep, gravelly voice as resonant and jarring as tom-toms struck inside a pickle barrel.

Lily jumped. "Scotch. On the rocks."

"Got a preference?" the man barked again.

"Preference?" Lily repeated.

"Yeah, lady. You want rotgut or label?"

"Chivas Regal?" she suggested tentatively.

The man's lips, which had been lost in the wealth of his luxuriant beard and mustache, appeared suddenly with his wide grin. "Good choice. Drink it myself. Name's Charlie, by the way. Owner, operator."

Unwilling to encourage conversation, Lily merely returned his smile with a nod, then swiveled on the stool to look around the room.

"Looking for someone?" Charlie asked as she leaned forward on the stool.

"No," she said quickly, turning back around and accepting the glass he was holding out to her. "I was trying to see if there was anyone sitting in the corner over there. But it's too dark."

"Hiding from someone?" he asked bluntly.

"No!" she protested. Then more quietly, "Of course not. I just want some privacy. I want to sip my drink undisturbed and be alone with my thoughts."

There was no one sitting in the corner she'd indicated and Charlie Wesmeier could have told her so at once, but he wanted to draw out the conversation. He didn't get too many females in the Striped Tuna, and certainly none as young and pretty as this one. "You the gal who's come down here from the Big Apple to bury her mama?"

Lily almost dropped her glass. Ice clinked loudly and the amber liquid splashed onto her fingers and the countertop. "I beg your pardon?" she asked, though she'd heard the question clearly enough.

"You Doc Hutton's little girl?" Charlie asked.

"Yes."

"Didn't know your old lady. Never had the pleasure. But me and the doctor was pretty good buds. He'd come in to the Tuna ever now and then when he was seeing to a patient down this way. Sit and talk for an hour or so. Never about anyone or anything 'ceptin' your mama and you. He wasn't a man to gossip or even to spill his guts about his own problems, you know? But he was too proud of you and his wife to keep quiet about that. Liked to brag that he was the luckiest feller in the Carolinas."

Tears that had been successfully held in check all day, filled Lily's eyes and spilled over her lashes. "Thank you," she said in a choked whisper.

Charlie grabbed a towel and began wiping the counter, clearly embarrassed by her tears. "Hey, ain't nothing. Just thought you'd like to know. I never did believe that crap about your mama doin' him in. Not unless the doc was a fool who didn't know her good as he thought. Which he weren't."

"Did he come in here often just before . . . just before he died?" she asked, moving her glass aside and leaning forward to rest both arms on the bar.

Charlie didn't hesitate. Tossing the towel over his shoulder, he leaned forward as well, unconsciously aping her position. "Matter of fact, he was in here that Friday night, just two days before. Didn't talk much at first." Charlie laughed deep in his throat, then explained. "Went over and sat in that corner over there like you was thinking of doin'. I brought him a couple of brewskies and left him alone. Most of the fishing boats was still out, it being summer and all, and the weather conditions being good. So it was quiet. Just him and me. Every now and then he'd hold up his empty bottle and glass and I'd bring him a refill. The last time, he patted the seat next to him and invited me to sit down.

"I asked him straight out, soon as I was sittin', what was bothering him."

Lily could feel her heart quicken. "What did he say?"

"Didn't say anything right off and when he did speak, he asked me a question as I recall. Wanted to know if I liked the way people was treated in Rosehill.

"I told him I didn't rightly understand the question."

"And did he explain?"

"Nope. Just said for me to forget it. If I didn't understand that was good 'cause that meant I didn't have a problem. I said, 'Yeah, but sounds to me like you got one.' He smiled real sad like and nodded. Then he said, 'I sure do, Charlie, but it's nothing I can't fix. All I have to do is move my girls out of this hellhole."

"Hey, Wesmeier, you gonna serve drinks or jaw with that gal all night?" a man yelled from the opposite end of the bar.

The bartender straightened, winking at Lily. "You drink your scotch, sugar pie, and I'll be back in a few."

Lily sipped the drink as she'd been directed, but her thoughts were on the conversation she'd just shared. What had she learned? That her father was planning to move away with her mother and her? So what? What did that prove? Nothing. Not a damned thing.

When Charlie returned he nodded in the direction of her empty glass. "Fill it again?"

"Sure," Lily replied absently, then almost without a beat between, asked, "How do you remember that conversation with my dad so clearly? I mean it was so long ago, and you must talk to scores of men every day."

The deep, booming laughter rumbled again. "Sure I do, but I don't get many customers like Doc Hutton in here. He was from up there on the hills, you know? Born and raised up there with the other big shots, but he never acted like he was no better than anyone else. Just a regular guy, and a man don't forget that. Neither did I forget what he talked about doing either 'cause I remember thinking what a loss it would be if he up and moved away like he mentioned. Then two days later there he was dead. Coincidence of that gave me the willies, let me tell you."

Lily opened her mouth to thank him for sharing his memory of her father with her, but the door opened suddenly, washing her in an icy breeze. A chill coursed the length of her spine as if someone had just passed over her grave . . . or maybe that of her parents.

Chapter Seven

At the moment that Lily was polishing off her first scotch, Eudora Rivers was sitting down at her dressing table for her nightly ritual of cleansing and moisturizing her delicate skin. Before she began, as always, she leaned toward the mirror, carefully and meticulously examining her eyes and mouth area for signs of new age lines. At fifty, she was still an inordinately handsome woman, thanks to the expertise of Dr. Harold Walthers, her plastic surgeon, and to the scrupulous attention she paid her cosmetic care.

Tonight she found lines not only around her eyes and mouth but creasing her usually flawless forehead. Signs of tension and worry, and all because Sara Two Moons-Hutton had died, and now her daughter was in Rosehill and apparently intent on staying around for a while.

Eudora had begun the process of smoothing her hair away from her face, but quickly slammed the silver brush against the table, causing bottles and jars to bounce and dance noisily. "Damn you, Sara!" she cried.

There was a sharp knock at her bedroom door. Eudora allowed herself one last hushed expletive before calling out, "Come in!"

One of her perfectly arched brows raised a fraction at her surprise. "And what do you want?" she asked.

Jason Rivers ignored the censure in his wife's tone. He knew it irritated her for him to enter her room after she retired for the night. She'd made her displeasure clear on countless occasions before he'd finally given up coming to her at all. But tonight he wasn't going to be put off. Striding past her, he grabbed one of the twin ice-blue watered silk chairs from its place by the window and set it beside her. He lowered himself into it, crossed his legs, and sighed wearily. "How did it go?"

"The funeral?"

"Of course the funeral. Or was there something more pressing on your calendar today? Like some grand mayoral duty too pressing to ignore? Or some poor clerk you had to dress down? Or perhaps the funeral conflicted with your appointment with your masseuse."

Eudora laughed. "Oh, Jason, don't try sarcasm with me. Acerbic wit is *my* specialty."

"Acerbic wit! Ha! That's a good one. Your euphemism for vicious cruelty?"

As her smile wilted, Eudora leaned toward the mirror while she smoothed the line from her face with her fingertips. "What do you want, Jason?" she asked on a deep sigh. "You know I don't like confrontations just before my bedtime."

"As I already told you, I want to know about the funeral. And the girl, Lily Dawn, how is she?"

"She's staying," Eudora said flatly, never taking her eyes from her reflection. Just the memory of the girl's declaration produced new lines. Something would have to be done.

"Staying? You mean in Rosehill? For how long?"

Giving up the inspection that was only adding to her frustration, Eudora turned on the stool away from her husband and stood up, walking to the window to stare out at the lights in the city below. Her city. Immediately, she felt calmer.

Her back to her husband, she answered him. "She didn't provide me with her itinerary, but I gather she intends to stay for some time."

"But why?"

Eudora glanced over her shoulder at him. "Why, darling, you sound almost worried. Why would you care how long she stays?"

Ignoring the question, Jason rose from his seat and crossed the room to stand behind her. "Was he there at the service?"

"You mean Sash?" she asked, her tone mild, though her stiff posture told another story.

"Was he?"

"Yes, but they didn't speak. He came after the service began. Left as soon as it was over. I invited Lily and her uncle to the house, and as far as I know, Sash was long gone by the time we left the cemetery."

"I don't want you to hurt him again, Dora," Jason said in a quiet voice.

"Why would I hurt him? I don't even see him anymore. He never comes up on the hills. His life is on that boat of his. When he's not fishing, he's drinking in some tavern or visiting one of his women friends in the Alley."

The Alley was a four-block strip of seedy motels, adult novelty shops, and strip clubs located in the heart of downtown Rosehill. A dozen or so hookers also resided in a small apartment complex that backed onto the Alley. For years, Eudora had tried to shut down the iniquitous operations. She'd almost succeeded once, but the ramifications of spreading crime were immediate. In recent years, she'd realized the wisdom of working with the slumlords instead of against them. As a result she knew that her stepson occasionally visited "friends" in the area.

Jason let loose a long, shuddering breath and sank down on the side of his wife's bed. "How do you do it?"

"Do what?" she asked, her blue eyes wide with genuine wonder. "What is it I've done now? Uttered the awful truth about your son? That he's happy in his existence working and socializing with the lowlifes of our society? Is it untrue? Any of it?"

"No," Jason said with an abject shake of his head. "But he's no mongrel, Dora, as you imply. Even a dog whose pedigree can be traced back for generations will learn to survive in the wild if it's cast out with no other home."

Eudora laughed and came to sit beside him. "You should put in long hours more often, darling. You're usually so uninspired, but I swear that was positively clever!"

She crossed her legs, purposefully allowing her dressing gown to fall open, revealing bare thighs that were still slim and shapely. She leaned back on her elbows and slowly uncrossed her legs so giving him a glimpse of her nakedness beneath the modest cover-up. Her head tossed back, she studied Jason covertly beneath lowered lashes. The pose was provocative, as close to a physical offering as she would ever make, and she wondered why tonight of all nights she had been aroused by him. Was it the funeral service, an overt reminder of her mortality? No, she thought rather it was his flagrant disregard of rules set down by her years before. After all, it was the first defiant, *manly* act she'd witnessed in him since . . . why, since Ali's death.

Wasn't that a fantastic irony? It had been the murder of Dr. Alison Hutton that had played such a significant part in the ultimate destruction of her relationship with

Jason. Odd that Sara's death might in a roundabout way influence their reunion.

Turning so that she leaned forward on one elbow, she wrapped her other arm around his neck and blew softly into his ear. "Forget about Sash for now, Jason. Come to bed with me. We'll help each other forget everything for a while."

Jason didn't move. Not for several long moments. Then he only grasped his wife's arm, pushing her away from him. She fell back against her pillows and lay there, most of her body exposed for him to see. He let his gaze rake over her, only once and quickly, and struggled to prevent his disgust from showing. "I didn't come in here to make love to you, Dora. I wanted to talk to you about Lily, and our children."

Furious with him, Eudora scampered from the bed, covering herself hastily and retying the sash with trembling fingers. With her back to him, she laughed bitterly. "Children? I don't have *children*, Jason. Only a daughter, and she's away with her husband. Sash is thankfully *your* progeny and your problem. Of course, I've been a good stepmother, helping you find a way to keep anyone from finding out that he was on that balcony when Ali was killed."

Jason stood up, anger twisting his features into an ugly mask of outrage. He grabbed Eudora roughly by the forearm, spinning her around and pulling her against him so that his face hovered only inches above hers. "I'll never believe the ridiculous scenario you painted for me, Dora. Oh, it worked at first. I actually believed he might have been involved with Ali's murder. Not anymore."

She laughed, never taking her eyes from his until he let go of her abruptly, causing her to stumble and almost fall. "But you do, poor dear. If you didn't, you wouldn't worry so that the Hutton girl is staying."

"No," he said, shaking his head then running his hands through his golden hair which was becoming more and more streaked with silver. "There were two witnesses who saw Sara kill Ali. Neither of them saw Sash on the balcony. You're the only one who claimed he was there."

"The only one?" she asked, sarcasm making the question sinister. "And what about Sash? If he wasn't there, why did he run that night? He was gone for *ten* years, Jason. And when he came back, did he ever deny being in that house when Alison was killed?"

"You know he didn't deny it! He wouldn't discuss it at all. But I'll never believe he killed anyone, not even as an accomplice who stood aside and let the murder take place."

Eudora tossed up her hands. "Fine, believe what you want. He's not my son. But remember, there's no statute of limitations on murder."

"Thank you, Madam Mayor."

Reclaiming her seat in front of her dressing table, Eudora twisted the lid from one of the jars of cream. "If there's nothing else, Jason," she said, seeking his reflection in the mirror. Then finding it as he moved behind her, "Ah, there you are. For just a second, I thought you might have reconsidered your sanctimonious refusal to go to bed with me. But since you haven't, why don't you leave me alone. I have a busy day tomorrow, no doubt simply brimful of all sorts of emergencies I wasn't around to handle today."

"There is one more thing," he said after opening the door to leave.

"And that is?"

"You'd best call your daughter, Dora."

"Why? I told you, she's away with her husband. Dixon had business in New York and Imogene decided to go along and get some shopping in. That's why she wasn't at the service today."

"She's not in New York either."

"What in heaven's name are you talking about? Of course, she is. She called me day before yesterday just before she and Dixon left. I told her I'd send a car to pick them up when they returned tomorrow morning."

"Well, then you'd better call Stu," he said, referring to Stuart St. Charles, the chief of police. " 'Cause someone's stolen her car and parked it in the Alley."

The jar slipped from Eudora's hand, crashing loudly to the glass-topped table. Imogene drove a ragtop candy apple–red Viper convertible. With its package of customized gold trim, including gilded spoke wheel covers, it was hard to mistake. The vanity plates that read NV ME made it impossible.

"Damn it!" Eudora shrieked.

Jason would have smiled with satisfaction if it wasn't all so damned sad. Silently, he pulled the door closed after him as he stepped from the room.

He was halfway down the stairs when it opened again. He looked up to see his wife leaning over the banister. "And what the fuck were you doing in the Alley? Is that where you're getting it from these days? That why you don't need to see to your own wife's needs anymore?"

Jason could have answered. He could have told her that he'd never been unfaithful. At least not in a physical sense. But what would be the point? She wouldn't believe him. Besides, it wasn't her he was being faithful to. It was to the others, the two women he'd truly loved. One had been Sash's mother. The other ... the other was the woman's whose grave he'd secretly visited before returning home tonight. His lips twisted in a sardonic grin. Faithful to a woman who had never even been his. Hell, she'd never even known how he felt. No one knew. Not even Dora. Especially not Dora.

That was why he hadn't attended the funeral today. That was why he didn't want to see Lily. Even as a child she'd been the spitting image of her beautiful mother. Jason didn't think he could bear it. And he was afraid the mask he'd kept in place all these years might slip and the whole world would learn his secret.

As he reached his den, he could still hear Eudora screaming at him. With his foot, he kicked the door shut behind him.

After a few minutes, he heard her bedroom door slam above. He hardly registered it as he crossed to the window and lifted his glass to the stars he could only imagine in the cloud-covered sky. "Rest in peace, Sara. God knows you deserve it after what we did to you."

Chapter Eight

Lucky Lucci, the owner of the Ruby Palace Motel, didn't need the caller to identify herself. He'd recognize the mayor's haughty tone anywhere, anytime. *Shit.*

"Yeah, Mayor, I heard the question," he said. "You want that I connect you to your daughter's room. Thing is, Ms. Mayor, she ain't here."

There was a heavy pause, the drone of the telephone line the only sound for several seconds. Foolishly, Lucky thought just for an instant that the autocratic bitch was going to let him off the hook. When she spoke again, she quickly disabused him of that notion. "I'm going to make you a onetime offer, Mr. Lucci. If you connect me with Imogene's room at once, the Ruby Palace will stay open. I won't close you down and neither will I send the police into the Alley to check on your neighbors. But if you stall for even ten more seconds, the Alley will look like a ghost town by the end of the week and your business associates will all know who upset their dreary little lives."

Sweat peppered Lucky's bald pate. He wasn't a man who was easily intimidated. But then Mayor Eudora Rivers wasn't your common, everyday adversary. She was one of those few up on the hills who *owned* the

town. Didn't matter that his name was on the Ruby
Palace Motel deed. If he crossed her, he might as well
put a match to it.

"Well, son of a gun, whatcha know about this? I just
found Ms. Imogene's signature in the register right
here, jes' as pretty as you please. Must have signed in
while I was at dinner. You jes' hold on there, Mayor
Rivers. I'll ring the room straightaway."

She didn't answer, but Lucky imagined he could almost see her cruel grin of satisfaction through the receiver. "I'll put ya on hold for jes' a minute while I
make the connection." He pressed a button, then dialed
room 219 with shaking fingers.

A sultry, whiskey voice answered on the second ring,
"What's up, sugar?"

"Your mother's calling you, Ms. Imogene. Insists that
I put her through."

Rich, smoky laughter answered his pronouncement.
"Then do your thing, honey."

"What is it? Who's calling you here?" a voice demanded from the background in the instant before
Lucky connected Eudora.

"Hush, darlin'. It's my mama," Imogene told the man
lying on the bed behind her. She'd sat up with the rude
peal of the telephone. Now, as naked and pale as a
Christmas goose, she sat on the side of the bed swinging
a slender leg.

She didn't speak for several minutes.

Boyd Humphries, his shaggy brows drawn together
with worry and irritation, scooted up so that he sat
against the headboard. As owner of Rosehill's sole lim-
ousine rental company, and lone operator since his last
driver had quit, he knew the dragon lady on the other
end of the one-sided conversation as well as he did
Imogene. Okay, almost as well, he amended as his eyes
tracked the sharp nubs of her vertebrae to the twin

dimples in her buttocks. Point was, he couldn't afford for Eudora to find out he'd spent the afternoon screwing her daughter.

He scratched at the hair on his chest, shaking his head. Why had he let her talk him into this? Stupid question! She hadn't *talked* much at all. Fact was, she'd let her fingers do her persuading as they sneaked right inside his pants, right around his schlong.

Genie's husband, Dix Price, had telephoned the office from New York to ask Boyd to pick up his wife at the airport. Boyd had arrived just as she stepped from the company plane onto the tarmac. He'd held the back door open for her. Only she'd ignored that, circling the long car instead and climbing into the front passenger side. "You don't mind if I ride up here with you, do you, sugar?" she'd asked.

That was the second he should have put his foot down. But, hell, he was a good-looking guy. Women came onto him all the time. Only difference was, no one had ever climbed all over him before like Imogene. Almost got him off then and there in the front seat.

By the time they arrived at the Price mansion on the hill, he'd been ready to tear her clothes off in the circle drive in front of God and everyone. That's when she'd suggested that she follow him back to his office in her car, then the two of them could find "a place to be together."

Boyd ran his hands through his sandy hair. They'd been together all right and now the shit was about to hit the fan. Eudora Rivers! Christ Almighty!

"I was bored," Imogene was saying, her tone not quite a childish whine. "After Dix got that award of his, he had meetings scheduled around the clock. It was his idea for me to come home."

Jesus, now he was going to have to lie here and listen to her marital problems. Leaning forward, Boyd started off the bed, but without looking back, Genie stopped him with an amazingly accurate grab for his groin area.

"I'm sorry I missed the funeral. I'll make it up tomorrow, and I'll be the epitome of propriety when I pay my respects to Lily and Dr. Two Moons. I swear it, Mama. I'm contrite, ashamed, and properly chastised. May I—"

Boyd could hear the buzz of Eudora's voice again, but his attention was focused on Imogene. He stared at the pale cascade of blond curls that ended just below her shoulders, amazed at her ability to sound so remorseful while so wickedly working her magic on him at the same time.

"I know I've been bad, Mama. I said I was sorry. So please stop fussin' at me. I'll go right home and pick out the perfect outfit for my condolence visit tomorrow." She listened another few seconds. "All right then, you go to bed, Mama. I'll talk to you tomorrow. Sweet dreams." She pulled her hand from his lap as she replaced the receiver in the cradle, and Boyd made a little yelping sound of mingled relief and desire.

"What a wrong, sugar?" she asked. "You're not worried 'cause my mama called, are you?"

"Damn straight! I might have enjoyed the hell out of spending the afternoon with you, Genie, but I'm still a happily married man."

Imogene had stood up and was already stepping into her panties, discarded several hours earlier. Next she slipped her arms into her bra straps, then stopped to glance at him over her shoulder. "So what? No one's threatening your marriage. Not my mother and certainly not me, honey bun."

In spite of his worry and jangling nerves, Boyd couldn't help but notice again how exquisite she was. He even felt himself getting hard again and reached out for her hand to draw her down to the bed.

"No way, lover," she said, sidestepping his grasp easily and slithering into a simple chocolate-brown jersey sheath. "It was fun, darlin', but you heard my promise. I've got to get home."

"You are planning on waiting for me, aren't you?" he asked. "You insisted we come in your car, remember?" His voice raised slightly, he glared at her as irritation replaced the desire he'd felt only moments before.

Genie took a brush from her handbag, ran it through her hair a few times, then stashed it away once again. "I've got to rush, sweetie, but I'll have Lucky call you a cab, okay?"

"Well, hell yes. Sounds just dandy to me," Boyd said sarcastically, his arms flapping. "I'll just show up in a taxi. No way that'll make my old lady suspicious. I mean she won't wonder where I left the limo or anything, or where in Sam Hill I've been all day since I haven't been at the office." Then in a milder, almost pleading tone, "You said you'd drive me back."

"And I would have. Now I can't."

"Great! And what about your mother?"

"What about her?" Imogene asked with exaggerated patience.

"She gonna just forget she found you here in this motel room with a guy who ain't your husband?"

Imogene was applying lipstick now and met his reflection in the mirror. "What are you getting at, Boyd? My mother's the mayor. She's a busy lady. She might not like the idea of me in a motel room with some john, but she doesn't have time to worry about *who* I'm with. She doesn't ask. She doesn't care." Shoving the silver cap on the lipstick tube, she stuck it back in her bag, then pulled her purse strap onto her shoulder. "Stop being such a worrywart. You're a big boy. I'm sure you can think of a story for your wife."

He had crawled across the bed so that he sat on the

side nearest her now. His hands clasped between his knees, he hung his head. "Yeah? And how do I know you won't decide to tell Patty?"

Imogene would have laughed if her patience hadn't been stretched so thin. "Now let me see. I'm not a brain surgeon, but I can probably figure this one out. Patty must be the little woman you're married to. And you're worried I might decide to call her up and tell her all about our extraordinary afternoon at the Ruby Palace, is that right?"

There was no denying the syrupy scorn in her tone, and Boyd flushed red with the implied insult. "Yeah? why not?"

"Why not? Why, because, Boyd, darlin' "—she leaned forward and patted his limp penis—"my poor memory's only as long as the last dick I played with . . . and sweetheart, you're already forgotten."

Moments later, Genie slid behind the wheel of her car, pausing only long enough to wave a cheery farewell to Lucky as he watched her from the window beneath the flashing red neon OFFICE light. *Nosy bastard.*

Inside the darkness of the two-seater, she turned on the ignition, punched in a number she knew by rote on the cellular phone, and yawned hugely. *Answer the damn phone.*

At once a voice replaced the insistent jingling in her ear. "Mission accomplished," she said with more spirit than she felt. Damn, she was tired.

"What did you find out?"

"Lily hired Humphries to take her and her friend to the house but there wasn't much talk going on in the backseat."

"So your afternoon was wasted."

Genie grinned and licked her bottom lip. "Not entirely. Humphries is a lot more resourceful than he seems."

"Jesus Christ—"

"Would you chill," Imogene interrupted. "There are a lot more unpleasant ways of finding out what we need to know. Besides, all fun and games aside, it wasn't a total bust. Boyd did overhear Lily say she's not planning on returning north for a while."

"Did he hear why?"

"Not really. He said her friend isn't happy about it. They argued some, though he thought Lily was being careful about what she said because they weren't alone."

"Anything else?"

"Yeah, a kind of funny thing her friend said just before they got to the house. I'm paraphrasing, of course, since it came to me secondhand. Something like, 'This place is too fuckin' weird for me, babe. Looks like paradise, smells like paradise, even feels like paradise. Now you gonna go playing Eve, looking around for some serpent. Only this one ain't gonna go down like the original script. This time you start stirring things up, you're gonna get snakebit. "

"She knows."

"Sounds like it," Imogene agreed. "So what now?"

"We scare her off like we planned. That doesn't work . . ."

Imogene stared at the blinking red light. "Yeah," she said. She didn't have to hear the alternative voiced. She knew what it was.

Chapter Nine

"You can't stand out here all night," Errol said to Jesse's back. "You'll freeze to death."

Jesse had started at the interruption of his thoughts, which had traveled years back in time. But he smiled as he turned to face his niece's guest. "I suppose not," he agreed, stepping from the third-floor veranda into the study.

"Don't worry about Lily. She'll be all right," Errol said as he followed the older man inside. "She has this thing about night walks. Says it clears all the clutter gathered during the frantic daytime hours.

"I used to worry about her penchant for roaming. At first, when we were just getting to know each other, she was so naive, trusting, I was sure she was always just a walk away from becoming some mugger's victim. After a couple of years she got more savvy, but more daring at the same time. Her walks at night were taken later and lasted longer. Still, I don't believe she's ever had so much as a threatening encounter. Guess if she's survived the mean streets of New York, she can handle anything she meets up with here in Rosehill." Errol gave a short, derisive laugh as if the idea of encountering evil in Rosehill were preposterous.

Jesse reclaimed the seat he'd occupied when he heard his niece's angry exit from the house an hour earlier. Crossing his legs, he picked up his pipe, using it as a pointer to usher Errol onto the sofa opposite him. As he puffed life back into his pipe, his expression remained impassive. Only the click, click, click of the beaded tassels on his moccasins betrayed his agitation as his feet tapped the floor. "Is it always arguments with you that send her out into the night?"

Errol shook his head in obvious irritation. He leaned forward suddenly, hands pressed together, his fingers steepled as he made his plea for understanding. "Look Dr. Two Moons, I know you don't like me. You made that clear on your first visit to New York after Lily and I moved in together. But don't you think for now the two of us need a sort of détente until we find a way to talk her out of this asinine decision to stay in Rosehill and look for a killer? I mean, we don't even know for sure that her mother didn't in fact die of a heart attack as the hospital claims. I don't happen to believe it for a second. But what if she did? My God, do we want Lily playing detective? And what about her career? Did she tell you that after six years of spirit-shattering, no-where auditions, dancing in off-Broadway productions, and squeezing in acting, singing, and dance lessons, she's finally gotten the break every hopeful in New York prays for?"

Jesse ignored the last question. No, in fact, he hadn't heard about her "big break," but when he did, he wanted it to come from Lily herself. "Are you telling me the two of you argued because you were trying to persuade her to go home to New York with you?"

Errol nodded, then shrugged. "At least that's the way it started. By the time she stormed out of here we'd moved on to my selfish fears."

Jesse waited. When Errol didn't elaborate, he pressed

for more detail. "Mind telling me what Lily Dawn thinks those fears are?"

Errol smiled. "I'm supposedly afraid of you, for one. And I'm afraid I'll lose my meal ticket if she misses her chance to star on Broadway, for another. And she said she thinks I'm concerned I won't benefit from all the money she's going to inherit from her mother."

As Errol spoke, rival emotions of amusement and sadness mingled in his eyes, and though his tone maintained a nonchalant lightness, his grin faltered from time to time. Perhaps, Jesse thought, he'd misjudged him. There was depth here that Lily had apparently discovered at once. Why then, Jesse wondered, all the effort to keep it hidden from him? Pulling at his pipe for several long seconds, he focused on the turquoise stone in the ring he wore. Without looking up, he asked, "And was she right? About any of her accusations?"

"Not about the money. Hell, she's been subsidized by her father's trust since long before I met her. You can believe me or not, but I've never taken a dime from her."

"Anything else?"

This time when it appeared, Errol's smile was steady and genuine, matching the laughter that sparkled in his eyes. "I'm not afraid of you, if that's what you're pushing for. Don't get me wrong. I know how Lily feels about you. If you told her you personally hung the moon and the stars, she'd buy it. And maybe when we first met I was afraid because your disapproval was so evident, but not anymore."

"Why not? Don't you worry that Lily Dawn still cares what I think?"

"Oh, sure, but let's face it, man, even you can't affect her feelings if she doesn't have them."

Jesse raised a brow, impressed with the young man's

candor and insight. "So you're saying my niece doesn't feel for you today the way she did a couple years back."

"Not exactly," Errol said. "Lily never loved me, Dr. Two Moons. She didn't when we moved in together and she doesn't now. She had one hell of a crush in the beginning. How could she not? Here was this handsome, sophisticated, brilliant actor offering her the chance of a lifetime. To be seen with me. No one could have refused me." His tone dripped with self-mockery.

Jesse smiled as he removed the pipe from between his lips. "I've no doubt."

"But?"

"No buts. Just a why."

"Why do I stay with her if I know she's never going to reciprocate my feelings? Why not? No matter what she feels for me, I still want to be around her. I may be all the glorious things I just claimed so immodestly, but it ain't gonna change the fact that the lady's heart just doesn't go pit-a-pat when I walk into the room."

"And that doesn't bother you?"

"Hell, yes, it bothers me, man. But not enough to let go gracefully. Hey, I flushed pride down the john years ago. I'll fight, beg, grovel even if it means staying with her." His grin now was thin, tight, and his eyes suspiciously bright as he suddenly pushed himself to his feet. He was halfway out the door when he stopped to speak again. His back still to Jesse, he said, "Anyway, now you know. You don't have to worry about me. I'm not here to take advantage of Lily."

"Thank you for telling me."

Errol spun around, took a couple steps into the room once again. "Hey, I'm not after appreciation, man. That's not what this is all about. I just want Lily out of Rosehill. She might be way out there with her theory about her mother's death, but the people in this town still give me the creeps. You notice that bunch gathered

at the Rivers place today? You ever see a whiter bunch
congregated in one building? I mean, Lily warned me.
She told me all about the weirdos here and their wacky
laws. Like property on the hills not being sold outside
the families who've owned it for more than two hundred years. And the intermarrying that goes on; almost
no one hitching up with outsiders. But, shit, man, for
a few minutes there this afternoon I was trying to decide
if I was at a Nazi Aryan gathering or a meeting of
the Klan."

Jesse didn't answer. He understood Errol's shock.
He'd experienced the same amazement when he'd come
to Rosehill for the first time. His entire family had been
upset when Sara eloped with the young doctor none of
them had ever met. Sara Two Moons, like all of her
Osage nation, was an extremely wealthy young woman.
Her parents, fearing that she may well have been married for her money, decided that Jesse should accept
the invitation to the wedding reception in South Carolina being given in the newlyweds' honor. Believing the
element of surprise would help him better gauge his
new brother-in-law's feelings for his sister, Jesse had
told no one he was coming.

Jesse had liked Alison Hutton, Sara's new husband,
immediately. But the others . . .

To his own people, Jesse Two Moons was more than
merely a licensed psychiatrist. He was a shaman, a seer,
and a man with special gifts of discernment. Though
only thirty years old at the time of his sister's sudden
marriage, he'd already demonstrated his rare psychic
talent with wondrous accuracy. So, when he announced
to his family and the tribal counsel upon his return two
days later that his sister needed him, no one questioned
his decision to give up his fledgling psychiatric practice
and move to South Carolina.

He'd remained in Rosehill for the next ten years.

He'd established a new practice, in fact, sharing an office with his brother-in-law. But while Alison's patients were comprised of the who's who in Rosehill society, Jesse's patients all came from poorer walks in life. It was an ideal arrangement. Through Ali, Jesse learned just how deep-rooted his sister's new family and neighbors' hatred was. Through Jesse's own patients he gleaned an understanding of how far-reaching, insidious, and dangerous were the effects of their hate. Over and over he saw dreams dashed, hearts broken, even lives destroyed by Rosehill bigotry.

The twelve families who lived in the palatial hills homes also governed the community, occupying every major seat from police commissioner and mayor to coroner and judge. As he'd quickly surmised, truth and fairness had little to do with how justice was meted out by the ruling oligarchy.

A few such as Ali had somehow managed to grow up untainted by the prejudice, greed, and contempt that seemed almost as inherent as any genetic flaw. Still, Jesse had known almost at once that neither his brother-in-law's goodness nor his love for his wife would be enough to save her from the hatred focused on her the moment she arrived in Rosehill.

Jesse didn't know if Lily Dawn was right about Sara's death. In the days to come, he would seek answers from his spiritual guides. He frowned as he absently stuck the pipe in his mouth once again. He would ask about Sara, but his attention must be focused on Lily Dawn now. Sara was past his need for help. She'd been destroyed by Ali's death as surely as if the knife had been driven into her heart along with his.

"Dr. Two Moons?"

Jesse gave his head a shake. "Sorry, son. I get lost out there sometimes," he said, sweeping his hand in a

wide arc as if encompassing the universe. "I was thinking about Lily Dawn's mother."

Jesse set his pipe aside once again, standing with the
ease of a much younger man. Putting his arm around
Errol's shoulders, he guided him from the room. "I feel
like a drive. Wanna come along?"

"Sure, but I've got to warn you," Errol said as they
descended the staircase to the foyer. "Lily gets pretty
pissed when she thinks anyone's trying to interfere. Says
it stifles her, threatens her sense of freedom."

Jesse chuckled under his breath. "It's an Indian thing.
I understand where she's coming from. So what do you
say we don't go looking for her. We'll just drive down
to the wharf. If we find a place that looks warm and
inviting, we go inside and make nice with the locals.
Soak up some of the Carolinas' southern warmth."

It was Errol's turn to laugh appreciatively. Lily had
taken off down the trail on the east side of the hill that
led to the wharf. It was a pretty good bet that since she
hadn't returned home by now, she had taken refuge
from the chilly winter night inside some bar or
restaurant.

Jesse detoured into the living room to grab the keys
to his rental car from the fireplace mantel while Errol
took their coats from the closet. Less than a minute
later the two men stepped through the front door, Jesse
pulling on his gloves retrieved from his cashmere coat
pocket as Errol hastily yanked up the zipper on his
parka. "Judas Priest, it's gotten cold."

"That's good," Jesse said. "This way if we find my
niece and she gets too mad, we'll threaten to make her
walk home."

"I don't know," Errol said dubiously. "I think you
may have forgotten how stubborn Lily is."

"Nope, I haven't forgotten, but I remembered something even more significant."

"What's that?" Errol asked.

"She hates the cold."

Both men laughed, but as they backed from the drive and turned onto the snaking road that wound down the hillside, their grins wilted. Something about the quiet of the night reminded them of the somberness of the occasion that had brought them together in Rosehill. There no longer seemed to be anything to laugh about. They were on a mission

Find Lily.

Bring her home.

Keep her safe.

A seagull flew across the windshield, screeching. Errol shuddered. Jesse's hands tightened their grip on the steering wheel. Silence folded in on them again. Somehow the night had turned lonely. Lonely and freezing and forbidding. All at once.

Chapter Ten

Melancholia. Lily snatched the word from the fuzz that had settled over her mind after an hour and a half and four double scotches on the rocks. Somewhere she'd read an article about melancholy and the Native American. Seems the author had done a study on suicide among Indians; about the deadly combination of depression and alcohol that afflicted one out of four of her mother's people.

Lily giggled, raising her glass to the author. "Make that one out of three," she said aloud, then pressed the back of her hand to her mouth as the hiccuping laughter threatened to turn into sobs.

She wouldn't cry! She'd devoted the past ninety minutes to drowning her sorrows, forgetting that she'd buried her mother today.

Lifting her glass once again, she quickly drained the contents. Amazing how much better it tasted now than the first couple had. Remarkable how much easier it went down. No longer tasted like gasoline that ignited once swallowed and then seared her insides.

But if the scotch had lost some of its heat, the room had recovered it, she thought. Damn it was hot.

She was still wearing the ribbed black wool jersey

dress she'd worn to the funeral service. The sleeves were tight-fitting to her wrists, but she pushed them up to her elbows. There was nothing to do for the rest of the dress, which hugged her torso like a second skin before flaring at the hips and ending several inches above her knees. But she *could* take off the smothering leather boots. Who would care? she wondered as she glanced around the semidark, smoke-filled room. If anyone was paying her any attention, she couldn't tell it. Hell, she couldn't even *see* anyone else in the dense gloom. Only silhouettes that swayed in the cigarette smoke that danced drunkenly toward the ceiling.

Lily curled her stockinged toes against the deliciously cool floor a moment later, her boots discarded. Leaning back in her booth, she slid down a couple of inches, stretching her legs, flexing her ankles, and testing the pull of her strong calf muscles. Still there. Not reduced to gel by the booze. Tossing her head back, she raised her glass and signaled the bartender for a refill.

A few minutes later Charlie set another glass of scotch in front of her. "Think I better call you a taxi, Miss Hutton?" he asked.

Her head still laid back, her body nearly horizontal beneath the table, Lily wagged a finger from side to side. "Never, ever, ever suggest to a drunk that she has had enough, Charlie," she managed, though her tongue was suddenly thick and uncooperative. "Them's fightin' words. First rule taught in every respectable bartendin' school." She giggled. "Even I know that, and I don't drink!"

Charlie laughed. "Could've fooled me, honey."

Lily frowned, just sober enough to catch the sarcasm. "Well, 'course I'm drinkin' right now. I mean, that's obvious. I was talking about my chara ... characterist ... Never mind. You know what I mean."

"Yeah, sweetheart, I'm reading you like a book." He

started off, hesitated, and backtracked. Leaning low, he whispered, "Just slow it down a little. I'm keeping an eye out for you, but these guys are regulars I don't wanna tangle with if I can avoid it. You get my drift?"

Lily didn't but neither did she care. "Gotcha," she lied, signaling A-okay and winking for emphasis.

Understanding broke through the mist a few seconds later as she glanced around the room at the shadowy figures seated at the bar and tables. Why, Charlie was afraid they were going to hit on her! And why not? She'd come into the Striped Tuna looking for forgetfulness, hadn't she? What better way to accomplish that than with a party and new friends?

Reaching for her glass, she scanned the room more purposefully. Through half-closed eyes, she subtly tried to make out the faces of those closest to her. The dimmed lighting, heavy smoke, and her blurred vision conspired against her, and a flash of sobriety warned against such rashness. And then, suddenly, she heard her mother's voice softly reminding her of the dangers of blind trust. *You're too generous, Lily Dawn. You look at a coral snake and see only its pretty colors.*

The quiet analogy had been offered on the afternoon of Lily's eighth birthday party. Imogene Rivers had stolen a bracelet given to Lily by her Uncle Sander. Lily had watched the other girl take it from its box and slip it into the pocket of her dress. Later, when Sara had asked where it was, Lily had explained that Genie had borrowed it. Sara had pressed, wanting to know if the girl had asked to take the bracelet. Lily had answered honestly, "No, but I know she wouldn't just *keep* it. She's too pretty to be like that."

Pain at the bittersweet memory knifed through Lily's heart, and she quickly gulped her drink. Every thought of her mother brought fresh bouts of agony.

Seconds later, Lily felt the hurt ebb and a wave of peaceful lassitude wash over her.

A soft smile on her lips, she stretched, arching her back and giving herself fully to the moment that was the first truly relaxed instant she'd known since her mother's phone call the week before. A hairpin bit into her scalp, reminding her that her hair was still knotted at the base of her neck. Seconds later, it tumbled down her back, and Lily closed her eyes and rested her head on the back of the booth as she stared at the ceiling. This was nirvana, she thought. Total paradise.

Wiggling her bare toes, she realized she could hardly feel them. Laughing, she tested her fingers, then remembering the true test a friend had told her about, tapped at her front teeth. Definitely numb. She laughed.

Why had she never gotten drunk before? It was wonderful!

And then she remembered. She'd always danced through her stress and nerves and heartache.

After every cattle call, she danced.

Following every argument with Errol.

When she came home from one of the sad visits with her mother in the institution.

New pain pricked at her heart, and Lily jumped to her feet. Even deadened by the sting of whiskey her heart managed to detect hurt. Tears stood in her eyes as she reached into her coat pocket, retrieved a quarter, and hurried to the jukebox.

Her fingers trembling slightly, she traced the cataloged songs and artists, then punched F1, G2, and S4.

Squeezing her eyes shut, she rested her forehead against the cool plastic covering on the stereo system. Seconds later the first strains of music began to reverberate against her face and her body answered its call with a subtle swaying motion.

She heard the first crystal husky strains of Michael

Bolton's voice, tuned out the background buzz of scattered conversation in the tavern, and felt the faint cracks in the hardwood floor beneath her stockinged feet. She heard her mother again, this time so clearly, so believably real against her ear, she felt Sara's breath against her hair.

Dance, little one. Give yourself to the music.

Lily obeyed. There was magic in music and dance that was more powerful than any alcohol or medication. It would deliver her from all the hurt, set her spirit free.

Soon the world around her disappeared. No longer did the murmur of voices distract her or the heavy veil of cigarette smoke burn her eyes and throat. Tears rose to her eyes, spilling over her lashes to cool her cheeks while her dance warmed her soul.

From his seat in the far corner of the semi-crowded tavern, Sash winced at Lily's selection. Jesus, was she *trying* to hurt herself? Did the words to the sad ballad somehow validate Sara's death for her?

Well, she might need this masochistic rite or whatever the hell it was, but he didn't need to sit here and watch.

Downing his beer, he grabbed his coat, then pushed back his chair as he stood up.

"I'm outta here," he said to the other three men seated around the table. "See you all *mañana*."

One of the men lifted his chin a notch in farewell, then jutted it toward the dance floor. "Now that's some hot little stuff. Shoowee, my old lady ever move like that, we'd never make it to the bedroom. Treat the kiddies to some mean ruttin' right there in the living room in front of God and everyone."

"I'm telling ya," another of the fishermen agreed with a soft whistle for emphasis. "I ain't never seen nothing that pretty or that sexy."

The third man, barely old enough to be sitting in the bar, looked up at Sash. "You ain't really gonna leave while this show is playing?"

Sash muttered a curse under his breath, dropped his coat back into his chair, and ran his hands through his jet black hair. Of course he wasn't. These guys might all be his friends, men he'd worked the nets with, braved storms beside, walked the picket lines for. Any one of them would risk their lives for him. But he *owed* Sara. No way he could leave her kid in here alone with this pack of wolves.

Cursing again under his breath, he crossed the floor in a few long strides. "Come on," he said in a low growl as he grabbed Lily's arm, spinning her around. "I'll take you home."

The surprise that registered on her face dissolved into pleasure with recognition. Her smile spread slowly and her eyes blinked a sleepy greeting. "Hey, Sash, I didn't know you were here. Long time no see, huh?" she asked, then hiccupped on a giggle. "Been a whole afternoon and at least a half-dozen drinks since this morning at my mother's grave. Guess it's true what they say about time flying when you're havin' fun."

Looping an arm around his neck, she canted her head slightly. "You come to dance with me, gorgeous?"

Sash started to shake his head, but one look into her eyes, and he knew she wasn't focusing. Neither was she waiting for his answer as she twisted her arm free of his grip, then stepped closer, wrapping it around his neck as well. "Hold me, Sash. Dance with me," she said in a breathless whisper against his ear.

Sash groaned inwardly, but didn't pull away. He couldn't. He'd passed the entire afternoon and the early hours of night in the tavern drinking beer, even downing more than a couple shots of eighty-proof whiskey in his quest for forgetfulness, numbness. But in the moment that he joined her, allowed her to press her lithe, well-muscled body against his, he was as sober as a sinner on Judgment Day.

A catcall that he recognized as coming from one of his friends reached them as he began to move his feet in time with hers. "Ignore 'em," he muttered.

Lily might not have heard or maybe she simply followed his instruction to pay the comment no attention, for her dancer's legs continued to move as she buried her face deeper into the hollow of his throat.

He knew he was playing with fire, could feel its flames, but he was merely protecting her, sheltering her from the lewd thoughts of the Tuna's patronage. Just this one dance and he'd help her into her coat and boots and out of the bar.

He told himself all this while the warmth of her breath stirred against his throat, the fingers of her hands toyed restively against the hair at his shirt collar, and the subtle sway of her body stirred a savage hunger in the pit of his belly.

With a quiet moan, he gave up the fight and surrendered to the command of the music and the pull of her body.

Tightening his grip around her waist, he lowered his face so that his lips brushed her hairline at her temples, and closed his eyes.

They moved together in perfect sync, each of them feeling the other's blood pulse as passion for the music and their dance surged and ebbed, then welled again. Neither spoke. Sash's hands roamed from her waist to her back, caressing her hips, then lingering on her backside for a heartbeat.

Every nerve in Lily's body tingled in response to his touch. Her breath caught in her throat as she pressed herself even tighter against him. Sara had taught her how to feel the joy of dance, how to experience the exquisite pleasure of giving oneself to the music, but never had she known such ecstasy. Raising her face to his, she looked into his half-closed dark eyes. Did he feel it? This rapture that was so sweet it was almost agony?

Sash could feel her heart beating against his chest, heard her breath catch before quickening, and saw the question in her eyes. He knew he should stop, but sweet Jesus, he couldn't. Not yet.

Chapter Eleven

Neither of them moved for a long moment after the music faded, then died. Lily was the first to pull away, though slowly, reluctantly.

Embarrassment, acute and fierce, suddenly washed over her. Oh, God, she'd made a complete ass of herself. "Thanks ... for the dance," she said, tucking her hair behind her ears and forcing herself to stop staring at the floor, to meet his gaze. She even managed a small grin. "Guess I was pretty conspicuous out there by myself."

Sash shook his head, setting free a rebellious shock of black hair that fell over his brow. "These guys just aren't used to anyone as pretty as you around here. Especially not in a place like the Striped Tuna and dancing like you do."

Lily's smile widened. "That was nice of you," she said softly. "Thanks." She started past him, stopping midway and backing up. "You're a good dancer, too. I didn't remember that. My mom teach you?"

Sash shrugged. The last person he wanted to talk about was Sara Two Moons-Hutton. He didn't even want to think about her. That was why he'd spent the afternoon drinking. But how did he avoid such an innocent question without provoking more questions? "She tried," he said, at last. "Said two left feet were better than none."

Lily laughed. "She must have been teasing. She had an eye for talent. I don't think she would have missed yours."

Sash felt suddenly angry. How could she laugh and joke with her mother buried today? He wanted to hurt Lily with his memories. "Sara wasn't interested in anyone's talent except yours. She was always saying how great you were going to be. Guess she was right, you dancing professionally and all in New York now. You on Broadway?"

Lily noticed the way he'd jammed his hands into his back pockets, and how his gaze flashed with some strange emotion. He was obviously uncomfortable; it was clear he wanted to get away from her. So, who'd asked him to stick around making polite chitchat? Not her! Abashed, she attacked.

One hand on her hip, she caught his jaw with the other, forcing him to meet her eyes. "Been a while since I attended any southern cotillions, Rivers, but I'm pretty sure it's still considered proper and polite to simply bow and walk away after thanking a lady for the dance. Conversation isn't obligatory even for the most chivalrous southern gentleman." Dropping her hand, she flicked her wrist in his direction. "So, good-bye. Shoo."

Anger sparked in Sash's dark, midnight-blue eyes, even as a contradicting grin spread into place. "In case you haven't taken a good look around, princess, this ain't no effing cotillion, and I've never been accused of being a gentleman. And sweetheart, whoever saw to your upbringing after your mama wasn't around to do it forgot to teach you that *ladies* don't wander into honky-tonks alone, get soused, then put on an exhibition that would tempt a saint."

Without warning, tears washed to the surface of Lily's eyes. How dare he judge her! Didn't he remember that she had buried her mama that morning? Didn't he understand?

The bar was merely the hole she'd crawled into to lick her wounds; the scotch, the Novocaine she'd chosen to numb her pain, and the dance, the release her soul always sought.

Her hands clenched into fists at her sides, she began to tremble with rage too long kept in check. "And what about you, Sash? You're one of the local nobility. This where the Rosehill aristocracy slink off to when they don't want to be bothered with nasty loose ends?"

Sash's confusion was too genuine to be contrived, but in spite of her razor-sharp anger, Lily's perception was still too muddled by alcohol for her to trust her judgment. "Oh, don't look like you don't know I'm talking about my mother. Sara. Remember her? She was the woman who treated you with love and kindness from the first moment she laid eyes on you. She was the woman you never once visited in all the years she was locked away in that . . . that hellhole. I'm talking about Sara, the woman we buried today. The woman you were in love with even though she was married to someone else. The woman you couldn't even bother to pay tribute to today." Tears streamed down her face now, and Lily was suddenly exhausted as if the last of her energy had flowed with them. Swiping at her face with the backs of her hands, she gave her head a shake and brushed past Sash. "Oh, never mind. Just go away, Rivers."

But Sash's own anger had been stoked into full flame by her ambush as well. Grabbing her arm, he spun her around, then drew her close so that she had to tilt her head back to see his face. When her sherry-brown eyes locked with his, she caught her breath at the rage burning in their ink-blue depths.

Sash laughed at her reaction. "What? All of a sudden you afraid you might have gone too far, princess? Guess what? You're right. You did." His voice was cold, icy with threat.

"Forget it," she said, trying to pull free of his grip. "I don't care why you didn't go see her or why you didn't join us at your mother's after the service. Obviously, Sara didn't mean what I thought she did to you." She raised her chin a notch, defiance swirling in her eyes in spite of the fear that churned in her stomach.

Music began to spill from the speakers again, and someone from the back of the room shouted a request for another dance. Sash ignored the slurred demand, and as abruptly as he'd grabbed Lily's arm, he let her go. Jutting his chin in the direction or the table she'd occupied, he said, "Get your boots and coat on. I'll take you home."

"What if I'm not ready?"

Sash shook his head as he grabbed her elbow and steered her across the room, then none too gently pushed her into the booth. With a loud sigh, he sat down beside her, picked up her boot, and caught one of her feet in his other hand.

"What do you think you're doing?" she said loud enough for her question to be heard even above Garth Brooks.

Sash didn't answer as he worked her foot into the boot, pulled up the zipper, then dropped it to the floor with a loud thud, and picked up the other boot. A moment later, he stood up, seized her coat from the opposite bench, and taking her hand, pulled her up beside him. "Put this on," he said, thrusting the coat at her. "I'll get mine and meet you at the door." He started to walk away, turned back, and said, "Settle your tab with Charlie, and be nice. He thinks you're some kind of classy lady. No sense disillusioning him."

For the first time in more than five minutes, Lily found her voice. "You're an asshole, Rivers."

"Just get your coat on and settle up, Hutton. The weather's suppose to take a turn by morning, and I need to be up by dawn."

He turned away on the last words leaving Lily to stare at his back. What did the weather have to do with what time he got up? she wondered, though she'd rather have cut out her tongue than ask. Shrugging into her coat, she pulled her billfold from her pocket and crossed to the bar. "How much do I owe you?" she asked Charlie when he looked her way.

"Not a penny, honey. It's on the house." He winked. "Consider it my way of paying my respects to your ma."

Tears filled her eyes again, and Lily shook her head. "Would you believe I haven't cried in years? Today I think I'd cry over spilled milk."

"Hey, you're entitled," Charlie said earnestly. "When my old lady passed, I bawled like a baby for a week."

Lily smiled, lifting her hand in farewell. "Maybe I'll see you again before I leave."

"Stop in anytime. 'Specially if you're plannin' to treat my customers to another show. That was some mighty pretty dancing you and Rivers was doin' out there. The guys loved it."

At the reminder of the spectacle she knew she'd made of herself, Lily felt her face heat. "We knew each other as kids."

"Yeah, I kinda figured."

"We're not friends or anything now," she went on, though why she didn't know.

"Too bad, Sash is one of the good guys," Charlie said.

Lily nodded. "My mother thought so, too."

Charlie pointed toward the door. "He's waiting for you."

"Insists on taking me home," Lily explained with a dismissive shrug. "I can take care of myself. I live in New York. Rosehill is hardly intimidating after that."

But Charlie didn't seem to be listening. Instead he was looking at Sash, a quizzical expression on his face. "Sonofabitch. Never thought nothin' would get him back up in them hills."

A man at the bar was staring at Sash as well. "No shit." Then with a sidelong glance at Lily, he added, " 'Course, ain't been nothing this fine up there . . ."

Lily walked away before he'd finished his sentiment. She was thinking about what Charlie had said. What did he mean he didn't think anything would ever get Sash up in the hills? Sash *lived* in the hills. He was a Rivers. His family was one of twelve of the most powerful dynasties in the Carolinas.

Without speaking, Sash guided them around to the side of the square building. Nudging her with his shoulder, he pointed to a gleaming black motorcycle. "It'll be cold, but I'll drive slow so the wind's not too bad. It'll beat walking. Sorry I don't have a nice, big, warm car."

Lily hardly registered his words. "Why do you have to be up so early?"

"Huh?" Sash asked, losing her in the U-turn back to his earlier comment.

"Tomorrow. You said you have to get up by dawn. I was just wondering why." She shrugged. "No big deal if you don't want to tell me."

Pulling on a black helmet and throwing a leg over the bike, he motioned for her to get on behind him. "We'll take the boats out in the morning. The weather's been unpredictable these past few days, which makes for contrary waters. Tomorrow promises to be dry and calm. Got to take advantage while we can until spring or our profits'll be for shit."

"Is this some kind of field work you do for your father? Going out with the fishermen from time to time to oversee their work?"

Sash's laughter was carried away from her in the breeze as he grabbed her hands, drawing them around his waist, but even so, she thought she detected bitterness. With one good kick, he brought the bike to life. Only then did he answer her. "You've been away too long, princess."

Just after Sash started northeast with his passenger, Jesse and Errol entered the Striped Tuna. Moments later, they exited again.

"I can't believe she'd go off with him," Errol complained as they stopped beneath the flashing neon sign while Jesse pulled on his fur-lined gloves and adjusted his cashmere scarf at his throat.

"What's so hard to believe? It's cold. He offered her a ride home."

"She coulda called one of us or taken a taxi. They do have taxicabs in this burg, don't they?"

Jesse chuckled as he slid behind the wheel once again. "Got a cab company, airport, even a motel or two. Only thing Rosehill doesn't have is smog and high-volume crime."

Errol pulled the door shut after himself and crossed his arms as part of his sulk. "Yeah, regular little Shangri-la. *Unless* you believe Lily's theory that someone other than her mother murdered her dad, and now that same person just killed Sara, too. If you believe that, then you have to believe there's a good chance it was one of the good folk up in the hills. After you digest all of that, think about the fact that she just rode off with one of them."

"Fasten your seat belt," Jesse said.

"That doesn't worry you?" Errol asked.

"Not particularly. Sasha Rivers was just a kid when Alison was killed. Even if Sara somehow did manage to call Lily Dawn and proclaim her innocence, I don't thinks she would ever have pointed a finger in Sash's direction. She loved that boy like her own."

"Well, it sure as hell bothers me," Errol mumbled.

Laughter rumbled from the driver's side of the car. "That bartender said they were on a motorcycle. Don't think you have to worry about things getting too hot."

"I'll stop worrying after we get back to the house and find her safe and sound." *And alone.*

Sander Hutton was alone. Picking up his cellular phone, he pecked out a number in the dimness of his luxury car. "Guess who's on his way up the hill?" he asked as the call was answered on the other end.

"Sander? What time is it?" a sleep-thick voice asked irritably.

Ignoring both the question and the irritation, Sander kept his eyes on the single reflector light in front of him as he slowly trailed it up the winding road. "Sash has apparently decided to end his exile."

"What are you talking about? Sash is on his way here? But he hasn't been home since he left fifteen years ago."

Sander's sigh was long and heavy. "I didn't say he was coming home. Only that he's on his way up the hill. I'm right behind him."

"Then where is he going?"

"Looks like he's on his way to my brother's house."

Silence.

"Did you hear me?" Sander asked.

"You think he's going to see the girl?"

Sander almost smiled at the fear he detected in the

other voice. Would have if he weren't so worried himself. "She's *with* him," he said.

"With him!" It was not a question but a sharp bark that betrayed panic. Then in a slightly calmer tone, "Why? How?"

"I don't know. I just spotted them at the four-way stop. Hardly paid them any attention until he pulled out in front of me when I had the right of way."

"Get rid of him, Sander. Don't make it obvious to the girl. Just make sure he doesn't stay."

Sash had no intention of staying. He hated the hills, hated the memories that still haunted him after all this time.

For fifteen years he'd avoided the past by staying away. Now here he was, for the second time in two days, back up here.

Even in the numbing cold, which should have consumed his attention, he was being assailed by the ghosts of his bittersweet childhood and regretting his decision to drive Lily home.

Bringing the bike to a stop in front of her house, Sash reached behind him for her hand, helping her dismount.

Lily wiped wind-induced tears from her eyes, and took a stab at smoothing her snarled hair from her face. "Thanks."

"Yeah. See ya," he said, already backing up and beginning to turn away from her.

Automobile headlights suddenly captured him in their bright beam, effectively pinning him for an instant.

Sash faced the approaching vehicle head-on. He recognized the car at once, knew who the driver was though of course it was impossible to see anyone in the interior. For a heart-stopping few seconds, he was certain the operator intended to run him down. The wind had picked up, yet even over its wail, Sash thought he heard Lily's cry of warning. And then the driver blared his horn angrily before veering wide and turning into the driveway a mere fifty feet past them.

"I thought he was going to hit you," Lily said, her fear still lingering in her voice.

Sash eased the helmet from his head, smoothing back his dark hair as he stared past her at the man climbing from the car. "I wasn't too sure myself. Sander holds the record for accidents around here. Don't think he's killed anyone yet, though."

In spite of the scare she'd just experienced, Lily laughed. "You're exaggerating, surely."

Sash shook his head. "No, I'm not. Ask him. But wait till tomorrow. He'll be in a better mood after he's slept it off."

Lily looked from Sash to Sander, then back again, her incredulity stubbornly written on her face. "You're saying he has a drinking problem? I don't believe it. He was always so disapproving of my father's drinking."

Sash settled the helmet back over his head and snapped the chin strap into place before answering with a shrug. "Who knows? Maybe he took up where the doctor left off, carrying on the family tradition."

"Why are you so . . ."

"Cynical?" he offered as she looked for the word she wanted.

"Surly." She hesitated, then laid a hand on top of his gloved fingers as she searched the opaque shield of his visor for his eyes. Though she couldn't see anything but the mocking grin on his lips, her tone was gentler when she spoke again. "I don't think you were like this as a boy. I don't remember you that way."

Sonofabitch! Of course he wasn't the same! Nothing was the same. Never would be again. Why didn't she get it?

Removing his hand from beneath hers to slide it

around her waist and pull her against him, he said, "I'm not a boy anymore, sweetheart. Why don't you climb on again, and we'll go on down to my place. I'll treat you to a little demonstration of just how much I've changed. I think you'll agree things have definitely taken a turn for the better."

Lily opened her mouth to object, but Sander called out to her just then, checking her response. "I'll be right there!" she shouted.

Headlights framed them in its beam again, and Sash let his arm fall away. "Never mind," he said. "Looks like the rest of your gang is home. You'd better get on inside where it's safe and warm."

"I don't understand you." She spoke so softly the words might have been only a whisper of wind.

The vehicle passed them by, slowing and making a right-hand turn into the driveway as Sander had moments earlier.

"Regular Grand Central Station around here. The witch lady must hate this. She prizes her privacy and quiet," Sash said, looking past Lily.

Following the direction of his gaze, she realized he was looking past her house to the Rivers home above them, focused on the light that shone from the highest window in the Rivers home, and for a crazy minute, Lily almost thought Eudora was actually standing on the widow's watch. But, of course, that was silly. Still, a chill ran the length of her spine. Forcing her attention back to Sash, she laughed nervously. "By the witch lady, you mean your stepmother?"

"One and the same," he agreed.

"She was very kind today."

Sash didn't answer and though Lily still could not see his eyes through the tinted visor of his helmet, she thought he studied her face as if searching for an answer to an unspoken query. Then abruptly, he revved the motor. "They're waiting for you, princess," he said with a slight jerk of his chin.

Lily didn't turn. She didn't have to. She'd recognized Jesse's rental car and realized he and Errol must have been out looking for her.

"Why do you keep calling me that? Princess, I mean."

"It's what your dad always called you. That's the way I remember you."

He twisted the handles beneath his gloved fingers again, provoking another whir of the powerful engine, and Lily suddenly wished she could climb back on and ride away; leave the mysterious phone call and the questions about her mother's sudden death behind. She laughed softly under her breath and put a hand to her brow. She must be coming down with something or else was still very drunk, though she felt pretty damned sober. Whatever. She didn't want Sash to go. "Stay," she blurted. "Just for a little while. I know you have to get up early, but I'd like to talk to you, and Jesse will want to say hello, too. We didn't have a chance to talk to you at the cemetery today."

She could feel his eyes on her as he considered her request. Then he moved his head slightly, and she felt Eudora's influence as keenly as if she were standing beside them.

"Sorry, princess, I don't belong here . . . and neither do you. Forget everything you ever knew about Rose-hill. Go back to New York." Reaching out, he cupped her chin in the palm of a black leather glove. "Don't walk away, Lil. Run."

Chapter Twelve

Lily brushed past the three men still clustered on the front veranda. "What? None of you ever seen a motorcycle before?"

Exchanging glances, they followed her inside the house.

Once out of the cold, her anger quickly dissipated. She suddenly felt more tired than she could ever remember. Intending to stop only long enough to hang her coat in the closet, she turned to face the trio knotted in the entryway behind her. "Look," she said, hugging her coat beneath her chin as she leaned against the closet door, "I know you all worry about me—especially you and Sander, Uncle Jesse—but you don't have to. I'm a real, honest to goodness grown-up now. Ask Errol." She frowned, then amended her statement. "On second thought, don't ask Errol. He's no judge of what constitutes maturity.

"Anyway, thanks for looking out for me. I know you love me. But I can't stand being smothered like this."

"No one's trying to smother you, Lily Dawn," Jesse said quietly.

"Maybe you don't mean to, but you do. So tomorrow I want you to go home, Uncle Jesse. Your pretty young bride needs you more than I do with a new baby on the way. And Uncle Sander, I still don't understand why you've been living here instead of at your own house with Marla and your daughters." When he opened his mouth to speak, she waved away his explanation before it could be made. "No, don't get me wrong. I'm not asking why. I don't care, but I want you to go home to them, too."

"You can save your breath if you're about to send me back to New York," Errol said. "I'm not leaving you here alone. I was at the Rivers house today too, don't forget. I met most of your neighbors, and they give me the heebie-jeebies. They're loony-tunes, babe." He glanced Sander's way, sending a message of apology with his eyes. "Not that I'm including you, man."

In spite of her weariness, Lily chuckled. "He was born with his foot in his mouth. He can't help himself, Uncle Sander."

She had expected Sander to laugh with her, at least grant a pardoning smile, but her paternal uncle was suddenly pasty white and beads of perspiration dotted his brow and upper lip.

"Uncle Sander?" she asked, dropping her coat and taking a step in his direction.

Jesse, too, had noticed Sander's sudden pallor and had a firm hold on his forearm. "Come into the living room and sit down for a minute."

But Sander shrugged him off. "I'm fine. Really. I have these bouts, but they only last a few seconds. Nothing to worry about." He'd pulled a handkerchief from his pocket and was mopping his brow. Then with a tight grin of reassurance, he stepped past the others, stopping on the landing of the staircase. "If you'll excuse me, I think I'll go on up to bed. It's been a long, sad day. My old body is merely reacting to the stress of saying good-bye to a loved one."

Lily quickly handed her coat and hanger to Errol and hurried to kiss Sander's cheek. "I hope you feel better in the morning."

"Thank you," he said in an oddly choked whisper, and Lily was surprised by the tears she saw in his eyes. "Sander . . ."

"I'm all right, my dear. Truly. As I said, it's a sad time."

Lily implored her Uncle Two Moons to do something, say something, for she was suddenly sure Sander was anything but all right as he kept professing.

"Why don't I go up with you, Sander?" Uncle Jesse offered dutifully. "Just make sure you get to your room safely."

Anger that was too sharp and bright to be mistaken for anything other than what it was flashed in Sander's eyes. "I'm fine, damn it!" Then in a milder tone, "If everyone will quit fussing, I'll just take myself to my room and to bed. In the morning everything will begin to return to normal."

Lily waited until he'd disappeared down the upstairs hall before speaking. Even then, she kept her tone hushed. "Could it be his heart? Sash seemed to think he has a drinking problem. Could he have simply over-indulged? He arrived home just minutes before you pulled up, and though he wasn't driving fast, he almost ran Sash down. Do you think he could have been having a spell like we just witnessed?"

Jesse hazarded an opinion based on his experience as a psychiatrist. "Maybe it's just what he claims. A reaction to stress." His eyes raised to the upper floor as if he could see Sander through the ceiling, he added, "Although I don't think he's as upset about your mother's death as he'd have us all believe. Don't get me wrong, he was always cordial to your mother, but why should he care that's she's dead? Don't forget that she was convicted of killing his brother. I doubt *he's* forgotten. I suspect that it was your request that he return to his own home that induced his odd behavior."

Lily looked from her uncle to Errol, who held up his hands as if in surrender. "Hey, don't look at me. I told you what I think. This town is spooky and it ain't the scenery that gives me the creeps. These people are bonkers."

"Errol, these *people* were my father's friends and family."

"So what are you saying? All of a sudden you changed your mind about your mom calling you last week and telling you she didn't kill your dad?" he asked.

"No, of course not. It was her. I'm sure of it."

"Then you have to consider that if your mother didn't kill your dad, one of these other folks did. They may be family and friends, but, hell, with kin and pals like them you don't need foes. And that includes dear Uncle Sander. As Jesse here also noticed, he didn't get that sicker than shit look until you bid him *adios*. Methinks the man's gotten real comfortable in his brother's house, and he ain't planning on going anywhere."

Lily busied herself with hanging her coat in the closet while she digested what both men had said. Her hands trembled as she worked the top button into its buttonhole. It was true that Sander and Sara had never been close, but she was his brother's wife. Sander would never have been a party to Alison's death. It wasn't possible. Brothers didn't murder brothers.

Caine murdered Abel.

But Sander loved Lily. He was always there for her. Presents from him arrived regularly at her New York apartment; thoughtful little reminders of his affection for her. He telephone every few weeks or so just to see how she was doing. He was even the executor of her father's estate. Her trust was paid through his law firm.

And what about when Sander had called to tell her of her mother's unexpected death? Hadn't he also told her, "I'm here for you, Lily. We'll get through this together. Just come home."

Were those the words of someone who wished her ill?

"Come into my parlor," said the spider to the fly.

Dropping coat and hanger into a clattering heap, Lily pressed her fingers to her lips and fled the foyer for the bathroom at the back of the house. It might have been all the alcohol she'd imbibed at the Striped Tuna that rose to her throat as thick and bitter as bile. Or maybe it was fear, pure and simple.

Chapter Thirteen

The following morning the grandfather clock was chiming in the foyer below as someone pounded on Lily's bedroom door. With a groan that nowhere near reflected the level of pain that shot across her brow, she pulled her pillow over her head and burrowed deeper beneath the heavy down comforter. "Go away," she implored.

Errol opened the door disobediently. "Sorry, cute stuff, but you've got callers."

Lily peeked from under a corner of her pillow, moaned louder, and buried her face again. "I can't, Errol. My head's splitting, and my stomach is promising a repeat performance to last night's if I so much as move."

Errol sat down beside her with a decided bounce, provoking a curse. "Come on, babe. It's almost noon. Besides, I don't think your company is going to budge till you show your cute little puss."

"Who is it?" she asked without removing her head from its hiding place.

"Eudora Rivers and her voluptuous, drop-dead sexy daughter."

"Imogene?" Lily asked incredulously, tossing both

pillow and covers off as she scooted up to a sitting
position on her knees and tugged her T-shirt over her
hips. "She didn't come to the service yesterday." She
crawled from the bed and pulled a pair of jeans from
the chest of drawers. Wiggling into them, she added
over her shoulder, "She was one of the witnesses who
testified against my mom. She was just a kid, only two
years older than me, but I harbored a lot of hatred for
what she said at the hearing."

"What about the old guy? The one who claimed to
have witnessed the murder, too? You didn't seem so
angry at him yesterday when he showed up at the
cemetery."

"Joe Joe?" She was sitting beside him on the bed
once again, pulling on socks. "No, I wasn't, but that's
because he didn't claim to actually *see* her stab him. All
he said was that Imogene screamed, and that's when he
saw my father fall over the railing on the veranda."

"He never actually witnessed the murder?"

Lily shook her head, only then realizing that her hair
was still a tangled mess from her motorcycle ride the
night before. Grabbing the brush from the dresser, she
began the painful task of freeing the snarls as she related
the old black man's testimony. "He saw Daddy fall. Saw
my mother rush to the railing after him. But he said
he never saw her stab him or even push him." Though
she'd kept her memories focused only on the surface
details, ignoring Joe Joe's observations about the knife
and the blood, and her mother's piercing screams, tears
burned behind her eyes again. Her head still bent, her
face turned away from Errol, she finally managed to
speak again without betraying the extent of her heartache. "The last person I want to see right now is Imogene Rivers."

"Hey, I don't blame you. I'll tell her to get lost."

"No, if I'm going to do this—figure out the truth

about what happened to my dad, and now my mom—
I'll have to face her sooner or later. Might as well be
sooner. No sense serving notice that I'm declaring war
before I have my weapons assembled." Surreptitiously
wiping the wetness from the corners of her eyes, she
tossed her hair from her face and smiled. "Thanks for
raising me from the dead. Do me one more favor? Tell
them I'll be a few minutes? My mouth tastes like a
thousand shit-eating camels walked through it while I
slept. I'll brush my teeth, then come on down."

"Take your time. I'll just be down there feasting my
eyes on your luscious enemy." He crossed the room,
opened the door, and stepped out. He stuck his head
back in with a question, "That didn't make you even
the least bit jealous, did it?"

A twinge of sadness pinched at Lily's heart. But that
was silly. Errol was making a big show of being devastated by her defection when in truth what had once
been between them—lust or love, she'd never been certain—had been over with for a long time. She shook
her head, laughing at his woebegone expression. "Nice
try, buster, but I'm pretty sure you'll be licking your
chops instead of your wounds as soon as you close that
door behind you."

"You injure me, madam!" Errol said dramatically,
clutching his heart.

Lily held the hairbrush over her shoulder as if ready
to toss it. "I'm *going* to injure you if you don't get down
there and deliver my message," Lily said on a laugh
that reminded her fleetingly of what happiness had once
felt like.

Jesse and Errol were seated in the formal living room
with Eudora and Imogene. Both men rose when Lily
entered the room, a gesture that she recognized as a
testimony to their loyalty rather than a statement of

old-fashioned chivalry. Lily noticed with some satisfaction that Eudora had raised an impressed eyebrow, and treated herself to a mental grin.

"I hope you'll pardon the wait—" she began.

Imogene interrupted the rest of her statement, sliding forward so that she sat on the very edge of the sofa. "Lily, sweet, I'm so sorry I wasn't in Rosehill yesterday. You must forgive me. I was away in New York when your poor mama passed on. Mother called me, of course, as soon as she heard, but there was just no way I could get home in time for the service. Dix—my husband?—was receiving a prestigious award from his alma mater, and I just couldn't abandon him in his brief moment in the sun. Can you forgive me for not being here for you?"

Imogene hadn't changed an iota in fifteen years, Lily thought as she watched the cerulean blue eyes fill with crocodile tears. She was still the perfect southern belle, sugar and spice all the way from her honey-sweet drawl and dainty mannerisms, to her feminine attire of pink angora sweater dotted with seed pearls and matching cashmere slacks, winter-white ankle boots and luxuriant shoulder-length blond hair that smelled faintly of lilacs and was tied away from her face with a candy-striped bow. Her makeup was flawlessly applied, and Lily had the absurd thought that even the tears that wavered in her Kewpie-doll blue eyes dared not spill over to disrupt its perfection.

Eudora was likewise impeccably dressed, and Lily struggled against the childish urge to tuck her head inside her oversized T-shirt and hide.

As if reading her mind, Uncle Jesse moved to the fireplace behind the sofa where the two ladies sat. Leaning against the mantelpiece where he could observe without being watched himself, he took advantage of his position to wink encouragement at Lily. She lifted a corner of her mouth in response, then turned her attention back to Imogene. "There's nothing to forgive. Mother would have been the first to agree that your place was with your husband."

"How sweet of you to say so," Imogene drawled.

"It's the truth," Lily said impatiently.

"Nevertheless, you're very generous," Eudora interjected as if sensing the short fuse that burned inside their hostess this morning. She flashed a wide grin, including both Lily and Imogene in a motherly look of approval. "I must say it is good to see you two girls together again after all these years."

Lily blinked with surprise. *Good to see us together again?* When had they ever been together? Never that she could remember.

Seeking a diversion, she glanced over her shoulder to where Errol half stood, half sat in the window. "How rude of me not to introduce my friend. This is Errol—"

"Mills," Imogene said. "We met. Your uncle most graciously did the honors."

"Oh, well, did he also offer you some tea or coffee?"

"He did," Eudora answered, "and as we told him, we didn't come to disrupt your day. Genie was merely concerned that you know how badly she felt about not being here for you yesterday."

Lily ran a hand over her brow where it felt like tom-toms were pounding out war messages loud enough for the Seminoles to read in Florida.

"Are you all right, sugar?" Imogene asked.

"Just a headache," Lily said.

"Probably from your late night at that shabby little bar on the wharf," Eudora said.

Lily's head jerked upright at that. "How do you know where I—" She broke off her own question to glare at her uncle.

"Oh, no, don't be angry with Dr. Two Moons, dear.

He didn't tell me a thing. I'm afraid Sander is the one who's been carrying tales, though I hope you won't be too angry with him either. He worries about you."

"That may be," Lily said, springing to her feet, jamming her hands into the back pockets of her jeans, and circling the chair she'd occupied so that there was more distance between herself and the Rivers women. "But where I spend my time is no one else's business." She sighed. She didn't have the energy to fight them this morning. "Please don't be insulted. I appreciate your concern, though it's misguided. I take care of myself, and I keep my own counsel. Uncle Jesse and Errol can both attest to that."

Eudora's answering smile was condescending, that of a tolerant parent dealing with a wayward, dim-witted child. "But surely you understand, Lily, dear, that you are one of us. Your great-great grandfather was my great-grandfather. One of your great-aunts was my cousin. So you see, we're more than merely neighbors. All of us, every member of the original twelve families is related in some way. We're really one big family. I loved your father very much, and your mother, well, she was a dear soul. I know they'd want me to look out for you as long as you're here in Rosehill."

Was that Imogene's cue? Lily wondered when the young woman stood up and closed the distance between them to ask if what her mother had told her about Lily staying in Rosehill was true. "Are you seriously thinking about giving up a career on the stage to live here in this provincial, prosaic little town where nothing exciting *ever* happens?"

"My plans are still sketchy right now, Genie. I've just lost my mother, and as it happens, I'm in a position to take a few weeks off from my work." She paused, glancing at her uncle, who seemed to be warning her with his eyes not to say too much. She looked back at Imogene. "I'm playing it by ear. That's all I can tell you for the moment."

Imogene's face was as blank as a porcelain mask for a long moment, and then she smiled warmly, surprising Lily and catching her off guard. "Well, at least it looks like you won't be bored, not with late-night rides on the back of my brother's motorcycle and all."

"This come from Uncle Sander, too?" Lily asked, not bothering to keep her annoyance from her voice this time.

"No, actually, Mother said she saw you from her house last night. Seems she was having trouble sleeping so she went upstairs and stood on the widow's watch for a few minutes."

So it hadn't been merely a figment of Lily's imagination. Eudora had been standing there. But if Lily hadn't been certain what she was seeing, how could Eudora have known who was riding the bike? She turned to the older woman to ask her, but the question was answered before she could make it.

"I told her, Miss Lily," the housekeeper said from the doorway as she carried a tray into the room and set it down on the coffee table in front of Eudora. "I know you said you didn't want any tea or anything, but I thought I'd fix up a few goodies, just the same."

"Thank you, Kitty," Eudora said. "Your mother would be proud of what a considerate, conscientious employee you've become."

Helen Star, Kitty's mother, had been Sara's housekeeper from the moment Alison brought his bride home until two days after Dr. Hutton's death when Helen had inexplicably disappeared from the face of the earth. Though rumors had run fast and free about the woman's fate, no one had seen hide nor hair of her again.

"Would you please explain why you would report

what I do to *anyone* else?" Lily asked, unable to disguise
her outrage.

Kitty opened her mouth to answer, but Imogene interrupted, taking the question as though it had been
posed to her. "Oh, please don't be mad, Lily, honey.
It's all just a big silly misunderstanding. Mama hired
Kitty to look after your daddy's house, and then your
Uncle Sander when he moved in here. Kitty has been
in the habit of reporting to her when something needs
fixing, or when someone comes around who shouldn't
be here. It's nothing more than an employment
agreement of sorts." Her smile asked if Lily didn't understand how foolish she was to get so excited over
nothing. "Everyone on these hills has always looked out
for one another and like it or not, they're not apt to
stop to accommodate your big city ways. You've been
away a long time, and couldn't possibly know who
should be up here on the hills and who shouldn't be.
We all *care* about you, after all, and we're honor bound
to look out for you."

Eudora stood up then as well. Crossing the room in
an efficiency of brisk strides, she wrapped her arms
around Lily, drawing her into a tight embrace. "I know
you pride yourself on your fierce independence, Lily
Dawn. Your Uncle Sander has remarked on it often
over the years. But as long as you intend to stay here
with us, you're going to have to accept the fact that we
are a family who takes care of one another."

Lily extracted herself from the embrace, then went
to stand by Jesse's side. Her arms folded over her chest,
she shook her head. "I can't do that, Mrs. Rivers. I
value my privacy too much." She turned to Kitty. "And
I'll thank you to keep your observations to yourself
from now on."

"Oh, my!" Eudora cried. "You are a stubborn one,
aren't you? Wherever did you get it from? Not your

mother. She was such a sweet, docile creature. And not from Alison. Why, he'd rather have died than stop his family and friends from doing their charitable duty."

Lily was shocked by the careless reference to her parents, whose deaths had been so abrupt and tragic, and then it occurred to her that Eudora had wanted to shock her, had chosen her words with care. Anger blazed inside her chest and she balled her hands into fists at her sides. "I am absolutely amazed that you would describe my mother as docile, considering that your own daughter accused her of murder."

"Ah, but any one of us is capable of being pushed too far and though Genie was unlucky enough to have witnessed poor Alison's death, none of us can know what happened between him and Sara that provoked her to such violence," Eudora said, totally unruffled by the anger in Lily's tone. "As much as I hate to even consider it, I can't forget that my own stepson had formed quite a crush on your mother. I've wondered many times if her obsession with him wasn't the catalyst that pushed your father to alcohol and anger, and your mother to her ultimate loss of control . . .

"Which reminds me, whatever were you doing with Sash last night?"

"Why, Eudora? Afraid another Hutton woman might fall victim to his charms?" Lily asked, relishing the satisfaction she felt when the older woman's face drained of color except for two unsightly purple patches that appeared on her cheeks.

"It was an innocent question," Eudora defended in a hushed tone, reflecting her injury.

Run, Lily. Don't walk.

"Was it?" Lily asked, remembering Sash's strange parting warning.

Jesse stepped forward, wrapping his arm around Lily's shoulders and taking control of the situation. "It's been a difficult time for us as you can imagine. Why don't we put this conversation on ice until our equilibrium has been regained?"

"Certainly," Eudora said stiffly. Then to his niece, "I'm sorry if I upset you, Lily Dawn. Your parents and I were very dear friends. I doubt they would have misinterpreted my concern for meddlesome interference."

"I don't know," Lily answered. "I'm not them. But *I* don't care for it."

Eudora's smile was slow in coming, but it appeared nonetheless as she turned her attention to Jesse once again. "Surely, *you* understand, Dr. Two Moons. After all, we're not so different from a tribal community where everyone looks out for each other."

"Now, that is an interesting comparison for you to draw," Jesse said, his tone carefully neutral though Lily felt the sudden tension in his body. Ducking her head, she allowed herself a secret grin as she silently rooted him on. It did her heart good to know that even with all his training, he wasn't immune to anger.

"Perhaps if tragedy hadn't claimed her father and mother when Lily was so young," Jesse continued, "she might feel more strongly about these bonds to family. As it is, however, I'm afraid my niece puts very little stock in blood ties merely for their own sake."

Eudora's smile faded a bit, but she quickly recovered it. "I see, and this doesn't trouble you?"

Jesse matched her grin. "Why, not at all. In fact, I've always discouraged blind allegiance. Fidelity should be earned, don't you think?"

"Obviously I wouldn't disagree that merit has its rewards. On the other hand, I very much believe in family pride and allegiance. After all, heritage is the one asset any of us is born with."

"Well, I'm as positive as I can be that Dr. Two Moons feels the same way, Mama. So let's not worry the point to death," Imogene put in, shrugging her pretty shoulders and treating everyone to one of her dazzling smiles. "Anyway, we have to be scootin' along."

Thank you, God, Lily thought, ushering the two women to the front door.

Errol was waiting there ahead of them, coats in hand. "Leaving so soon, ladies?" he asked, causing Lily to nearly burst out laughing. She sent him a warning glare, which he ignored. "But you didn't even have any of the refreshments Kitty prepared."

"Put a sock in it," Lily whispered, yanking the coats out of his arms.

"We're delighted to have you back with us, Lily Dawn," Eudora said as soon as she'd slipped into her coat and pulled on her gloves. "I only wish it was under happy circumstances. Ah, well, perhaps your stay here away from that Sodom and Gomorrah will provide you with some peace and comfort."

"It's not exactly peace that I'm looking for," Lily couldn't help saying.

Jesse clamped her shoulder with his hand, applying pressure. Lily merely shrugged it away. She'd had enough. She wasn't going to lay all her cards on the table, but it was high time she let them know she was in the game.

There was only one way to get to the truth about her mother's death and maybe even the facts surrounding her father's murder, and that was to start beating the fields. She was certain there were at least two blue-eyed snakes she could stir up.

"Then what is it, sugar?" Imogene asked.

"Answers. I intend to find out what *really* happened in this house the day my father died."

"But I'm sure every available detail was shared with you, dear," Eudora said. "Of course, none of us can ever really *know* what went on between your parents before . . . well, before Sara lost control." She held up her hands in a gesture of helplessness. "I'd always hoped that one day Sara might snap out of that trance she was in and tell us. Unfortunately, now with her death, even that possibility is gone."

Lily was suddenly aware that she was flanked on both sides by Errol and Jesse. Glancing at each of them, she could feel their tension and realized that they held their breath. She smiled, wondering at the serenity she suddenly felt. "In many ways, you're right of course. None of us will ever know precisely what occurred when my mother went flying out of the dance studio as Imogene testified that she saw her do. We can only guess. Did my father call to her at the exact moment that her music stopped? Was she working on the choreography for my new dance when it suddenly occurred to her to stop and run upstairs and kill him?"

"Don't be absurd," Eudora snapped. "No one's suggested that."

"I know," Lily said quietly. "And I have to wonder why. Why weren't alternative theories presented at the hearing? She couldn't argue for herself. Why didn't someone—any one of you, her loving family—pose these questions?"

"Because," Imogene said, "Mr. Joseph and I saw what we saw, Lily. I'm sorry, but nothing can change that."

"Wait," Lily said, ignoring her cousin's reasoning. "There's another plausible explanation for why a woman in the middle of working out a dance routine would suddenly stop and rush upstairs. What if she heard someone else up there? Another voice other than her husband's?"

No one spoke or even moved. Only the ticking of the clock behind them gave evidence that time had not stopped. That and the way the blood slowly drained from Eudora's face.

"But that's impossible," Eudora said finally in a strangled whisper.

"Why?" Lily asked. "Genie was watching from the back of the house. What if someone came in the front and left the same way. Neither she nor Joe Joe would have seen him ... or her."

Eudora rubbed her brow with trembling fingers. "It just doesn't make any sense."

"Of course it does," Lily insisted. "It makes all the sense in the world because she would never have killed my father. She loved him. No matter what you claimed, Genie, I think we're missing part of the puzzle. The key piece that would exonerate her."

"Would ... would you escort my daughter and me to the car, Doctor?" Eudora asked, turning her back on Lily.

Without answering, Jesse gave his niece's shoulder another tight squeeze, this time clearly signaling his support, and followed Eudora and Imogene from the house.

He was surprised at how quickly the older woman regained her composure when she motioned her daughter into the car, then turned suddenly and said, "I'm very worried, Jess."

A brow lifted with his surprise. *Jess?*

"I know how painful this is for you. Sara was your sister, after all. But we both know that things were not—how do I say this? Exactly copacetic between dear Ali and his wife. Lily is their daughter. She'll never accept that sometimes things go wrong in a marriage; in a person's mind as it did in poor Sara's. You're going to have to help her understand that what is past is over and done with and no matter how badly we wish we could change the past, it's impossible.

"Of course, I realize Lily is an artist, and everyone understands how unstable creative types can be. She has already demonstrated an impulsive derring-do that I think could be a very serious sign of underlying symptoms. Why, just look at the company she keeps. First that dreadful actor and now my stepson."

Jesse pulled his lips back in a grin that he hoped resembled encouragement and at the same time disguised his mounting aggravation.

Eudora smiled in return, then tilted her head slightly to the side. "I suppose I'd be whistling in the wind if I asked you to use your influence to persuade her to go home, back to the stage where fantasy is an art form and not a nuisance?"

"Pissing against it, more likely."

Eudora's appreciative smile lit all the way to her eyes. "Am I missing the distinction?"

"Absolutely. Whistling in the wind is merely an exercise in futility, while pissing against it can make for some pretty nasty consequences."

Rich, full laughter bubbled from Eudora's lips. "Oh, my word, that's good! You know, Doctor, I'd quite forgotten how entertaining you are. Rather the Native-American equivalent to Confucius, aren't you?" But just as quickly as the laughter began it ended, and a look of pure hatred was left in its wake like charred rubble in the path of glorious fire. "Remind her that we're family. We'll stand by her even as she makes a fool of herself. We won't allow her to make fools of us, however."

"Is that a warning, Mrs. Rivers?"

Laughter tinkled through her lips once again. "Good heavens, no, Jess, darlin'. I'm just talkin' to hear my own voice. It's what my husband says we southern women do best."

*   *   *

When Jess reentered the house a few minutes later, Errol and Lily were waiting for him in the living room again. Both turned their heads expectantly when they heard the front door open and shut.

"Well?" Lily asked, turning around completely in her seat so that she peered over the back of the couch. "Did I put my foot in it so good I won't be able to pull it out again?"

"Believe it or not"—Jesse dropped into an easy chair beside the fireplace and automatically reached for his pipe and the pouch of tobacco that lay near it—"the lady's pretty damned quick on her feet. Recovered as if you'd never given her a fancy surprise dance step to learn."

Lily laughed. "I'm not worried. I'm the one who's hosting this dance, and I'll dictate the tempo."

Jesse sighed. "Could you make it a slow dance? This old guy isn't up for too many quick maneuvers."

"Come on, Errol," Lily said, slapping his knee when she noticed the dark frown on his face. "Lighten up. It all needed to be said. I'm glad the truth about why I'm staying is out in the open."

Errol shook his head, then jumped to his feet. "No, I'm not doing this. You know me, babe. I'm all for good times, a party-a-minute kind of dude, but if you're right about this, you're dealing with cold-blooded murder. You'll forgive me if I don't sit here yucking it up with the two of you, while you congratulate each other about how cleverly you've put yourself in danger."

He left the room, and Lily and Jesse heard the closet door open and shut, then the front door.

"He's right, Lily Dawn."

"I know," she said quietly, standing up and walking to the window. She rubbed her forearms briskly as a shiver traipsed the length of her spine. Without turning, she added, "But I've spent fifteen years pretending this wasn't real. If I stop now, I won't be able to fight them because I'll have to accept that there aren't really any happily-ever-afters and that good guys don't always win."

Chapter Fourteen

"*Son of a bitch*," Errol muttered under his breath. He'd stormed from the house without car keys or billfold. Now here he stood, ass in one hand, pride in the other. Well, he sure as hell wasn't going back in there to get them. Reaching into his jacket pocket, he came back out again with ... a dollar eighty-two in change. Enough to buy a cup of coffee and beat a loitering charge. Fine, *if* he could find an IHOP or a set of golden arches and *if* he didn't freeze his balls off on the hike down the mountain.

Unlike Lily, Errol wasn't much on cardiovascular exercise.

He frowned. Come to think of it, that was probably the least of his and Miss Hutton's disparities. Not that he hadn't realized that before today. After six years, he'd pretty much deduced that their shared love of the arts might well be their only commonality. But damn it, their differences hadn't seemed to get in the way so much until they arrived in Weirdsville, USA, two days before.

Since then, though, her heritage had become more than the tidy check she received every month from her trust. Here, in the aristocratic bosom of her father's family, and under the guidance of her wise and equally wealthy maternal uncle, Errol could pretty much hear the chains creak as the drawbridge was being raised to protect her royal fucking highness from the bloody riff-raff of which he was clearly deemed to be a bona fide, card-carrying member. Fucking A, he thought with a burst of rebellious pride. Born the eighth child just six hours south of here to fourth-generation Florida crackers, he'd arrived in the world with his own birthright of forty-two dollars a month in additional welfare benefits to his grateful parents.

Huffing pretty significantly with exertion and wincing at the fire that burned in his calves as his anger fueled his descent, he laughed at the comparison. Ridiculous. There *was* no comparison. That was the problem. That and the fact that Lily didn't love him anymore.

Arriving at the four-way stop at the bottom of the hill, he turned right, away from the ocean and wharf, and headed toward what he hoped was town. He was careful to check street signs, register landmarks, and keep his eye on traffic which should increase as he approached the heart of the Rosehill business district. Only minutes later, however, his thoughts turned away from his destination and returned to his troubles with Lily.

Admit it, he told himself. *Lily* never *loved you.* Once upon a time, she'd confused a hopeful, young actor with a knight in shining armor, and developed a pretty fierce crush. True. But that was many moons ago, to borrow from her uncle's vernacular, before the tarnish began to show.

Jamming his hands deeper into his pockets and tucking his chin into the collar of his jacket, he cursed the frigid temperatures and the short straw he'd apparently drawn in the love department.

Maybe he should face the inevitable; pack his bags

and return to Manhattan. He'd never been a quitter, but wasn't there a difference between making a timely exit and tucking tail and running?

Sonofabitch, he was getting cold. Hungry, too.

Glancing around him, he realized that he had in fact been walking toward downtown Rosehill. He now stood at the intersection of Third and Broadway. He laughed, sending rolling gusts of steamy breath into the atmosphere. Broadway, huh? Not exactly!

He wished Lily was with him to share the humor, he thought on another amused laugh. But these days, he doubted she'd crack a smile. These days she was pretty damned humorless. Probably get on him about poking fun at her hometown.

Stomping his feet, he glanced around, looking for a restaurant or diner, anyplace where he could grab a hot cup of coffee and hide out from the cold for a time.

To his right, a cluster of gleaming, bronze or silver mirrored high-rises competed for attention. On the left, the buildings were older, plainer, clearly leftovers from a more modest day and age. And looking down Third, he caught a glimpse of an intersecting street that promised another facet to downtown life. He read the sign: THE ALLEY.

Neon lights flashed though it was barely after noon, and muted blasts of raucous music could be heard even from a distance of more than a block.

Ignoring the signal light he'd been waiting on, Errol sprinted down Third and cut across it at a jog.

Two minutes later, he was sliding onto a stool in a diner called Eddy's and leaning his elbows on a counter. A pretty little waitress with a bouncing auburn ponytail and laughing bottle-green eyes appeared from behind swinging doors with a menu in hand and a friendly smile in place. Her crisp blue-and-white checked uni-

form fit her body in all the right places, showing off
lush curves on a petite frame.

"You sure don't look like no Eddy to me," he said,
already starting to thaw from his long walk.

She wrinkled a lightly freckled nose and giggled. "Do
I look like an Eddy's daughter?" she asked.

"That could work," Errol agreed, shrugging from his
jacket and placing it on the empty stool beside him.
"But I bet you got a pretty name to go along with your
cute little face."

She rolled her eyes as if to say she'd expected better
and handed him the menu. "Lunch rush is gonna start
picking up any minute so Pop says you better decide
quick."

Errol laughed as he glanced around the tiny restaurant. He was the only customer in the room. He liked
this girl. Reaching for his jacket, he pulled out the
pocket change, confirming the dollar eighty-two he'd
counted earlier. "Okay, Eddy's daughter, bring me a
cup of java and a bowl of soup."

"Potato or vegetable?"

"Surprise me," Errol said with a shrug.

"Ooh, a man who likes to live dangerously," she answered, placing a generic white porcelain mug on the
counter in front of him. Reaching behind her for a glass
coffeepot, she rested her free hand on her hip as she
filled the cup. "Name's Nancy. A few folks call me Nan.
Nickname's Rusty. Most of the guys—regulars—call me
that." She turned away, replaced the pot, then pushed
open the aluminum swinging door with her hip. She
paused. "Tell you what, you figure out why, and I might
just find y'all a BLT to go along with that ol' soup and
coffee. On the house."

Errol wrapped his hands around the steamy mug,
wincing at the sting that began in his fingertips and
worked its way up to his knuckles. *Probably frostbitten*

he thought gloomily. But within seconds, the redness began to disappear and the burning began to ease up. He sipped the coffee and let his thoughts return to his problematic relationship with Lily.

Maybe he should read the proverbial writing on the wall. After all, it wasn't like he hadn't known the end was near. For months now, she'd been telling him she wanted him to look for another apartment, a new roommate, anything as long as it meant he would move. Hell, he didn't even blame her. They hadn't been sleeping together for at least a damn year. As an actor, he was still an undiscovered genius. His contributions to room and board depended on whatever his current part-time job was at the moment. Mostly, he handled the cleaning and cooking. Not much of an inducement to allow him to stay on indefinitely.

Not that she hadn't been fair. Shit, she'd allowed him to hang around long after it was clear they weren't going anywhere as a couple. But then they were great and supportive friends to each other.

And the truth was, he couldn't even claim a broken heart. He loved her in his own selfish way. She was beautiful, talented, and unusually thoughtful for one so young. She was also on her way to stardom. She'd always been destined for greatness. He'd seen that at once. Now, it had come knocking, and frankly he'd been determined to stick around for the party. Errol Stanley Mills was a narcissist, but he was also honest. He knew his faults and his strengths and freely admitted both. He was one hell of a talented thesbian. No doubt about it. But he wasn't lucky. He needed someone like Lily to take him with her to all the right places where he could meet the right people. She'd once accused him of being nothing more than one of those fish that attached themselves to sharks, always along for the ride and around for the feast after the kill. Fucking A, he'd answered. Damned straight.

But the truth was, even the most persistent takers had to know when the ride was over.

"What you frowning about?" Nancy asked, startling him from his reverie as she placed a steaming cup of vegetable soup and a thick, triple-tier sandwich in front of him.

Ignoring the question, Errol inhaled deeply. "Umm, smells great. You sure the sandwich is on the house? I left home without my billfold. Only got enough to cover the—"

"Hey, I understand. No big deal, okay?"

He started to answer, but she was already moving away, smiling at newcomers as they entered the diner. Cops.

Pretty cool uniforms, he thought as he bit into his sandwich, then absently licked a dollop of mayo from the corner of his mouth. Especially the Stetsons with their confederate insignias. He'd once thought about law enforcement. For about two seconds.

The two men spoke to Nancy for a few minutes. Though they stood within ten feet of him, he couldn't make out what they were saying, but he sure didn't like the way they kept looking at him. It was a good bet they knew all the faces in the area and would be quick to recognize a stranger. They were no doubt wondering where he'd come from.

Well, screw 'em. Let 'em wonder. He turned back to his food, giving it his undivided attention until one of the police officers clapped a hand on his shoulder a moment later.

Errol sputtered on his coffee, and angrily brushed the man's hand away. "Hey, man, I almost choked. You mind letting a guy finish his lunch before you surprise him like that?"

"Not at all if the man's got a name and some ID to back it up," the young officer said in an easy drawl that contrasted sharply with the serious frown on his face.

Errol had picked up the last quarter of his sandwich. With an impatient sigh, he set it back on the plate, wiped at his mouth with the paper napkin Nancy had given him, and turned on the stool so that he faced the two uniformed men. Nancy stood off to his left at the end of the bar; he didn't think he liked the worried expression he read in her eyes. "Look, guys, I'm not breaking any laws. My name's Errol Mills. I'm down here from New York with a friend. Her mother died a few days ago. I only came down here with her for moral support. So let me finish my food while it's still hot, okay?"

The older and bigger of the two men took a step forward so that he stood within inches of Errol. Freeing the snap on his holster, he pushed back the leather cover and placed a hand on the butt of his gun. He stroked the smooth wood handle slowly with his fingertips, letting a mean smile spread across his face at the same time. "Well, we sure wouldn't want to upset your meal, buddy." He laughed. "Tell him, Lonnie. We don't go around ruining folks' meals for 'em, do we?"

The other man snickered. "Not unless they give us reason."

"Come on, guys, he's not doing anything wrong," Nancy interjected.

"And we haven't accused him of any wrongdoing, Rusty," the older cop said. "We just want to see some identification. Once we do that, we'll wish him a pleasant visit here in Rosehill, and mosey on outta here."

From the corner of his eye, Errol caught a glimpse of a face peering through the glass window in the kitchen's swinging door. It wasn't too hard to figure out what was going on. The waitress must have mentioned something to her father about Errol's lack of funds, and the old man had then called the cops. But why? Were these people really that paranoid? Evidently.

He held up his hands. "Listen, my name's Errol Mills. I'm a friend of Lily Hutton's, and I'm a guest at her house. I went for a walk and forgot to grab my wallet from the dresser before leaving this morning. But if you'll just let me make a phone call, I'll get in touch with her or her uncle and ask them to bring it here."

The bigger, older, uglier one signaled something with a jerk of his chin. Next thing Errol knew, he was being shoved from the stool, his face pressed against the countertop, and his legs kicked wide. In a matter of seconds, his hands were bound behind his back with a pair of handcuffs, and he was being pulled to a stance. "We've got strict vagrancy laws, pal."

"Fuck this! I'm not a vagrant!"

Something hard was jammed into his kidneys, and Errol grunted against the pain.

"We don't take kindly to that sort of vulgarity around our ladies, mister," the younger one explained though it was his partner who had delivered the punishment.

Involuntary tears had immediately flooded Errol's eyes, blurring his vision, but he detected a flash of russet-colored hair as Nancy disappeared into the kitchen. He guessed he wasn't going to get any support from her. Turning his attention to the young cop once again, he summoned an ounce of courage and dared another question. "Correct me if I'm wrong, but Rosehill *is* located within the United States, isn't it? I've still got federal rights guaranteed me under the Constitution, don't I?"

This time, his corporal discipline was delivered between his legs, swiftly and fiercely. Errol retched as his knees collapsed. His head dropped to his chest, and he flinched reflexively as the man holding him raised his nightstick again. But the blow he'd expected didn't come. Instead the man suddenly released his grip on Errol's forearm, allowing him to crumple painfully to the floor.

"Come on, Barrett," Errol heard the other one say. "Put it away. We're not supposed to beat him to death, just bring him in."

"I don't think anyone's gonna complain 'cause this piece of shit has a few bruises," the one named Barrett growled. But he grabbed Errol under the armpit all the same, while the other one got a hold on the other side.

Several seconds later Errol was tossed into the backseat of a black-and-white patrol car. He worked his way to the far side, rested his head against the window, and closed his eyes. A steel mesh wall divided him from his captors. Protection from the bad guys.

Errol thanked Jesus, then recanted it when he heard Barrett tell Lonnie, "Get on the radio. Tell 'em we got the lamb, and he's all trussed up for the sacrifice."

Errol groaned. It was definitely going to be a bad day.

Chapter Fifteen

Sash knew all about bad days and on a scale from one to ten, today was a mother.

He wore a dew rag on his head, a scowl on his face, and a tourniquet on his arm.

"Hey, Rivers, leave the rest to us. We'll unload the catch. You go on to the hospital and get that arm stitched up."

Sash glanced at the long gash just above his elbow, which was still oozing blood. It was going to have to be sewn closed all right. *Shit!*

Mopping sweat from his neck and chest with the back of his uninjured arm, he acknowledged his boss's advice with a modified salute, pulled his jacket on with care not to touch the wound, then leaped over the side of the boat onto the pier.

The day had been jinxed from the start. Six of the fishing fleet's crew had called in sick with a flu bug, then one of the trawlers had blown an engine. They'd made adjustments, rotating fishermen to able vessels, and headed out. A tuna shoal had been spotted just after daybreak and for a while, everyone forgot that trouble usually came in threes.

The net on the purse seiner Sash was working was

lowered without a hitch, but as soon as the order was given to haul the surrounded shoal aboard, it became apparent that the winch had seized up.

Sash hadn't hesitated. He was already halfway up the crane to examine the power block by the time most of the crew realized there was a problem.

After more than a decade on the seine netters, he knew every square inch of the powerful net-handling equipment, every potential for trouble, and every remedy. In only minutes, he had the winch free and was shimmying back down the mast. Halfway down he stopped to watch the net being drawn from the sea. A frown furrowed across his brow as he spotted the illegal bounty captured in the purse seine. Cupping a hand around his mouth, he yelled down to the men gathered at the stern awaiting the load. "Dolphin!"

The graceful sea mammals were protected from capture, and the men worked efficiently and competently to free them and return them to the ocean.

Once order had been restored, the men returned to their normal routine of sorting their booty. Some of the crew shared jokes or talked about family problems. Sash worked in silence. It wasn't unusual. He was never garrulous. But neither did he ordinarily wear such a dark scowl. From the corner of his eye, he saw one of his shipmates jab another guy in the ribs and raise a questioning brow. Sash ignored him. A man had a right to his own thoughts.

But he wished *he* could escape his thoughts. Wished he could turn back the clock and erase the day before entirely. Then he wouldn't have to remember the sight of Sara's daughter at the cemetery, her expression voicing more clearly than words her heartache and struggle against her grief.

He wouldn't be remembering his fierce reaction to the sight of her lithe, toned body moving in a provocative dance alone on the dance floor, or the way she'd felt in his arms minutes later. He wouldn't still feel the warmth of her breath against the hollow of his throat, or have been permitted a glimpse of her soul through those exotic amber eyes in her most vulnerable moment.

Damn it, why had she come back? Why had Sara died now when he'd just started to forget?

It had taken him almost fifteen years to escape the nightmares of that terrible night when Alison Hutton had been mortally wounded with a knife buried in his chest, then pushed from the third-floor veranda.

The horror of that moment had only begun to fade in recent months. Memory of the agony he'd seen reflected in Sara's eyes would probably never dim, nor would the guilt that had kept Sash awake night after night for years. But at least he'd been able to push the horror from the foreground until Lily's return. Now, it was all back, occupying his thoughts, refusing to stay buried in his subconscious any longer. And the worst part was he wanted Lily as he'd once desired her mother. If that wasn't depraved—

A surprised howl of pain tore from his lips as he suddenly lost his balance, slipping on the slick deck floor, and somehow managing to fall on the long, wicked serrated edge of the knife he'd been working with. A four-inch long horizontal wound slashed across his bicep. Blood poured profusely.

Ten minutes later, a tourniquet had been applied just above the cut and the bleeding stanched for the most part. But Sash was done for the day. He'd gone forward to the wheelhouse where he'd stayed for the remainder of the voyage while the last of the fish were stored in the chilled tanks of seawater.

Now, he was going to Rosehill General Emergency Room to have the wound closed. After that, he was going up on the hill once again. He wished to hell that

Lily Dawn Hutton hadn't come home to stir up ghosts and guilt. But he was going to make certain she didn't stay. He owed Sara that much. But damn if it wasn't costing him to go up there. He'd sworn never to set foot on those hills again, and for fifteen years, he'd kept that vow. Now, Lily was there, and that changed everything.

In spite of the intense fire that burned from his shoulder to his wrist, Sash managed a tenuous grin. He might not like the noblesse oblige he owed to Sara's girl, but there was some satisfaction in knowing that his stepmother and the others had to be hating it worse. He'd seen evidence of it last night when Sander had aimed his car straight for him. Sash had felt the other man's hatred as tangibly as the frigid winter night air, and for an instant believed Sander might well lose control.

Straddling his bike, he was jerked back to the present. There was no way he could handle the powerful machine with only one arm. Looking around him, he climbed off again, and yelled at one of his crewmen. "Hey, Foster. I'm gonna have to leave the bike. You and Reed get it to my place for me?"

"Sure. Toss me the keys," the man named Reed answered for his crony. "Hey, you want one of us to drive you over to General?"

Sash shook his head. "No, man, I've already disrupted the schedule enough. I'll call a cab."

Greg Foster snatched the keys from the air one-handed. "Hey, Rivers, one more thing."

Sash raised his chin a notch in acknowledgment. "Shoot."

"Since you're probably gonna be laid up for a few days, what d'ya say I go find that pretty little gal you was dancing with last night and sort of fill in for ya?"

Sash was surprised at the anger that sparked in him with the question. Balling his hands into tight fists, he caused the muscles to flex in his arms and fresh blood to spurt from the wound. But Foster was a friend. They teased each other about women all the time. Remembering that, Sash grinned. "Who you kiddin', bro'? The lady's a first-class act all the way. She wouldn't give your sorry ass the time of day."

Several of the crewmen had gathered on the bow, and they all laughed. Reed answered for his friend. "Yeah, we was all saying how she'd sunk lower than snake spit to dance with a bum like you."

"Hey, what can I say? Some of us just get lucky every now and then."

"Probably doesn't hurt that you was born up there in the hills with the other high-and-mighty blue bloods, Rivers, or that Daddy owns most of Rosehill," interjected a man usually assigned to the ailing vessel.

Sash knew little about the guy other than that his name was Doug Brewster, and he'd been suspended from the docks two or three times for fighting. "Doesn't hurt at all," he agreed, careful to keep his tone moderate, knowing the others would set the bastard straight after he left.

"Didn't think so, but it sure as shit bothers some of us," Brewster said.

"Sorry to hear that," Sash said from between clenched teeth.

"Back off, Doug," Reed said.

"Yeah, Brewster, you got a problem with Rivers, you work it out for yourself. He don't ask for no special favors, and he don't get none handed to him."

"That right? Then how come he's the one ended up taking that gal home last night? She didn't even look at the rest of us. You think it's cause he's packing more between his legs than we are or 'cause Daddy's a big fuck around here?"

"You looked in a mirror lately, Brewster? You really

think someone like Lily would look at you twice?" Sash said, giving up his carefully practiced neutrality.

"Why, you—" Brewster lunged toward the railing. Three seamen grabbed him, holding him back.

"Get out of here, Rivers," one of them shouted. "You two can settle this after your arm's been seen to."

Sash's temper was already cooling. He had a short fuse but an equally quick recovery period. He'd learned a long time ago the cost of losing control. A picture of Lily flashed across his mind. He winced. For nearly fifteen years he'd governed his emotions. He wasn't going to lose it now. He forced a grin. "Hey, I'm sorry, man. Guess this arm is making me irritable. Tell you what. Why don't I buy you a beer tonight?"

"Fuck you," Doug said, jerking his arms free of the other men's grasp and stalking away.

"Watch him, Sash," Reed said. "He's a fight lookin' to happen."

"Well, he's gonna have to keep looking. I'm not the right place. Leastwise not today. I've got more important things to attend to than that loser."

A devilish grin spread across Greg Foster's face. "Yeah, I hear ya. Maybe after you get your arm stitched, you should think about attendin' to that gal you was with last night. Who knows, maybe you'll get lucky, and she'll make the same offer Brewster just did."

Sash laughed. "Say, give me my keys back. I'm just gonna ride my bike on over to the hospital." Five minutes later, as he climbed onto the cycle and pulled his helmet onto his head, he remembered Foster's parting shot and grimaced. "Yeah, don't I just wish, pal."

He turned his gaze to the hill nearest the ocean where he'd grown up, where Lily most likely was right at this moment.

He *was* going up there to see her as soon as his arm was fixed up. But not to ask her out. Somehow, he had to talk her into leaving, and he had to do it without telling her the truth. Not about Sara and not about himself.

And then he had to start forgetting all over again. Only this time it wouldn't be Sara's face who filled his dreams. This time when he closed his eyes the face he saw would be lighter than Sara's; the color of lilies at dawn as Alison Hutton had poetically described his daughter's complexion in the first few days of her life once the redness of birth had faded.

The eyes would be more exotic; almond shaped, and larger, and like warmed sherry instead of dark chocolate.

The lips would be fuller; sultry and soft, and slower to smile.

And this time, just like last time, she was forbidden fruit.

Chapter Sixteen

Lily paced the front room. It had been several hours since Errol had taken off. At first she hadn't worried. Errol was temperamental. It was a part of his artist persona. Tantrums and dramatic exits were common.

She stopped to stare out the window, and a smile flitted over her frown. He raged and stormed about insignificant little nothing matters, then always returned later with some romantic doodad in hand. Like a bouquet of wilted flowers he'd conned some vendor out of for the change he had in his pocket. Or a silver star he'd fashioned from wire and aluminum foil to hang on her bedroom door in honor of her first dancing part in the off-Broadway production. Once he'd brought home a kitten with a big red bow tied around its scrawny little neck. The fact that the bow was made from a red plaid flannel strip torn from the hem of his shirt or that the tiny cat had to later be returned to their landlord from whom she'd been "borrowed" hadn't marred the moment for Lily.

It was for all of his crazy, impulsive traits that Lily had once believed herself to be in love with Errol. She still loved him, though as a friend or the brother she didn't have. And as frustrated as she often was with him, she couldn't help but worry that one day he was going to tear out in a rage and never be heard from again. That's why she'd sent Jesse out looking for him more than two hours before. Now both men were missing and she was very near panic.

It was fast approaching four o'clock. Sunset would occur just after five. Shadows were already settling over the hills and the valley below and a low-hanging fog was drifting in from the ocean.

Positioning herself in front of the large picture window once again, Lily hugged herself. Goose bumps dotted her arms as she conjured worst-case scenarios in her mind.

What if he'd followed her example and cut through the woods? He might have fallen and still be lying out there, alone and freezing to death. Kids took the shortcut to and from school every day, but they might easily pass Errol by if he was unconscious or too weak to call for help. Or what if he'd turned the wrong way and ended up in the swamp? No. That was too horrible to even contemplate.

"You're being ridiculous," she told herself aloud. "You always do this. In a minute, you'll be planning his funeral."

Car lights turned into the driveway, passing over the living room window before being extinguished. Lily was already opening the front door before Jesse stepped from the car. "You didn't find him?"

"No, and I swear, I drove over every road in this town at least three times."

"I'm going to call the police," Lily said, turning around and going back inside. "Something's happened. He wouldn't stay away this long."

"He's probably in a bar sweet-talking some cute little cocktail waitress," Jesse said, following after her and closing the door behind them. "Let's at least give it till supper. That's only two hours from now. If we haven't heard from him by then, we'll call out the police, the National Guard, *and* the Coast Guard until we find him."

"How could he be in a bar, Uncle Jesse? I told you, his billfold is still upstairs on his dresser."

"I know," he said, purposefully keeping his tone low and even. "But you said yourself he could have a few dollars with him."

"I said it was possible, not likely."

Ignoring that, Jesse asked if she'd heard from Sander, and was immediately sorry for posing the question when he saw the misery in her eyes intensify.

She sank to the ottoman, laying her head on her knees and hugging her legs. "I've screwed everything up."

"Don't be silly," Jesse said, hunkering down in front of her and lifting her chin so that she was forced to meet his gaze. "We've talked about this guilt complex before, haven't we?"

Lily nodded as her chin quivered beneath his gentle touch. Suddenly she felt every bit a child again, and she wished she could slide off the stool and into her uncle's arms as she had years before.

"Errol is a grown man. He has a quick temper, and he flies off the handle without much motivation. Am I right?"

"Yes," she said, misery returning to her tone. "But what about Uncle Sander? He's lived here all this time, and I come home for a few days and tell him to get out." Pressing her face into her hands, she groaned.

"Stop this, Lily Dawn!" Jesse snapped.

Lily jumped at the sharp rebuke, but she straightened as he'd meant for her to do and even managed a crooked smile as she realized how effectively she'd responded to his ploy.

"You're right. I'm overreacting." Standing, she crossed the room to pick up the telephone. "Don't worry, I'm not going against your advice of giving Errol another couple of hours. I'm just going to try to reach Sander at the law firm. I want to apologize. Retract my suggestion that he move."

"Good enough," Jesse said, starting from the room.

"Hey, where are you going?" she called after him.

"Just gonna stroll around the yard for a while," he said, giving in to the sheepish grin tugging at his lips.

Lily laughed softly under her breath as the telephone rang on the other end of the line. So Uncle Jesse was worried about Errol, too. That must mean he was beginning to like him.

As the phone was answered on the other end, Lily's brows drew together in a tight frown. She asked to be connected to Sander Hutton's office, then turned back to thoughts of Errol. *Please be okay*, she told him silently.

Errol wasn't okay. But he was alive, which was more than he had thought he would be a couple of hours before.

The two uniformed officers who had brought him into police headquarters for questioning had continued their harsh treatment, even running him into a door-jamb as they pushed him roughly into the station. "Oops," the older cop said. "Sorry about that, bro'."

"Hey, it wasn't your fault, Barrett," the other one named Lonnie said. "Our friend here just tripped on the step all by himself. Ain't that right, Mr. Mills?"

Blood trickled from the bridge of Errol's nose along his cheek and into the corner of his mouth. With his hands still cuffed behind him, he couldn't do more than wipe it off on his shoulder. His right eye was rapidly swelling shut, but he canted his head far enough to make out the younger officer's face. "Yeah," he said. "Clumsy of me."

"See," Lonnie said. "I told you. For a Yankee, this one's pretty smart."

Now, two hours later, battered and sore as hell, he had been taken from his cell and led into a room with a long, glossy wooden table and chairs. Errol raised a brow. This certainly didn't resemble any torture chamber of his imagination. On the other hand, Errol didn't doubt that the R.P.D. wouldn't much care where they abused him. They'd already pissed on his right to make a phone call. But this looked like some kind of conference room. Maybe they'd all get together and discuss his punishment while he sat there shackled to the chair, forced to listen. Some kind of psychological torment these creeps had dreamed up.

The man who'd ushered him from the cell wasn't Barrett or Lonnie. This was one he hadn't seen before. But that didn't mean he wasn't capable of the same brutality as his comrades.

"Give me your hands," the man said, turning him so that Errol stood with his back to him. Seconds later, Errol was amazed to find the handcuffs removed.

"Thanks," he said, cautiously optimistic as he rubbed the chafed skin on his wrists.

"Sure. Take a seat. I'll bring you a cup of coffee. You take it black or sweetened?"

"Black," Errol answered though with renewed suspicion. What were they up to now?

Fifteen minutes later, his fears neither allayed nor confirmed, the door opened. With his one good eye, Errol watched as a procession of four men marched into the room.

The first through the door stopped dead in his tracks only a few feet inside the room, almost causing a collision with those following after him. "Good God, man, what in the hell happened to your face? Tell me you weren't injured while in the custody of the Rosehill Police Department!"

Errol didn't know the man speaking to him, had never seen him before. He was sure of that. No one would forget meeting this guy. For one thing, he was extraordinarily handsome. Almost beautiful with his perfect, chiseled jaw and chin, the strong roman nose, royal-blue eyes, and thick, white-blond hair. But it was a beauty that was wholly masculine. Maybe because of the superb athlete's physique that was accentuated by the elegant lines of a dark custom-tailored suit. Or perhaps it was the powerful, self-assured way he carried himself. A deep, softly modulated voice didn't hurt, Errol thought. Radio announcer's voice. A very *southern* announcer's voice, he amended, recalling the rich, syrupy drawl.

The second fellow, a heavyset, balding man with pasty-white skin and pale eyes that were magnified a hundred times with thick, bottle-glass lenses, was likewise a stranger to him. But he knew the last two.

One was Sander Hutton. The other, Officer James Barrett. Errol ignored the glare the uniformed patrolman directed his way. He didn't need further coaching to know how to answer the shocked query. His hand automatically going to the injury, he lied, "I did it myself. Fell."

"Well, thank God for that," the handsome man said before glancing around at the other three and asking, "Has anyone called for a doctor to examine Mr. Mills's face?"

"We called Dr. Tiennerman, but he was on rounds at the hospital," the second man explained. "His nurse suggested we take Mr. Mills to the emergency room."

"So why isn't he there?"

"You told us to bring him here," Officer Barrett said.

The man who seemed to be in charge ignored the patrolman's explanation and rounded the table to place a hand on Errol's shoulder. "Mr. Mills, I'm Dixon Price, the district attorney in Rosehill. I've come here to offer my sincere apologies. There's been a terrible injustice done you that I'm having trouble dealing with. I'd like time to talk with you, explain how this . . . this mistake came about. But first, I must ask you if you'd like to go to the emergency room before we speak?"

Fuck, no, he didn't want to go to the hospital. Hell, the cops had almost killed him already. He had no doubt the doctors could finish the job with drugs and scalpels. He shook his head firmly from side to side.

The D.A. flashed perfect white teeth and motioned to the chair at the end of the table to Errol's right. "Good. I think it best if we talk. Mind if I sit down?"

Errol shrugged.

Dixon Price motioned for the others to do the same, then turned back to Errol. "I believe you know Officer Barrett. He was the senior arresting officer. And you're acquainted with Sander Hutton, of course." He flicked a wrist in the third man's direction. "And this is our chief of police, Stuart St. Charles."

So what was he supposed to say to that? Errol wondered. Pleased to meet you? He decided not.

Price placed his manicured hands flat on the table side by side, as if suggesting that they lay all their cards on the table.

The D.A.'s perfect grin spread with scintillating brilliance once again. "I want you to know, first off, Mr. Mills, I understand how you must feel. One minute there you are minding your own business. The next thing you know, you're being shoved into a jail cell. Pretty damned confusing and upsetting, wasn't it?"

Errol clenched his own capped teeth and hoped his

one visible eye didn't reflect his urge to punch the man's lights out. What the hell was this, anyway?

The smile on the tanned face disappeared. "You have every right to be furious. You may even be considering legal options available to you. We don't blame you. Not in the least. In fact, that's why I telephoned Sander and asked him to meet me here at the station. He's a highly respected attorney in private practice, who also happens to be someone you will trust because he's the uncle of your girlfriend. I only hope you'll give us a chance to explain before you decide what you want to do about this unfortunate misdeed."

Errol opened his mouth to tell him exactly where to shove his concerns and apologies, but Sander began speaking before he could get it said.

"Come on, Errol, hold on a minute here. Just give 'em their say and think of Lily a minute here. The girl's just lost her mother. I know you don't want to add to her troubles."

Mention of Lily sobered him. He straightened in his chair. "Look, Mr. Price, Sander, I appreciate you both coming over here to get this mess squared away. You're damn right, I'm pissed off, but I'm willing to forget it all for now if one of you will just give me a ride back to Lily's house."

"Of course, we'll do that," Price agreed. "But before we do, I want to explain how this ... this injustice came about."

Errol laughed, not bothering to keep the ring of sarcasm from it. "You'll pardon me if I tell you I don't give a fuck why or how this 'injustice' happened. I am sore and tired and in need of a good stiff drink, and you gentlemen will please forgive me for pointing out that I don't want to spend one second more than necessary with any of you."

"We certainly do, Errol—you don't mind if I use

your first name?" Dixon asked. Then without waiting for permission, "But you have to forgive us for insisting that we have our discussion first.

"That's the way it works here in the South. Especially in our little corner of the South. We're very big on tit for tat. I do something for you, you do something for me. I wash your hand, you wash mine. Understand?"

"Perfectly. So what is it I have to do in exchange for my freedom?" Errol asked.

"Only one tiny little thing," a new voice, a feminine voice said from the doorway. Every head turned in that direction and every man except Errol jumped to his feet.

"Imogene, what on earth are you doing here?" the district attorney asked his wife.

Errol thought he detected the first hint of anger the man had allowed in his tone, but apparently Imogene heard nothing, for the smile she directed his way was wide and happy.

"Why, aren't you the forgetful one, Dix? I was supposed to pick you up at your office so we could go shopping for Mama's birthday next week. When I got there, your secretary told me you were over here interrogating a suspect, so here I am. But I had absolutely no idea you'd be browbeating this poor man." Without giving her husband time to explain, she turned toward Errol. "What in the world happened to your face?"

"He fell," Dixon explained, his voice flat and without charm for the first time. "Mr. Mills has assured me it happened before he was taken into custody."

"Well, I'm glad to hear that, but are you all right, Errol, honey? You look positively ghastly."

Errol touched the wounded bridge of his nose, then his swollen eye with tentative fingers, wincing with pain. "It hurts pretty good, too."

"Well, then, just tell them what they want to hear so I can take you back to Lily's house."

"They haven't told me what they want yet," Errol said.

"Why, that one's easy. They want you to promise to get out of Rosehill and not come back," she said.

"Why?" Errol asked.

Dixon Price answered for his wife, and there was no mistaking the fury in his voice now. It quivered with rage. "You'll pardon Genie's sick sense of humor, Errol. She thinks she's amusing, but you'll notice no one is laughing." Grabbing her arm, he steered her from the room, pulling the door closed behind them.

No one spoke while they awaited the D.A.'s return, and Errol wondered what would happen when he did. The cool composure the attorney had maintained throughout the interview had slipped during the bizarre episode with his wife. Errol still wasn't certain what her point was. Oh, she'd been laughing, but at whom? Errol or Dixon?

Before he had a chance to delve any deeper into the meaning of Imogene Rivers-Price's visit, or her remark about what was expected of him in exchange for his freedom, her husband slipped inside the room once again. Errol sighed with relief at the prosecutor's recovered even temper. The pearly teeth gleamed with the return of his bright smile that reached even the blue, blue eyes. "Women." He laughed by way of a one-word explanation.

Chapter Seventeen

"Men! That's our topic today," a well-dressed talk-show host told her television viewers. "Women have been complaining that they can't live with 'em and can't live without 'em since Adam first ragged on Eve about eating that damned ol' apple."

Lily muttered amen to that sentiment as she hit the off button on the remote control and reached for the pealing telephone at the same time. *Please let it be Errol*, she prayed as she put the receiver to her ear. "Hello?"

"Lily, it's Sander."

Her heart sinking with disappointment, she shook her head at Jesse's raised brow. "Hi," she said, unable to find even a modicum of enthusiasm.

"Honey, I'm at Rosehill General Hospital. I'm with Errol."

"Oh, my God," she said in a choked whisper. "Wait. Tell Uncle Jesse."

She thrust the phone at Jesse, her hands trembling violently. "Errol's at the hospital. Find out if he's—"

"He's all right," Jesse told her two minutes later as he hung up the phone.

"Then what is he doing in the hospital?" she asked.

"He's been hurt," Jesse admitted in his most soothing, professional tone. "But it doesn't appear too serious. I don't know all the details. Sander said he took a bad fall. Smashed his nose and is sporting a pretty ugly shiner. They're taking some x-rays just to make sure there's no concussion. Sander offered to drive him home as soon as they finish up."

Tears of relief threatened but Lily refused to give in to them. "I'm so glad he's all right, Uncle Jesse. I've been doing this 'if only' routine all day. You know, if only I hadn't let him come with me to Rosehill. If only I had gone after him this morning. If only ... well, it doesn't matter now. The only thing that counts is that he's all right." Stepping past him, she motioned for him to follow. "Drive me to the hospital. I'm still too weak-kneed to trust myself behind the wheel."

Jesse was grinning as he followed her down the stairs. "Somehow I knew you wouldn't wait here. I told Sander we'd meet him in the emergency waiting area."

Lily laughed for the first time since Errol's disappearance. "You think you're pretty smart, don't you?"

"As a matter of fact, I'm pretty proud of my intuition, yes."

They were both still chuckling as Jesse backed the rental car from the driveway minutes later.

Sander had just hung up the pay phone when Sasha Rivers walked through the emergency ward doors. What the hell was he doing there?

Taking a step backward into the recesses of the booth, he watched as Rivers talked to the receptionist, shrugged off his leather jacket after a minute or so, then pulled his sweatshirt over his head. From his vantage point, Sander couldn't quite make out what Sash was showing her, but he could see clearly her reaction to the sinewy chest and powerful arms. Sander's mouth curled downward with disgust. Were all women fools for a few muscles and a sexy grin?

With a muttered curse, he reached inside his trouser pocket for a quarter. Better let a certain someone know that Rivers was here and Lily on the way. He dreaded the ice he would feel all the way through the telephone line when he imparted the news. Then reconsidering, he *hoped* his bad tidings would be received with the usual arctic reserve. His hands trembled as he pushed the buttons. He knew well what happened when control snapped. Someone always paid.

From the corner of her eye, Lily caught sight of her father's brother. She slowed, raised her hand in greeting, and continued on through the double doors. She stopped before the crescent-shaped nurses' station. "Errol Mills. Where is he?" she asked of a harried-looking woman passing behind the counter.

"Room six," the nurse replied, pointing to a curtained-off area in the far corner of the large room.

Lily took off in a half-run, her heart pounding. Despite Sander's assurances that he wasn't seriously hurt, she expected the worst. She couldn't help it. It was always that way until she saw for herself. Ever present fear of sudden death was baggage she'd carried since her father's fatal fall fifteen years before. Inhaling sharply, she slung back the drape that surrounded his cubicle.

Tears immediately flooded her eyes, and before she could check them, sobs of relief were choking her.

"Hey, babe, I'm okay. Just bruised is all. Nose isn't even broken," Errol reassured her as he climbed from the bed. "Sore as hell, but that's no big deal. You know me, honey. I stub my big toe, I'm in bed for a week."

And then Lily was laughing. Hiccupping, weeping,

and giggling all at the same time. Was this hysteria? She didn't care.

Gripping the metal railing at the foot of the narrow hospital bed, she reached into her pocket for a crumpled tissue. She dabbed at her eyes and blew her nose. "I should blacken your other eye, Mills. You scared the hell out of me today!"

Usually Errol backed down without argument. Why not? He was always the one in the wrong. Today, though, he'd had enough bullying to choke a horse. He wasn't going to take any more. Not even from her. "Hey, babe, chill."

"*Chill?* Damn it, Errol, I've been worried sick!"

Errol's temper flared. "Look, why don't I do us both a favor and get the hell out of your life?" he asked, grabbing his shirt from a plastic basket. "That's what you've wanted for a long time now and to tell you the truth, I don't know why I've hung on. It's not like I've been having too much fun at the party to leave. Someone turned the fucking music off a long time ago and you stopped dancing. Guess I was trying not to notice." His head was pounding and every muscle in his body ached. But it was the effing proverbial knife he drove into his heart as he met her eyes and saw the surprise and hurt and confusion in their tawny depths that almost made him cry out.

Damn it, Lily, don't look at me like that. I'm doing what's right for both of us. I'm finally letting go just like you've wanted.

He turned his back to her as he pulled on his slacks, discarded the hospital gown, and shrugged into his shirt. "Go on home, Lily," he said softly. "I'm sure your Uncle Sander will bring me by the house to get my things."

But Lily didn't move. "This is crazy. Dynamite couldn't shake you loose before today. You're scared,

Errol. Why? Who did this to you?" She grabbed his arm, trying to force him to turn around and face her.

"Let him be," Jesse said from behind her.

Lily turned. "You heard? He's leaving. Just like that."

Jesse nodded. "I heard, but this isn't the place to discuss it. Let him ride with Sander. The two of you can talk at home." He put an arm around her shoulders, but she shrugged it away.

"I'll be in the waiting room with Sander when you're ready to leave," Jesse said evenly.

Lily didn't answer. She whirled and barged out of the curtain, only to find she was not in the hall but in the adjoining partitioned cubicle. Sash Rivers was sitting on the bed, wearing nothing from the waist up except a red kerchief tied around his head. A nurse was wrapping his upper arm with gauze bandaging, while a second one gathered up an aluminum basin, an instrument tray, and some blood-soaked cotton swatches.

Sash met Lily's gaze with a crooked grin. "Trouble in paradise, huh?"

Lily ignored that. "What happened to you?"

"Fishing accident. Needed a few stitches. Nothing serious. How about your friend? From what I could hear, sounds like he ran into a Mack truck."

Lily smiled despite her depressed mood. "If someone had told me that's exactly what happened, I'd believe it. He looks like hell."

The nurse who'd been wrapping his arm, stood back. "Okay, Mr. Rivers, you can put your shirt on. We're all done here. I'll go get your release papers and be right back."

As soon as she stepped from the tiny room, Sash hopped from the bed and tugged the curtain along the track, closing off the rest of the emergency ward.

"What are you doing?" she asked as he suddenly lifted her from her feet to set her on the bed. Her hands were flat against his chest, and she felt blood surge to her face as his muscles rippled beneath her palms and fingertips. Still she didn't take them away, even when he covered them with his own and stepped nearer so that he stood between her slightly parted legs.

"You look like you're about done in," he said in a low, soothing voice. "I want you to sit here a minute till you feel better."

Lily's breath quickened as she felt the hard lines of his hip against her leg. She was immediately reminded of their dance the night before.

His heart beat beneath her palm.

Last night it had beat against her breast.

Last night his warm breath had stirred the baby-fine hair on the nape of her neck. Now it brushed her cheek.

She met his gaze, then let her eyes roam the perfectly chiseled planes of his face. There was something frightening about his beauty. Something pagan and savage.

His deep-set, dark blue eyes glittered like sapphires against the bronzed tan of his skin, never blinking as they met her probing gaze. The nostrils of his long, aquiline nose flared slightly, and his full lips parted just a little with his slow, even breathing. A muscle ticked in his powerful jaw, and his racing blood was visible in the pulsing vein in his neck.

He's like a powerful, sleek cat. Lily sucked in air at the dizzying thought.

"Don't look at me like that," he said in a hoarse whisper.

"Like what?" she asked, her voice as breathless as his.

"Like I'm going to eat you."

"Are you?"

His hands had moved to her legs, though neither of them could have said when it had happened. But she felt his thumbs caress the tender flesh of her inner thighs through the coarse denim of her jeans, and she pressed the heels of her hands against the rock hardness of his bare chest.

She'd closed her eyes for an instant, but they flew open as his fingers moved higher, nearing the apex of her legs, and she felt his hot breath shift to her lips. His face was only inches from hers. She had only to lean forward, and his mouth would be on hers, his teeth nipping at her lips, urging them to part for him.

This was crazy! But even as she thought it, she moved her pelvis forward to greet his hands. Then she craned her neck as she heard him inhale sharply and almost forgot to breathe when his lips finally claimed hers.

The metal hooks that held the drapes jingled noisily as the nurse returned with his release papers.

Lily jumped as if doused with ice water, but Sash gripped her waist, refusing to let her go. "Goddamn it, Lil!" he whispered. "Go away. Please. Before someone gets hurt too badly to fix."

"Why?" she asked, grabbing hold of his wrist and feeling against her fingers the thin gold bracelet she'd noticed the night before when they danced.

Sash jerked his hand from hers and turned his back as he reached for his sweatshirt. When he looked back, Lily was gone.

Damn it!

He balled his hands into tight fists as he half-listened to the nurse's instructions to return in six days to have the sutures removed unless there were signs of infection such as redness, drainage, blah blah blah.

A minute later, he stepped from the examining room. He paused outside number six. The curtain was drawn. Was she in there with her boyfriend?

Fuck it, he thought as turned on his heel, wadding the release form as he strode from the emergency ward. Outside, he stopped on the sidewalk, inhaling deeply of the cool evening air. What had happened to him in there? Hell, he'd almost made love to her right then and there on that hospital bed! No one had ever affected him that way before.

Maybe she'd listen to him this time and leave. Leave him to the guilt and torment he'd lived with for too many long years. At least he wouldn't have her on his conscience as well.

Glancing down at his hand, he realized he still held the crumpled hospital form, and tossed it toward the wire trash bin a few feet away, not bothering to notice whether or not he'd made the basket.

She'd looked a lot like her mother today. Maybe it was the way she wore her hair pulled back in that loose braid. Or her clothes. The baggy, oversized shirt, the faded, straight-legged jeans, and those dingy tennis shoes. Sara had dressed like that more often than not when she was around the house.

But this wasn't Sara.

And he wasn't a boy with a teenage crush.

And that was the problem in a nutshell. He'd loved Sara with childlike adoration. Now he was a man, and there was nothing even remotely adolescent about his feelings for Lily. He wanted her, pure and simple.

As he stepped from the curb and turned up the collar of his jacket, he laughed. Fuck that. There wasn't anything pure about what he wanted to do to Lily Dawn Hutton . . . and when he got right down to it, neither did it have anything to do with her mother.

Chapter Eighteen

"Litterbug," Lily complained, scooping up the wadded release form Sash had tossed away in front of the hospital emergency entrance. She shoved the paper ball into her pocket absently as she glared after the departing motorcycle. From the corner of her eye, she saw Jesse's brow quirk. "Not one word!" she snapped.

"About what?" he asked innocently. "You mean about what went on between the two of you behind closed curtains back there in the emergency room? I wouldn't dream of intruding on your privacy, Lily Dawn."

Lily opened her mouth to rebut the false statement with examples of his interference in the past, but the doors behind them parted and Errol was wheeled outside. "Where's Uncle Sander?" she asked, looking past the hulking orderly standing behind the wheelchair.

"I told him to go on," Jesse explained. "No sense in him waiting around since Errol's going to ride with us. Incidentally, while we're on the subject of Sander, I mentioned your change of heart about him moving out. But you're off the hook. He says it's something he and Marla agree should have happened long ago . . . it's time they worked out their problems." Turning his attention to the patient, he patted Errol's shoulder. "I'll go get the car and bring it around."

Errol held up a hand in acknowledgment. "Thanks."

"You okay?" Lily asked, crouching in front of his chair. "Not too uncomfortable?"

"Jesus Christ, Lily, do I look all right to you?"

Hurt, Lily pushed herself to her feet. "Stupid question, you're right."

The man standing behind the chair winked. "Hey, sometimes the meds they give 'em for pain make 'em cranky. He don't mean it. Shake it off."

Lily smiled her gratitude but the sting from Errol's verbal slap stayed with her even after they arrived at the house twenty minutes later.

Kitty appeared in the foyer as Lily and Jesse flanked Errol on either side, helping him up the stairs. "Wow! How's the other guy look?" she asked.

"Ha ha," Errol managed. "Your talent as a comedienne is wasted here in Rosehill, honey."

"Any calls?" Jesse asked though he didn't look back or stop as they continued to the next floor.

"Yes, sir, that's what I came out to tell you. Your wife called from Oklahoma. Said it was important."

"Think it could be the baby?" Lily asked over Errol's shoulders.

"I hope not. He's not due for another month."

"I can help Errol the rest of the way. Why don't you go call her?"

"Whatever it is, it'll keep a few more minutes," Jesse answered calmly, but even with Errol between them, Lily felt the tension in him.

"You had a few calls as well, Mr. Mills," Kitty called from the landing below. "Mrs. Rivers and Dixon Price and Rusty from the diner. All three of them said they were checking to see how you were."

Lily raised a brow, bending forward slightly to look

into Errol's eyes and make a silent query: *How do Eudora Rivers and Dixon Price know about your accident?*

Errol turned his head slightly, avoiding her gaze, and Lily let it go for the moment. As soon as Jesse went to call Rebecca, she'd ask again, this time aloud, and if he didn't want to tell her what was going on, she'd simply return the phone calls herself.

A couple of minutes later, their patient stretched out on his bed, Jesse hurried away to telephone Oklahoma, and Lily took a seat on the mattress beside Errol.

"All right, pal, what the hell really happened to you today? You didn't just fall, and Uncle Sander didn't just miraculously stumble over you."

Maybe it *was* the medication they'd given him at the hospital or maybe it was just plain old-fashioned relief to still be alive that provoked Errol's reaction to her questions, but he was mad as hell. Scooting up against the headboard, he gripped his raised knees with white-knuckle intensity. "Ah, where to start? Not in the back-seat of a Rosehill police cruiser listening to the cops talk about how lucky I was I hadn't wandered off into one of the infamous Carolina swamps. Maybe when they arrested me for vagrancy, then smashed my kidneys and balls with a nightstick. 'Course that was just a pre-view. Rammed my head into the end of a metal door at the station and treated me to a strip search—"

"Stop! Oh, God, I don't want to hear any more!" Lily cried, her hands over mouth. "Just tell me why! And how Sander found you."

"Not tonight," he said, his voice suddenly reflecting his weariness. "I've hit the wall, babe."

"All right, but I'm going to find Sander and make him tell me what the hell that was all about. They just can't arrest a man for no reason, beat the shit out of him, and expect us to just back off without a fight!"

Errol pushed himself up on an elbow and focused his

one undamaged eye on her. "Listen, I don't want you saying anything to Sander or anyone else. It's over. Done with. *Finito.* I'm not going to give anyone any reason to hassle me again, and I don't want you to get hurt either."

Lily folded her arms over her chest. "Fine. You're leaving anyway. I'll wait until you're safely out of Dodge. But then I'm going to have Sander file some sort of complaint against the police department. Charge them with false arrest, excessive force, harassment, whatever it takes."

"Ain't gonna work, babe. You're forgetting who runs this town. These uniformed guys are just doing what they've been told to do. And your Uncle Sander is one of the honchos making up the rules."

Lily frowned as she considered what he was saying. Remembering the messages he'd received, she pressed him about those. "Kitty said Eudora Rivers and Dixon Price called you. Are you saying Uncle Sander was in on your arrest with Dixon and Eudora?"

Errol shrugged. "I'm not saying anything except your Mr. Price visited me along with Sander at the police station. Price is the district attorney, did you know? His gorgeous wife just happened to come by too while our little parlay was going on. They were all real solicitous. So damned sorry I was unjustly detained. But I'd bet every nickel you have, they not only knew about my arrest before it went down, one of them ordered it."

"What about Eudora? Was she there, too?"

"Mama bear wasn't around, but since she's the mayor of this fine town, I imagine she's heard all the gory details by now. Probably calling to find out how well the lesson was delivered by her boys in blue."

Lily sat down on the edge of his bed. She ran her hands nervously through her hair then said, "I'm scared, Errol."

"Good. Then you can go home with me tomorrow. Give up this crazy notion of trying to prove someone else killed your old man. You can't bring either one of your parents back no matter what, but you can end up out there past the city lines in that cemetery right beside them."

Lily was suddenly cold and trembling, but she clasped her hands tightly in her lap and shook her head. "I know I can't change the past, but I'm not leaving until I know what happened to my father fifteen years ago, and to my mom last week. At least until I feel certain that the phone call was a prank."

"Jesus Christ, Lily, you just said you're scared. Why would you hang around when you know there's a chance you could end up hurt or even worse?"

"Maybe you're wrong," she said, slowly slipping off the bed. Sticking her hands into the back pockets of her jeans, she crossed the room to stand in front of the window and stare out at the starlit night. After a time, she said, "Last night the cloud cover was so thick, I couldn't see a thing. Tonight it's beautiful out there. Like black velvet splattered with diamonds and centered with a big milky opal." She sighed. "It's hard reconciling such beauty with the evil that seems to be here."

Errol didn't answer, but he was wondering if he could look outside that same window and see anything beautiful about a Rosehill night. He didn't think so. He was pretty sure he'd see only images created for him by two cops following someone else's order to deliver a message; images of corpses swallowed by swamp mud that never gave up the dead. He shuddered with the thought, then started when Lily abruptly spoke again.

"Do you think they did this as a warning to me?"

"Jesus Christ, Lily, what do you think I've been trying to tell you?" Then in a calmer tone, "But I could be wrong, I guess. I've told you from the first that these people give me the creeps, but as bad as the vibes I keep picking up are, we haven't uncovered a single thing that even remotely backs up your suspicions, so maybe I'm off base."

Lily turned then. He'd expected to see flames spark in those amber eyes, but instead, excitement flashed. She crossed the room to plop down on the end of the bed, landing on both knees. "Well, I think you're right. I think I'm making someone nervous by staying. And if that's true, we have to ask why. Nothing to worry about if there's nothing to hide, right?"

Errol held up his hands in surrender. "Tell you what, I'm too fucking sore to travel for a couple of days. Why don't you settle this for yourself once and for all. Only please, babe, do it on the q.t. Go see the doctors at that loony bin—" He shrugged an apology and mouthed the word *sorry* at her glare, then continued along the vein he'd begun to follow. "Find out if there is even the remotest possibility the call you got came from Sara."

"That's a waste of time. You know I already talked to Dr. Lepstein and she insists there's not."

"So who says she knows everything there is to know. Talk to someone else. Hell, talk to a lot of someone elses. Talk to the nurses and aides, security guards, even the maintenance people. Look at that registration book you had to sign when you went to visit her. See if she had any visitors that week."

Lily opened her mouth to speak, but Errol was on a roll and flagged her off.

"If you don't turn up anything there, go see the old guy—what's his name?"

"Joe Joe?"

"Yeah. Maybe if you talk to him for a while, kind of take him back through everything that went down the day your dad was killed, he'll remember something."

"I've thought of that, Errol, but if there was anything

to remember, why wouldn't he have thought of it before now?"

"Maybe because no one asked him the right questions. Why should they? They had your mom and dad on that balcony. Your mom with a knife in her hands. Your dad with a knife wound to his heart. When two and two add up to four there's not much reason to check the equation a second time."

Lily grinned. It spread slowly across her face as appreciation for him grew. "You're really something, you know it? Thanks."

Inexplicably embarrassed, Errol waved away her gratitude. "Hey, I just want you to satisfy your curiosity so we can get back home. You've got a new gig to get ready for, remember?"

There was a knock at the door and both of them turned toward the sound, simultaneously calling, "Come in."

"Oh, Uncle Jesse, you look upset. What's wrong?"

"It's Rebecca . . . and the baby. Seems her blood pressure is sky high and the doctor thinks the baby's stressed. He's put her in the hospital for complete bed rest. If things don't turn around, he wants to do a C-section on Friday."

Lily scampered from the bed, hurrying to her uncle's side to wrap her arms around his waist. "I'm so sorry, but I'm sure everything will be all right. You have to go home as soon as possible. I'll drive you to Charleston. Have you called the airlines?"

Jesse shook his head. "No, I'm not going to leave you here alone. With Errol leaving, and—"

"He's not. Leaving, I mean. At least not for a couple of days. But even if he was, I wouldn't let you stay here when your wife needs you."

Jesse returned his niece's hug, but his gaze was focused on Errol. "You sure you're okay about staying? I can be back as soon as the baby is either delivered or the crisis is past."

Lily answered for her friend. "Don't be ridiculous. You're going to go home to Broken Arrow and stay with Rebecca and my cousin once he gets here. As a matter of fact, I'd like to come for a visit before going back to Manhattan."

Jesse held her away from him as he studied first her face then Errol's. "Why so cheery all of a sudden? What's happened since the two of you came up here?"

"We've come up with a plan," Lily offered. "At least, Errol has. I'm going to go to Tremont and talk with the staff. See if I can't find out absolutely once and for all if Mother could have made that phone call. I'll do that when I take you to Charleston to catch your flight. Then I'm going to talk to Joe Joe and maybe even to Genie."

"And if she doesn't come up with some kind of evidence that confirms any of her suspicions pretty fucking—sorry, sir—conclusively, she's going to close the book on this place and get the hell out of Dodge."

"He wrote the last part of that script without consulting me," Lily said.

"But he's right, isn't he? If you come up empty on all accounts, you'll settle the last of Ali and Sara's estate and go home to New York?"

Lily jammed her hands into her front pockets as she shrugged her acquiescence. "I guess so. What would be the point of staying if I'm wrong?"

"There wouldn't be any," Jesse said sternly. Then he smiled. "Well, I guess I'd better go call the airlines, see what I can line up." He turned away, but at the door, he stopped. "Kitty said to tell you she'll be glad to bring your dinner up here, Errol. I suggested something light and easy like soup and Jell-o."

Errol started to wrinkle his nose with distaste, but

flinched against the pain instead. "Jesus, my schnoz is sore."

"It looks it," Jesse agreed. "Which reminds me, how did you fall, and how in the hell did Sander find you?"

"Long story. But in a nutshell, the police picked me up, someone connected me to Lily, Lily to Sander, and *voilà!*"

"Aha, well, then, maybe there's something to be said for small town grapevines after all," Jesse said.

As soon as the door closed behind her uncle Lily said, "Thanks for not telling him what really happened. He has enough to worry about with Rebecca and the baby."

"Kind of amazes you that such an insensitive jerk could think of that, huh?"

Lily frowned. "Don't start an argument. Not tonight."

"Okay," he said lightly. Too lightly. "Then how about bringing me the phone. Think I'll return one of my phone calls."

Something had changed in Errol today. Something inside that she suspected had nothing to do with the cruel beating he'd been treated to.

Matching his tone, she asked, "Her name wouldn't be Rusty, would it?"

"Oh, hell, now I have to add psychic to all your talents," he groaned playfully.

"*Errol!* Who is she?"

"Just a cute little waitress I was getting to know before Johnny Law interrupted us." He pointed toward the door. "The phone, babe. Please?"

"Be back in a jiff," she promised.

Errol signaled a-okay, closed his eyes, and held onto his grin until the door opened. But he let it slip too soon. Lily saw the shadow that fell across his features.

With a frown, she slipped from the room, pulling the

door closed after her. She leaned against it, brow to wood, and her hand went unconsciously into the pocket of the jacket she still wore. She curled her fingers around the wadded release form she'd picked up just as she heard Errol mutter bitterly from the other side of the door.

"Yeah, baby, maybe the four of us can even work a double date before we blow this fuckin' paradise. Me and little Rusty, and you and the Ruskie."

Chapter Nineteen

The moon does more than hang in the sky with a complacent expression on its face. It influences the tides and, Jesse believed, the moods of men. Even the word *lunatic* was derived from lunar. And as he paced the floor of his bedroom, he knew without looking that there was a full moon tonight. Either that or something significant was about to happen.

Ceasing his restless progress back and forth, he picked up a framed photograph he'd only moments before laid in his suitcase. His sister's tranquil face smiled up at him, and he felt the knife in his heart twist as it had every time he thought of her for more than fifteen years. "I'm worried about our Lily, sis. I have to go home to Broken Arrow in the morning, but I'm anxious about leaving her alone. I couldn't stand it if anything happened to her."

He stared at the picture, wishing his sister could speak to him. Promise him in that soft, breathless voice he still remembered so vividly, that she would watch over her daughter in his absence. Reassure him that the evil he felt around him would not touch Lily.

On a deep sigh, he placed the photo in his bag again, zipped it closed, and moved it from his bed to a place on the floor near the door. Sleep would not come easily tonight, but he should at least try to rest. Tomorrow promised to be long and tiring. Rebecca needed him, and though he would leave part of his heart here with his niece, he had to be alert in case it was the day his son chose to arrive.

Ten minutes later, he lay on his back, his arms folded over his chest, his face toward the ceiling. Though his eyes were closed, he wasn't asleep. Yet suddenly he was dreaming in that half state between slumber and wakefulness.

The air around him was colder and a sweet olio of familiar scents filled the room. Jasmine and lavender, cinnamon and spearmint, tangerine and peach nectar.

The scent of flowers he remembered from Sara's perfume, the smell of spices from her kitchen, and the pungent tang of fruit from the delicate dwarf trees she'd tended and babied in her atrium.

Bells tinkled, yet faintly, as if from a faraway distance, and Jesse smiled as he realized it was Sara's lilting laughter he heard and not the sound of bells at all.

A warm breeze stirred against his lips like breath gently exhaled, and he heard words in the whisper. *I'm with her, Jesse. I'm here.*

Jesse drifted off into the first deep, peaceful sleep he'd found in days.

Terrible dreams kept waking Lily from sleep. Nightmares of men wearing ghoulish masks and dressed in police uniforms all hovering over Errol shouting and brandishing nightsticks. Dreams of Sasha lying on a stainless-steel examining table to her left, Errol on another one to her right. Both of them reaching for her with icy fingers and then grabbing hold to tear her apart in a to-the-death tug of war.

She awakened screaming from the last.

Tossing aside the covers, she sat up and snapped on the lamp on her nightstand as she pushed away the last clinging residue of fright.

She needed to dance. A good, vigorous routine around the studio floor a few times, and she'd sleep like a baby with nothing worse than images of sugar plums prancing around in her head.

Less than ten minutes later, Lily sat down on the edge of her bed again, this time clad in silver leotard and black tights as she slipped her feet into black ballet slippers. She skipped down the stairs, already relaxed and energized by the prospect of doing what she loved best in the world, though she hadn't even stretched out yet.

But that was the power of dance. The magic began in the mind even before the body began to perform.

Lily went to the cassette case that had belonged to her mother, rifling through the tapes with her fingers for a tune familiar enough to dance to. Maybe she should run back up to her bedroom and look through the tapes she'd brought with her from—

Theme song from *A Star Is Born*. Sara's longtime favorite.

How many times had mother and daughter danced to the routine Sara had created for the powerful piece? But did Lily dare try it now after all these years? She'd been only a child the last time she danced alongside her mother, and dancing with a lot more heart than accomplishment. Would she remember even thirty seconds of the complicated number?

Only one way to find out.

She slipped the tape into the stereo system, then went to the exercise bar to begin the process of limbering up. She was always careful to spend enough time with head bends, leg lifts, stretches, and splits, but tonight she was jittery and anxious to start the music. She de-

cided to cut the warm-up short and began pinning her
hair into a twisted knot at the top of her head.

Going to the stereo again, she pushed START.

She hurried to the far right side of the room, taking
her position as she remembered it, and she could almost
hear Sara call to her. *Fifth position, Lily. Shoulders relaxed,
head high, neck long, and tummy in. Atta girl . . .*

Lily smiled as the music arrived on the note she and
her mother had started on. Side by side. *Piqué* turns.
Four of them. Then leaps. Legs extended parallel to
the floor! Toes pointed! Back straight!

She was remembering! Every step surfaced in her
memory right on cue.

Barbra Streisand's voice filled the room from the
speakers, rich, clear, crystal pure, and Lily danced with
matching perfection.

The room disappeared. Stereo, speakers, exercise bar,
everything faded except for her likeness reflected in the
floor-to-ceiling mirrors . . . and the beautiful woman
who danced like a graceful swan to her left.

Tears trickled along Lily's cheeks and the twin dancers blurred before her eyes like images in a rippling
pool.

Never had she danced so well. Never had she felt so
free. And never had she been more at peace than now
with Sara beside her, and then she saw Sara back away,
moving to the edge of the floor, yet encouraging Lily
to keep dancing.

Brava! Brava, Lily Dawn! Today you are a true dancer.

Lily laughed at the praise yet didn't miss a step until
the music ended. Then she sank in a graceful heap on
the floor.

"Oh, Mama, that was wonderful!" She cried once the
music ended.

But it was her image alone that looked back at her
from the mirror now and for an instant, Lily wondered

if she hadn't imagined it all. Had her mother been beside her, dancing and moving in perfect sync? Had the ecstasy inspired tears?

She touched her cheeks. They were still damp. She couldn't have made it up. Not all of it.

She bowed her head and hugged her knees as her breathing slowed and then she felt it, the most tender caress. Arms draped around hers, and fingers brushing the backs of her hands.

She squeezed her eyes against the joy so intense, so fiercely bittersweet that pain accompanied it.

"I love you, Mama. Don't leave me."

No one spoke. There was no need. She knew. Sara would always be with her.

Sash hadn't even tried to sleep. It would have been a waste of time. He was restless. His arm throbbed from the wound all the way to his fingertips. He had a headache. And worst of all, he had a terrible need to finish what he'd started with Lily Dawn Hutton in that emergency ward examining room.

He'd been trying to watch TV. Some Van Damme flick. Jesus, the guy made him nervous. Besides, tonight Sash felt every blow Jean Claude took. Sash hit the off button on the remote control.

Maybe he would take a ride along the coast on his bike. That always calmed him down.

Or maybe he'd drive up East Hill Drive.

And what? Just stop in for a little visit? See how Lily's friend was doing and ask if she'd like to pick up where they'd left off? Sure.

He looked around his house. Okay, so maybe he'd clean up the place. Or maybe he'd sketch a study that he would paint in oils later. It had been days since he'd gone upstairs to his converted attic studio. And his art had always mellowed him. Even as a child when Eudora confined him to his room for days on end as a punishment, he would lose himself in his sketchbook, many times hardly noticing how long he was imprisoned there.

As he climbed the steep, narrow staircase to the studio, he remembered that it was Sara who had first encouraged him to pursue his talent as an artist. A smile twisted his lips as he recalled the first time she'd peered over his shoulder and looked at one of his doodlings.

"Oh, Sasha, you're wonderful! Do your parents know how gifted you are?"

He'd been embarrassed and crumpled up the sheet of paper he'd been drawing on. But later, after everyone else was in bed, he'd sat up most of the night, sketching pictures of Sara. He gave her the best one for Christmas that year. Her present to him was an easel, two dozen tubes of oil paint, assorted brushes, canvas, and a pallet. He was ten years old that year. Too old for tears and too young to know how to control them. But Sara had come through for him even then. She'd taken one look at his glistening eyes and insisted Ali and Lily Dawn go with her to the kitchen to help her make hot chocolate. By the time they returned to the living room several minutes later, Sash had recovered his equilibrium.

Now, he stepped into the attic, pulled the string to turn on the overhead light bulb, and walked directly to a sheet-draped canvas and easel in the far corner. Though the entire studio was usually bright with sun that poured in through skylights, at night shadows bathed this part of the room. Sash hardly noticed, for even in the dimness he could make out every feature in the portrait he'd painted sixteen years before.

Sara. The most beautiful woman he'd ever known.

Until Lily, his mind corrected.

With his fingertips, Sash traced the lines of Sara's image and felt the too familiar pangs of longing and loneliness. But for the first time he found a new kind of guilt had made a place within the collection of feelings he'd carefully nurtured all these years. Guilt for his defection in favor of Lily?

He'd been staring at the portrait, yet not really seeing it until it seemed the lips parted slightly. Of course they hadn't. Not really. The smile, which was ever so slight, mocking and amused, wasn't real either. And neither did he hear her laugh and speak.

Silly man. Didn't I always promise the right woman would come into your life? She's here. She is the best of what I was, and now I give her to you. With my blessing, Sasha Rivers. With my love.

It was all merely the figment of his imagination. Even the touch of her lips on his brow. None of it was real.

Still, he sat in front of a new canvas for hours, sketching an outline, then changing to oils as he began to flesh out the features. And at times, he'd talk as he had years before. Explaining why he was changing brushes or the color he hoped to achieve by mixing a combination of paints or why he'd decided on a certain texture.

Sara didn't answer, but he knew she sat beside him and listened, and he knew she approved of the picture he was creating.

At dawn, he finished the portrait he'd painted from his heart. He looked to his left and grinned. He'd captured her, hadn't he? And she was beautiful. Lily.

Chapter Twenty

"You sure you're going to be all right here without me?" Jesse asked his niece the following morning. His flight had just been called and they'd stepped to the side of the boarding gate for a few last minutes of conversation.

"I'm fine, really. In fact, like I told you on the drive over, I feel invigorated today." She hunched her shoulders. "Don't ask me why. Maybe it's simply that I have a plan or maybe it's the deadline I've set. Just knowing that I'm going to put this all behind me once and for all in the next couple of days has made all the difference."

"I'll come straight back if you need me, Lily Dawn. You remember that. I'm only a telephone call away. I can be back here in a matter of hours."

"Will you stop worrying," Lily said with a small laugh. "I told you, I'll be fine. Now go on, give me a hug, then get on that plane and home to your family. And give my new cousin a kiss for me as soon as he arrives."

The parting embrace out of the way, Jesse picked up his suitcase and started for the door. He stopped, set the bag down, and gathered her to him once more. "Be careful. I truly couldn't stand it if anything happened to you. I love you like my own, little one."

Lily felt tears prick her eyelids as she returned the fierce hug. She stepped from his arms only to capture his broad face between her hands. "I love you too, Uncle Jesse. But stop worrying. I wasn't going to share this with anyone. It was so personal, but I think it'll help you leave with a good feeling in your heart.

"Last night after you went to bed, I went down to the studio. After Errol's, um, accident, I was uptight. I needed to dance. As soon as I started to move with the music, I knew I wasn't alone. I felt Mom there with me. I felt her spirit dancing alongside me. Oh, Jesse, I thought I even saw her! You can't imagine the joy! Her spirit was so free, so happy! I know now I'm going to be able to resolve all my doubts. And you know something else? When the music ended, I just sat there wanting to keep her with me, but knowing I couldn't, and still I was happy, because I knew she was telling me that she will always be with me in my heart."

Never before had she seen tears in her uncle's eyes. Not when he'd come to tell her about the tragic losses of both her parents. Not as he exchanged wedding vows with Rebecca the year before. Not even at Sara's funeral.

At first, Lily was afraid she'd somehow hurt him, but then he was grinning and even laughing. "It wasn't a dream, Lily Dawn. Sara spent a few minutes with me last night as well. Now that I know you understand, I can go happily to the birth of my son. You are going to let go of the past, so I know you'll be safe."

Lily started to argue that point, to remind him that she was still going to Tremont and then was going to pay a visit to the old retired school janitor. But what did it matter? She knew now that she was only going to go through the motions. She wouldn't find anything that confirmed any of her suspicions. Her parents were content. It was time for her to move on with her life.

"You're right," she answered with a bright smile. "I'm going to be safe and happy and star on Broadway!" She clapped a hand over her mouth as she remembered she'd never told him about the role she'd been promised. "Oh, Uncle Jesse, the big news I had to tell you! I almost forgot—"

"Final call for flight 485 to Oklahoma City, sir," a flight attendant said with an impatient smile.

"I'll call you, Lily! You can tell me then!" Jesse said, picking up his luggage again and hurrying through the door.

Lily stared after him until he disappeared down the jetway and for just an instant, her lighthearted spirits flagged.

Since the day her father had died and her life had taken such a profound turn, she'd protected herself. She'd learned the value of never giving fully of herself so that when she was hurt it was only the surface that was wounded and the scars didn't run too deep. She'd guarded her independence just as carefully, reasoning that if she didn't need, she couldn't lose.

But as she walked away from the gate, out of the airport, and across the parking lot to the car, she wondered if she hadn't been a little too vigilant.

Her parents were both gone now. Uncle Jesse had a family of his own. And hadn't Errol told her he would be moving on as well once they returned to New York in a couple of days?

No, damn it, she thought as she turned the key in the ignition. She might be truly alone for the first time in her life. That didn't mean she had to be lonely. She had her career and finally after so many years, she was about to discover peace of mind once she buried all the niggling doubts and questions with the past.

"And when I get back to Rosehill, Errol, you and I are going to have a talk," she said aloud as she slipped through the exit gate and turned onto the access road. "You're going to stop feeling sorry for yourself long enough to do some serious auditioning and start landing some good parts. Then I can let go of you, too, like I should have a long time ago."

As Lily pulled out in traffic on the interstate, Errol was just stepping from the shower. As he began to towel off, he tested the soreness in his battered body. Except for the bridge of his nose and the left eye that was still closed, he had to admit he didn't feel too bad. Not that he was exactly up for a 200-meter sprint, but at least he thought he could navigate the stairs and get to the kitchen for a cup of coffee.

Damn, he'd slept well. He remembered the sedative the house doctor had prescribed for him at the hospital and promised to see about getting a refill before he and Lily left for New York.

The phone rang, making him jump. Who in the hell ever heard of a telephone in the bathroom?

Pulling on his underwear, he ignored it as it jingled again. Let the housekeeper get it.

But on the fourth ring, he picked it up with an angry growl. "Yeah?"

"Mr. Mills?"

"You got me," he said, recognizing Eudora Rivers's exaggerated drawl. "What can I do for you?"

"First of all, how are you this morning? My daughter told me about the horrible misunderstanding yesterday. We—everyone from myself to the police commissioner—are so sorry that such a mistake was made."

Yeah, I hear ya, lady, and my nose smells the baloney, Errol thought.

"Are you there, Mr. Mills?"

"Hanging on every word."

"I was wondering if you would come to my house today? I think we should talk."

Errol scratched his wet scalp. "To tell you the truth, Ms. Rivers, I can't think of a single thing we got to talk about. And honestly, I'm not feeling my best today. Kind of sore."

"Please, Errol," she said. "We'll have lunch in the living room in front of the fire. And as added inducement, my cook's just baked a cake we can enjoy for dessert. Chocolate fudge." She waited, then added, "It's important, Errol, or I wouldn't ask."

Errol didn't miss the way she'd slipped so easily from last name to first *or* her cajoling tone. In fact, both irritated him, but it occurred to him that maybe the old battle-ax would inadvertently provide some clue that would help Lily. Now that would be worth an hour or two of his time. "Yeah, okay. But I'm not moving too fast. Give me about thirty minutes to walk over. Lily's got the car."

"Would you like me to come in my car to pick you up?"

Errol raised a brow. *Damn!* The lady was certainly going all out to make this easy for him. Well, he wasn't impressed. But he *was* curious. What the hell was she up to?

"No, I can walk. Might do me some good. Get the kinks out. But I just got outta the shower. Give me thirty or forty to get it together."

He went into the bedroom after breaking the connection to finish dressing, and fifteen minutes later was seated on the edge of the bed tying his shoes.

He glanced at his watch. Still had time to spare. It couldn't take more than what? Five or six minutes to walk to the Rivers's house?

Lily should be home around three or four. Maybe

the two of them could do a movie. Jesus, how long had it been since they had just hung out together? The more he thought about it, the more it grew on him. Reaching for the phone on the nightstand, he dialed information for a phone number, then the Pier Theater for a schedule of features and showtimes.

All right, a new Val Kilmer flick. Lily was crazy for the actor.

Errol replaced the receiver, knocking his keys behind the nightstand in the process. He started to reach for them, changing his mind at once when his bruised back muscles raged at his thoughtlessness. Forget it. What did he need his keys for today, anyway? They only worked on the locks in his other life in New York.

On to his date with the dragon lady. Find out what the hell she was up to. Then he and Lily could relax a little tonight. God knew they both could use a little R and R.

"Where is Lily this afternoon?" Eudora asked politely as she sat across from her guest.

They'd already done the "Oh, you poor thing," routine, gotten past talk of the weather and the approach of spring, even covered a few news headlines. Now, it looked like they were going to get down to business. Errol was surprised to be enjoying himself. He took a long sip of the rich, black coffee, then answered her question. "She's gone to Charleston. Should be back this afternoon."

"Charleston?"

"Yes, ma'am," Errol said, enjoying watching the wheels spin and wondering how long it would take her to get to the question she really wanted to ask. But he wasn't going to help her out. Call him perverse, but seeing a proper southern lady like Eudora Rivers squirm in her prissy panties was fun.

"And what about that charming uncle of hers? I would have included him in my invitation had I known the two of you were home together."

"As a matter of fact, he's gone to Charleston with her."

"Oh? Whatever for?"

Bingo! Errol resisted the urge to laugh. "Lily was taking him to catch a plane to Oklahoma. He and his wife are expecting a baby, and it looks like the little guy is going to arrive ahead of schedule."

"Well, how delightful. It's a shame he had to leave so soon, though. I know Lily is going to miss having him here with her."

"Suppose so," Errol said, raising his cup to his lips before providing the rest of the reason for Lily's sudden trip to the city. "She's also going to that hospital where her mother was."

Eudora didn't bat an eye, and Errol suspected for the first time that she'd known all along the purpose of Lily's trip. Jesus, did they have the house bugged?

"What did you want to see me about?" he asked, not even trying to disguise his disgust.

Eudora raised her hands, palms skyward. "Now, I can't say it was nothing, can I, after telling you it was important. But I really just had to see for myself how you are. I felt simply terrible about what happened yesterday. It was so unfair for you to be arrested. Then when my daughter told me how you'd been hurt as well, why I was absolutely horrified. I don't think you can appreciate how responsible I feel, in my position of mayor, and this being my little corner of the universe."

"Yeah, well, I survived. I'll just be careful to keep my ass tucked up here on this hill till we head back north."

Eudora smiled in response as a hand toyed with a cameo pin at her throat. Errol remembered that she'd worn the same brooch the day of Sara Hutton's funeral and commented on it.

"That's a good-looking piece of jewelry. Looks like an antique. An heirloom?"

This time, Eudora's smile was wide and genuine. "Why, yes, it is. It was my great-grandmother's. I was told her husband brought it home from a business trip to England as a wedding gift. . . . You have an eye for good jewelry, young man. Is your family in the business?"

Errol almost sputtered coffee all over his shirt at the question. "My family? No ma'am. The only thing my folks knew about jewelry was how much they could get on a loan from a pawn shop."

"I see," Eudora said. She straightened her plaid wool skirt over her knees, uncrossed and recrossed her ankles, then folded her hands in her lap. "So your family was poor. Is that why you wear such a heavy chip on your shoulder?"

"Maybe. Or could be they just never bothered to teach me good manners."

Eudora laughed. "You see, that's exactly what I'm talking about. I'm only making polite conversation, but you find it necessary to come back at everything I say with some clever quip or outrageous remark. And there's no need. Especially not in your case. You are such a handsome young man. Blond, blue-eyed, tall, and fit. Very like my son-in-law, as a matter of fact. Of course, I can't deny that Dix was born with certain advantages. But on the other hand, you have the advantage of great creative acumen. There's no need for you always to be on the defensive. All you do when you attack is alienate the very ones who could best assist you in realizing your goals."

"Is that what you wanted to talk to me about?" Errol asked. He leaned forward to set his cup and saucer on

the table between them. As he sat back, he placed a
foot on his knee and began to toy with the shoe string
of his Air Jordan sneaker. " 'Cause I have to tell you,
ambitious as I am, there are—believe it or not—some
things even a greedy bastard like me wouldn't do."

"Like make your home here in Rosehill?" Eudora
asked with a comprehending grin.

"Or wrestle alligators. Or scuba dive with great
whites. Or hypnotize cobras."

"You do us an injustice," she said, her cold blue gaze
piercing his. "We're not evil or dangerous. We don't
eat our young, and we don't even recommend the practice to others no matter how ill-fated their progeny."

"Now we're getting to it. You're talking blacks, His-
panics, anyone you consider inferior? Yeah, I noticed
how white bread your little group was at Mrs. Hutton's
funeral. I bet you just about swallowed your twenty-
four-carat teeth the day Allison brought home a squaw.
Even one as filthy rich as Sara Two Moons, huh?"

Eudora had leaned forward to spoon sugar into her
cup. The silver spoon clattered noisily against the fine
bone-china saucer but neither of them paid it any attention as they faced off. "You are an arrogant, rude man!"
she said in such a perfect hiss Errol was tempted to
search his neck for fang marks.

"What I can't understand," she continued, "is who
in God's kingdom ever led you to believe *you* could
judge anyone else?"

"You mean because I can't trace my pedigree?"

"Exactly!" she almost screamed.

At once, two uniformed servants appeared in the
doorway. "Are you all right, Miss Eudora?" one of
them asked.

"Of course I'm all right, Hanna. Mr. Mills and I are
merely enjoying a debate on social propriety."

The servants exchanged glances, then walked away.

Errol watched Eudora and knew the second he left, she'd be delivering a stern lecture about forgetting what they'd heard.

"You must get stressed maintaining that balancing act all the time," he said. "How can you do it? And how in the world do you get all the little people down in the valley to let you guys up here in the hills control their lives, convince them that you really care about them, and still kick them around without even a whisper of complaint?"

"It's very easy. We feed them well, give them an occasional pat on the head, and punish misdeeds sternly."

Errol rubbed the bandage on his nose. "Yeah, I know that's right. So let me see if I've got this straight. Basically, you just treat them the way any good owner handles his pet."

"You see, I knew you were quick," Eudora said dryly.

"Okay, but let's get back to situations like the marriage between Alison Hutton and Sara Two Moons. That sort of thing doesn't happen too often to the families up here on the hills, huh?"

Eudora stood up and walked to the mantel. Decorum and good breeding too firmly instilled for her to turn her back entirely on her company, she nevertheless almost seemed to forget he was there as she stared at the collection of framed miniature portraits arranged before her. After a time, she selected one of them and turned it so that Errol could see it. "This is Rose Price, Errol. She came to America with her husband and three children in 1703. They arrived with a company of 214. One month later, everyone save Rose, her oldest daughter, a man named Hutton, and two boys named Rivers was dead. They'd all been butchered by savages."

Errol's disbelief must have registered on his face, for she held up a hand and shook her head. "No, I'm not saying that's why we were unhappy when Ali married Sara." She set the picture back on the shelf, then reclaimed both her seat and her smile. "The story that has been carried through the decades is that when the Indians attacked, Rose saved her daughter and the two Rivers boys by hiding in the swamps. Not just for a few hours, but for several days.

"They were more dead than alive by that time, but Rose pulled them all through it, and even saved Hubert Hutton's life after he'd been badly wounded and left for dead.

"The community had been named Victoria Hills, but Hubert renamed it Rosehill in her honor."

"You should write a book," Errol said.

Eudora ignored him. "The point is, we're all descendants of that woman."

"Was she rich?"

"She was descended from royalty."

"Ahh," Errol said with a slow nod of his head. "And every now and then someone comes along to dirty up the gene pool. What then, Eudora? Do you try to scare them off or do you usually just kill them straight off?"

"Don't be absurd!"

"Hey, genetic cleansing is an accepted practice in some parts of the world. Why not here where you admit bloodlines are everything?"

Eudora's blue eyes were positively frosty. "We discourage marriage between races as well as social subordinates. I won't deny it. Normally, our children share our views and by the time they've matured and gone away to school, they automatically flock with their own."

"Did it ever occur to you that your little Shangri-la hasn't prospered and grown because most people find your bigoted, narrow-minded views repugnant?"

Eudora smiled and spread her hands like a Catholic

priest granting benediction. "There! You see how little you understand. And I thought we'd been so vulgarly obvious about everything, the simplest fool would have figured it out."

"There are still a few of us morons out here."

Her weariness with his obstinate behavior suddenly manifest in her smile, Eudora continued. "*We've* stifled our growth by discouraging outside industry. Almost every square acre of Rosehill is owned by one or more of the twelve governing families. *We* have refused offers from Marriott, Hilton, Holiday Inn, and so on to put hotels in. We've turned down countless lucrative offers from movie companies to film here. Our zoning restrictions are the toughest in the country, and—as I'm sorry you learned—our laws are enforced to the letter."

"And all so you can keep tight-fisted control on the minions," Errol finished for her, tasting his disgust on his tongue. He was just about to tell her how much she sickened him when she started again.

"Please, Errol," she said, pressing her hands together in a plea for understanding. "Just listen.

"We're not Nazis as you'd make us out to be. We're simply proud of what and who we are, and we strive to see that the values we've inherited are passed on to generations after us. We discourage outsiders from settling in Rosehill as I've admitted. Especially those who would change our way of life. We're happy the way we are. And how are we? Clannish? Absolutely. Narrow-minded? All right, I suppose that's true. But we're God-fearing, taxpaying Americans. Why, do you know none of my friends and family on these hills would dream of buying product made outside the USA?"

Errol had heard enough. Slapping his thighs with his hands, he rolled his eyes. "Why is it I can hear the faint strains from Greenwood's 'I'm Proud to Be an American'?"

Clearly angered by his sarcasm, Eudora took a long stabilizing breath before continuing as if she'd never been interrupted.

"Have you ever heard of white flight?" she asked, trying a new tactic.

"Of course. It's the politically correct term for what's happening in the suburbs when people try to integrate the neighborhoods and the WASPs move out."

"Exactly so. Here in Rosehill there will never be the need for such overtly offensive measures to be taken."

"Anybody ever notified the NAACP about you guys?"

Eudora went on. "Here our neighborhoods remain segregated, for the most part, but nobody complains. And do you know why? Because everyone is happy. We make certain of that by anticipating their needs and finding solutions before problems occur."

"Bullshit, lady. Slave owners tried that tune more'n a century ago. It didn't play then, and it ain't gonna play today." Errol stood up, straightening his jeans legs and smoothing back his hair as he struggled to control his anger. "You are a piece of work, Mrs. Rivers. No wonder Lily's glad to be away from here.

"You'll excuse me for changing my mind about lunch. I've suddenly lost my appetite." He stepped past her and crossed the room without looking back. "I'll show myself out. You just go on sitting there telling yourself how you're making your little slice of the world a sweeter place to be. Maybe one day you'll get past the sour taste in your mouth every time you say it."

He was halfway down the driveway when a sleek, low-riding red car turned in. In spite of his anger, he couldn't help slowing down long enough to let loose a long, appreciative whistle. "Now that's a car!"

"Thanks," Imogene Price said, sliding from behind the wheel and leaning on the top to let her eyes roam just as appreciatively over him. "You've got some pretty sleek lines, yourself," she purred.

"Not today, honey. Your mother just tried to sell me a snow job. I wasn't buying then, I ain't buying now. Unfortunately for both of you, I'm ready for spring."

Genie laughed appreciatively. "That's good! You're funny."

"Yeah. Har har har, and all that."

"Hey, wait a minute. I know you've still gotta be sore from your, um, accident. At least let me drive you around the bend to Lily's. Only take a minute and save you from putting hurt on top of hurt."

Errol shook his head without looking back at her. He hadn't worn a jacket and even though the weather had warmed considerably in the past twenty-four hours, it was still cooler than he liked. He wasn't going to accept a ride from Eudora Rivers's daughter or any of her other upstanding neighbors, but he wasn't going to hang around debating it while his balls shriveled up either.

"Not even if I promise to keep both hands on the wheel?" Genie teased, surprised at his refusal.

"Especially not then," Errol called back, but she noticed that he laughed.

"Well, at least walk on the road. It'll take a little longer, but your bruises will thank you later."

He shouted something again, but it was lost on the breeze that carried it south with him, and then he disappeared around the bend. Well, you couldn't win them all, but, my, oh, my, that was one she'd have liked a stab at.

"Wonder what he was doing here at Mother's?" she said out loud.

She shrugged and slipped behind the wheel once again. She could ask Eudora, she supposed, but then again she could have so much more fun pestering Errol.

She was backing down the drive when she caught sight of her mother on the widow's watch three stories above. Backing all the way onto the road, she stopped and rolled down her window. "Got an important appointment! I'll come by later!"

Eudora didn't appear to hear as she stared directly south to the Hutton house.

Genie closed the window and tooted her horn as she shifted into first. She hadn't released the clutch all the way when she heard the sharp squeal of tires ahead on the street, around the curve. Her brows drew together in a perplexed frown. She shifted into neutral, letting the car roll slowly down the street, around the bend.

She was shaking and her heart pounding out a fierce tattoo by the time she stopped a couple of hundred yards north of Lily's house. Nothing. But that was impossible. Where was the car she'd heard? And where the hell had Errol gone? He couldn't have made it to the house already, could he?

She wasn't imagining things. Not things that loud and nerve-jarring. The car she'd heard hadn't passed her going north, and it couldn't have been heading south. East Hill Road ended in a small, dead-end circle at the end of her parents' drive, so unless . . .

She craned her neck to look out of the back window. There was a narrow strip of gravel just off to the west that maintenance vehicles sometimes used when working on power lines or telephone poles. Maybe someone had pealed off the gravel too fast and skidded out of control for a second or two.

And then she saw the flattened foliage on the west shoulder. Oh, Lord, if someone had driven off right there, they'd be at the bottom of a hundred-and-fifty-foot cliff.

Legs trembling, she climbed from her car. She hugged herself as she neared the edge and almost lost the nerve to peer over the side. In the next instant, she giggled on a note of hysterical relief when she didn't find any automobile wreckage. And then she saw him. Errol. Not at the bottom where she'd been looking, but about three feet below on a narrow ledge. He was lying facedown, his left arm and leg beneath his body, and his right limbs hanging over the side. Blood was spreading from beneath his head and chest, staining the earth. "Oh, my God," Genie whispered as she turned unconsciously to stare up at the place where she imagined her mother still stood, though of course she couldn't see the house from here. *Damn it, Mother! How dare you?*

Chapter Twenty-one

Lily slowed the car as she approached the Tremont State Prison Facility. Though technically a hospital for the treatment of mental disorders, the only patients were prisoners of the state of South Carolina who'd been declared guilty of a crime by reason of insanity.

Rolls of barbed wire topped the miles of ten-foot-high fence that surrounded the grounds, and heavy mesh wire covered every window.

The hospital itself consisted of one central three-story building and several single-floor appendages where the incarcerated residents were actually housed. All were painted battleship gray. Not more than a dozen trees and shrubs dotted the grounds, and more than half of those were placed strategically close to the main building where visitors were always brought. No tax-payer would ever complain that his money was being wasted on frivolity here.

It was even worse on the inside where the odors of antiseptic, furniture polish, and pine cleaner never quite managed to camouflage the underlying stench of illness.

Lily's hands trembled on the steering wheel as she sat parked along the curb on the opposite side of the street. For the first time, she doubted she could do this. Not alone. If only Uncle Jesse or Errol . . .

And what about Sara? She'd been alone in there for fifteen years.

Lily shifted into drive and pulled back into traffic, crossing to the center turn lane, then into a long divided drive that was interrupted by a guard station.

An imposing black man with legs that looked like tree trunks stepped from the booth, motioning for her to roll down her window.

"There are no morning visiting hours unless you are an attorney for the inmate you wish to visit or physician assigned by the court. All other visitation—spousal, parental, sibling, religious, and good neighbor—is strictly kept to afternoon hours. Two to five-thirty.

"All parole hearings are held on the first Monday, Tuesday, and Wednesday of each month. Sanity reviews are on the third Monday of every month." The man recited the schedule in a deep baritone. His ham shank–sized arm resting on the roof of Lily's car, he went on. "If you have business other than the aforementioned, state it now and hand me two pieces of ID, at least one with picture and one with social security number.

"Should access to the facility be granted, you will be asked to sign a registration book, have your picture taken, and searched."

Lily handed him her driver's license and her Actors' Equity card. "I'm here to see Dr. Janice Lepstein or Dr. William Teggs."

"No appointment?" he asked, studying the information on the cards in his hand.

"No," Lily said wearily. "But it's important that I see one of them. My mother was a . . . a resident here for fifteen years. She passed away last week. I have some questions."

The man, whose badge identified him as Rowland

Foxx, stooped lower to meet Lily's gaze. "Dr. Teggs is in Washington, D.C., today and tomorrow. Dr. Lepstein is in a meeting, but I'll see if she can work you in."

"Thanks. It's very important."

Rowland grunted. "Yeah."

Lily tapped her fingers on the steering wheel while she waited. She was composing her argument to persuade the doctor to let her talk to staff members when the guard returned. She jumped at the unexpected intrusion of his voice.

"Sorry. Dr. Lepstein's assistant says she's got an appointment in Charleston in an hour. She can't see you today. You wanna make an appointment for next week, I can set it up with Mizz Randolf, her assistant."

Lily slapped the steering wheel with the palm of her hand. "Damn it." She looked up at the patient face of the guard. "Look, would you ask Miss Randolf if I could talk with her? It really is very important."

He hunched his shoulders and disappeared inside the booth again. Seconds later he was back, shaking his head and handing her her ID back. "Strike three. Sorry."

"Why not?"

Rowland scratched under his chin. "Don't know, but maybe Dr. Lepstein doesn't think you should be talking to the secretaries about her patients, if you catch my drift."

"Yeah, I catch it," Lily said, shoving her license and union card into her wallet. "Do I just go up here to the end of the divider and turn around? I've never been turned away before."

He drew an inverted horseshoe in the air with the longest index finger Lily had ever seen.

"Okay, thanks."

"No problem. Peace."

Lily shook her head. "That's one thing I won't have any of until I can get inside this damn place."

"You'll pardon me for asking, but if yo' mama's already passed on, why are you so desperate to talk to the doctors? I mean, ain't she kinda past the need for their help?"

Lily opened her mouth to explain that she was looking for information, not help for her mother, when she remembered Errol's advice. *Talk to the nurses, aides, security guards. . . .*

Excited, she slammed the gear into park and opened her car door. "Look, Mr. Foxx," she said as she climbed from behind the wheel, "you've worked here a long time. I remember you from visits as far back as three or four years ago."

"Yeah, so?"

"So, maybe you can help me."

"Uh-uh," the guard said with a firm shake of his head. "I don't know what you're wantin', but I *know* I ain't gonna be the one givin' it."

"Oh, please, Mr. . . . Rowland, please just listen. I don't want you to do anything that might jeopardize your job. I just want to ask you a couple of questions. I've driven more than a hundred miles to talk to someone. This won't take you five minutes."

"Whatcha wanna know?" he asked begrudgingly.

"My mother's name was Sara Hutton. I just want you to check your book, see if she had any visitors between two and three weeks ago."

"*Lady*," the big man said, managing to whine as he rolled both head and eyes at the same time.

"Please, Rowland! It's so important."

"Okay, but I'm not sure I can tell you what you want to know."

"Why not? Everyone signs in with you, don't they?"

"Naw. Only when they show up without an appointment like you doing today. If they meeting with some-one by arrangement, they just show me their ID, I call in to the front desk, and they sign at the front desk."

Lily's hopes flagged. "You're right. I knew that. Well, would you check anyway? See if just maybe someone came by on an unscheduled visit."

A car leaving the compound honked its horn for Rowland to press the button inside his control booth and open the gates. "Be right back," he told Lily.

As the gates opened, the car proceeded through at a very low speed, stopping on the far side of the guard station. Lily held her breath. If it was Dr. Lepstein leaving for her appointment in Charleston, she just hoped Rowland wouldn't tell her what Lily had asked him to do. She'd already figured out that both Doctors Teggs and Lepstein didn't like anyone looking over their shoulders or questioning their authority. She was certain the good lady doctor would take offense at Lily's investigation no matter how superficial. But the woman who climbed from behind the wheel was not Janice Lepstein. Even though Lily had never seen the doctor face to face, she knew this girl was too young to be Lepstein.

As thin as a sapling, the young woman was positively dwarfed by the massive security guard. Lily watched them talk for a few minutes, hoping against hope that she wasn't the subject of their conversation. A moment later the young woman stepped past him and motioned for Lily to join them on the other side of the station.

"Miss Hutton? I'm Mary Alice Randolf, Dr. Lepstein's assistant. I don't know exactly what's going on, but I'm afraid she's sent me to ask you to leave. She said that I should tell you that any further requests for informa-tion, meetings with herself or other staff members should be made through your mother's attorney." She smiled, her eyes apologizing.

Lily struggled against her anger. No sense taking it out on the assistant or the guard. Neither one of them were to blame. "All right, I'll leave, but could I ask you one favor, Miss Randolf?"

The girl's eyes darted to the top floor of the central building where Lily knew the administration offices were located. "No, really—"

"I just want you to take my phone number back to Dr. Lepstein along with a message." She turned back toward her car for a paper and pen, but Rowland was ahead of her and handed her both. Lily quickly scribbled her phone number and name and pressed the slip of paper into Mary Alice's hand. "Please. Just give her this and tell her she's misunderstood my visit. I'm not here to cause trouble for anyone associated with Tremont. I'm only trying to resolve some personal issues for myself, and I think she or someone here at the . . ."

Mary Alice looked sympathetic, but Lily knew she wasn't going to go against her superior's instructions. At least not in front of another employee.

"Okay, look, don't give her the number. Keep it yourself. And if you can help me in any way, call me, please. I just want to know who visited my mother the week before she died. That's all."

Suddenly choking on impassioned tears, Lily hurried back to her car, quickly climbing in and shutting the door before she broke down and embarrassed herself. Without daring a look at either the administrator's assistant or the guard, she started the car and pulled away. She still had to pass them on the rebound—a whipped pup, tucking tail. Not hardly! She forced her lips into a semblance of a smile and waved as she passed them by. *Then* she let the tears come.

The two-hour return drive to Rosehill helped restore Lily's good humor. For much of the time, she listened to a soft rock station, humming along or even singing familiar lyrics. In the remaining minutes, she delivered a firm lecture to herself about the necessity of keeping a stiff upper lip. No more blubbering. No more caving in under pressure. She was from better stock than that. The Two Moons-Hutton union was a formidable one and she was the by-product. Not too shabby.

She was just approaching the Rosehill city lines when she remembered her intention to visit old Joe Joe. Only problem with that, she didn't know his address.

She spied a Chevron station on the right, made a quick, unsignaled turn into the parking lot and went inside to ask the clerk for a phone book. If he wasn't listed, she was sure his grandson's law practice would be.

Minutes later, an address in hand, and directions provided by a very accommodating clerk, she pulled back out in the light, mid-afternoon traffic.

Lily checked the number on the small sheet of paper: 4226 Georgia Peach Terrace.

She followed the directions without a hitch, arriving in front of a small, well-kept bungalow.

Though the house was located in the least prosperous section of town—the northwest end—Lily noticed that most of the houses reflected their owners' pride.

She was just stopping the car at the curb when a midsized black sedan turned into the driveway. Lily resisted a smile as she slipped the keys into her purse. She hadn't spoken to Abe Joseph when she called the office. Only to his secretary, who had obliged with the address after an abbreviated explanation from Lily. But she had no doubt Abe had left his office the moment his employee told him about the call.

He was already approaching across the small patch of front yard by the time she got out of Jesse's rental car.

She held out a hand, which he accepted at once. "I'm sorry I interrupted your day, Abe. I didn't mean to."

"That's all right," he said, smiling easily, and placing a hand lightly on her back as he motioned her up the stairs to the front door. "It's just that my grandfather doesn't hear like he used to. I make it a practice to be here for him when he needs me."

A ball went sailing over their heads, banging soundly on the front door, then bouncing back at them.

Abe snatched it from the air and tossed it back to a group of adolescents crowded at the end of the driveway.

"Sorry, 'bout that, y'all," one of them said with a wide grin that appeared anything but repentant. "Ball jes' sorta got away from me is all."

"And besides, they wanted a closer look at my grandfather's pretty company," Abe told Lily with a knowing wink.

Lily laughed, turned to the youth, and waved. When she turned back, Abe was holding the door open for her.

There was no entryway. As soon as they crossed the threshold, they stood almost in the middle of the tiny living room.

"Pop's probably in bed. Says he likes to doze for thirty minutes or so every afternoon," Abe said. "Truth is, I haven't found him out of bed in the past two years anytime I stop by between noon and three. He's always up by then, though, because he's a dyed-in-the-wool fan of that soap opera *Days of Our Lives*. It's approaching that now, so he's probably just waking up. I'll just go tell him he's got company."

Though he was trying hard to mind his own business and be a good host at the same time, Lily could see the worry in his eyes. She laid a hand on his arm, stopping him for a moment. "I don't want you to worry, Abe.

As I told your secretary, I just want to talk to him for a few minutes."

"About the day your father was killed?"

Lily nodded.

"But why? You were there in the courthouse when he testified. You heard everything he had to say."

"Please, just let me talk to him. Tell him why I'm asking questions. You're probably right, and he won't tell me anything new, but I have to ask."

"All right," he said, motioning to the well worn sofa against the far wall. "Have a seat."

While he was gone, Lily looked around the room, which was a charming clutter of too much furniture, too many books and magazines, bric-a-brac of every description, and family pictures covering almost every square inch of wall. Lily could not believe her eyes when her gaze fell on a tiny framed photograph of her own family. She'd been only a babe in arms when the picture was snapped and her mother and father looked like teenagers. Especially her father.

Lily was laughing at the bell-bottom trousers Ali wore when Abe returned. "Don't they look weird?"

"Nope. But they look happy."

"How'd he get this snapshot?"

"He took it. He was up at your folks' place to fix something and they were leaving for the church to have you christened. Your mother asked him if he'd do the honors. After they were developed, she gave him a copy."

"They'd be so pleased he thought enough of them to frame it and hang it along with his family photos," Lily said.

"You can tell him that in a minute. He was already up. Plannin, to tar some kids for slamming their ball against the front door."

Lily laughed. "I don't imagine they're any more

afraid of him than we were in school. You know, I think he retired when I was only in first or second grade, but I still remember him fussing at us for running in the halls or splashing water on the floor in the bathrooms."

"Did you quake your boots?"

"Saddle oxfords. Black and white. I wore them all the way through elementary school."

"Mine were black leather wing tips. Shined till I could see my pupils in the reflection. I thought I was one real cool dude till I looked around and noticed the really cool guys were wearin' big ol' army boots and high-top sneakers."

"What you two kids out here goin' on about?" Joe Joe asked as he shuffled into the room.

Lily's laughter immediately faded away as she noticed how frail he looked. She'd seen him only days before at the cemetery, but today he looked eons older. Maybe it was the oversized, wrinkled khaki slacks and faded flannel shirt that was half-tucked, half-out, or the grizzled beard on his face.

"I'm sorry to bother you, Joe Joe."

"Turn on the TV, Abraham. Don't wanna miss *Days*. I think Marlena's gonna do away with Stephano. Now, don't get upset, missy. He's had it comin' for some time. Lawd he's bad. Been terrorizing them folks for years."

"It's not quite time yet, Pops. Why don't we let Lily ask you her questions then you can watch your show?"

"What questions you got to ask ol' Joe Joe, missy? I don't do nothin' anymore worth knowin' 'bout."

He'd sat down in the vinyl recliner nearest the television, but Lily pulled a footstool with an embroidered padded cover over beside his chair and sat down to talk to him. "I want to ask you about the day my father was killed."

"Who?"

"My father, Joe Joe. Alison Hutton. You were up there fixing the sprinklers, I think."

"Nope, I was takin' a nap by then. Right in that gazebo Dr. Alison built for his little bride, Sara. Pretty as a wildflower, that one."

Lily smiled patiently and nodded her head. "Yes, she was."

"She's gone now, too, I hear. Abe, did you hear anything about Miss Sara dying up in that place where they put her after she done killed Dr. Alison?"

Abe came to stand on the other side of his grandfather's chair. A hand on his back, he leaned down and spoke into his ear. "Yes, Grandfather, we went to her funeral earlier this week. Don't you remember?"

"Nope!"

Abe shrugged on a smile. "Sometimes I don't know if he's being contrary or if he's really forgotten." He'd hushed his tone and spoke over Joe's head. "I think it's a little of both. He gets embarrassed because he doesn't remember what I'm talking about, so he gets belligerent. Says I'm making up things to confuse him."

"But you remember the day you went to sleep in the gazebo after fixing the sprinkler system," Lily said.

" 'Course I do. I'm old, missy. When I woke up that pretty little Rivers girl started hollering and carrying on and that's when I seen your daddy fall off that terrace."

"And you saw my mother up there on the terrace, too, just before my father fell. Is that right?"

"Yep. Jes' like I tol' the police. There she was, up there screamin' and cryin' and holdin' that knife that she done killed him with."

Several seconds passed before Lily spoke again. She was trying to decide how best to get him to remember everything that happened without leading him and confusing what was real with what she might suggest.

"Could you see the knife all the way from the gazebo, Joe Joe?" she asked at last.

He thought about that for a minute or so, then he shook his head. "No, ma'am, I can't say as how I really could. I could see she was holdin' something, and I could see he was bleedin'. Or maybe I jes' knowed it was blood from some deep-rooted instinct. I don't know!"

"It's all right. That's not important. But I wanted to ask you if you saw anyone else besides Genie Rivers? On the terrace near my mother and father or even downstairs around the outside of the house? Anyone at all, Joe Joe?"

"No. No, ma'am. The police asked me the very same question and I told them the same as I'm tellin' you. There wasn't nobody on that there terrace 'ceptin' yo' mama and yo' daddy. When he fell, I told the girl to run and git help. Send an ambulance, and I'd go see after Mizz Sara 'cause I knowed it was already too late for Dr. Alison."

Abe shook his head. "I'm sorry, Miss Hutton, I know that's not what you were hoping to hear."

Lily stood up, patting the old man's forearm as she did. "That's all right. It was a long shot, but worth asking." She smiled. "And I'd say the timing's just about perfect. Only a couple of minutes until three o'clock and time for his show."

"Go git yer mama, honey!" Joe Joe cried suddenly, wiping his brow with the back of his hand as if swiping away perspiration. His eyes seemed to be staring intensely at something, but it wasn't in this room. "Don't you be worrying about what's happened to yo' brother. Sasha's a good boy. He'll be home directly. Right now we gots to see 'bout gettin' help for Mizz Sara."

Abe and Lily exchanged excited glances. Lily sank back down to the stool, and Abe rushed around the back of the chair to crouch at her side. "Whoa, Pops. Hold up. Let's go back to Imogene. Was she out there with Sasha? Were they playing out there when Dr. Hutton fell?"

"No, Abraham! I already tol' you, no one was there 'cept me and that chile. She was lookin' for young Sasha but he wasn't there anymore. I tol' her to forget him and . . ."

Abe stood up, giving his grandfather's shoulder a squeeze. "All right, Pops, that's cool." He reached around the chair for the remote control and put it in Joe Joe's hand. "It's just about time for your soap. Go on and turn it on. I'll show Miss Hutton to the door and be back in a few minutes."

"I'm sorry, Lily," Abe told her as they walked to her car. "He's talked about what happened that day for years and I never once heard him mention Sasha Rivers. Do you think it's possible he saw what happened? Maybe he—"

Lily stopped him. "We still don't know that he was there. Only that Imogene was there because she was looking for him. Her mother probably sent her out to call him for dinner. He was always at our house, hanging around, doing errands for my mom. That's probably just the first place she was going to look."

"And if he was there?" Abe persisted.

Lily stalled by digging in her purse for her car keys. Once they were in hand, she raised her gaze to his again. "If he was there I think he would have told someone. He . . . he loved my mother very much. He wouldn't sit by and let her be committed without rushing to her defense. Even if all he could do was try to justify what she did."

"You're probably right, but on the other hand, if he was there and saw something he didn't report, justice wasn't served. I'm going to talk to Pops some more.

Keep a dialogue going over the next couple of days or so. See if I can't pry some more loose. I'll call you if I get anything at all."

Lily hugged him quickly. "Thank you, Abe." Her chin had begun to quiver and she knew it wouldn't take much more before she gave in to the tears lumped in her throat. She gave his hand a quick squeeze and opened the car door. "I'll see you again before I leave."

"Count on it," the suddenly somber lawyer said.

Lily didn't look back, not even in the rearview mirror, but she knew he watched her until she'd turned out of sight. She knew he was wondering why she'd waited all these years to start asking questions. She could have told him about the phone call she believed her mother had made to her in New York, but then she'd have to explain about the fear. The truth was she was terrified of the past; desperately afraid of what she might find if she looked too closely at the monsters that haunted her dreams. For years, she'd been afraid of who she'd find hiding behind the hideous masks. Did she want to believe now that one of them could be Sash?

Chapter Twenty-two

Lily was shrugging from her coat when she spied the note taped conspicuously to the top of the balustrade as she started up the stairs. She stopped, grabbed the piece of lined yellow notepaper, and sank to a step to read.

She recognized her roommate's cramped scrawl immediately.

> Babe—
>   *Hanging around was getting to be a drag. Needed some action, so I'm outta here.*
> Be cool,
Errol—as in Flynn—Mills

Lily was disappointed that he'd gone out. She'd been anxious to tell him about her conversation with Joe Joe. Get his take on the meeting.

Realizing that this was the first time she'd been alone all week without a man hovering over her, she decided to take a long, hot, relaxing bath, wash her hair, and manicure her nails—fingers *and* toes. Using one of the newel posts, she pulled herself to her feet and was just turning to go upstairs when Kitty suddenly appeared at the top. Both women let out loud shrieks of surprise, and Kitty almost dropped the oversized load of bed linens she was carrying.

"Oh, my gosh, Kitty, you scared the wits out of me. I didn't know anyone was home," Lily said, placing a hand over wildly beating heart.

"I'm sorry, Miss Lily. I didn't hear you come in."

"No, that's all right. I startled you, too." Lily shook her head. "Obviously, I was wrong, but I could have sworn Uncle Sander said today was your day off."

Kitty's gaze darted for the floor as she answered. "It is. Usually. Today and Sunday. But since you're only going to be here for a short time, I thought I'd try to be here to help you out."

"Gee, thanks," Lily said, touched by the thoughtfulness. "But you don't have to work your days off. Not on *my* account."

"I don't mind," Kitty said, still not looking at her employer. "If you'll excuse me, I'll just get these sheets in the washer."

"Freshening the room Uncle Jesse used?" Lily asked, following the other woman down the stairs.

"Uh, no. I already finished his room. Mr. Hutton's, too. I'm cleaning up Mr. Mills's room now."

"Errol's? Oh, Kitty, you don't have to do Errol's and mine. We've only been here a few days. Besides, I don't think we'll be staying too much longer. Now that you've already stripped his bed, go ahead, but don't worry about mine unless I change my mind and decide to hang around a little longer."

Kitty stopped on the bottom step, seeming to consider a dilemma.

"Does that sound okay?" Lily asked tentatively. Maybe she was stepping on some unwritten housekeeping rule by telling Kitty when to change the linens and when not to.

"Sure, fine," Kitty said, continuing to the foyer then down the hall to the laundry room.

Lily tagged after her, leaning against the dryer while the woman sorted the bedclothes and loaded the washer. She was about to ask if Kitty knew where Errol had gotten off to when she noticed a long smear on the other woman's cheek. "Kitty, you've got blood on your face. Have you cut yourself?"

Kitty shoved the sheets into the washer and stepped past Lily into the hall, then disappeared into the bathroom one door down. Lily could hear water running in the sink. A moment later, Kitty was back absent the streak of blood. "I had a nosebleed on the way over here," she explained. "I didn't know I had it on my face. That's gross. I'm sorry."

"That's okay. I was just worried that you might have hurt—"

"I know, but I'm fine," Kitty interrupted in a tight voice. "I would like to get the laundry in and get back upstairs to make the bed, if you don't mind."

Lily was taken aback by the girl's sharp tone and a little angry as well, though she warned herself not to overreact. Kitty was probably just tired and maybe unconsciously resenting her decision to work on her regularly scheduled day off.

She said, "Well, then I'll just get out of your way."

Kitty busied herself measuring detergent, stain boosters, and fabric softener, but Lily didn't leave at once. There was something very wrong with the normally unflappable Kitty Star. It was also blatantly evident that whatever it was, the girl did not want to talk about it. Still, Lily couldn't help but feel responsible for her. No matter who had hired her, it was still Lily's estate that paid her wage.

But just as Lily turned to go, Kitty was suddenly talking. "Miss Lily, wait. I didn't want to tell you. I thought when you found the note telling you that he left, you'd understand, but I can see you don't."

"What note? Oh, you mean the one Errol left saying he was going out for a while? It's okay. I understand. He doesn't like it here, so he gets a little crazy sitting around thinking about New York and wishing he was there. I've got to admit I'm not happy that he's wandered off again, especially after what happened to him yesterday, but I—"

Kitty was shaking her head from side to side. "No, no, no. That's not what he was telling you. He's gone, Miss Lily. He went back to New York."

"But that's impossible. He wouldn't do that. Not after . . ." But she knew better. Errol would do whatever he felt like at the time. He was like that. Mercurial and unpredictable. Still, he'd promised.

"I'm sorry," Kitty said, turning her back to Lily once again and starting the washer.

Lily walked away. She couldn't believe Errol would just take off without saying good-bye. Besides, if he'd known he was going to leave today, why hadn't he gone to Charleston with her and Jesse? Because he was a coward, that's why. Lily kicked the wall, wincing as pain shot from her toe to her ankle. Damn him!

She was halfway up the stairs when it occurred to her to wonder how he had traveled to Manhattan. And how had he even gotten away from the house? He could have called a taxi, of course, but that just didn't wash. Errol was a tightwad.

She heard Kitty coming from the laundry room and leaned over the banister. "Just one more question. How did Errol get to Charleston to catch his plane?"

Kitty didn't answer at once, and Lily sighed impatiently. Damn it, what was the girl so afraid of? Did she think Lily was going to blame her because her jerk friend had run out on her? "Look, it's no big deal. I'm not mad at anybody. I'm just trying to make sense out of one more crazy thing here in the land of Oz."

Kitty smiled a little at that. "I used to think this place was like that, too. Especially after my mom took off. Everything was so crazy for a while. The police coming around asking all kinds of questions, then all our neighbors looking at us—my dad and us kids—with these real hound-dog expressions like we was the most pitiful folks around." She shrugged. "Anyway, it got better. It always does."

Lily had forgotten that Kitty had lost her mother at almost the exact same time that her dad was killed and Sara was taken away. Kitty had been a couple of years older than her. Maybe sometime they'd sit down and talk about those days. Just not today. She smiled at the girl below her in the foyer. "You're right. Time has a way of healing the hurt."

She started up the steps again and was almost to the top when Kitty called up, "I took him to the train station. He . . . he said it was cheaper than flying. Said he was going to cash in the return airline ticket and save the difference."

Lily remembered the way he'd signed the note he'd left. Errol—as in Flynn—Mills. *My foot!* Errol—as in first-class jerk. Asshole. Scum-bucket—Mills.

"Well, I hope you're miserable, buddy," Lily muttered.

Chapter Twenty-three

Lily didn't like the big house at night when she was all alone. It was creepy. Boards creaked and wind whistled down the chimney flue. The big clock in the foyer ticked loud enough to be heard all the way back in the kitchen, and even the furnace kicking on and off startled her. "Damn you, Errol, for running out on me!" she stormed for the umpteenth time.

She stood at the center island in her mother's big kitchen, lathing mayonnaise on bread with a heavy hand, then licking the knife and dropping it into the sink. Slapping the slice of bread on top of her ham and cheese sandwich, her thoughts returned to her runaway friend. "All I've gotta say is, he'd better have enough sense to be moved out of my apartment when I get back."

But as angry as she was with him, she already missed him, too. "Like a nail in my foot," she amended with a rueful smile. Errol was many things—and most of them bad—but through everything, he'd been her friend and confidant. She supposed that was what made his defection so painful to accept.

Her long jet hair hung loose around her face and shoulders as she poured a glass of milk and grabbed a bag of chips from the pantry. She was reaching for a plate when she glimpsed a greasy dollop of mayo clinging to the end of one long strand. She set the plate on the center counter and walked to the sink in front of the window to turn on the water. She had just finished rinsing away the sandwich spread when she saw the face staring back at her from outside the window.

She screamed, loudly and with ear-ringing pitch. It wasn't until she'd grabbed the most lethal butcher knife she could find and run to the back door to check the lock that she realized who it was staring back at her.

Sash!

Damn him!

"You scared ten years off my life!" she railed almost before she'd opened the back door.

"Jesus Christ, princess, you did a good job of your own in that department. Where in the hell did you learn to scream like that?"

Lily stepped aside as he came in. She still held the knife in one hand, and Sash pointed at it as he walked past her. "Put that thing away, okay?"

"What's the matter? Afraid I might take after my mother?" She was immediately sorry for the remark that was both careless and ugly. She apologized quickly. "Sorry. That was stupid."

"You said it."

Returning the knife to its place in the cutlery rack, she turned and leaned against the stove. "I just made myself a sandwich. Want one?"

Sash shrugged. "Sure. Need some help?"

Lily shook her head, then went to work gathering the makings from the fridge again and creating a second lavish concoction. "Mayo or mustard?" she asked after a few minutes.

"Either."

"Got soda—Pepsi, diet, I think—beer, and milk."

"I'll have milk, too, but I'll get it myself."

Lily raised an eyebrow as he went to the cabinet for a glass, then helped himself to the carton of milk in the refrigerator. "You still know your way around in here. Guess it's like riding a bike. Some things a person just doesn't forget."

He stood at the refrigerator, holding the door open. "And other things a person doesn't get over."

"What do you mean?" Lily asked.

"It still bothers you that I was here so much, doesn't it?"

"Of course not! That's silly."

Sash laughed. "No it's not. You were so jealous of me, you couldn't stand it. If I closed my eyes right now, I could still see you hiding behind that door over there, glaring at me."

"I'm surprised you noticed me at all," Lily said as she fished a handful of potato chips from the bag and scattered them around his plate. "You never seemed to see anyone but my mother."

"See, that's just what I mean."

Lily wrinkled her nose at him, then picked up the plates, indicating the glasses of milk with her chin. "Grab the drinks and napkins and follow me."

She set the plates on the coffee table in the study, then sat on the floor, crossing her legs and motioning for him to sit across from her.

A fire blazed in the hearth.

"Cozy," he said, his dark blue gaze on her face. "Nice."

"Why did you come over?" she asked at last.

"I wanted to be with you."

Lily smiled at the answer. She knew it wasn't the entire truth, but for the moment, warmed as she was by his reply, she didn't want to hear the rest of his explanation. He would tell her when he was ready. In the meantime, she was going to enjoy the way he made her feel when he looked at her. Like there'd never been anyone else. Especially not Sara.

They ate in silence that was both comfortable and relaxed. As the fire heated the room, just being together warmed them with a glow that emanated from within.

When they finished eating, Sash straightened his long legs and folded his arms behind his head as he closed his eyes and leaned against the sofa.

Lily stacked their plates to the side, propping her elbows on the table, and cupping her face with her hands as she studied him in repose.

He was every bit as gorgeous as the memory she'd retained from the day before, but he didn't seem as dangerous tonight. Maybe it was the way his sharply chiseled features softened while he rested, or just that like any wild animal, at times even he enjoyed unbending from the hunt. The analogy surprised her, and she wondered if she had stumbled across his true nature. Was he that? A hunter?

He opened his eyes, smiling when he found her gaze on him. He looked incredibly young in that instant. His cheeks were flushed from the warmth of the fire and his lids heavy over those sapphire eyes, and she saw him as the handsome child who had curled up on the floor to watch TV with her family on those rare occasions when Eudora consented to him spending the evening. He no longer resembled the predator, and she wondered who he really was, what he really wanted from her.

"Penny for your thoughts," he said.

"I would have offered more for yours," she countered.

"No. I couldn't have taken it. Too easy. Like taking candy from a baby. Your mother always said it was impossible for me to hide my feelings. I don't think I've gotten better with time. That's why I never gamble."

"Don't you?"

"Not for money."

"Then for what?" she asked.

"I gamble on my intuition; feelings I get in my gut. Sometimes I see something worth putting myself on the line for and I go for it."

His eyes were locked on her lips as he spoke and though she was piteously without experience except for her relationship with Errol, she knew he'd just announced the reason for his visit. Her breath quickened with the understanding that he'd come to finish what had been begun the day before, and a new hunger that had nothing to do with food began to gnaw at her.

"Come here," he said in a hoarse whisper.

Lily didn't stand, but crawled around the table to the other side until she was in front of him still on her hands and knees.

Slowly, like a sleek, black panther unfurling from sleep, he released his lean, powerful arms from beneath his head. One of them went around her back and pulled her against him. The other hand captured her face beneath her chin, drawing her mouth to his.

Lily had never been kissed the way Sash was kissing her now. His lips were as hot as firebrands, and his tongue as demanding and cruel as a lashing whip.

Moving his hands, he took the backs of her thighs, pulling them toward him so that she straddled his hips, and the incredibly sensitive place between her legs rested against his swelling, throbbing manhood.

She inhaled sharply as she ground her hips and wrapped her arms around his neck.

The kiss deepened, and Sash's breathing grew ragged and hard as his hands caressed first her back, then came between them to cup her breasts. "I need you, Lil."

"I know," she breathed against his neck. "Me, too."

Without disturbing their embrace, he leaned her back and drew his legs up beneath them so that he held her in a half crouch as he moved plates and glasses to the floor. Then he laid her on the table. His eyes only half opened, he ran his tongue over his lips which were parched with fire and slowly began unbuttoning her blouse.

The telephone rang, startling them both.

Lily tried to sit up, but Sash pushed her down again. "Let it go," he whispered.

And God, she wanted to. "I can't. It might be Jesse or Errol."

At the mention of the man who had accompanied her from New York, Sash sat back on his haunches, giving her room to stand. He didn't offer to help her. It was one thing to move aside for her boyfriend. He wasn't going to hand her to him.

He watched her as she drew her shirt closed over her breasts and picked up the phone, careful to keep her back to him as she spoke. She ran her hands through her hair and walked a few feet away into the hallway.

She was back a moment later, but she stopped just inside the door, leaning against the jamb as she explained the call. "That was Marla Hutton. She wants me to come to a dinner party tomorrow night. Would you . . . would you go with me?"

Sash let his eyes roam slowly from her head to her toes. God, she was exquisite. But she was Sara's daughter. He'd allowed himself to forget that in his lust for her.

He hadn't come to her house tonight with the intention of making love to her. That was just something that happened every time he got within a few feet of her. Ever since they'd danced. She'd started a fire inside him that he knew only she had the power to put out.

But not now. Not until he'd repaid his debt to her mother.

He stood up, crossed the room to stand in front of her, his eyes drinking in her beauty in spite of the warnings his mind was shouting. Legs braced, he hooked her waist with his arm and drew her toward him for one last kiss.

A moment later, he stepped away.

Lily put a hand to her swollen, bruised lips, her eyes questioning. She'd felt good-bye in that kiss, and experienced disappointment all the way to her toes. "What's wrong?"

"I've got to get going, princess. I just came by to make sure you were okay now that your men are gone."

Lily felt her anger begin a low, roiling boil. "That may be the excuse you gave yourself, but that's not why you came," she said.

"I'll be damned," he said with a crooked grin that didn't quite make one side of his face. "You're as clever as Sara."

"But I'm not Sara! Why do you keep throwing her up at me? Do you just want to use my body while you pretend I'm her? Okay!" she cried, hurriedly unbuttoning her blouse with trembling fingers. "Close your eyes and make love to me and we'll both play make-believe!"

He covered her hands with his, stilling them. "Don't."

"Why not? You know I want you, just as I know it's Sara you want. So okay, we'll compromise."

"You're wrong," he said softly, tenderly, wiping a tear away as it escaped the corner of her eye. "I don't want Sara, but I won't make love to you as long as she stands between us."

His lips covered hers, yet so briefly, so lightly, she cried out with disappointment. "Please, Sash!"

"I can't. Sorry. Like I said, I only came by to see if you were okay now that your uncle and friend are gone." He laid a hand against her cheek. "Lock the door after me."

"Go to hell," she told him in a strangled whisper.

He hesitated, then shook his head and walked away.

She didn't move as he left the room. Not when she heard the front door close after him or even after she heard his motorcycle roar to life, then fade away in the distance.

"What about the party?" she asked as she continued to lean against the doorjamb. Tears streaked her cheeks but they were going to be the last. She was getting damned tired of crying.

Chapter Twenty-four

Lily hadn't brought anything fancy with her from New York. For sure, nothing suitable for a formal dinner party. In fact, she hadn't brought much except casual wear—jeans, T-shirts, sweats, and the like. She'd packed her dance and exercise togs, of course. And two dresses. One, she'd worn to the mortuary on Monday; the other to the funeral on Tuesday. She'd laid both on the bed as she tried to decide between them for the dinner engagement at Marla and Sanders'. Both black. Both simple. So, which one?

She eventually selected the first because she thought the satin piping, buttons, collar, and cuffs made it a little more dressy than the one she'd worn to the cemetery. She'd wear Sara's pearls and maybe go all out with sheer black stockings. Not that it mattered much. It was just a dinner party with people she'd probably never see again once she returned to New York.

Still, she took great pains with her makeup. She was good at applying it though she rarely wore more than a dab of lipstick and a touch of mascara. But she'd learned how to apply it artfully and with a heavy hand for her stage appearances. Her thick, glossy hair was easily arranged in a sophisticated-looking French twist with a few long, cascading tendrils.

t six-thirty, she stepped away from the mirror in
e bathroom to examine the overall achievement. "Not
ad," she admitted with a quick little spin that caused
he softly pleated skirt to flare and swirl, revealing her
long, shapely legs.

Fifteen minutes later, she was parking the rented
Ford Sable in the wide circular drive in front of Sander
and Marla's house. Taking the keys from the ignition,
she leaned forward to stare up at the colossal structure
through the windshield.

Though in actuality not much larger than her parents' house and very nearly the same size as the Rivers',
this one had always seemed bigger than life to her. The
twenty-eight room structure was three stories high and
more than twice as long with twin rock turrets on either
end, creating an image of grandeur that was both awesome and intimidating. Lily remembered her uncle
boasting that he'd built his wife a castle, and he
hadn't exaggerated.

She smiled in the darkness of the car interior as she
recalled her father's quip to her mother on the drive
home following the housewarming soon after its building was completed. *All Sand needs now is a moat and a
drawbridge. Then he and the queen bitch could rule in real
style. Throw a couple gators in the mix and their subjects
would be properly dragooned.*

Lily remembered, too, that her mother had chastised
him for making such a tacky joke in front of Lily, but
she hadn't forgotten that Sara had giggled while she
fussed.

Lily had laughed with them, but she'd dreamed of
dungeons and thrashing reptiles that night and had
hated the house ever since.

Though the hands on Lily's watch were pointed exactly to seven o'clock, it appeared everyone was already gathered in the oversized living room by the time she was shown in by a very British butler.

Every face turned her way as she stopped in the doorway, and she fought the urge to back out again.

"Oh, Lily darling," Marla called from the far side of the room, already starting her motorized chair in motion and wheeling toward her. "I was just telling my son-in-law, Davis, how thrilled we are that we're able to bring everyone together before you return to New York."

"Thank you," Lily said as she bent to kiss her aunt's cheek. "It was very kind of you to invite me, though I hope you didn't go to all this trouble just for my sake."

"Of course, she did," Sander said, too loudly, too energetically, as he approached from another direction. "And she loved having an excuse to entertain. We've had far too few reasons for celebration in the past several years, and we rarely party in the winter, don't you know?"

Lily smiled and nodded. "As my mother's people say, winter is a time for death and rest; a time of quiet."

No one seemed to know what to say to that and Lily noticed the quick exchanges. *Is she reminding us that Sara was just buried four days before?* they seemed to be asking themselves.

Marla spoke up. "How right they are. And speaking of your Native-American heritage, where is your delightful uncle, Dr. Two Moons? And that handsome young man of yours, too? I hoped you understood my invitation included all of you."

Lily wondered how long it would take the party to return to normal pockets of conversation, but she kept her smile in place as she explained that both men had left and the reasons for their abrupt departures.

"So you're all alone?" Belinda, her cousin, asked as she joined her parents. "Poor baby. Maybe you'd like

Daddy to move back over to your house so you're not so isolated and lonely."

"That's very sweet of you, Bea, dear," Sander said, slipping his arm around both his daughter's waist and Lily's. "She has a housekeeper, don't forget. Besides, we all tend to forget that she's lived in the Big Apple for years unlike you and your sister and the other young ladies from around here, who I'm afraid are disgracefully cossetted."

Lily was grateful when a handsome man she didn't remember joined their circle, kissing her on her cheek and giving her hand a tight squeeze. "Ten dollars says you don't know who in the hell you've just been kissed by."

And then she had it. Well, almost. "I know you're one of the Price twins. I just don't know whether it's Oliver or Dixon."

Everyone froze. Not a smile slipped, nor a single eye blinked until a deep, familiar voice spoke from behind her in the doorway. "Oliver's dead, princess. Died in a boating accident three or four years after you left."

Torn between apologizing to Dixon and greeting Sash, Lily looked back and forth between the two men. Everyone else, she noticed, was staring at the newcomer with stunned expressions, and she turned her attention there as well.

Sash was dressed as formally as the other men in the room, though his powerful, athletic body certainly filled out the white dinner jacket and black slacks with much more exciting results. Lily let a smile of welcome spread slowly as she slipped an arm through his.

"What are you doing here, Sash?" someone, a man with a soft, menacing voice asked.

Lily turned her head, ready to attack in Sash's defense. His father stood at her side, his face almost as pale as his white jacket.

"I invited him, Mr. Rivers," Lily said before Sash could answer.

"But—"

"But nothing, Jason," Marla said, expertly wielding her chair so that she was suddenly positioned between father and son. She looked up at the younger Rivers. "I'm so glad to see you, Sash. It's been too, too many years."

A brilliant smile flashed across Sash's face, and Lily thought even his eyes brightened from midnight blue to sapphire. "Thank you, Mrs. Hutton. It has been too long, you're right. If Lily hadn't asked me to come, I might never have ended my self-imposed exile." His grin turned enigmatic.

"Then we all owe her a debt of gratitude," Marla said uncertainly.

"Hey, bro," the man whom Sash had identified as Dixon Price said. "It's good to have you back." He clapped Sash on the shoulder and steered him into the room.

Her arm still linked through Sash's, Lily followed. She was confused and made a mental note to get Mr. Sasha Rivers in a corner later and make him explain some things to her.

Like where he'd been all this time.

And why he'd been gone.

She jumped as cold fingers clamped over hers. "Oh, Eudora, you startled me. You're hands are like ice! Are they normally so cold?"

"You know what they say, dear, about warm hearts and cold hands."

Lily could have argued that point. Her mother was the most warmhearted person she'd ever known, and the warmth went all the way to her fingertips. Instead she chuckled. "In the Village where I live, the cliché is 'Show me a guy with cold hands, I'll show you an out-of-work artist. Show me a guy with warm hands, I'll show you an artist whose father owns the building.' "

Imogene joined them. "Careful, everyone's going to be jealous if the two of you keep laughing and having so much fun."

"Lily was entertaining me with colorful saws from her world in the theater," Eudora explained. She turned back to Lily. "How is it that you happened to invite my stepson to join you tonight?"

"Mother!" Imogene interrupted. "I hardly think it's any of our business how or when or why Sash and Lily agreed to attend Aunt Marla's party together."

Lily was grateful to Sash's half-sister and just as amazed that she'd forgotten that Marla was Genie's aunt as well. She told her as much. "It had completely escaped me that your mother and Marla are sisters."

"That's only because dear Marla has aged so since the tragic operation that left her confined to a chair," Eudora said, looking at her sister across the room beside Sash and Sander and the youngest Hutton girl, Caroline.

"You're referring to the surgery my father performed to remove a malignant tumor that saved her life?" Lily asked, wondering how it was that Eudora always managed to find just exactly the right words to make her temper flare.

"Oh, now, Lily, honey, ya'll know I didn't mean anything by that. Every single one of us—Marla, Sander, their two girls, and myself—were grateful to your father for saving her life. But, *of course*, that doesn't mean we aren't mindful of the price she had to pay."

No matter how much honey the woman spooned onto her words, Lily could still smell the vinegar. It was a saying from her childhood, and Lily lowered her face to hide the smile that came with the memory of one of her father's favorite expressions. It seemed to her now, he'd been speaking of Eudora Rivers more often than not when he used it.

"I'm sorry," she said quickly when she noticed the frowns spoiling the perfection of both women's brows. "I wasn't smiling about what you were saying, Eudora. I was thinking about something else."

"Why don't we go get a drink from the bar," Genie suggested. Then to her mother. "Could I get you something?"

"No, you girls go on. I'll just stand back here and let you reacquaint yourselves. It'll do me good to see the two of you together enjoying one another."

As soon as they were out of earshot from Eudora, Genie stopped. "You go ahead to the bar. I need to say hello to my brother. Mother would rather cut out her tongue than speak to Sash, and Daddy dances to her tune."

"I'll go with you," Lily suggested.

"I'd really like a drink if you wouldn't mind getting it for me. Besides, that way I can talk to him alone for a few minutes." Imogene's eyes were almost pleading, and then she did an about-face by laughing. "And anyway, he's sure to die of boredom if I don't rescue him from Dix."

"What are you drinking?" Lily asked.

"Scotch and water."

"I'm disappointed," Lily said. "I thought for sure it'd be mint julep."

Imogene responded with laughter that was genuine and appreciative. "You'd be surprised, sugar, just how far we southern belles have come. We not only drink real alcohol, we no longer faint dead away at curse words, or deny that we love sex. Why, we've had ourselves a bona fide revolution down here in the south, and we've emerged positively victorious. It's downright glorious!"

Without another word, Imogene spun around and began to wend her way through the crowd. Lily stared after her. No doubt about it, Genie had more than lived up to her adolescent promise of beauty, and Lily still experienced a twinge of envy at her flawless porcelain skin, dollar-size cornflower-blue eyes, deep dimples, and glorious smile that revealed toothpaste commercial teeth. Her pale corn-silk hair was curled around her face in the kind of artful disarray that Lily never understood how anyone managed. Genie's designer blue-and-white striped taffeta dress emphasized her full breasts and tiny waist, and the full skirt whispered with her walk as if calling attention to her long legs.

On a sigh, Lily turned away.

"It's all right," Caroline said as soon as Lily stepped up to the bar beside her. "We all hate her."

Lily's face flamed, and her cousin laughed.

"I'm joking, silly. We love her. She makes our otherwise mundane little lives brighter with her pizazz and incredible beauty. And even if we really did hate her just a little, we'd still keep her around simply because life is so exciting when Genie's in it."

"She definitely fills up a room," Lily agreed, looking to where the subject of their conversation was talking to Sash.

"And he's not exactly hard on the eyes, is he?" Caroline said.

Lily escaped that one by answering the bartender's request for her order.

Caroline stood with her back to the bar, resting both elbows on the counter as she watched the Rivers siblings. "She's quite notorious for her affairs." At Lily's amazed expression, she nodded. "Yes, really. Eudora Rivers's daughter cheats on her husband. When the gossip first started, I thought it was just petty jealousy provoking mean rumors, you know? But it's true."

"Doesn't Dixon—"

"Care?" Caroline shrugged. "Guess not. But then, the rumor about him is that he's got some sort of medical problem, if you get my gist."

Lily thought she did, but Caroline apparently wanted to be sure and explained it succinctly.

"Can't get it up. But then Oliver was gay, so maybe there's some connection."

"How do you know that?" Lily asked.

"About Oliver? 'Cause he said so. Came straight out and announced it at his and Dixon's eighteenth birthday party. His mom and dad almost died right there on the spot. And poor Dix. He was devastated. We were at the country club and everyone had been making toasts to the guys. The next thing we know, Oliver is telling the world that he's a fag, and then Dixon hauls off and punches him out. Two days later, poor Oli was dead. Killed in a freaky boat accident. Dix wasn't the same after that, of course. Kind of cold and distant and I guess it went all the way to the bedroom."

"I haven't seen Dixon's parents since I got here. How have they been since then?"

"Wow, when you go away, you go away, don't you? They were killed in an automobile crash just a few weeks after Oliver's death."

Lily was stunned. So much tragedy in one family! She accepted the drinks from the bartender and smiled in Caroline's direction. "Thanks for bringing me up to date. I'm glad I didn't ask Dix about his parents, too."

"Oh, he's pretty cool about it now. After all, that was a long time ago. Like Mom's illness. It was bad at the time, but life goes on."

"You look like you've seen a ghost," Sash said a moment later when Lily joined him and his half-sister.

Lily handed Genie her drink as she explained her pallor. "No, I'm fine. Caroline was just telling me about

Dixon's family. It's so sad and in a way, I was reminded about what happened to my parents. I know it's not the same, but I feel a kinship with him." She gave herself a shake and found a smile. "But that's enough talk about tragedy and death for tonight. I promise not to cast a pall on the entire evening. Besides, I want to hear all about you," she told Sash. "Where have you been all these years?"

"Dinner is served!"

Sash laughed at the timely interruption. "Saved by the bell," he said, offering an arm to each woman. "Trust me, princess, it's a long, boring story."

Lily didn't argue, but she doubted he was telling the truth. Somehow she didn't think anything Sasha Rivers ever did was boring.

Chapter Twenty-five

Dinner was a veritable feast of southern dishes from the split pea soup to the raspberry dumplings, which were served for dessert. Like the food, conversation was rich, southerly, and puffed up. Lily was surprised that she enjoyed both as much as she did. But by the time the dessert plates were cleared and coffee served, she was leaning back in her chair, relaxed and comfortable.

"This was so nice, Marla. Thank you for going to so much trouble on my behalf."

"Nonsense, sugar, it was my pleasure. I just wish the circumstance of your homecoming wasn't so tragic, and I hope ya'll come down our way again before too long."

Several faces around the long table were nodding their agreement, and Lily smiled her gratitude. "Thank you. You've all been very gracious." She paused on a long breath, then added, "Especially since you all believe that my mother killed my father. I know you loved him, and it must have been difficult for you to attend the service on her behalf."

"Are we to understand, Lily, honey, that you *don't* believe Sara killed poor Ali?" Eudora asked, her tone reflecting her astonishment.

Lily let her gaze rest on each face for a moment as

she composed her reply. Most of them—all of them, in fact—except Sash, Imogene, and Jenny Lynn were staring at her, mouths slightly agape, eyes disbelieving. Jenny Lynn seemed sad as if for once in her slow little world, she'd understood something someone more clever had missed. Sash appeared amused, damn him. And Imogene was worried. No question about it. But why?

Dismissing the question, Lily turned her focus back to the reply she'd formed. She'd been about to play it safe, explain that she had doubts though they were probably silly and unfounded. Instead, she heard herself say, "I *know* for a fact she didn't, Eudora."

"But what about Genie and that old Negro fellow? They witnessed it. Don't you trust what they saw with their own eyes?"

Lily smiled patiently at the mayor's obvious dismay. "Don't get excited, Eudora. I didn't say that. I believe they *think* they saw her kill him. I just know they're wrong."

Lily took a last sip of the delicately blended coffee, then wiped her lips with her napkin. The only sound in the room in that tense instant was the gentle clink of china against china when she returned cup to saucer. "I didn't mean to upset everyone," she said. "In fact, I don't understand why you all look like I've just delivered bad news."

"It's not that," Marla hurried to explain. "It's not that at all. Ours is a very normal reaction to shocking news, I declare. We, of course, believe what we heard at the time of the tragedy. Even if there were the slightest chance what you're saying is true, how, after all these years, can you hope to prove it?"

"I've already started. I've been to see Joe Joe. He's old and feeble, but his grandson has promised to keep talking to him. Maybe he'll jog a memory."

"But Genie was there, too," her father said. "She's always been quite firm about what she saw."

Lily cast a sidelong glance at Imogene. Her normal peaches and cream complexion had paled significantly, and her blue eyes were fixed on Sash and wide with fear.

"Just tell us one thing, Lily, dear," Eudora said. "Why? Is it merely your fierce loyalty to Sara that has fostered these totally unsubstantiated doubts?"

"Not at all. I have proof."

A collective gasp resounded around the table.

"What proof?" Sash asked quietly.

"Sara told me," Lily said, going for broke. "She didn't kill my father."

Chapter Twenty-six

Sash escorted Lily to her car twenty minutes later. "You didn't ride your bike here tonight, did you?" she asked, looking around.

"Absolutely. It's the only way I travel."

Lily tilted her head to the side, a disbelieving grin on her face. "There's no way you could have arrived looking like a *GQ* cover model after riding on that bike."

With a smile and what she thought might be a flush of pleasure, Sash pulled a comb from the inside pocket of his dinner jacket. "Took me ten minutes squinting into the little side-view mirror to get it just right. I packed cologne in the saddlebag. Biggest problem was the white jacket. Had to wear a jumbo trash bag over it to keep the dust off. I would have packed it along with the patent dress shoes, but I knew it would wrinkle too bad."

She was delighted by his teasing and leaned forward to kiss him affectionately on the cheek. "Thank you," she said.

"Hey, don't thank me. I knew you'd look like a million bucks. I didn't want to show up looking like something the cat drug in."

"And here I didn't even go buy a special dress. Now *I'm* the one who's embarrassed."

Sash brushed a wisp of hair from her face, holding it against her throat with his hand as he stared into her incredible sherry-colored eyes. "I don't believe that," he said softly. "You don't get embarrassed about unimportant things like clothes. You're deeper than that."

"Thank you," she said. She looked down at the keys in her hand. She should have pretended coyness, claiming that he'd embarrassed her with the compliment, but he hadn't really. He'd made her giddy with the thrill of his words, made her insides churn, and made her want to wrap her arms around his neck and not let go. She satisfied herself by covering the back of his hand with hers. "You're a very nice guy, Sasha Rivers. My mother had very good taste in friends."

He grinned. "So, I guess that means you're not mad at me about last night anymore."

"No, you've redeemed yourself by showing up tonight for me."

Sash took the keys from her hand and reached past her to unlock her car door. "Wear your seatbelt. It's the law." He grinned at the roll of her eyes. "Drive carefully. I'll ride past in a little while to make sure you got inside your house okay."

She could have told him that she left the theater district in the wee hours every night in New York, then went all the way to the Village without incident. Instead she said, "If you're worried, you could stay with me tonight."

"Jesus," Sash groaned. "How in the hell do I turn that down?"

Lily laughed, but she felt the rejection all the way in the pit of her stomach. "Forget it. It's still pretty early. You probably have plans."

"I do, but not like you're thinking. It's not another woman or—"

"Don't!" she said, putting her hands over her ears. "It's none of my business. I spoke without thinking." She slid quickly behind the wheel and reached for the door handle, but Sash was there before her, stopping her from closing it.

"I've got business that'll probably keep me pretty much tied up for the next day or so. Do me one favor till I can get back up to your place?"

"What?" she asked impatiently, hurt and disappointment still niggling at her.

"Don't go talking to Abe Joseph or anyone else about your father's . . ."

"Murder," she said harshly. "It's all right. You can say it. I know he didn't just topple over the railing by himself."

Sash ignored that. "Promise me, Lil."

"Why?"

"I haven't got time to explain right now. Just tell me you'll back off this amateur investigation of yours until I call you or show up at your door. I'll try to get there tomorrow night. Sunday at the latest. Okay?"

"But you won't tell me why."

"Damn it!"

"All right! I won't go around asking any more questions until I hear from you, but—"

Sash checked her next objection by bending down and capturing her face between his strong hands as he covered her mouth with his.

Then he was gone without another word.

Lily watched him stride along the well-lighted drive until he was swallowed in the shadows cast by the hedges and trees.

As she started the car and drove along the same path he'd just taken, she searched the darkness for him but he'd vanished. Maybe he'd gone back inside for something, or perhaps he'd parked his bike away from the long row of automobiles.

Lily pulled out onto Central Hill Road seconds later, her fingers touching her lips where she could still feel the pressure of his. She wondered momentarily why he'd exacted the promise from her not to ask any more questions about her dad's death. She brushed away her doubts and misgivings. It didn't matter why. All that was important was that Sash had asked. She trusted him. And that was enough.

"Isn't it bad enough that she's running around asking questions about what happened in that house fifteen years ago?" a voice hissed from the purple shadows along the side of the house where Sash had left his motorcycle. "Now you've started playing kissy-face and encouraging her to stay! How stupid can you be!"

Sash picked up his helmet and straddled the bike as he answered the charge. "You don't know what you're talking about. She's promised not to do any more investigating until I give the go ahead."

"Oh, great! You think just because you flash her one of your sexy grins, kiss her a few times, throw in some tongue, and make a couple promises, she isn't going to question where you're coming from later? You really think she's not going to figure out that maybe it's to your advantage to keep her in the dark?"

Sash peeled off her fingers that were suddenly gripping his upper arm. The stitched flesh beneath coat and bandage was still tender. "Go back inside to the party. We don't want anyone discovering us out here together."

"Which reminds me. Why the hell didn't you tell me you were coming here tonight? I almost lost it in there when you walked in."

Sash's teeth gleamed bright and white against the

black backdrop of night with his sudden smile. "Naw. Your reaction was perfect. You looked like you were going to pee your pants same as everyone else. Wish I'd had a camera."

Two hours later one of the guests at the Hutton's lavish dinner party answered the shrill peal of the telephone, listened, then smiled. "Fine. So, if everything is taken care of, I'm going to bed. By this time tomorrow night, you should be able to report that two more of our problems have been neatly disposed of.

"Oh, one more thing. If no one's discovered Mills's body by then, I think an anonymous telephone call to our boys in uniform might be in order. It's satisfying to eliminate problems after they occur *if* we catch them in time and nip them in the bud. But I much prefer heading them off before they become troublesome. How can we stop our Lily from bringing disaster on her own head if she doesn't even know about the warning we sent? Why, the poor girl thinks that jackass boyfriend of hers has simply gone home to New York! She needs to know the truth."

Chapter Twenty-seven

For the first time in nearly 200 years, hysteria threatened the impassivity of those members of the secret association that governed Rosehill, South Carolina.

A chain of telephone calls that began just after sunup started the upset, and it was almost out of control by the time the last communication was made just ten minutes later.

Six calls were placed. In every one the communiqué from the calling party was almost exactly the same:

"There is no body." Each word was enunciated with excruciating care. "We have scoured the floor beneath the cliffs for a mile in each direction, the foliage along both the east and west shoulders of East Hill Road, as well as the wooded area to the north of the Rivers estate. The conclusion is this: Either Errol Mills got up and walked away under his own volition or someone else found him and carried him out.

"It doesn't matter which. *We are in jeopardy.*"

For the first time in thirty-six hours since his rescue from a narrow shelf of rock, a sickening hundred and fifty feet above the chasm separating East and Central Hills, Errol regained consciousness.

It was seven thirty-eight, Saturday morning. The first thing he saw was Lily's face. Beautiful, compassionate Lily.

Errol's eyesight was blurred. She kept swimming in and out of focus. And his face . . . Jesus Christ . . . it hurt like a son of a bitch.

"Lil?"

"Hey, handsome."

Errol had just about slipped back into that peaceful void of unconsciousness when the semi-familiar voice penetrated the fog enveloping his brain. Who'd spoken? Not Lily. A woman but with a deeper voice . . . husky like . . . like that broad . . .

It was right there on the selvage of his mind. *Blonde. Beautiful. Sexy.*

Shit, it wouldn't come.

Then, there she was. Imogene Rivers. Leaning over him. Smiling. Laughing.

Hey, what the fuck's so funny?

"You, silly!" she said.

Had he spoken aloud?

She kissed him.

"Ow! Watch it, that hurt!" What was the matter with his tongue? It sounded like someone had cut it out, ground it up into hamburger, then reattached it.

"Good! You want to hurt. If you stop hurting, ya'll are dead, sweetie pie, and *you* I definitely want to keep alive."

"What happened?" he asked, this time noticing that his speech was clearer though weaker.

"Someone tried to kill you," she said, her voice too chipper for his liking.

His eyes moved from her face, trying to find Lily again. Instead they stopped on a pair of the plumpest and prettiest boobies he'd ever seen. Maybe he'd died and gone to sweet hell. Maybe he was going to hurt for eternity and be tempted by luscious hooters like these that he couldn't quite muster the energy to reach for.

Genie laughed again as she followed his gaze and his thoughts. "Believe me, honey, it'd be my pleasure, but I think you'd better concentrate on getting your strength back first." Then she surprised him by cupping both breasts in the palms of her hands and lifting them all the way out of the bodice of her silk wrapper. "Say good night, boys. Tell the nice man that you'll be waiting for him to take you out to play soon as he's feeling up to it."

In spite of the pain, which he now felt all the way to the bottom of his feet, Errol chuckled when her gaze dropped meaningfully to his groin. He licked his parched lips as he closed his eyes.

He let his grin slip as he felt a blanket being drawn up under his chin. He was exhausted, and he hurt! Everywhere. The pain was taking over and he heard a groan slip from between his clenched teeth.

A hand that was soft and gentle brushed his hair from his brow. "Try to sleep. The doctor will be by later to give you another shot."

"Lily?" Errol muttered.

"No, honey, it's me, Genie, remember?"

"But . . . I . . . I saw her," Errol argued. He tilted his face to the side and cracked his eyelids. *There!*

The blond babe was telling him something. Explaining about Lily. Something about her not being real. But that was crazy. He could see her clear as day smiling at him from that canvas.

Eudora ignored the peal of the telephone. It was only minutes before eight A.M., but she'd been up since dawn. She'd stood on the widow's watch as the sun rose into the sky. As always, she'd been enthralled by the majestic event.

Rays of purple, mauve, and cotton-candy pink bled through the heavens in dazzling rays that kissed the earth good morning. There was nothing in the world as beautiful or awesome as the dawning of another day over her city.

Except that today fear accompanied the awe. Icy tendrils of terror coursed her arms to her fingertips.

They were losing control. Might well have already let it slip away. And she'd told them! She'd warned them that they were going too far. Not just too far! In the wrong direction. The threat they'd feared wasn't from Lily Dawn Hutton. Not really. Even if what she claimed was true—that Sara had called her—there was no proof of anything. Not one single shred.

And Eudora had told them to let the girl look. Let her talk and question to her heart's content. When all was said and done, she'd give up.

Damn them! Damn them all!

Why hadn't they listened when she told them that her stepson was the devil they'd better be watching? He was the one who posed a threat. And wasn't it true? Hadn't he even begun to turn her own daughter against her?

Oh, they didn't know, Sash and Genie, that Eudora was aware of the time they spent together.

Her arms hugging her shoulders as the cool, late winter breeze picked up, Eudora laughed. Why, if he hadn't been Imogene's half-brother, Eudora would have sworn her hot-to-trot daughter was fucking him just like she was every other man in Rosehill.

The phone rang insistently again and again. Eudora cursed it as she picked it up. "What!" she demanded.

"Your *daughter's* what!" Dixon said. "The question is *where?*"

Contrary to her depressed mood, Eudora laughed. "What a man you are, Dix. How many men in all of Rosehill do you know who can't keep their wives in their beds? And none of them as handsome and charismatic as you. What do you think the problem is, Dixon? Could it be you're as limp-wristed as your brother was?"

"You're a vile bitch, Eudora!" Dixon almost screamed.

From her end of the telephone line, Eudora could hear his rapid, ragged breathing as he struggled for composure. She smiled with the first real pleasure the morning had brought.

Having regained a modicum of composure, her son-in-law spoke again. "Just find her, Eudora. We can't afford any complications this morning." There was a heavy pause, then he said, "Not with everything about to come down around our ears."

Eudora sighed. "We both know where your wife most likely can be found. Why don't you drive over to the Alley and see if you spot her car outside the Ruby Palace?"

"I have to go to Charleston. I have depositions to take. I'll be back this evening. Find her, Eudora. We don't need the distraction."

The receiver on the other end clanked loudly in her ear, followed by the rude droning buzz across the lines.

"Find her yourself," Eudora said. She had more important things to attend to. Like tuning her fiddle. She looked around her at the spectacular horizon. Yes, indeed, she had the best seat in the house to watch from while Rome burned.

Chapter Twenty-eight

The next morning, Lily was awake and downstairs by seven o'clock. A night person by nature and her profession, she rarely crawled from bed before ten in order to make her first dance class at eleven. Here, in Rosehill, it was another girl who climbed from beneath the covers every morning in the early hours because sleep was fitful and dreams pervasive; who preferred days to the lonely nights.

As always when she sought tranquility, Lily danced. But this morning serenity was elusive, and more than ninety minutes elapsed before she stopped. Then she grabbed a towel from the exercise bar and sank to the floor. It had been a good workout. She'd pushed herself hard. Her breath came in ragged gasps, and her heart was beating a real drum roll inside her chest. Her face glistened with perspiration and fine wisps of baby hair clung to her damp brow and nape.

But the taxing routine had done the trick. She felt great!

Relaxed. Peaceful. Hungry!

She bounded to her feet, laughing as she rushed to the kitchen. She *never* ate breakfast! Nothing more substantial than a piece of melba toast munched on the way to the subway. But this morning she intended to feast. She was already licking her chops when she rounded the corner and came face to face with her housekeeper. Both women braked sharply.

"I'm sorry! My fault!" Lily said on a bark of startled laughter. "I keep forgetting that you're here every day. I don't know why. Uncle Jesse had a full-time housekeeper, too. But here, I simply cannot seem to remember that I'm not alone."

"I know how you feel. I keep expecting you to be Mr. Hutton. I'm always shocked when it's you who comes through a door instead of him." She made a little circle and headed back into the kitchen, adding as she went, "Of course, this morning I heard your music. As a matter of fact, I was coming to ask if you were ready for your coffee."

Lily hopped up on a stool at the breakfast bar. "Sure, but not just coffee. Believe it or not I'm starved this morning! I was going to cook some eggs, bacon, potatoes, the whole nine yards. Since you're here and I don't want to encroach on your territory, do you mind if I sit here and talk to you while you fix it?"

Kitty took Lily's order as she placed a mug in front of her employer. "Coffee's ready. You get started on that while I get everything else going."

Lily laced her fingers around the hot ceramic mug and inhaled deeply of the rich aroma steaming from the cup. "Do you like working for Uncle Sander?" she asked, more for the sake of conversation than out of interest.

"Sure. He's pretty rigid—likes everything just so and right on schedule—but believe it or not, that makes my job easier."

"How do you mean?" Lily asked as she sipped her java.

"Well, for example, he's up and showered and out of

the house every morning by seven-thirty. He doesn't come home until almost six. He likes dinner at six-thirty and always has a snack in the study at nine. He's in bed by ten.

"I know just when I should be cleaning, when it's okay to make noise, when I should be doing quiet work. I know just when to start cooking and exactly what time I'll be home at night.

"Weekends are just about as inflexible. He has dinner in town with business associates every Friday night unless there is some kind of social affair like the one he and his wife hosted last night. He plays golf on Saturdays, spring, summer, and autumn. Winter, he goes to the gym to play racquetball. He putters in the atrium Saturday afternoons and usually meets friends at the country club that night. On Sunday he leaves for church at eight, spends the day at the Central Hill house with his wife, daughters, and their families. That's one of my scheduled days off, but I'd bet my last dollar he goes to bed at exactly the same time he does Monday through Thursday." She looked over her shoulder and added, " 'Course, I'm off on Thursdays, too, so who knows? Maybe he's a real maniac that night, staying up until eleven or twelve." She grinned.

"And here I come messing up everything," Lily said.

Kitty shrugged as she stood over the crackling bacon and broke eggs in another skillet. "It's different. I'll hand you that."

The telephone rang, and Lily reached for it. "Hello."

"Hey, kiddo," Jesse said.

"Uncle Jesse! How's Rebecca?"

"Not quite as round as she was two hours ago. She delivered the baby at six fourteen this morning; a boy as we already knew from the ultrasound. Six pounds one ounce. Eighteen and a half inches long."

"Oh, that's so neat." She put her hand over the receiver for a second to tell Kitty the good news. "I'm a cousin again! I feel more like I should be the kid's aunt—hey, wait." She spoke into the phone again. "What's his name?"

"Daniel Hutton Two Moons. Rebecca thought of Hutton. Said it was the name of an honorable man." He paused for a second, then said, "You're crying, aren't you? I told Rebecca you'd start bawling!"

Lily laughed through her tears. "No, I'm not"—she lied on a sniffle—"but I'm happy for you and very moved by the tribute."

"You're welcome," Jesse said. Then, "How are you doing?"

"I'm fine. Really. Marla and Sander threw a party for me last night. I had a good time. Surprised even myself."

"Errol go with you?"

Lily bit her bottom lip, then avoided a second fib with some pretty fancy sidestepping. "Actually, you'll be surprised to hear that my date was someone else. Positively blew everyone away!"

"I'll only be amazed if you tell me it wasn't Sasha Rivers."

"How did you know?" Lily cried.

"I didn't, but if you didn't go with Errol, who else other than Sash? The two of you could hardly take your eyes off each other the first time you met again last week. Then you showed up on the back of his bike the following night. It doesn't take a rocket scientist to figure that one out. Just tell me how your actor feels about this?"

Lily was distracted by the heavenly aroma of breakfast as Kitty set the plate in front of her and had to ask Jesse to repeat his question. "I'm sorry. What did you say, Uncle Jesse?"

"I was—never mind. I've got to go. They're moving

mother and son from the birthing room to their private quarters. Just tell me you're safe and well and not getting into trouble."

"All of the above. Kiss, kiss, and one for mommy and baby, too." Lily hung up the phone on a long sigh. She was thrilled for her uncle. If anyone deserved happiness it was Jesse Two Moons. She thought of Errol as she cut her eggs and spread marmalade on her toast.

She hated lying to her uncle about him, even if it had been one of omission rather than commission. But she wasn't going to worry the proud new papa. Not now.

"What's the matter?" Kitty asked.

"Um, nothing," Lily said, absently munching a piece of toast. "Just thinking about Errol. Wondering why he didn't even call to tell me he got home okay and why he hasn't answered the phone in the apartment. I called him last night and again this morning. No answer either time. He should have been home yesterday morning. No telling where's he's gone or what he's up to. I guess I'll hear from him after he's made the rounds with all his friends." She raised her gaze to the other woman. "He's like that—inconsiderate, selfish—but I still thought he'd spare me one little minute to at least let me know he got there okay."

"Why do you care if he's such a jerk?" Kitty asked.

"I don't know. He *is* a jerk. First class, but he's also ... how to explain it?" She thought a minute, then said,"He's like a naughty puppy that runs around tearing up. Then when you pick him up to scold him, he covers your face in wet kisses and about twists his back end off with his wagging tail. How do you stay mad at that?"

"So you have this love/hate thing going with Mr. Mills?"

"No. Not really. At first, a long time ago, we did.

But now we're pretty much just buddies, you know? And I miss him and wish I could yell at him and have him pull one of his crazy tricks to make me laugh and forget why I was ever mad."

Her breakfast hardly begun, Lily pushed the plate away.

"Come on," Kitty coaxed, "finish your breakfast."

But with refound worry for Errol, Lily's appetite had disappeared as suddenly as he had.

Abraham Joseph arrived at his grandfather's house just before noon. The old man was shuffling along the sidewalk to the mailbox, which brought a grin to Abe's face. Who did Joe Joe expect to hear from? It wasn't like he ever got anything but junk mail and utility bills. That wasn't exactly right, Abe amended. At Christmas, a few people still remembered him with cards wishing him happy holidays. Then in January, he always got one of those contest packets suggesting that he could be the latest ten-million-dollar winner. But the rest of the year was sadly predictable.

Abe made himself a promise to have his kids draw their great-grandfather a picture that he could mail to him.

"Hey, Grandpa Joe!" Abe called. "What's happenin'?"

Joe Joe stopped in his tracks. "I was jes' gonna git the mail, then go in the house and call you. Have some lawyerin' business to throw yo' way."

Abe suppressed a grin and kept his dark brows from quirking as he asked, "That so? What kind of legal problems you having, Grandpa Joe?"

"Not a problem. Not exactly," the old man said as he pulled a grocery flyer from the mailbox. "Jes' been thinkin' on that visit I had with Mizz Lily. I been tryin' hard to remember if I seen anythin' at all I forgot to tell the police about. And I'll be doggone if I didn't jes' do it this mornin' while I was sippin' my o.j.''

Abe stopped dead in his tracks halfway up the steps to the front porch. "What're you sayin', old man? You sure this ain't something you just dreamed up 'cause you're wanting to help that gal?"

"No, suh! I *remember*!"

Abe helped his grandfather into the house and into his chair. He sat on the sofa opposite him, then leaned forward, his arms between his legs, hands together, and fingers steepled. "Now, Grandpa, this is real important. You can't be inventin' things that never happened, you hear?"

"I'm old, boy," Joe Joe said irritably, jerking his arm as if wishing he could backhand the impertinent youth. "Sometimes I stand in the middle of this room for fifteen minutes tryin' to remember where I put the mornin' paper when all the time it's right here in my hand, but I ain't started imaginin' things that didn't never happen. I remembered what I seen when I went runnin' into that house after Mizz Sara pushed Dr. Alison over that there railin'.''

"Who, Joe? Who'd you see?"

"Now don't push me, boy. I gots to figure out how to esplain what it is I seen and what I heard, 'cause they wasn't one and the same."

Abe pursed his lips and pressed his hands against them as he offered a silent prayer that what the old man was remembering was not simply a figment of his imagination. "Okay, Grandpa, take your time."

"I saw the boy. Young Sash. He wasn't in the house. He was out front, hidin' behind a tree, and oh, lawd, that boy's eyes, they was big as silver dollars. He was scared, that one was." Joe Joe pressed the heels of his gnarled hands against his eyes, and Abe thought he'd finished. But just as he started to ask his grandfather when this was—before or after the murder—Joe Joe told him. "I remember how my heart hurt for that boy 'cause I knowed he'd seen what happened same as me and his little sister. I didn't have time for him though. I had to git to Mizz Sara. But I'd stopped. Undecided, ya' know? And in that one second I coulda sworn to Almighty God that I heard footsteps, movin' real quick like. Yes, sir, I'm sure as I can be now that I'm thinkin' on it, that there was other folks by that day. At least two, maybe more. Somebody else besides me and that chile . . . and young Sash Rivers knows what happened in that house when Dr. Alison was murdered."

Chapter Twenty-nine

Sash was a little crazy this morning. Maybe it was the way his house had been turned into both bed-and-breakfast and infirmary in the past two days. Or maybe it was the secrets he was keeping from Lily.

Lily. That was *who* was bothering him, and everyone knew it. His sister Genie. Kitty Star. And Rusty. Even the guy lying upstairs in his attic studio.

"Why don't you just go get her?" Rusty had asked only that morning. "Bring her here and tell her everything."

"You know why I don't!"

"Because you don't want to put her in danger, but she's been at risk since she arrived last Monday," Rusty said.

Sash was seated on the sofa, and Genie came over to sit beside him. "Come on, Rusty, you know we can't tell her the truth. Not when we're this close to having it all."

Rusty stood near the bedroom door, her back against the wall. She folded her arms over her chest in a gesture of clear defiance. "I don't believe we're that close. Sorry."

Sash ran his hands through his dark hair. "Look,

things are about to break. I didn't want Lil in the middle. I thought she'd come home for the funeral, then go right back to New York. But none of us knew about the phone call from Sara."

"Wasn't that awesome?" Genie said excitedly. "Could you believe it? I bet she just about lost it when she heard her mother's voice on the phone after all those years."

In her enthusiasm for the topic, the silky wrap she'd tied around her opened slightly revealing her lack of clothing underneath.

"Why don't you go get some clothes on?" Sash asked tersely.

"Because I'm probably going to lie back down if Rusty can keep an eye on our guest for a couple of hours more. I was up with him all night."

Rusty shrugged. "Sure, I don't mind, but you didn't tell me how you got out of the house after the party without Dix getting suspicious."

"Easy. My wonderful, faithful husband didn't come home with me after the party. Said he had business with Sander and Stuart. I called Sash as soon as I got home. He sent Kitty to pick me up and here I am." She winked at the other girls before adding, "Dixon never comes to my room after I've been sleeping 'cause he knows it makes me furious to be disturbed, so he wouldn't miss me."

Stretching out on the sofa, she yawned widely, then went on, "This morning, he's on his way to Charleston to take depositions on a case he's prosecuting. He won't be home until tonight. By that time, I'll be sitting in front of the TV pouting and bored to bitter tears because I've been left too long all by my lonesome."

Rusty laughed. "He should know what you're really up to!"

"Don't look so thrilled at the prospect of what he'd do to me, sugar," Imogene said.

"Okay," Sash said, heading off a potential catfight. "Let's talk business." The phone rang on the wall just inches from Rusty's head. "Get that," Sash told her unnecessarily.

"Surprise, it's for you," she told him seconds later. "Guy says it's important."

"Who is it?"

"Some dude named Abraham Joseph. Says he's an attorney with urgent business."

Sash took the phone and listened a few minutes, then said, "Come right on over, Mr. Joseph." He gave him the address and hung up. "*Yes!*"

"Yes, what?" the women chorused.

"That was old Joe Joe's grandson. Remember him?"

Both women nodded, and Imogene prodded him along. "Of course, we remember Joe Joe. So what? Tell us!"

Sash let a slow grin spread, then turned to explain to Rusty what Genie already knew. "He was one of the witnesses the day Alison Hutton was killed. Along with my sister, here."

Rusty nodded her understanding, and Sash continued. "Last night at the dinner party, Lily announced that she was trying to jog the old guy's memory. See if he remembered seeing anyone else around the murder scene."

"You should have seen the scowl on Sash's face when she made her little announcement. I thought he was going to explode," Genie told Rusty.

"Because you were afraid she was going to get in the way of what we're trying to do," Rusty deduced.

Sash shrugged. "That and because I don't want her getting hurt. But it's too late now. She inadvertently tossed out the bait, and someone's already taken it. And guess who?" It was a rhetorical question, and he paused only a beat for effect before providing the answer. "Dear ol' Mom, that's who. She just called Joe Joe's house. His grandson was there and got the call, which seems to have suited Eudora fine. She's asked him to come to her house tonight for a visit."

"Okay, but I don't get it. Why call you? Mother didn't mention your name, did she?"

"Nope. I wish she had, then at least we'd know where we stand. Why Eudora wants to see Abe Joseph," Sash said, rubbing the day-old stubble on his jaw thoughtfully. "But it looks like the princess has done more to shake things up in the past week than we've been able to do in the last five years. She went to see the old man, and he's had a memory of me being there. Abraham says he wants to talk to me about that before he goes to see my stepmother."

"Nice of him," Rusty said.

"*Smart* of him," Sash corrected. "Don't forget this is a *black* man practicing law in Mayor Rivers's neck of the woods. He doesn't want to cross her, but he knows enough about her not to trust her either."

"You think he trusts you? Why?" Genie asked pragmatically.

"I don't know that he does. Maybe he's heard about my status as persona non grata with the powers that be. Or maybe he just wants to hear my reasons for being at the Hutton house that day." He shrugged. "We're just going to have to play wait and see, but I've got a feeling the game's begun in earnest now. No more hide and seek or blind man's bluff."

A crash that sounded like metal against metal startled them all. Rusty recovered first. "Guess who's awake? I'll go check on him." She was halfway to the door leading upstairs when she stopped. "What time is that doctor coming by today?"

Imogene shook her head. "Who knows? Your guess is as good as any. He said whenever he can get away from the hospital."

"I'll stay upstairs till he gets here." Then to Sash, "Want me to change the dressing on your arm?"

"No, it's okay. Genie did it earlier. But thanks."

Dimples appeared with the waitress's grin. "Next time wait for me. No sense pulling your shirt off for your sister. Your gorgeous body is wasted on her."

"I'll remember that," Sash said.

"You do that and don't forget to call me when that lawyer shows up. I don't want to miss that."

"You've got time. He won't be here for a couple of hours. Said he'd stop by on his way to see the great lady."

Rusty disappeared behind the door, and Genie stretched, arms wide and head tossed back with an accompanying loud yawn.

"I'm sure all this gorgeous, milky-white skin is doing wonders for your patient's recuperation," Sash said sarcastically, "but as Rusty just pointed out, I am your brother, Genie. Put some clothes on when you're around me, okay?"

"How did the same man sire such different kids?" she teased as she stood up and went toward the bedroom where she often stayed when she sneaked out of her husband's house. "Who would believe Imogene Rivers has a prudish sibling? It positively boggles the mind!"

Sash laughed. "Go to bed!"

"I'm going, but what about you? You going to try to catch a few winks while you got the chance?" Genie asked, all teasing aside.

Sash shook his head absently as he sat forward on the edge of the sofa. He was already opening a thick, expandable folder. "I'm going to go over all the evidence we've gathered. See if I can make a few more pieces fit the puzzle."

By four o'clock, Lily was still puzzling over Errol's whereabouts. She'd telephoned the apartment four times. Each time, the answering machine had come on. It was still the same silly message Errol had programmed before they left for La Guardia five days earlier.

If there was one thing he was on top of, it was the answering machine. Like he always said, the discovery that put him on the show-biz map could well be only one phone message away.

Lily decided to call the apartment building super, ask him to use his passkey to go in and check for some sign that Errol had been there.

Fifteen minutes later, she had her answer and fear replaced concern. Errol had not been back to the apartment. Something was very, very wrong.

Lily was halfway up the stairs when she remembered Kitty. What had the woman said about Errol's sudden departure? Lily tried to remember her exact words as she turned on the step and reversed her direction.

She found the housekeeper cleaning the mirrors in the dance studio.

"Hi," Kitty said, smiling into the mirror at Lily's reflection. "I'm almost done if you're wanting to dance."

"No, not now. I want to talk to you about Errol."

"Sure," Kitty said, though Lily noticed that she no longer met her gaze. "What do you want to know?"

"You said you took him to the train station. What time did the train for New York leave?"

Kitty shook her head. "I don't know. He must have had the schedule, 'cause he was in a hurry to leave."

"So you didn't actually see him get on the train?"

"Geez, what is this? The Inquisition?" Kitty asked, tucking the roll of paper towels under her arm and climbing down the ladder. "No one told me I was responsible for when and where your friends go." She dropped the bottle of glass cleaner in a bucket along with the towels and sponge mop. "I'm all done. If it's all right with you, I'd like to get home a little early today. Need to do some cleaning there before my old man crawls all over me."

She didn't wait for an answer as she picked up the stepladder and started from the room.

"Kitty, is something wrong?" Lily asked.

The girl stopped, but didn't turn. She sighed loudly, then answered through what sounded like clenched teeth. "I'm a maid, Miss Hutton. You pay me six dollars an hour to keep your house spic-and-span. I throw in the cooking 'cause I enjoy it, but I ain't no friggin' detective."

Lily didn't answer. She didn't know what to say except that she was sorry, and she didn't feel she owed Kitty an apology for worrying about her friend.

But damn it, she was going to find out what the hell was going on one way or the other.

Hands balled, Lily brushed past Kitty and headed up the stairs, forcing herself to take them at a moderate pace that wouldn't betray her frustration.

She headed down the hall toward her bedroom, passing the room Errol had occupied, stopped and backtracked. She stood there, outside his room, her hand on the doorknob. What was the use of looking in an empty room? Kitty had even changed the sheets already, for heaven's sake.

She was opening the door as she argued with herself. But what the heck? What could it hurt to check out the closet and the chest of drawers? Maybe Errol had left some clue behind as to where he'd really gone.

But where would that be except New York?

And then she remembered his family in Florida. He had seven older brothers and sisters strung from one end of the state to the other, not to mention his parents who still lived in Jacksonville, last Lily had heard. Maybe he'd called one of them.

With reborn hope of discovering some kind of clue Lily began a search of his room in earnest. With hands and eyes, she swept the dresser drawers, stood on tiptoes to peer over the ledge of the closet shelf, and crawled on hands and knees to inspect the area beneath the king-sized bed. Nothing!

Plopping down on the bed, she combed her hair away from her face with her fingers, sighing with exasperation at the same time. She pulled open the drawer on the nightstand. Empty as Errol's pockets most days.

The telephone! She grinned as she remembered a trick she'd seen in some whodunit flick. Ignoring the open drawer, she picked up the receiver and hit redial. Maybe, just please, God, maybe, he'd called someone before he left.

"You've reached the Pier Movie Theater," a recorded voice droned. "The following schedule will provide featured—"

Errol had been checking on what movies were playing? Hardly the thing a guy would do if he was leaving town in the next couple of hours.

Lily grinned, pleased with her clever sleuthing. "In the vernacular of the very witty, very charming Errol Mills, 'exacta mundo, baby!' "

The grin didn't stay in place for long as fear replaced her excitement, slamming into her chest like a hammer blow. "Damn it! Where the hell are you, Mills?" she asked, pushing the bedside table drawer shut with a frustrated bang. The hand-painted porcelain lamp on top of the table rocked and teetered uncertainly, and

Lily jumped to her feet just catching hold of the glass chimney in the nick of time before it toppled to the floor. But Lily lost her own balance in the rescue of one of her mother's favorite pieces and caught herself with some fancy footwork and a hand to the wall behind the table. And then she saw them. Errol's keys.

Fear knotted her stomach and coursed through her arms, sending pin prickles to her fingertips as she squatted and stretched for the gold lion key ring she'd given him for his birthday the past August.

A moment later, her hands trembling, she examined the key ring. They were all there. Five of them. Keys to the apartment building, loft, mailbox, gym locker, and bike; passports for access to Errol's life. There was no way in hell he'd leave without them.

Chapter Thirty

Lily had always prided herself on her cool demeanor. No matter what the crisis, no matter what the provocation, she rarely let anything or anyone incite her to anger. She'd always attributed her even keel to her Native-American heritage. But the moment she found Errol's keys, another inherent idiosyncrasy manifested itself. Lily wanted blood, and a certain lying housekeeper's scalp.

"*Kitty!*" she screamed from the third-floor landing. She repeated the girl's name four times on her way downstairs to the ground floor.

No answer.

Lily checked the kitchen, laundry room, study, living room, and dance studio. And then she remembered Kitty's request to leave early.

"Damn it!"

Lily opened the front door. The red truck that the housekeeper drove was gone from the driveway.

"Damn it," she repeated, this time in a softer tone in keeping with her deadly temper.

The gold astrological cat on the key ring was biting into her palm as she hurried into the kitchen for her purse. Damn her, Kitty Star wasn't going to get away with this. Lily would track her down if she had to knock on every door in Rosehill.

A glance at the telephone book on the shelf beside the wall phone almost made her grin. No doubt looking up the girl's address would be more efficient than a house-by-house search.

She found the only listing for Star. An H. E. Star. Lily frowned. What was Kitty's father's first name? She seemed to remember Emmitt or Everett. This had to be the right—

She nearly jumped when the phone rang only inches from her head.

Errol! And then a new possibility occurred. What if he didn't realize he'd dropped the keys until after he was already in New York? Knowing him the way she did, she doubted he'd call her right away. He might wear egg on his face often; that didn't mean he wore it well.

She snatched the receiver from the hook, holding her breath instead of speaking as she prayed it would be the missing actor who spoke from the other end.

Disappointment rose to her throat as bitter as gall when a woman spoke instead. "Hello? Is anyone there?"

Her forehead against the wall, Lily answered in a strangled whisper. "Yes, I'm here."

"Miss Hutton?" the stranger asked.

This time Lily waited. Who was calling? Someone making a "courtesy call" as the latest telemarketing firms euphemistically referred to their sales pitches. *Not today!*

"Hello? This is Mary Alice Randolf calling for Lily Hutton. Is anyone still there?"

"Yes!" Lily said as name recognition dawned. "Ms. Randolf, its me. This is Lily."

"Call me Mary Alice, please."

"Sure," Lily said, twisting the telephone cord around

her wrist, then letting it go again. "What can I do for you?"

"Well, actually, I think I may be able to help you." This time, her words were offered hesitantly, and Lily hurried to offer reassurances.

"I appreciate whatever you can tell me, Mary Alice."

There was a slight pause, then a sharp intake of breath before Mary Alice spoke again. "You have no idea how I've been battling with myself over this since you came to Tremont the other day. It isn't just that I'm going against Dr. Lepstein's wishes by speaking with you, it's that I think I may be directly involved in something I had no idea I was getting into."

Lily's heart began its drum roll again. "You mean with my mother's death, don't you?" she asked in a hushed, scared voice.

"No!" There was nervous laughter, then a repeated denial. "Good God, no! At least I hope not—"

"I'm sorry," Lily quickly put in. "Look, you just tell me what you called to say. I won't interrupt."

True to her word, Lily didn't break in, but the two or three seconds that she waited were nerve-racking.

"Lily, you asked if anyone had been to see your mother during the week before she died. The answer is yes. She had a visitor on three occasions between that previous Sunday and the Thursday that she succumbed to the heart attack. But I have to explain."

Lily's brows drew together in a perplexed frown. "Okay, go on," she agreed hesitantly.

"About two years ago, I met a guy. He was rugged, handsome, moody-broody, sexy as hell." She laughed. "I know you don't care about my social life, but this is all germane to what you want to know, so bear with me, okay?"

"Sure," Lily said, more confused than ever.

"This guy said he'd traveled the world as a sailor

first, then a merchant marine. Now he was a fisherman living in Rosehill.

"I've never been farther away than Atlanta, and never had anyone even half as good looking as this guy talking to me. After a while he started asking me about myself. What was to tell, right? I'm single, untraveled, not exactly cover-model pretty. Not exactly enjoying an enviable lifestyle. On the other hand, some of the patients at Tremont are pretty notorious, so I talked about them. That's when he said he knew Sara Two Moons-Hutton."

Lily squeezed her eyes shut and slid along the wall to sit on the floor. She felt her suspicions beginning to churn in her stomach and clamped a hand over her mouth as she willed herself not to be sick.

"Anyway," Mary Alice went on, "to make a long story short, I guess he knew who I was all along. He wanted a way into Tremont that would allow him access to Mrs. Hutton without any record being made. I'm ashamed to say I helped him."

"Why?" Lily managed in the barest of whispers.

"I don't know," the woman sighed. "He said they'd been friends before she ... well, before the incident with her husband. But he said his family was disapproving and he didn't want them to know he was visiting her. He claimed they'd try to stop him."

Lily's whole body was trembling now, and she had to hold the telephone with both hands to keep it steady enough to hear. "Go on."

"That's about it. He came every Sunday night just after visiting hours. I arranged with the regular aide and nurse on duty for him to see her in her room—strictly against regulations, as you can probably guess."

"Why ... why would the others go along with you?"

"I don't know," Mary Alice said. "Maybe Sash was promising them the world, too, like he did with me."

Sash! There. She'd identified him and Lily could no longer practice denial.

"There's one more thing," Mary Alice said. "I hope you won't think I'm trying to justify what I did by telling you this. Believe me, that's not it. I just think it might make you feel better to know."

"What?"

"I don't know what his motives were, but I know he helped your mother. Somehow, he was able to do what all the doctors who treated her couldn't. I watched them a couple of times through the window in the door, and I swear she was almost smiling when he was there."

"When . . . um, when was the last time he saw her?" Lily asked.

"I don't have the exact date. Like I said, we sure didn't write down the dates of his visits for anyone to see. But I know he was there three times that week because it was the first time he ever did that. In the two years that he came to Tremont he never came except on Sunday night till that week. And I remember that everything was crazy the last night. Bonnie and Flo— that's the nurse and the aide—and me were real scared we were going to get caught. There was a fire and the office in E-2 Wing was broken into. Someone called Dr. Lepstein, and we almost didn't get Sash out of the hospital before she arrived."

"But you're sure he wasn't there the night she had the heart attack?"

"I don't think so, but I can't swear he wasn't there. Bonnie or Flo, either one, might've arranged a visit I didn't know about. They were pretty impressed by him, too."

"Oh, God." Lily dropped her forehead to her knees and squeezed her eyes shut.

"His name is Rivers. Sash Rivers. Do you know him? Was he telling the truth about your mother? Were they friends?"

"She thought they were," Lily answered quietly.

Chapter Thirty-one

As Lily climbed out of the rental car, she was stunned to realize she didn't remember a single minute of the drive from the East Hill Road address to the Overview Drive waterfront property where she now stood.

She recalled hanging up the phone after talking with Mary Alice Randolf, going to the hall closet and searching the pockets of her jacket for Sash's hospital release forms, and copying down the address. After that, nothing.

For the first time, Lily understood how her mother could witness something so horrific, so excruciating, as her husband's murder, that she'd escaped inside her mind where pain couldn't follow.

For the first time in her young existence, Lily knew what pain was.

And betrayal.

And rage.

She'd fallen in love with Sasha Rivers. And into hate.

She gazed up at the wood frame house, built just a hundred yards or so from the water's edge, yet high and untouchable on stilts.

With balled hands, she rounded the side of the house to the board stairs, pausing for a steadying breath before the climb.

Her legs trembled as she mounted the first steps, and she stopped again, bending at the waist and inhaling deeply. The pungent ocean scents of saline and brine did the trick as ably as smelling salts, stinging her nostrils and restoring her resolve.

She made the rest of the climb rapidly. She noticed for the first time that a light burned over the doorway and wondered absently who Sash was expecting. A thin smile spread at the prospect of ruining his plans whatever they were. It had already disappeared again by the time she raised her hand to pound on the screen door. She didn't stop until it was opened.

As she'd guessed, Sash was expecting company. His expression revealed as much when he discovered her standing there. Lily allowed herself a fragment of pleasure at having caught him unawares.

"Lil—" he said, pushing the door open and reaching for her hand to draw her inside.

Lily didn't wait. She launched her attack the moment her feet crossed the threshold. "Did you kill my father, Sash? Is that why you went to Tremont? Were you afraid Sara would remember? *Did* she remember? Is that why you killed her, too?"

Sash shook his head, denial and anger flashing in his midnight-blue eyes. "Lily, I swear to you—"

Lily slapped him. "You lying bastard! She trusted you!"

Suddenly she was shaking uncontrollably. She had to get a grip. It had been a mistake to come here. She couldn't stand it. Not yet. Tomorrow. Tomorrow she'd be able to face him knowing what he was. Knowing how he'd destroyed everything that mattered to her. Even her love for him. Tomorrow, but not tonight.

She turned, reaching for the door and fumbling clumsily with the handle.

"Lily, wait. Please. I don't know where you got these crazy ideas, but you're wrong. I swear it."

She spun around, pushing her hair away from her face, ready to attack—verbally, physically, anything. But then she saw the others.

Imogene Rivers and Kitty Star!

Oh, God, were they all in it together? And what about Errol? Had they killed him, too? Was that why he hadn't come back for his keys? Because he was dead?

Brushing past Sash, she crossed the room in long, angry strides. She grabbed Kitty's arm when the woman tried to back away from her. "*You lying bitch!* Errol didn't take a train to New York!" She pulled his keys out of her pocket, holding them in front of the stunned woman's face, jingling them for effect. "These are his keys. He wouldn't have left them behind."

Kitty didn't answer, but her face had paled and her gaze had darted past Lily in an obvious plea for help from Sash and Imogene.

"You're right, Lil," Sash said. "Your friend didn't leave. He's still here in Rosehill."

Someone was knocking on the door behind her, and Sash paused, glancing over his shoulder, his attention diverted.

Lily ran trembling fingers across her brow. "Damn it, Rivers, don't you move toward that door until someone tells me where Errol is exactly and why I was told he went back to New York."

Sash hesitated, torn between satisfying her and getting on with his business with Abe Joseph. He compromised. "He's safe, Lily. That's all I can tell you right now. I wish I had time to sit you down and explain everything to you, but I don't. You opened Pandora's box last night when you told everyone at the party that Sara didn't kill Dr. Hutton. And, now, sweetheart, all hell's breaking loose." He jerked a thumb over his shoulder. "As a matter of fact, that'll be Abe Joseph."

"What is Joe Joe's grandson doing here?" Lily asked, her confusion retarding her anger. "Don't tell me he's involved in this, too."

"Oh, Jesus," Sash said, throwing his hands up in exasperation. "You've got this all mixed up, Lil."

She wasn't going to argue with him. What she wanted was simple. Answers to the questions she'd asked. Had he killed her parents, either of them, or both of them? And where was her friend? But before she could reiterate that, Sash had the door open, and Abe Joseph was stepping inside looking wary and nervous.

The black man's eyes widened. "What're you doing here, Miss Hutton?"

"She thinks I killed her parents," Sash said, brushing the reason aside with an irritated shrug.

Abe wasn't as quick to let it go. "Then she and I've got something in common, Mr. Rivers, 'cause I'm wanting to know the same thing before I go meeting with your mama."

"Eudora is not my mother," Sash ground out. "Don't make any mistake about that. And don't think she'll take kindly to you calling her that in her presence. She hates me even more than I do her. There's not a single maternal instinct in her body where I'm concerned."

"And yet your *half*-sister is here with you," the lawyer observed, raising his chin in Imogene's direction.

"Caught in the middle," Imogene explained, stepping forward and speaking for the first time. "I'm helping my brother, but that doesn't mean I don't love my mother, Mr. Joseph. Sash thinks she's messed up in some bad things." She looked at Lily for an uncertain second. "Yes, Lily, like the death of your father." Then back to the attorney. "Sash may well be right. I hope not, and he knows that even though I'm helping him, I'm working to disprove my mother's involvement."

Abe nodded thoughtfully. "Well, Mrs. Price, that definitely puts a different spin on things. Beggin' your pardon, but I've never believed in spelling out a case in front of the other side." When she opened her mouth to interrupt, he held up a hand. "I know you're trying to be loyal to your mama, while you're also helping your brother. But to me, that just means you're standing there with your feet on both sides of the line. I'm not trying to be rude, Mrs. Price, but I think, until I learn why your mama asked me to come to her house for a meeting tonight, I'll just keep what I got to say for Mr. Rivers's ears only. No offense intended."

Genie grinned as she folded her arms across her chest. "Suit yourself. Sash and I don't have secrets, but the important thing for now is that you be comfortable." She started from the room, stopping to lay a hand on Lily's forearm. "Hang in there. Sash is right. Your friend is safe, and I've got a feeling we're very close to all the answers you've been looking for. Just try to be patient a little longer. It's very important that everything be in place before we play our final card."

Like Abe, Lily wanted to believe her. Right now she didn't trust anyone. She turned to the lawyer. "I don't understand what Eudora is after, Abe." She shook her head. "It doesn't make sense. Why would she call you out of the blue to come to her house and talk to her? If this is on the up and up, why not meet in her office in the middle of the day instead of in secret at her house at night?"

Abe grinned, slow like and appreciative of the points she'd made. "Exactly what I thought. That's why I called Rivers, here. My grandfather remembered something today." He looked at Sash. "He remembered seeing you outside Dr. Hutton's house just after the

man was killed. Said he thinks you were hiding behind
a tree. Told me you were real scared."

Rage heated Lily face, and her hands trembled
though she tried to hold them in tight fists. "Then it's
true," she said in an accusing whisper.

"That I was there, yes. Not that I killed him. You
have to believe that."

"I think he's telling the truth, Miss Lily," Abe said.
"I questioned Grandpa Joe at great length this afternoon. His recollections are spotty, but he's sure young
Sash, as he still calls him, was scared not by something
he'd done, but by something he'd seen." Abe shot Sash
a questioning glance.

"How would he know that?" Lily scoffed. "Forgive
me, but your grandfather's an old man who's mixed
everything up in his mind."

"He may be old, Lil, but he's right," Sash said. "I
didn't kill your father."

Lily's gaze locked with his in a long measuring moment. She was the first to look away. She might be
letting her heart influence her, but she suddenly believed him.

"What time's your appointment with Mrs. Rivers?"
she asked Abe.

"At seven o'clock. In exactly fifteen minutes."

"Then we'd better get going," she said firmly.

Sash raised a dark brow. "*We?* I don't think so,
princess."

Lily let a slow smile spread. "Then I'm glad I don't
need your permission."

"This is not a game. For God's sake, Lil, think about
it. On one hand, you're convinced that your mother is
innocent of your father's murder. But on the other hand
you're not worried that your little announcement at
dinner last night didn't scare the shit out of whoever
did kill him? You don't see the coincidence of Eudora's

invitation out of the blue to Abe to visit her at her house at *night*. What if he's walking into a trap? Do you want to be caught in it with him?"

"So, what am I supposed to do? Just go back to my house and twiddle my thumbs till you decide to let me in on everything?"

"Yes," he said, gripping her shoulders and meeting her gaze with his, which was intense and pleading.

"Okay," she said after a moment. "But tonight, Sash. I don't want to wait until tomorrow for answers. I want to know what happened the day my father died." He held up his hands, but she shook away the disclaimer she sensed he was about to make. "I know you don't have all the answers. That's okay. I just want to know what you remember. I want to know what you've found out since then, and I want to know where Errol is." She fired the words without pause, then stopped to inhale deeply before adding, "Or so help me, Sash, I'm going to start shaking things up, and I don't care who gets caught in the middle."

Five minutes later, a rough plan formed between Sash and Abe, Lily preceded the two men down the steps to the driveway. At her car, she opened the door and looked at Sash, who was about to climb in on the passenger side of Abe's black sedan. "What happens if someone sees you lurking outside Eudora's house while Abe's inside?"

Sash hunched his shoulders. "Then I'll improvise." He raised his hands as if poised for a boxing match and shuffled his feet quickly in a parody of a dance. "Do a little fancy sidesteppin' and hope I'm better than the other guy at ducking punches."

He was grinning.

Lily tossed his words of earlier back at him. "This isn't a game, Sash. If you don't want me charging in there like a one-woman cavalry, you'd better get your ass back to my house before I get too worried."

That sobered him. Letting go of the door, he crossed the three or four feet of pavement that separated them. He caught her hair in his hand at the nape, bending her face up toward his as he cupped her chin with the other hand and kissed her. His lips were rough, warm.

She groaned as she gripped the fabric of his jacket sleeves, holding him there, not wanting to let him go.

"I promise," he said as he gently untangled his coat from her fingers and stepped away to climb into Abe's car.

Lily leaned against the door of her rental car as the dark sedan backed from the drive and turned onto the road. She didn't move as they drove away and the tail-lights grew smaller and smaller and smaller. Not until they disappeared.

Then she lowered her face to where her hand rested atop the car door. "Damn you, Sash, I love you. Don't you dare get hurt. Don't you *dare*."

Chapter Thirty-two

"You got it?" Sash asked Abraham as they started across the lawn behind Lily's house.

On the drive from Sash's house, he'd changed plans. Instead of driving to Eudora's, they would wait for Lily, stash the car in her garage, and walk to the Rivers house. "Safer that way," he'd explained.

"Why?" Abe had wanted to know.

"Because if we have to make a run for it, we've got more options on foot. We can take off through the woods to the pier, or get to Lily's, or run straight down the road. In the car, we've got only one way out."

Abe had grinned and needled him. "You pretty much worked out this Rambo image for yourself, huh?"

Sash had laughed, but not for long. "Okay, smart ass, but I'm telling you there's danger in these hills. I know. I was hiding in that house right behind us when they killed Alison Hutton. Since then, I'm pretty sure they've done the same thing to at least four others."

There was a silent pause as the ghastly number sank in. Then Abe said, "Look, Rivers, I believe these people are control freaks. Hell, what person who's lived in Rosehill for more than a few months doesn't know that? But some kind of a secret *murdering* society?" Abe shook his head. "I'm a lawyer, man. I deal with hard facts and irrefutable evidence."

"Bullshit! You deal with supposition and circumstantial evidence."

"Sometimes," the attorney conceded. "So, okay, when I get back from my little powwow with Mrs. R., you can argue your case, and I'll be your jury."

"What time is it?" Sash asked.

"Five till. I've gotta get going."

Sash shook his head. "You can be a few minutes late. Eudora will appreciate you not kowtowing. I want you to hear me out before you go in there so you know what you're dealing with."

Abe turned to face him. He folded his arms across his chest, and raised his chin. "Okay, counselor, let's hear it."

"When I came back to Rosehill five years ago, it wasn't because I suddenly got lonesome for family and home turf. I read a piece in a magazine about Tremont."

"Where Mrs. Hutton was incarcerated," Abe said.

"Yeah, only I didn't know she was even alive. I thought she'd been murdered along with her husband."

"So that's why you took off."

Sash nodded. "You got it. But then here I am reading this piece about people who go over the edge and commit murder. And there's her name. Only I know she didn't do it. I don't know who *did*, but I know she's innocent.

"So, anyway, I hopped a bus and came back. Took a room in the Alley at the Ruby Palace Motel for a few days. A couple of days later I'm talking to a gal who makes some comment about her mother disappearing. I make all the right sympathetic sounds, you know, and she confides that her family believes she was murdered to keep her from telling what she knew about Dr. Hutton's death."

Abe whistled. "So now you're off and running."

"Well, sort of at a fast walk, but at least we're moving," Sash said. "And then she said something real off the wall—at least, that's what I thought at the moment. Later, after I got back to my room, it made a lot of sense."

"So?" Abe prodded. "What did she say?"

"I was sympathizing, saying something about racial or social equality not existing in Rosehill. She laughed and shook her head. Said, 'Make no mistake, buddy. My mother may have been in the wrong place at the wrong time, but I wouldn't live up in those hills with those folks for all their gold. It's not a healthy place to live, especially if you're the least bit different.'"

"So, you're saying they killed Dr. Hutton because he was different?" Abe asked dubiously. "It was his wife who was Native American. Why didn't they kill her instead?"

"My *guess* is, they intended to kill her, and something went wrong. But listen, there's more. My mother was Russian—a gypsy according to Eudora. I was only four when she died, but I never bought the coroner's conclusion that she committed suicide. Then there was Dan Lucas. He owned a pharmaceutical business."

"Yeah," Abe said. "I remember that one. They said he went crazy in the grocery store one night for no apparent reason. Started shooting at cans and the police ended up killing him in a gunfight."

"Yep, and did you hear the rumor that went around after his funeral?"

Abe shook his head.

"That he'd met a pretty little senorita on a trip to Mexico and was going to bring her home as a bride the next week."

Abe scratched the back of his neck. "I don't know. That sounds pretty farfetched to me."

"Okay, what about Oliver Price? You were about the same age as him. Did you know he was gay? Came out of the closet and ended up a casualty two days later. Killed in a boating accident. I've been told his parents made accusations about the boat being sabotaged. A week later, they both died in a car accident . . . You need more?"

"Just one thing," Abe said, tugging thoughtfully on his earlobe. "Have you been able to come up with any evidence that links a specific person or persons to all this?"

"I've got a list of suspects with Sander Hutton and Eudora Rivers right at the top. Genie keeps her ear to the walls, and she's pretty sure her husband is involved. Stuart St. Charles, our police chief, too."

"Yeah, that makes sense. With the mayor, D.A., and chief of police all in it together, they wouldn't have too much trouble covering up the facts. But you don't think everyone who lives up here is automatically implicated?"

"No. If they were, Genie would have been brought into their confidence by now."

"Yeah, I guess that's right."

"So you understand why you have to tell them your grandfather hasn't remembered anything. You have to make them believe you were just letting Lily get off steam by listening to her. Convince them Joe Joe's too senile to ever be of any help to her."

"Hey, don't you worry. By the time I leave Mrs. Rivers's house, she's gonna wonder if I got my license to practice law outta some Cracker Jack box, that's how dense and naive I'm gonna be."

Sash grinned. "Good, but don't try for an Academy Award. Just get in, say your piece, and get out. Don't give her time to set you up, Abe."

"I hear you," the attorney said, jamming his hands into the deep pockets of his jacket. He started forward up the last few feet of lawn then stopped again to add one last observation. "After tonight I might even think about moving my family somewhere else. I don't want to end up buried in Cotton County." He shook his head. "Speaking of weird, that's a crazy one, ain't it? Having a law prohibiting folks from being buried here in Rosehill. Wonder who thought that one up? Wonder *why?*"

"You can blame my great, great, great-something grandmother, Rose Price, for that one. Legend has it she claimed she could hear all her friends and family screaming from their graves years after they were massacred in an Indian raid. Made her grandsons go dig up every single body and rebury them outside the city limits before she died. Made all her living descendants swear they'd never bury their dead inside Rosehill again." He glanced at the lawyer. "Surprised you didn't learn that one in high school history class."

"Seems to me I recall something spooky like that. 'Course I was a might impressionable at that age. Didn't like listening to tales about ghosts crying from their graves."

"I know what you mean," Sash agreed.

Abe glanced at his watch. "Well, it's a quarter after the hour. I'm fifteen minutes late. You think that's fashionable enough for the mayor?"

"Yeah, we don't want to get her too pissed off."

"You got that right. If this lady's up to the kind of bad shit you're talking about, I don't wanna make her mad at all," Abe said, his eyes looking as big as silver dollars against the darkness of night.

"It's not too late to change your mind. We can go back to Lily's and you can call her. Give her a telephone interview instead."

"No. I think the lady gives an invite, she means for the man to show up in person. 'Sides, you wanting to put an end to all the evil going on, I figure this might just be our chance to do that. Another reason? Until I decide where I'm gonna move my family, I kinda fancy the notion of being able to practice law without worrying what kind of accident the lady's going to arrange for me."

Sash offered his hand. Abe's grip was firm and steady though Sash knew he had to be scared shitless. "You cover your ass in there, Joseph. When everything comes down, I'm probably going to need a good lawyer."

Abe grinned at that. "Well, I am that. In the meantime, where you going to be while I'm inside playing mouse with a smart old cat?"

"Right here," Sash said, pointing to a thick clump of evergreen shrubs. Dropping to the earth, he bellied under the heavy cover of foliage, then peered up at his companion from beneath a sweet-smelling pine branch. "You think she can see me down here?" he asked.

"Not unless she's got some of them newfangled infrared glasses hunters use at night." Dried needles crunched beneath his heel as he took a step, then hesitated. "Here goes nothing ... I hope."

Sash dittoed that as he worked his way forward a couple of inches to see the house.

From his cramped hiding place, he watched Abe cross the street and a moment later, enter the house through the front door.

A flicker of movement on the roof of the Rivers' home caught Sash's attention just as the door closed behind the attorney. Eudora had stepped onto the widow's walk, and Sash frowned, wondering what she was doing up there.

Sash kept his eyes focused on his stepmother as she

paced in a tight square around the perimeter of the diminutive terrace. Where was Abe?

There! About damn time, Sash thought as the attorney stepped out of the door onto the widow's watch. He strained his ears trying to catch even the sound of their voices if not what was being said, but it was no use. From the distance that separated them, he couldn't hear a thing.

He wondered what she was up to and how Abe was handling himself, but after a time, Sash was distracted by his own discomfort. The ground was damp and cold even through the heavy fabric of his jacket and his sore arm was starting to hurt like a son of a bitch because of the strain he was putting on it. He shifted position slightly, relieving some of the pressure but froze in mid-movement when he heard a skittering noise to his left. Seconds later, his shoulders sagged with relief as a squirrel darted past.

He inflated his cheeks, holding his breath for a long moment, then sighed loudly. *Damn it, man, hurry up!* Sash hated waiting. Maybe he could just sneak out of there, creep in the shadows to the other side of the street, and get to the lawn under the roof line where he'd have a chance to catch what was being said. But as soon as the thought was formed, Eudora stopped her restless pacing to stand at the very edge of the widow's watch.

Leaning forward, she clasped the railing, and it looked to Sash as if she were staring directly at the clump of bushes where he hid. That was ludicrous, of course. He knew that. No way could she see all the way across the street and under the heavy thickness of fir branches. Hell, she stood bathed in the moon's glow, and he couldn't even make out *her* features. Not really. Only impressions. Still, his mind sketched in her eyes and nose and mouth. And he imagined that she was grinning; mocking him.

The conversation looked like it was becoming more animated as Abe began to wave his arms excitedly.

Sash elbowed his way forward a couple of inches and listened.

Nothing! Damn it!

Eudora was gesturing, pointing at something to the south past the point where he was lying. But at what? Lily's house?

Abe stepped around her, following the direction of her finger, then turned back, raising his own hands in apparent question.

But what the hell were they saying?

Sash hated this.

He was getting a crick in his neck, canting his head at such an odd angle so as not to miss anything.

"Hurry up, man," he said in a whisper. "Find out what the bitch wants and get the hell—"

Something glinted silver from the narrow door. Too quick for Sash to decide what it could be and then too late to do anything about it.

Eudora seemed almost to leap in the air suddenly. She staggered, two, three feet back until she was suspended over the railing that didn't quite reach her waist.

Sash saw Abe rush toward her, seeming to catch hold of her hands. And then Eudora was toppling over the side like a rag doll flipping head over heels.

Abe pitched forward in a last effort to catch her and even from the distance of his hiding place, Sash could hear his scream mingle gruesomely with hers as Eudora fell to the concrete driveway sixty feet below.

Sash twisted awkwardly beneath the low-hanging branches of the hedge, catching his jacket, then scraping his forehead painfully before finally managing to free himself. He sprang to his feet, lost his balance, and crashed into the bush, injured arm first. Cursing, he righted himself and darted across lawn and street to where his stepmother lay still and lifeless.

"Oh, my God, Eudora," he said in a choked cry as he fell to his knees beside her. She was dead. No doubt about it. A knife protruded from her chest, and blood spilled from the back of her head. But Sash's gaze was locked on the cold blue eyes staring lifelessly back at him.

"Oh, Jesus, sweet Jesus," Abe said in a breathless chant over and over as he tore from the house and out to the walk.

Sash glanced up, surprised that he'd forgotten all about the man in the horror of witnessing his stepmother's fatal fall.

The attorney was shaking from head to toe, and clearly on the verge of losing it.

"Hey, man," Sash called, pushing himself to his feet and racing for Abe. He grabbed his arm. "Let's go."

But Abe didn't move. Just stood there, tears running down his dark cheeks as he called on the Lord again and again.

Sash heard a woman screaming from somewhere inside the house.

"Come on, Abe, we gotta get out of here."

"I didn't do it, Sash," the man said through chattering teeth. "I don't know what happened, but as Jesus is my witness, I didn't kill that lady."

Now, a man was shouting from inside the house and lights had come on in the windows directly below the fourth-story widow's watch. Sash wondered if it was his father yelling for someone to call 911. He couldn't tell.

"Damn it, Abe, come on. Run!" he hissed in the lawyer's ear. "I know you didn't kill her, but it doesn't matter. You've been set up! In a few minutes, this hill is going to be crawling with cops out to get your ass. We've got to get you outta here."

But Joseph had found the body on the driveway with his eyes, and his face had paled almost white. Sash could see he wasn't going to move. He had no choice. That's what he told himself as he landed a fist squarely on Abe's chin.

Joseph was considerably smaller than Sash, so it wasn't a surprise when the punch sent him reeling backward. Sash caught him, pulled him forward again, then picked him up and slung him over his shoulder. Then he ran.

Sash stumbled over a fallen tree limb. He tried to catch himself, but with the dazed attorney still hanging over his shoulder, he couldn't recoup his balance. Both men fell to the ground, and began a roll down the steep incline.

Abe was the first to stop. A second later, he grunted as Sash tumbled into him.

Sash crawled to his knees, then got to his feet, though he remained doubled over for a long moment. He was winded and hurting.

"You okay, Rivers?" Abe asked as he got to his feet.

Sash nodded. "Just got the air knocked out of me," he managed finally. "Come on, we've got to get to Lily's."

Someone shouted behind them, and both men found a last burst of energy.

"They're gonna hang me," Abe said more to himself than to Sash.

A minute later, they were on the terrace at the back of Lily's house, Sash banging on the door and rattling the handle. "Nobody's going to do anything to you, Abe. We knew they were up to something. That's why I'm with you. We're going to get you out of here, but we have to stay calm," he said while they waited. His legs felt like rubber and every breath started a new spasm of pain in his side. He wondered if he hadn't cracked a rib in the fall. "We're going to get through this," he said firmly, though he knew it was himself he was reassuring.

Lily opened the door and both men rushed past her into the house. "Sash—"

"Close the door, Lil! Lock it!"

Lily did as she was told then demanded an explanation. "What happened?"

"Eudora's dead," he said shortly.

"Oh, my God! How? What did you do?"

"We didn't kill her," Abe answered. "But someone did, and now they're gonna come looking for me."

Sash was moving from window to window, peering out, checking the horizon for any sign that they'd been followed or that the police were already approaching. But the night was dark and still outside.

"All right," he said, unzipping his coat. "Give me your jacket, Joseph."

"Why?" Lily asked. "What are you going to do?"

"You're going to drive Abe out of here. Take him to the Ruby Palace Motel. Abe, you know where it is. You can direct her. Tell Lucky I said to go get your wife and children and old Joe Joe. And then you all stay hidden until I give the all clear, okay?"

The black man nodded. "Okay, but what are you going to do?"

But Sash was shaking his head. "Wait, tell me this. Did you touch anything in that house?"

"Nope, not a thing. I had my gloves on the whole time, just like we agreed. The lady didn't seem to notice, 'course I wasn't there that long before— Oh, Jesus, I just witnessed a murder!"

Lily grabbed Sash's arm, releasing it again when she

saw him wince and realized she'd hurt him. "Sorry, I forgot about your arm.

"But, Sash, I'm not moving till you tell me what you're going to do. Why are you switching jackets with Abe?"

"Look, princess, I don't know why Eudora was murdered except that someone wanted Abe set up. Now, whoever it was in that house who threw that knife, he or she is going to tell the police Abe did it. They'll have a description of a black man wearing sneakers, jeans, and a royal-blue jacket. I'm going to make them chase me long enough for you to get Abe and his family to safety. Then if they catch me, they'll be caught up short. Can't very well claim they were wrong, that it was Eudora's stepson they saw throw the knife."

"She was stabbed?" Lily asked, her face reflecting her horror.

Abe opened his mouth to say more, but Sash flashed him a warning glance. "Come on, Lily," he said instead. "We'd better get going."

"No, wait. Not until I figure out what's going to happen to you," she told Sash.

"I'll be okay. I'll try to keep them busy for a while, then double back here."

"Promise?" she said through trembling lips.

"I'll do my best," he said, bracketing her face between both hands. He kissed her soundly, then started to unhook the gold bracelet on his left wrist. "Here, you can wear this for me. It's always been lucky for me. With you wearing it, I know it'll get me back to you."

She stopped him, closing her hands over his. "No. If it's lucky for you, you need to be wearing it. You'll get back here, and I'll be waiting."

He kissed her again, then circled her shoulders with his arm as they walked toward the garage. "One more thing. Don't take Abe's car. We'll have to figure out a way to get rid of it tomorrow. And if you get stopped, don't argue. Explain that the two of you have been together going over some legal business all evening. But if they insist on taking Abe in, don't try to stop them. Just get to a phone and call Kitty or Genie or Rusty at my house."

"Rusty?" Lily asked, remembering the name from somewhere else.

"Never mind. Just do it. One of them will figure out what to do until I get back."

"This is crazy! Murder and conspiracy, decoys and contingency plans! This is not something that happens in real life."

"But it does. Here in Rosehill it's been happening for too long and people have been getting away with murder. Literally."

"But we thought Eudora was one of them. Now she's dead, too. How do we explain that?" Lily asked.

"I've got a theory, but it's going to have to keep," Sash said. "We've got to get going."

He'd heard something and now Abe and Lily heard it too. Sirens. A lot of them.

Sash kissed Lily once more, then the two men embraced. "You're a good man, Abraham Joseph. You stay safe until we get this all straightened out."

"I'm not ever going to forget the chance you're taking for me, man," Abe said.

Sash shook his head. "You got this a little backwards, buddy. *We* involved you, not the other way around."

A grin spread across the attorney's face. "Well, I guess we'll have to debate the who did what after this is all behind us. In the meantime, you keep your head low and out of the line of fire, ya hear?"

Sash watched the car roll away minutes later. He depressed the garage door control, stepping out into the night just as the first police car neared. He could see the flashing red-and-blue lights as he slipped around the side of the house, disappearing into the shadows.

"Well, looks like the dance is about to get under way." He inhaled deeply, wincing against another twinge of pain in his side. Not as sharp as before. Ribs were probably just bruised . . . like the rest of his aching body. In the morning, he was definitely going to treat himself to a long, hot, steamy bath.

If he lived that long.

Chapter Thirty-three

Imogene was just letting herself into her house when the telephone call came in. Dixon took it in the living room she started past the double doors. "Genie, wait! This concerns you."

With an impatient sigh, she dropped her coat and handbag in one of the twin water silk Chippendale chairs in the foyer. "What is so important that I couldn't even change my clothes before dealing with it?" she asked, pulling her high heel shoes off and padding barefoot across the thick Aubusson carpet.

She saw the color drain from her husband's face and felt tension knot in her shoulders. What now?

Hanging up the phone with studious care, he raised his gaze to hers, and she saw the tears that stood in his eyes just as his mouth crumpled. "Oh, darling, I'm so sorry," he said as he gathered her into his arms. "Something terrible has happened, Genie, darling. Your mother . . . Eudora has been . . . has been murdered."

Imogene stiffened in his arms. What in the name of God was he talking about? It was impossible that someone had killed Eudora. Why, right at this very moment, Abe Joseph was most likely sitting in her parlor suffering one of the mayor's famous "Shame on you" lectures.

Genie shrugged his arms away and stepped back to look at her husband's tearstained face. "No, Dix, honey, that simply can't be. I spoke with her just an hour ago. She said she was expectin' company and when her business was completed she would call me here," she concluded decisively. She smiled and raised a hand to wag a finger in his face. "And I have a bone to pick with ya'll. Mama was miffed with me 'cause of your little ol' tattletale phone call to her this morning. She—"

"Damn it, Genie, stop this!" Dixon said harshly, gripping her arms and shaking her. He lowered his voice, and his expression gentled. "I know how you dislike bad news, sweetheart. Ever since you were a little girl, you've managed to pretend bad things can't touch you. But this time, we're going to have to face it together."

Imogene slapped him with all her might. "Don't you dare tell me such a vile lie! No one would kill my mother!"

"The police are there now. At your parents' house, that is," Dixon said quietly, though he'd backed away from her after she struck him and continued to maintain the distance when he spoke again. "They've taken her body to the county morgue."

Genie was beginning to believe him. But how could this be? It just didn't make sense. She sat down on the edge of the sofa, letting the shoes she still held in one hand drop to the floor. "Was that my father who called?" she asked in a strangled voice.

Dixon sat before her on the heavy marble coffee table. Leaning forward, he took both of her hands in his, rubbing the back of each as he told her what he knew. "No, that was Stuart. Your father wasn't there when it happened. He arrived home just minutes ago, but the chief said he's having a pretty hard time."

"But Stuart was there when it happened. Isn't that what you said?"

Dixon frowned. Is that what Stuart had meant? That he'd actually witnessed Eudora's murder? "I don't think so. No, surely not. Else it wouldn't have happened, would it? I mean, he is the *chief* of police. A person doesn't commit a murder in front of a law enforcement officer."

Genie had been staring at the oil painting of her mother that hung on the far wall over the deacon's table. She looked at her husband now. "They do if the officer is involved in the plot to commit the murder, now don't they?"

"*What*—? Oh, God, Genie, think about what you're saying. Stuart wouldn't condone killing one of our own, much less sit by while it happened and not do anything."

"Just tell me what you *know*," she said. "Tell me what happened."

"But I don't really know that much, sweetheart. Not that much at all when I think about it. Why, you heard now long I was on the phone. Not more than a minute or two. Stuart said only that she'd been stabbed. Apparently Eudora had an appointment with a young attorney. She asked that one of her servants show him upstairs to her private studio when he arrived. A few minutes after he got there, the man was running from the house, and Eudora was dead on the driveway below. She'd fallen or was pushed from the widow's watch after being stabbed."

"Sounds to me like you're more clear on what happened than you realize, sugar," Imogene said with a disingenuous smile. "At least on all the important details that will go into the police record." She stood and glared down at him. "Tell me, doesn't it strike you as an amazing coincidence that her death is so astonishingly similar to Dr. Hutton's? I mean, doesn't it seem to you that the same people who orchestrated that poor man's death, might just have had a little something to do with my mama's?"

"Jesus Christ, Genie! Think what you're saying!" he said, rubbing his hands together as if suddenly chilled by the implication.

"Of course it would be necessary to come up with a different scapegoat this time. Not much you all could do about that, Sara being dead and all."

"This is crazy! You're in shock and not responsible for what you're saying," he said, getting up and striding hurriedly to the bar. "I understand, sweetheart. I'm pretty devastated by this myself. I think we both need a good stiff drink to calm us down. When we've recovered our equilibrium, we'll go sit with your poor daddy."

"So where's the lawyer? The one who had the supposed meeting with Mama? The police shoot him while he was making his escape?" she asked as if he hadn't spoken.

"Good Lord, Genie, how would I know where he is or if the police shot him. Damn it, how many times have I said I don't know anything more than what Stuart told me on the phone." He gripped the edge of the bar until his knuckles shone white. After a minute, his composure recovered, he said, "I'm sorry, Imogene. I apologize for raising my voice. It's just that this peculiar behavior of yours is unbecoming, and frankly, dear, a little unnerving." He'd spoken with his back to her, braced for another verbal attack. He was encouraged by her silence and turned with a smile in place. It slowly wilted when he discovered her gone.

Picking up a crystal goblet from the bar, he threw it at the marble fireplace. He derived little satisfaction from watching it smash into tiny shards. Contrary to what he'd admitted to his wife, he understood quite well where she was coming from with her questions.

But how in the hell did she know about the way life-and-death decisions were resolved in Rosehill? Clearly someone had ordered Eudora's execution and decided to blame it on the attorney who had an appointment with her.

But why? Death was always a last resort, a sentence handed down only in the most dire emergency and under pressure of the gravest threat.

No, it absolutely didn't make any sense. Even if Eudora had blundered across something damaging to the group, she would have kept it buried in her heart until her dying day.

Dixon shuddered on the last thought, remembering that today had been just that.

So, okay, if that wasn't it, than what? Was it possible that she had turned?

No way! That was even more absurd than his first wild theory. One of the others maybe if they were nailed to the wall. Even him, but not Eudora. If anything, her loyalty had always bordered on fanaticism. Besides, there was no way she could have turned without bringing ruin to herself. She was as guilty as any of them. More than some. No, something wasn't right.

He gulped down a shot of whiskey, refilled his glass, and repeated the action. The fire it started in his chest spread to his arms and legs, warming them and soothing his shattered nerves. He cast his eyes toward the ceiling, imagining his wife in her suite upstairs. He'd better go see to her. Calm her down somehow, and then he'd better be able to pull a satisfactory murderer out of the proverbial magician's hat.

Dixon poured himself another shot of the Canadian whiskey. His hand shook as he raised the glass to his lips.

Tears stood in his eyes and he realized for the first time that Genie hadn't shed even a single one. Shock?

Outrage? Or just because she was Imogene? Too self-centered and coldhearted to cry for another human being, even the woman who'd given her life?

Damn you, Genie, he thought as he crushed the delicate crystal glass in his hand.

He stared at the blood that bubbled from a dozen cuts, yet saw only his wife's perfect, flawless beauty.

She was everything a man should detest. A narcissistic, egomaniacal bitch who lied and sneaked behind his back, whoring around town and laughing in his face about it afterward. But she was beautiful and God help him, he loved her.

Chapter Thirty-four

Eudora Rivers was dead. Sash shook his head, struggling to accept such an impossible truth. He'd watched her fall, had knelt over her body and stared into her lifeless eyes, but it was only now, almost an hour later, that the reality of it slammed into his gut with the force of a battering ram. She'd been his stepmother for *almost* longer than memory served. Almost, not quite. Since he was four years old. Since only six months after his own mother had died. She'd been everything bad and ugly and mean that he'd known in early life. The lessons she'd taught with heavy-handed injustice had left scars that would never completely heal. And now she was dead.

He hunkered in the dark, watching the parade of official vehicles arrive outside the Rivers mansion, and he eulogized her. Bitch. Child abuser. Liar. Monster. Murderer. Mayor.

Mayor. He guessed it was a big, fucking deal when the top city official was murdered. That's why they'd brought out the militia. Jesus, there had to be fifty men traipsing over the grounds.

Sash's eyes widened as the back door of a van was opened and a team of bloodhounds piled out.

He shouldn't have hung around, waiting to see what was up. *Nosy and stupid*, he cursed himself as he turned around, still hunkering and trying to sneak away without alerting the dogs either by sound or sight. Scent he couldn't do much about. He could only hope it took them a while to get on to the one they were supposed to be sniffing out.

He crossed the outer boundaries of the Hutton property at a low crouching gait until he reached the woods. Then he straightened. His escape through the woods to the pier wasn't going to be easily navigated, not in the dark with the ground slippery with wet fallen leaves and mud left behind by the recent rain. Those guys with their trained mutts had a lot going for them that Sash didn't. Hiking boots for one thing; flashlights for another.

Sash grunted as he slid to the ground, landing soundly on his backside. He was going to have to do better than this if he was going to get away. Haul ass rather than scoot ass.

Above him he heard the dogs begin to bay, and his heart sent back a loud responding tattoo.

Sash could see the amber mercury lights along the pier in the distance below, but already flashes of light from above were glinting off the trees around him and he was starting to doubt his ability to make it to safety in time. If he could just—

He fell again, rolling several feet until he crashed into a boulder, stopping his fall. He lay there stunned for ten or fifteen seconds, then pushed himself to his feet again.

Why hadn't he gotten into that car with Lily and Abe? But no use asking that one. The answer was easy. Because of Lily. Because she'd come back and put the bad guys on notice that she wasn't leaving until she'd cleared her mother's name. Because with her quiet declaration, she'd effectively rattled their cages and made them mad. Because he'd fallen in love with her. And now he had to keep her safe . . .

But first he had to get away from those fucking dogs.

Lily stopped the car at the intersection approaching East Hill Road. The night was overcast and chilly, so she had the windows rolled up. The radio was turned on as she listened for word of Eudora's death. But even still she heard dogs barking in the distance. Not just the ordinary yip of penned pets, but the strident, yawping wail of dogs on the trail of their quarry. She cracked her window, straining an ear toward the sound she remembered so vividly from her childhood years in Oklahoma. Many of her Native-American relatives hunted with hounds, and though she'd always abhorred the sport, she'd long ago learned to recognize the different pitches accompanying each stage of the hunt.

The dogs' barks were insistent yet spaced apart and Lily knew they'd found the scent of their game; Sash's scent.

Her hands gripped the steering wheel with white-knuckled intensity as she remembered the chilling sounds of plaintive yowls and wails that signaled cornered game. She knew what happened to even the most gentle, mild-mannered hunter when his quarry was caught by the pack. A true sportsman always used his gun before the dogs' razor-sharp canines did too much damage.

But the men pursuing Sash weren't sportsmen. They were a search party on the trail of a man they believed to be a cold-blooded killer. She doubted they'd demonstrate much compassion.

She had to get to Sash before they did.

A car behind her at the stop sign tooted its horn angrily, and Lily quickly sped through the intersection, pulling over to the shoulder to let the driver pass. As soon as it was clear, she maneuvered a U-turn, heading southeast this time.

As she neared the pier, she could see lights in the wooded hillside to her left; flickering rays that she was sure were beams cast by flashlights. The dogs were yelping more stridently, and Lily let loose a ragged, stuttering breath with her fear.

She parked the car in the same parking lot she'd first revisited with her uncle the night before her mother's funeral, and climbed quickly from the car.

Behind her, a crowd was gathering outside the Striped Tuna. She remembered the bartender's claim that most of the men who frequented the bar were fishermen. Like Sash.

For just a second, she considered petitioning them for help. She discarded the idea just as quickly. It would take too long to muster their support. By the time she rallied his coworkers, he could well be mauled to death by the dogs or shot by one of the eager posse.

Lily judged the searchlights to be only a hundred yards or so above her now. She squinted against the darkness, searching the foothills and bottomlands for a glimpse of Sash. Nothing. But the night was as dank and black as pitch. He could be there somewhere, still ahead of the dogs ... terrified but alive.

"Oh, please, God, keep him safe," she murmured as she pulled the hood of her coat up and started off at a sprint across the parking lot, avoiding the boardwalk that was well-lighted, and heading into the woodlands. This was where he would emerge. Somewhere along the beach ... unless they cut him off, she thought with sinking optimism as revolving blue-and-red dome lights of arriving police cruisers flashed through the trees.

Hiding behind a tree trunk, she saw the marked cars pull to a stop behind the red Chevy in the beach park-

ing lot, forming a chain of vehicles that would prevent
anyone from crossing their lines without detection.

There! Above her to the left, she thought she'd
caught movement, something dark and at least as tall
as a man. She stared for several seconds. Nothing. Her
shoulders sagged with disappointment.

Where are you, Sash? Please, please, be okay. I need you.
Her eyes widened with the silent admission. It had been
a long time since she'd confessed dependence on another human being. Even to herself. And even in this
moment of terror a smile found its place on her face. It
felt pretty damn good to want a man to watch over her.

He didn't know it yet, but she was handing him her
heart. She pressed her forehead against the cool bark
of the tree trunk, squeezing her eyes shut. "Find me,
Sash," she whispered.

They were getting too close, and it wouldn't be long
until they found him. Sash knew that his time and options were running out. He'd discarded Abe's jacket earlier, hoping to slow the dogs down. And it had worked
for a few minutes, but they were back on his trail now
and not too far above him. At times when the wind
shifted, he could even hear the voices of the men tag-
ging after the dogs.

He was crouched low, analyzing his options. The pier
and the ocean were straight ahead to the south. Two
minutes earlier, that had been an option open to him.
Now, some clever tactician had blocked his way by
forming a chain with police cars.

To the east, a rock wall separated him from the sea.
He'd climbed it many times, but never with dogs baying
at his heels and expert riflemen training their weapons
on him. Once he left the thick foliage of trees and
waist-high brush, he'd be completely exposed and a perfect target.

To the north, just over the rise, the woods changed, became thicker, denser, dripping moss and mired in mud, water, and quicksand. Sash pulled his lips back in a grimace at the prospect of going in there at night.

He hated the swamps. Just thinking about going into them made his skin crawl.

A shaft of light fanned above his head with only inches to spare, and he fell to the ground, pressing his cheek against the cold, wet soil. He could feel the earth tremble against his ear as the posse approached, and he thought he could even make out the sound of the dogs snorting and sniffing at the air. Too close. Time was running out. He had to decide. He didn't think they'd follow him into the swamps. He wasn't worth the loss of their precious dogs. Besides, odds were the swamps would take care of business for them.

Or he could give himself up. 'Course that wasn't really an option. Not since he'd heard one of his stalkers call out to another man, "Ya'll hear Stuart say he didn't care if we brought the bastard back dead or alive? Suits me just fine. I see the murdering fucker, I'm gonna blow his freakin' head off!"

The light that had flashed just above his head moved away, fanning the trees to his right. Sash raised himself up to sprint position, ready to run.

But a sound directly below him, less than ten yards away, caused him to abort his dash. Judas Priest, were they coming up from the bottom already? Did he have time to make a run for it?

Straining his neck, he searched the inky darkness for sight of the person or critter that had made the noise. A light caught a copse of trees, illuminating them for just a second before passing on by, but long enough.

Holding his breath, Sash circled behind the trees, coming up on the dark figure too quickly for anything but a startled cry which he cut off almost before it was born with a hand clamped tightly over the mouth. "Be quiet!" he hissed. "It's me. It's Sash."

Lily thought she was going to be sick. He'd scared the crap out of her, but it was the words he was whispering in her ear that were inspiring the nausea.

"They're going to kill me, Lily. There's no chance to surrender. I'm going to have to try to cut across the back of the hill and run into the swamps."

His hand still covered her mouth, so Lily nodded her understanding, twisting her head and trying to see his face.

"I don't think I can leave you out here, princess," he continued, his voice still as soft as a whistled breeze. "But the swamps could be worse."

She placed a hand over his fingers, tugging them and signaling her need to respond. He took them away from her mouth. "I'm going with you."

Their eyes locked for a long, eloquent moment. His asked if she was certain, hers responded with trust. She slipped her hand inside his and mouthed, "Let's go."

The night had seemed dark in the forest under the cover of ancient oaks, stocky palmettos, and leafy magnolias. But Lily had never experienced blackness like that which closed around them when they entered the swamplands. There was evil in a world as shrouded and tenebrous as this. She felt it touch her spirit, and she feared they were never going to emerge alive.

As if sensing her thoughts, Sash tightened his hold on her, drawing her closer, and she could feel his tension in the rippling of the heavily corded arm that encircled her.

Lily wasn't sure how long they'd walked since entering this wet marshland. They couldn't have come far. Each step they took needed testing. Was the ground beneath them solid, not sinking like quicksand? Was it slimy with moss that lined the water's edge? And what about above them, where snakes curled from tree branches?

They hadn't spoken a single word for fear of drawing the dogs or men in after them, despite the risk. But Sash seemed to know that terror was threatening Lily's sanity, for he suddenly kissed her brow and said, "We're staying on the periphery, moving west."

"How . . . how do you . . . know?" she asked.

"Feel the breeze on your cheek. It's coming from the ocean at the east. After a time, we'll be too far away to feel it, but by then we should be able to hear the brook that runs between the hills. Don't think about where we are, think about where we're going. Close your eyes if you have to. I won't let go of you."

And she believed him. She turned to him, wrapping both arms around his waist, waiting and trusting, and after a time of focusing on where they were headed, she even quit smelling the brackish water and stopped hearing the terrifying night sounds.

It seemed as if days passed rather than minutes and hours. Lily's legs grew heavy with weariness and mud caked to her ankles. Insects bit her tender skin and, twice, moss clung to her hair and covered her face. She screamed the first time, refusing to quiet until Sash had freed her from it. The second time, she merely mewled like a kitten too weak to fight anymore. But just when she thought Sash must have led them in the wrong direction, deeper into the bowels of this nightmare, she heard the splashing, gurgling sound of water dancing over rocks.

"I hear it, Sash," she said, pulling free of his arm and trying to run toward the beautiful noise. Sash grabbed for her, catching the back of her coat and pulling her backward against him.

Lily struggled with him, but he held fast. "Stop it, Lily! We're almost out, but not yet. We still have several hundred feet of dangerous bogs to cross. One wrong move, and I could lose you."

Lily heard the logic of what he was telling her, but she'd had all she could take. She fell against him, sobbing and screaming. "I can't! God help me, I can't stand the darkness!"

Sash picked her up in his arms, cradling her like a baby. He crooned to her, making promises, reciting silly childhood poems, then coarse limericks learned in his work as a merchant marine.

Lily continued to weep, but her cries became quieter, and after a while, incredibly, her tormented mind found escape in sleep.

And then Sash was suddenly shaking her and calling her name. "Wake up, Lily. It's all over. We're safe."

Lily opened her eyes. She was lying on the ground, curled up in a tight ball. She saw the grass and the sparkling water. She blinked, turned her head, and saw the sky. Stars winked back at her, and then she saw his face above hers. She wasn't dreaming. It was true, she could *see*! She could see *him*. His face was filthy, covered with mud and muck and he looked wonderful. She giggled. "Do I look as bad as you?"

A slow grin spread and laughter rumbled. "Baby, you look like a million bucks!"

Chapter Thirty-five

"What now?" Lily asked her reflection in the bathroom mirror several hours later.

This time yesterday, she'd been a different person. A woman looking for reasons why a tragic miscarriage of justice had been perpetrated against her family, yet prepared to accept that sometimes life doesn't grant answers to every question one poses. She'd planned to return to New York in a few days, resuming her career, and putting the past in its proper perspective. She might have failed to change it, but that didn't mean she had to accept the account written in the history books.

That was before all hell broke loose. That was before she knew Errol was missing. That Sash was in the house the night her father died. That someone was so afraid of the questions she was asking, they'd murdered Eudora and framed Abe Joseph in the hope of getting rid of him and shutting up his grandfather. And that was before she realized she'd fallen in love with Sash.

She sat on the edge of the bathtub. What was she going to do about that?

She jumped when someone knocked on the door. "Lil, you all right?"

Sash. Who else? She grinned. "Be out in a minute.

Why don't you go on down to the kitchen, and see what Kitty left in the fridge?"

"Uh-uh," he said. "I'm not budging till you open this door and let me see for myself that it's really you and not some swamp thing I carried out of there."

Lily laughed, but a frisson of leftover fear coursed through her at the reminder of the nightmare they'd shared. "Give me a couple of minutes. I still have to brush my teeth. I'll meet you in the kitchen and fix us something to eat. I promise."

"Are you a woman who can be counted on to keep her word?" He teased through the door.

"Absolutely," Lily said on a giggle.

"Okay, you're down to ninety-five seconds," he said, and she heard him walk away.

She lowered her face, covering it with her hands. They still hadn't talked, and he owed her some answers. About Joe Joe's seeing him there the night her father died. About Errol's disappearance, Kitty's lies, his relationship with Imogene that had seemed so superficial at the dinner party yet was obviously much more involved. Eudora. *My God, she's really dead.*

And was it only coincidence that she'd died in almost the exact same way Lily's father had?

A shiver ran the length of her spine. Just like before, the police had a suspect, and again the obvious wasn't obvious at all.

Only now, Lily wasn't a little girl any longer. She was old enough to fight back.

Everything is changed forever after today. You're going to find all the answers you've searched for, and no matter what happens, you won't be left unchanged.

Where had that come from?

And then she remembered something Uncle Jesse said to her years before when she was leaving for New York.

You're going to be alone for a while until you get settled and start making friends, Lily Dawn. But remember that our ancestors have handed down a precious gift through the ages. They've given us the knowledge that we are never alone. No matter where we walk, our spirit guide goes with us. If we take the time to listen, we'll hear his gentle whispering.

Lily smiled. She understood what her spirit guide had murmured to her heart.

Standing before the mirror once again, she removed the towel she'd wrapped around her head, letting her tangled, wet hair tumble loose. She combed it with patient concentration until it fell in a silky veil around her face and shoulders. She brushed her teeth and gargled with mouthwash. She leaned into the mirror for a final inspection, and was pleased by what she saw.

Though there were dark hollows beneath her eyes, a lively glow sparkled and danced in her warm sherry gaze. The golden perfection of her coloring was marred by insect bites, bruises on her brow and jaw, and a scratch on the bridge of her nose, but they paled against the glow in her cheeks and the flush that reddened her lips.

Opening the bathroom door, she hesitated only a moment to listen for her spirit guide again, then smiled at the quiet that answered her. She didn't need it to tell her what to do now. She had no doubts.

She entered the kitchen, stopping just inside the door.

"Wow," Sash said, looking around from the stove where he was spreading bacon in a skillet. "You look beautiful."

Lily smiled. He really didn't see the ugly souvenirs of their ordeal the night before.

"Hey, old Uncle Sander's rags fit me pretty good,"

he said of the sweat pants he wore without the shirt. "Top was a little too tight. But at least I'm decent."

"Sash—"

"You hungry? I'm frying up some bacon and scrambling eggs. Benefits of baching it all these years. I'm a hell of a good cook. I make a mean omelette, but it takes time, and I thought you were probably starving."

"Sash?"

He'd been talking with his back to her as he broke eggs into a bowl, but he looked at her now and the smile he'd worn was gone. "I know, princess. We've got to talk. I owe you a lot of explanations, and I swear I'll give you every one. But let's eat first." A grin started. "I talk better when I'm sated."

"Good, 'cause I listen better, too," she said, a smile teasing the corners of her lips.

"Okay, then I'm just gonna—"

She'd come up behind him when he turned his attention back to the meal he was preparing. Her body pressed against his back, she covered his hard, muscled chest with her hands. She splayed her fingers and dug the heels of her palms into his warm, smooth flesh. A long red gash sliced across his shoulder blade, and Lily kissed it gently. "Make love to me, Sash."

Sash turned off the bacon, and turned to face her. He held her face between his hands and looked into her eyes, which were amber with passion. "I'm going to make love to you, Lily. But not yet. I told you, I won't have your mother or anything else between us when we—"

"She isn't between us. Not anymore, Sash. And I want to hear the truth about why you were here in this house the night my father died, why you didn't stay to talk to the police, all of it. But none of it matters more than what I feel for you and what I think you feel for me."

Sash searched her face for a long moment, then scooped her up into his arms. He carried her up the stairs to her room and laid her on the bed.

"You are the most beautiful woman I have ever known," he said as he placed a knee on either side of her hips and threaded her fingers with his. He eased her arms over her head, and leaned down to kiss her.

His lips were tender and patient, not hurrying but tasting and savoring, like a delicacy never before sampled. He drew her full bottom lip between his and let his tongue slide over it.

He was starting a fire using the most persuasive kindling, and Lily groaned as a smoldering warmth spread in the pit of her stomach.

She arched her neck and opened her mouth wider under his, silently pleading for more.

Sash refused her, taunting her by taking his lips from hers and brushing the hollow of her throat with feathery kisses.

Then he pulled away from her, sitting up and gazing into those pools of liquid fire. Taking his hands from hers, he gripped the hem of her shirt with his fingers and said, "I want to see you. When my hands discover every inch of you, I want to see you with my eyes and record it in my mind to be remembered later."

She didn't answer, and he accepted her silence as acquiescence. He moved off of her, to the side as he undressed her.

He raised her shirt slowly, an inch at a time, his fingertips barely grazing the creamy, smooth skin of her sides and stomach. He raised it halfway over her breasts, stopping for a moment to let his thumbs trace their soft, plump curves, then grazed her swollen nipples with his nails.

Lily trembled and licked her lips with her tongue as she silently begged for more. And then she felt his hot breath on one of her nipples just before his tongue moved over it, teasing and flicking. His mouth closed over it, sucking and nipping as his hand closed over the fullness of her other breast.

Lily raised herself to him as she ran her hands through his hair and urged him on.

With a loud groan, Sash raised his face. "I want to take my time," he said in a strangled confession. "I want to look at you before . . ."

Lily shook her head. "We have forever to look. Right now, I want you, Sash. I think I've waited my whole life for this. Don't make me wait any longer." She reached between his legs, circling his penis through the thick flannel of his pants with her hand.

Sash closed his eyes and reared back as scorching flames shot through his groin.

He pulled her shirt over her head, then peeled her pants from her hips. His eyes followed every inch that his hands moved, stopping just above her legs at the thick nest of black curls. He wanted to cup her buttocks in his hands, force her hips up and bury his face in her wetness.

Not yet, not yet, not yet.

He pulled her pants the rest of the way past her knees and off her feet, tossing them to the floor beside her shirt.

Lily's hands were moving over his belly, to his chest, as eager and inquisitive as his own. Raising up on his knees, he pushed the sweat pants from his hips, freeing his manhood and feeling it pulse wildly as her eyes discovered its magnificence.

"Oh, God, I want you, Sash," she said, shutting her eyes as her hand closed over him again, this time with nothing separating her from his throbbing hardness.

Sash nudged her thighs apart with his knee, lowering his mouth to the slight swell of her belly. His fingers parted the lips of her womanhood, and slipped inside her. With her free hand, she covered his, urging him deeper.

She nearly cried out as he skillfully brought her close to her first climax, then drew back. She lifted herself up onto her elbow to protest, but he only grinned wickedly. "Lie back," he said. "I want to taste you."

And before she could respond, he spread her legs and savored her sweetness.

Lily writhed and bucked, begging him to stop the exquisite torture, but he was a relentless and selfish lover, exploring her hidden core to his heart's content.

He felt her tense with another powerful climax, held her against his mouth until it passed, then raised himself above her. "I love you, Lily Dawn Hutton," he said just before he covered her mouth with his and buried himself inside her.

Lily cried out as he filled her and dug her nails in his back against the exquisite agony he was creating in her.

A tidal wave of passion rose up to claim them, and they rode it together. Her legs locked around his hips, she closed her muscles around him tighter and tighter with every powerful thrust. He reared back and plunged into her one final time, his lips parted in a snarl of ecstasy.

When his release was complete, he collapsed, exhausted against Lily's chest.

Lily held him in her arms, smoothing his damp hair from his brow and cradling his head like a mother with a child at her breast. Proof of their shared passion still filled her with its warmth, and she closed her eyes with a smile on her lips.

She had almost dropped off to sleep when he called to her. "Princess?"

"Hmm?"

"You sleepy?"

"Mmhmm."

"Okay, I'll let you rest. But, first, two things I want you to know."

She waited.

"What we just did? That was making love," he said.

"It certainly was," she agreed.

"When we wake up, we're gonna fuck."

She grinned. She liked the sound of that promise. Sort of naughty and definitely nice. "I'll look forward to it," she said, and closed her eyes.

Chapter Thirty-six

By the time Lily and Sash crawled from bed nearly six hours later, and showered again—this time together—they knew the true meaning of the word *starving*.

The telephone rang as they sat at the kitchen table scarfing down their meal. Her mouth full, Lily could only signal her decision to let it ring with a wave of her hand. A moment later, her bite swallowed, she explained. "The answering machine will pick it up, and we can return the call later."

"Fine with me," Sash said, shrugging his shoulders indifferently.

He was just about to shovel in another mouthful of hash browns when Lily's fork clattered to her plate.

"Oh, my gosh, Sash, I forgot all about Imogene. Her mother was murdered last night. She must be devastated. That was probably her looking for you."

She was halfway out of her chair, when Sash caught her wrist, drawing her down again. "Now, wait a minute. Let's say you're right, about her being upset, I mean. I'm sure you are. No matter what a depraved bitch I thought Eudora was, she was still Genie's mother ... and a good one far as I know. But Genie's tough. If I know her at all, which I do, she got all her crying done last night. Today, she's busy arranging an elaborate funeral complete with eulogies and scriptures to be delivered by heads of state and celebrities."

"That's terrible," Lily accused as the phone quieted.

"You're missing the point. I'm just being honest. Besides, it's not an insult. Eudora was a bitch with a capital B, but she was still the mayor and married to the CEO of a Fortune 500 business. I'm only saying that my sister will do up Eudora's funeral the way she would have wanted it." He paused, his expression grave. "You and I have some talking to do. After we're done, I'll call Genie. See how she's doing and fill her in on what I saw and how it went down."

"If she's interested," Lily said.

"What does that mean, if she's interested? Why wouldn't she want to know how her mother died?"

Lily shook her head. "She would, of course, but maybe not today."

Sash thought that one over for a few seconds, then nodded. "Yeah, I can see that. So, if I don't have to tell her all the gory details today, I don't have to worry about calling her back."

Lily put the last of her toast in her mouth, washed it down with milk, and wiped her mouth. "You're right. You're a very good cook. But now I'm tired again," she added, stretching seductively.

"Tired. Hmm, is that a euphemism for what we—"

"*No!*" She reached across the table and slapped his hand.

"No? Then how come your cheeks are so rosy all of a sudden?"

"It's called afterglow, smart-ass, and it's not all of a sudden."

"Aw, don't get mad," he said, standing up and leaning over the table to kiss her.

She grinned. "But I'm ready if you are."

Sash chased her up the stairs, capturing her on the second-floor landing and pinning her to the floor.

"Not here!" Lily squealed.

"Why not? You too delicate to take it on the floor?"

"No, I'm not too delicate, but I am prudish enough not to want someone walking in on us."

"Who could walk in on us? It's Kitty's day off and Sander has moved out."

He expected more teasing argument, but the laughter had gone out of her eyes, and Sash knew what had happened. Letting go of her wrists, he sat on the top step, his hands between his knees, and his back to her. "You want me to tell you about Errol first?"

He heard her moving and knew she was sitting up. After a moment, she sat on the step beside him. "He's my friend, Sash. That's all. We're not involved ... romantically. That was over a long time ago, but that doesn't mean I don't care about him. I care a lot, and I was worried sick when I realized he hadn't gone back to New York."

"Someone ran him down," Sash said shortly, then hated himself when he heard her sharp intake of breath. "He's going to be okay. He was lucky. Genie found him right after it happened. And Kitty was here. Between the two of them, they were able to get him in the back of Kitty's truck. Genie called me. Went over his injuries as far as she could tell from a cursory exam. I told her to bring him to my place. Then I got a doctor friend of mine to come there and look him over."

"But why? Who? Where?"

"We think someone was trying to send you a message: 'See what can happen if you don't mind your own business and stay out of ours.' The who was Eudora. At least we're pretty sure she's the one who gave the order to do it. I don't suppose we'll ever know for sure now that she's dead. Just another unsolved mystery to add to our list."

"But why didn't you tell me? Why have Kitty go to all the trouble of packing up his things and fabricating an elaborate story about a train trip home to New York?"

"Because I didn't want you getting hurt, and that's exactly what would have happened if you'd found out. Don't tell me it isn't, 'cause I've already seen you in action. You act first, think second."

Lily thought about that. "Okay," she said at last, "how badly is he hurt?"

"Like I said, the man got real lucky. A broken femur, two cracked ribs, and some fairly nasty cuts and bruises. Had to have stitches on his head." He decided not to tell her just how far Errol's luck ran. Three feet either way, he would have missed the ledge that saved his life. Lily didn't need that on top of everything else.

She pulled herself to her feet using one of the stair dowels. "Well, now that we're into it, why don't we go downstairs to the den? There's a lot I want to know, and it's probably going to take some time to tell. We might as well be comfortable."

Sash followed her down without comment. In the early moments inside the swamp the night before, he'd wondered if they would make it out alive. The one thought that had comforted him as he faced the prospect of death, was the consolation that then he wouldn't have to tell Lily about his cowardice the day her father died. Now, it couldn't be avoided.

"Where do you want me to start?" he asked as he stood at the window looking out through the sheer lace curtains.

"Come sit down," Lily invited.

"Naw, I think better on my feet."

"Okay, well start anywhere you like." She stretched

out on the sofa, tucking her hands beneath her head. It was a relaxed pose, but on the inside, her stomach was churning with dread.

It took Sash several minutes to begin, but Lily waited, not pushing or prodding. She lay there with her eyes closed, so she didn't know that he'd come to stand behind the couch and was looking at her with love and regret mingling in his dark blue eyes.

"I've never forgiven myself for what happened the day your father was murdered, Lil. You have to know that first of all." He saw her stiffen, and hastened to add, "I didn't kill him, but I could have stopped it if I just hadn't been so afraid."

Lily remembered how brave he'd been the night before in the swamp. "I don't believe that," she said. "But go on, tell me all of it."

"I was grounded. No big deal, I was always being punished for something. Eudora and Dad were gone. Dad had business to attend to. The bitch was supposed to be at a church meeting. Genie and I were home alone.

"She was watching TV so I decided to sneak out, go see your mom for a while. I knew you'd gone to the city with your uncle, and I thought Dr. Alison would be at the hospital on rounds. But he was there, too. I almost changed my mind about going. He was upstairs, coming in and out of the bedroom onto the gallery. She was in the studio, working out a new routine, I guess. She kept testing a move, then adding it to what she'd practiced earlier. I watched her for a long time before deciding to go on over there.

"I went around to the front door because I didn't want your dad coming downstairs and thinking I'd just sneaked in. I was going to ring the bell, but the door was open. Not just cracked. Wide open like someone was in such a hurry they forgot to close it. I remember thinking someone must have been there earlier, 'cause I knew they weren't having company now. I'd just seen her dancing, and he was ... well, he didn't look like he was expecting visitors."

"He was drinking," Lily said, filling in what he hadn't wanted to tell her. "I know. It was in the autopsy report. Go on."

"I closed the door, and started off toward the studio. I was just about there when I realized the music wasn't playing anymore. Then I heard a noise upstairs, and I thought, 'Great, Rivers, you've probably just walked in on an argument.'" He sat down in the chair across from her, letting his long legs stretch out in front of him as he stared up at the ceiling. "I just stood there, looking up like that was going to help me figure out what to do. Talk about stupid. I didn't want to leave without seeing her. But neither did I want them to catch me there and think I was snooping.

"I decided to get out of there. Come back later if Eudora didn't come home too early. That's when I heard the screams." He covered his face with his hands as he explained further. "His first, I think. Then Sara's. Hers was terrible. A long, pitiful wail. I ran for the stairs, but before I got there, I saw them coming down the steps. Running."

"Who?" Lily asked.

Sash shook his head and dropped his hands. "I don't know. There were three of them. They all had black robes on, and hoods. I keep trying to remember their shoes, but I don't see anything. I must have seen them, though! I was standing just below the staircase."

"What happened then?" she asked, her voice as tight as her fists at her sides.

"I ran," he said simply. "I thought they'd been murdered, Lil. Both of them. There wasn't a sound upstairs, and I was afraid whoever murdered them would come back, find me, and kill me, too."

He didn't speak again for several long seconds, and Lily opened her eyes to look at him. Tears poured from his eyes and his face was twisted in a mask of such raw anguish, Lily thought her heart would break for him. She pushed herself off the sofa and fell down in front of him on her knees. "You were sixteen years old. You weren't a coward. You reacted the way anyone would have. I don't blame you. I just wish you'd been here to tell the police that Sara didn't do it."

"Oh, my God, Lil, don't you think I've wished the same thing every day of my life since I found out she was still alive? That's why I went to see her all the time. Two or three times a week whenever I wasn't out on the boats."

"But why so secretive about it?"

Sash wiped the wetness from his cheeks, and Lily noticed again the thin gold chain that he wore on his wrist. It had a single gold bead with some kind of inscription written on it. She was curious, but now was not the time. They were talking about her mother, and she had to hear it all.

"I knew she was catatonic. I'd read about it . . . I was afraid if your father's killers found out I was going to see her, they might think there was a chance, however slim, that she'd respond to me and tell me who was there."

"She called me," Lily said quietly, her arms resting on his legs, her face turned up toward his. "Did you make that happen?"

"I think so. I'm not sure, but I think I finally penetrated that wall she'd erected around her mind. The last couple of weeks that I went to see her, she began to move a little here and there. First a finger, then her entire hand. And a little later, her feet. I even swore she looked at me, but the night charge nurse argued against the possibility. Then, one night, she whispered my name, Lil. It wasn't real clear and it wasn't strong, but I understood what she said. And as God is my witness, she tried to smile."

Lily was weeping, now. Crying and laughing and choking on the emotion that had filled her heart and was spilling over. "Thank you," she said, reaching for his neck and pulling him down so she could hug him tightly.

Sash gave her the time she needed, then gently untangled her arms, clasping her hands in his and holding her there so he could look into her eyes. "She died because of me," he said, slowly, carefully enunciating each word so there could be no mistake that she heard him.

"What is that supposed to mean?" she asked. She shook her head. "No, I believe someone killed her, making it look like a heart attack, but you'll never convince me it was you. Not when you loved her like you did." She laughed sharply. "That's ridiculous. Why would you even suggest such a thing?"

"Lily, stop! They—whoever *they* really are—didn't kill Sara. And neither did I. At least, not the way you think."

"But why ... ? I don't get it. She was only forty-seven years old. Her heart was strong, wasn't it?"

"She was heavily medicated for fifteen years, Lily. The drugs used in the treatment of mental illness are unpredictable. Long-term use can cause irreversible damage to every major organ in the body. Liver, kidneys, *heart*. She died of natural causes." He inhaled deeply, then said, "Only I think she'd still be alive if I hadn't interfered. What did it matter that she came out of that ... that trance she was in if I didn't find out anything and she died because of it?"

"You're wrong!" Lily said, her expression reflecting her passion. "She *wasn't* alive all those years. Not like she was before. You released her from that hell *they* sent her to. If she were here, she'd thank you as I do."

"She was everything to me, Lil. I don't mean I was in love with her. Not in the way I thought when I was a kid. I had a hell of a crush on her though."

Lily laughed. "No kidding."

"Yeah, guess that's no surprise, huh? I was over here every chance I got." He stared off in space for a moment, then laughed. "You hated me always hanging around."

"Sometimes," she admitted with a shrug. "But other times, I didn't really notice. Daddy called you Mama's shadow, but he wasn't ever jealous of you like I was at times when I didn't want to share her."

Sash shook his head and his eyes had that faraway look again. "No, he wouldn't have been jealous. He wasn't like that. Besides, Sara was nuts over him. I remember once when I was thirteen or fourteen, I came over for dinner. You let me in, and as I usually did, I went tearing for the kitchen. I was going to offer to help her. That way I could be with her the whole time, but they were kissing. She was embarrassed when they saw me. But Dr. Ali was cool about it. Said something about hoping I got as lucky as he had when I was ready to fall in love."

"What did you say?"

"Nothing. I just kept looking at her looking at him and I thought, 'No way, man. You already got her.'" He smiled then, shaking off the memory. "But I was wrong. I just didn't have the foresight to realize I was obsessing over the wrong Hutton woman."

Lily sat on his lap. "Hold me."

"You finished talking? You don't want to know about my tragic childhood, or my investigation into all the 'accidental deaths' that always seem to benefit one of our illustrious family members here on the hills?"

"That's right. You and I are related, aren't we? How distant is it?"

"Distant enough that we don't have to even think about it," he said.

"Good, 'cause I'd hate to feel guilty about anything as yummy as sex with you."

He grinned, slowly, suggestively. "So, I guess we're done talking, huh?"

"No," she said, sticking out her bottom lip in an attractive pout.

Sash kissed her, capturing her jutting lip between his teeth and running his tongue over it before standing up with her still in his arms. "This isn't going to work, princess. If we're going to talk, there's got to be at least a few feet between us. I can't think straight when you're tempting me like that."

"Thinking straight doesn't seem to be your only problem," she said, her eyes on the swelling bulge in his pants. Then she was laughing fully, like she hadn't done in a very long time, as his face darkened from a deep bronzed tan to purple.

"You didn't think it was so funny in the bedroom," he grumbled.

"I'm sorry," Lily said, struggling against her amusement. "Sit down and tell me more. I'll be good, I promise."

"I'm going to go get me a beer. You want one?"

Lily shook her head, fighting to keep her expression blank until he left the room. Then she placed a pillow over her face, holding it against her mouth to muffle her gales of laughter.

By the time he returned she was sitting crossed-legged on the sofa, her arms wrapped around the pillow. "You're cute when you're embarrassed," she said, holding up a hand to stop his protest when he scowled at her. "Wait! I'm not going to tease you anymore. You just looked like a little boy and I realized while you were in the kitchen that I don't remember you until you were a teenager. Do you think later, after the funeral, Jason would mind if I looked at some of your baby pictures?"

"There aren't any," Sash said, leaning against the fireplace and tipping up the bottle.

"What do you mean, there aren't any? Everybody has snapshots of their kids when they're little. Are you saying your mother didn't ever take any?"

"Nope. I'm saying Eudora burned them all. Tossed them one by one into the fireplace while I was forced to sit and watch. Said something like 'nobody likes bad little boys, so why keep pictures of them?' "

"But that's appalling!"

"You have no idea."

"What about your father? Didn't he ever stick up for you?"

"Mostly, he wasn't around so he didn't know. He worked all hours when he was in town, and traveled two or three weeks each month. Besides, Eudora used to threaten me if I ever bothered my 'poor, tired father.' "

"No wonder you liked being at our house," Lily said, her voice reflecting her horror and awe. Were there really demons out there like that?

"That was the one thing I ever really wanted that I got, and that was only because I was smart enough to go to my dad with a story about Sara helping me with my homework and my art.

"You remember how I was able to guide us out of the swamp last night?"

Lily nodded as a shudder rocked her.

"That's because I was in there by myself once. Eudora took me there one morning. Parked the car as close as she could and marched me to the edge. I'd made the mistake of asking to become a Boy Scout. Eudora asked me how badly I wanted it and I said a lot. She asked if I was willing to earn my way in and stupid me, I told her yes."

"So she took you into the swamp? Why? As a punishment for wanting to play with other little boys?"

"No, it was to test my instincts and ability to reason; see if I was Boy Scout material." He shrugged. "It wasn't as dark as last night. I mean it was full daylight, so even under the shroud of all that foliage, I could make out shapes. I could see the snakes and gators, and I never wanted to tell someone I'd changed my mind so badly in my whole life, even to today. But I looked into her eyes and I knew it wouldn't have mattered. So I went on and I didn't look back, and I made it, Lil, just the way I did last night."

It was Lily's turn to cry. Tears for that terrified little boy, who'd dared to ask to be a scout, rivered down her cheeks and dripped to her hands which were clasped together on top of the pillow. "I'm so sorry," she said in a voice choked with heartache.

"Yeah. Me, too, but it could have been worse if your mother hadn't been there. And your dad."

"What about your own mother? Were you old enough to remember her?"

His eyes brightened as he nodded, and Lily felt a sob knot in her throat at how little it took to make this man she loved happy. "Tell me about her," she said.

"She was dark like you. Only her eyes were blue. She was small, and she laughed all the time. She was an artist. Always sitting at her easel, capturing the wonders of the world. That's the way she put it."

"How did she die?" Lily asked.

"The official reason according to the police investigation was suicide. Death by asphixiation. They said she killed herself in the garage."

Lily watched him toy with the chain on his wrist as he spoke, and she asked him about it. "Was that hers?"

"Yeah. She told me my dad gave it to her when I was born. They were going to add another bead on every special occasion. Like when I graduated from high school, and college, and got married . . ." He held up his arm. "Only one bead. She didn't have enough time left for any more landmark events.

"I stole this from Eudora when I was eight. I saw her looking at it and trying it on her neck. 'Course she was too big for it and I watched the fury in her eyes when she slammed it back into the jewelry box. As soon as she left her room, I sneaked in and took it."

"And she didn't find out?"

"Oh, yeah, there was nothing Eudora didn't know. She used to claim she had eyes in the back of her head, and I was positive she had horns under all that hair."

Lily laughed softly. "Too bad you never got a look."

"Well, she's dead now. I guess it's really true what they say about what goes around coming around, huh?"

Lily didn't answer. She didn't like to see the darkness that came into his eyes when he spoke of his step-mother. She turned the subject back to his mother and watched for the light to reappear.

"There's something inscribed on the bead. What does it say?"

"Tina. Short for Valentina. My father called her that; said she was perfectly named because she'd stolen his heart and was so tiny. She was Russian. A descendant of refugees from Stalin's reign of terror. Her full name was Valentina Pavlovich. They met in Paris when my dad was there after graduating from college. It was love at first sight. He was engaged to Eudora, but he brought my mom back to the States and married her in New

York before ever coming home to South Carolina. I guess he knew they would have stopped him if he hadn't." He stared at the bracelet a long time before adding. "At least then they wouldn't have killed her. I wonder if he ever thinks of that?"

"Maybe he doesn't believe that, Sash," she suggested gently. "It could be that she really did suffer from some kind of chemical depression that caused her to lose perspective."

"No, they killed her, Lily. I was only four years old, but I can still remember waking up in the middle of the night and hearing her cry out, over and over. And a vase was knocked to the floor. I heard it crash. I even came out of my room and looked through the stair posts trying to see what had happened. My dad was on one of his trips, so I was frightened. And then it got real quiet, so I went back to bed. In the morning I thought I'd had a bad dream." He stopped abruptly. "Well, that's all I know, except that they lied when they said she killed herself. She was murdered the same as your dad and several others. I know the names of the victims. I just don't have the proof to identify the killers."

"But how do they get away with it? Why haven't you or one of the other family members gone to the state authorities? Ask them to come in and make an independent investigation."

"Because we don't even know who all is involved. We *suspect* who they are, but without proof, we can't make a move. Think about who these people are, Lily. Some of the most influential people in the state . . . even America."

"But we can stop them, can't we?" she asked.

"I don't know. We may have waited too long."

Lily frowned. "What do you mean?"

"Think about it. Eudora was murdered right in front

of my eyes. And someone went to the trouble of creating a parody of your father's murder."

Lily's eyes widened. "You mean someone may be exacting revenge?"

"That's what I think."

"That frightens me even more."

"It should, princess. It means none of us are safe. Maybe you'll understand why I'm sending you back to New York in a couple of days as soon as the doc says your friend can travel."

"New York? Errol? What the hell are you talking about? I'm not—"

"Come here," he said, grabbing her hands and pulling her to her feet. He kissed her passionately, then held her face while he looked into her eyes. "Smoke gets in your eyes every time I kiss you. Did you know that?"

"Stop flirting with me to get me to forget what you just said," she snapped.

"Okay, I won't flirt with you. But there's something I want you to do for me."

She was hurt and angry, but so in love, she didn't want a single minute of this one day ruined. Whether he had his way and she went back to New York until it was finally safe to come back, or if she won the battle and stayed, the perfection of today wasn't going to be marred.

"What?" she asked.

"Dance for me."

She blew out a long breath and rolled her eyes. "Okay, come to the studio with me so I can pick out some music."

Sash sat down, folding his arms over his chest. "I want to stay right here."

"There's no stereo in here," she pointed out.

"So what? Haven't you ever danced to music in your mind?"

Lily shrugged. "Sure, but not if there's real music just three rooms away."

"Well, pretend there's not and dance for me to music you create in your head."

Lily folded her own arms in stubborn refusal. "Sorry, no can do."

"Why not?"

"Because whenever I dance to music I hear in my head, I'm always dancing with my dream lover."

"Okay, so dance with him," Sash said amicably.

Lily's smile was wide and slowly spreading; a Cheshire cat's very satisfied grin. "Come on then, dream lover. Let's dance."

Sash laughed as he allowed her to pull him to his feet. "Have mercy, woman. I'm still sore and aching from carrying you out of that swamp last night."

"Oh, but the best remedy for working out aches and pains is good old exercise." She placed his arms around her waist and wrapped hers around his neck. "Oh, don't look so grumpy. You're going to love this. And just to show you how caring I am, I've selected music for a *very* slow dance."

She could feel the rumble of the laughter in his chest against her breasts as they began to move, but soon the only sound that existed was the music that played in their minds.

Lily closed her eyes and sighed contentedly as she followed him around the living room. "Do you remember any Russian?" she asked.

"Only one thing," he murmured against her brow.

"Tell it to me," she whispered.

"Ya tyebya loubou."

Lily sighed. "I love you, too, Sasha."

Chapter Thirty-seven

Sash stopped moving and leaned back to look at her when he asked, "How did you know what I said?"

Lily giggled. "Two of the guys in my dance company a few years ago were Russian defectors. They were also gay and very much in love. They said those words to each other at least a dozen times a day."

They were both laughing when the phone rang again.

"I think we better answer it this time," Lily said. "We haven't checked our messages and no one even knows we're safe."

Sash held his hands up in surrender. "Hey, it's your party. You want to stop the music, I'm not going to argue."

Lily rolled her eyes as she crossed the room to pick up the receiver. "Hello?"

"Lily! Thank God," Imogene said in a breathless rush. "I've been calling you all day. Have you seen Sash since—"

"Yes, Genie, he's right here." She held out the phone, then brought it back to her ear for one quick postscript. "I'm sorry for your loss, Genie."

There was a brief hesitation, then, "Thank you."

"It's your sister," Lily explained unnecessarily.

"I got that," he said, stopping long enough to kiss the tip of her nose. "Hey, Genie? You okay?"

"I'm okay, ya know? Not good. Not bad. I want to find who did this and I guess I feel a little more empathy for what Lily went through." She lowered her voice as if afraid of being overheard and changed the subject somewhat. "Sash, were you there? I mean, your plan was to go with Abe and wait. He didn't do this, did he?"

"No, but convince the police of that. I won't go into it now, but suffice it to say they had a hungry lynch mob after him last night."

"So I heard on the radio. But obviously they didn't catch him. I would have had word right away. Where is he?"

"He's safe," Sash said carefully. "Listen, I don't want to go into it on the phone. I'll tell you everything when I see you. How's that?"

"Fine. But when?"

"Anytime," Sash said, turning and raising a brow at Lily. "We don't have to go over this right away. I mean, whoever ... did this, he's probably not going away."

"You're right, of course. I need to see you, though. Reinforce myself with family. I need my big brother right now, Sash."

"Okay, sure. Come on out to the house—my house, that is. I'll meet you there."

"Is Lily going to come with you?"

"I think she'd like to see Errol. Will that bother you if she's there?"

"No, of course not. I'd like to talk to her anyway."

"Okay. Give me an hour." He started to hang up, changed his mind, and asked, "Genie, you still there?"

"Yes."

"How's Dad?"

Silence answered his query.

"Genie?"

"I don't think he's doing too well, Sash. He's locked himself in the house. Won't see anyone. Not even me. Maybe you could call him. Just check on him."

"Yeah, maybe," Sash said. But he knew he wouldn't do that. There was too much animosity between them. Jason had been hurt when his only son left town, never calling, never sending even an "I'm alive" postcard. When Sash returned, Jason had come to his son when Sash refused to come to him. He'd offered the younger Rivers stock in the company as well as a position in the corporate office and a vice presidency. Sash had turned it all down, and Jason had been hurt by the rejection and furious when he learned that Sash had accepted the money left him in trust from his mother's estate. Sash added salt to the wound when he interviewed with one of the Rivers Fisheries foremen for a job on the boats. The two men hadn't spoken three times since.

"What're you thinking so hard about?" Lily asked as she laid a hand on his shoulder after he'd hung up the phone. "Genie all right?"

"Yeah," he said, seeming to snap out of his somber reverie. "I think she's doing pretty good. 'Course I told you she would. My sister's resilient."

Lily smiled and laid her head where her hand had been. "You're going to meet her at your place?"

"We're going. I know you're about to bust to see your friend, and besides I want you two to be friends. Now's a good time to start."

"Is that an order?" she asked.

He could feel the spread of her smile against his shoulder and grinned as well. "Damn straight."

"Ooh, a macho man. I'm trembling."

"Speaking of trembling, you think we got time—"

"No!" she shouted incredulously. "Men! Is that all you . . ."

He reached under her shirt, covering one of her

breasts with his hand. His thumb flicked over her nipple, and she felt desire bloom in the pit of her stomach. "I think we ... ooh ... might have a little time."

"Not a lot?" he asked as he backed her against the wall and worked her sweat pants down her hips.

"Just a few minutes," she said on a harsh breath.

"Then we won't be able to make love," he said, spreading her thighs with his hand and inserting a finger into her hot center. "We'll only have time for a quick fuck."

Lily didn't argue.

Chapter Thirty-eight

"Hey," Sash said as he stopped the car in the driveway in front of his beach house.

"Hey, what?" Lily asked, a smile on her glowing face.

"I forgot to ask. Did you mean it? Do you really love me like you said?"

"Deeply, and completely, and profoundly, Sasha Riv—"

"Shh," Sash hissed, turning up the volume on the car radio.

"—*spokesman for the Rosehill police department has confirmed the discovery of six bodies in the hill area of the city. A middle-aged white male and female were discovered at 14 Middle Hill Road by one of their daughters.*"

"Oh, Sash! That's Marla and Sander's address."

"I know. Listen."

"—*body of police chief Stuart St. Charles was found by his wife in his garage early this morning.*

"*As the day's horror continued to unfold, the bodies of Belinda and Davis Jackson were discovered in their bedroom by their housekeeper.*

"*And just twenty minutes ago, the Rosehill district attorney, Dixon Price, was gunned down in his driveway. A barking dog alerted neighbors who telephoned police.*

"All six victims, all prominent Rosehill citizens, died from gunshot wounds. When asked if they believe the homicides today could be linked to the murder of Rosehill mayor Eudora Rivers, police said they weren't ruling anything out. However, they have pointed out that all of today's victims were shot by a 9-millimeter semiautomatic weapon. Mrs. Rivers, you will recall, was stabbed with a hunting knife.

"At this time, police have no suspects."

Sash cut the motor, shutting off the broadcast. Lily was weeping almost soundlessly at his side. He reached for her, circling her with his arm and drawing her close.

"Why?" she whispered.

Sash shook his head. "I don't know. It's crazy."

Lily looked out the window, noticing the other vehicles parked side by side. Imogene's red Viper was on the far end. "She must not know," Lily said.

Sash groaned as he remembered one of the names just mentioned in the broadcast. "Jesus Christ, would they release a victim's name before notifying the next of kin? This world is really screwed up." He opened his door. "Come on, we've got to tell her before she hears it like this."

Imogene opened the door as they mounted the last steps. Her eyes were puffy and red from crying and Lily's heart went out to her. She knew what it was to lose one's mother. And now Genie's husband and aunt had been murdered as well. Tears filled her eyes as Sash gathered his sister into his arms and hugged her fiercely.

"I'm so sorry, sis," he was saying.

"I know," Genie said in a strangled cry. "Me, too."

"We'll get through this," Sash said, and Lily heard the tears in his voice now.

Genie stretched a hand out for Lily, drawing her into the circle. "Thanks for coming," she said.

Lily looked away. God, she'd just lost her mother. How were they going to tell her about Dixon?

"Genie, I've got something I need to tell you," Sash said, keeping one arm around his half-sister's waist.

"I think I know," she said with a strange smile. "Let's go inside where we can talk." She looked at Lily. "And you can see your friend. He was real excited when I told him you were coming."

Lily and Sash exchanged worried glances over Genie's head. Despite her assurances on the telephone earlier that she was doing all right, she was obviously strained and upset.

Lily wondered how Sash was going to find the words to tell her that six more of her friends and family had been murdered, including her husband. She thought she'd offer to go visit Errol in the bedroom, thereby giving brother and sister time alone.

As soon as they were inside, however, she saw Errol sitting on the far side of the room in a wheelchair. Kitty sat beside him, and another woman Lily didn't recognize was standing beside the others.

Lily forgot all about Genie as she ran to his side. "You look like shit," she told him, laughing and crying at the sight of him, pale and weak yet grinning that devil-may-care smile of his.

"Hey, you don't look so hot yourself," he said teasingly, though Lily noticed the slur in his speech.

"Medication," the stranger explained. "Makes him fuzzy and thickens his tongue. Errol seems to enjoy it."

Lily laughed. "He would."

"I'm Nancy Star, by the way," the woman with the auburn ponytail said. "Most folks call me Rusty."

"Rusty?" Lily repeated, and then her eyes widened with dawning. "Rusty! Errol's pretty little waitress, Rusty."

The girl laughed. "The guy's got good eyes."

"Wait a minute. Did you say your last name is Star? Then you and Kitty—"

"Are sisters," Kitty finished for her.

"Okay, now it's all starting to make sense," Lily said.

"Good, now that everybody knows everybody else, we can get this party started," Imogene said.

"Genie," Sash said quietly, "we need to talk first."

"You're right, honey, but we're going to talk about what I want to talk about."

Sash frowned. What was the matter with her? Grief, sure, but there was something else. He stepped closer to her, laying a hand on her shoulder. "Hey, you okay, Genie?"

"No, I'm not okay!" she cried in a shrill voice that didn't resemble her normal husky tone. And then she laughed. "Mother was right about you, Sasha. You are really one dumb gypsy. I used to argue the point with her. Shit, you were so good looking, I thought anything that beautiful couldn't be as stupid as Mother always said, but she was right. She almost always was."

"He doesn't deserve that," Lily said, taking a step toward Sash's sister.

Genie whipped a gun out of her oversized purse. "Just step back little Miss Goody Two-shoes. And you, too, brother, dear. Go stand over there by your squaw and the rest of the losers."

"Did you kill all those people today?" Sash asked quietly as soon as he was across the room with the others as she'd ordered. "If you did, it's okay. We can help you. No one's going to hurt you. Just put the gun down, Genie, and let me call for an ambulance."

"Shut up! I don't need an ambulance. In fact," she said on a thin, piercing laugh, "no one is going to need an ambulance when I'm done."

"But why?" Lily asked. "Your husband, your aunt and uncle, your cousin—"

"I don't need a recount. I'm quite aware of who they are."

Errol and the two women beside his chair were exchanging confused glances, and Sash told them what he knew. "We just heard it on the radio. Six people were found in the hills, all shot to death, all murdered today. And I guess we know who did it. The question is why?"

"Because, *stupid*, they betrayed us. Mother and me. One of them killed her last night. And do you know not one of them had the courage to admit it to me. What did they think? I'd just say 'okay, you must be innocent, so you get to live'? How crazy did they think I was?"

"Pretty fucking nuts, if you ask me," Errol said under his breath.

Imogene laughed, head back and with genuine amusement. "You're a very funny man, Mr. Mills. I'm really going to regret killing you. Handsome, witty, talented. And me a patron of the arts. Pity."

"Yeah," Errol said, "Effing shame."

"Shut up," Lily said.

"Lily's right, Errol. You're amusing, but you're beginning to get on my nerves," Genie snapped. She pulled a chair out from the table and positioned it so that it faced the others yet maintained the distance of ten feet or so. "Okay, so let me tell you what's going to go down here."

"I think we've pretty much figured that out," Sash said quietly.

"Would you all shut up!" Imogene screamed. "Either you let me direct the party the way I want or it's over! Got it?"

No one moved.

Genie smiled. "Okay, then." She looked at the gun in her hand, her head canted at an odd angle and her swollen eyes blinking rapidly as if she'd forgotten all about the lethal weapon she held. "Isn't it pretty? TEC9 nine-millimeter semiautomatic. It's flashy and powerful and favored by drug runners and gangs. The silencer just makes it all more civil. Not so *noisy* and rude."

"That the gun you used on your family?" Errol asked.

Imogene chuckled, apparently no longer angry that someone else was talking. "Uh huh. Wacked 'em each twice just to make sure they were dead. But don't get your hopes up, there's still plenty bullets left for ya'll. There are thirty-six rounds. That's why I was so delighted to buy this little ol' thing."

"Yeah, okay, I think I can see how this is going to go down," Errol said. "You're gonna make it look like some kind of drug buy gone sour. But what about the murders on the hills? If you use the same gun, won't that confuse the issue?"

"No, silly, it won't because I left a couple souvenirs behind that will link those deaths to some very naughty boys in Colombia."

"Let me guess. They sold you the gun," Errol said.

"Damn! Not only cute but smart, too," Genie said.

Errol shrugged, holding up his hands as if to say he couldn't argue with that. "Well, since I'm on a roll, can I ask one or two more questions?"

"Sure, sugar," Imogene said.

"All these folks you killed today, were they part of some sort of secret club?"

"Yes!" Genie said, laughing and stomping her feet with glee. "You're very good! I like this. Go on, ask me another one."

Sash and Lily were looking at Errol with amazement. "Where is this all coming from?" Sash whispered to Lily.

"Quiet! Errol's asking me questions," Imogene said, her tone that of a whiny, petulant child.

"Sander was the ringleader?"

Genie's bottom lip jutted out with her disappointment. She made a sound like a game-show buzzer. "Wrong. *I* am the grand oligarch. A woman has always been the leader, ever since Rose Price realized that men are our inferiors.

"So you've got one strike against you. But go again. I'll give you three more questions. If you can get one right, the game will continue. If not . . ." She shrugged her shoulders.

"It was this . . . this secret society that killed Dr. Hutton, wasn't it?" Errol asked.

"Dingalingaling! You're right!"

"Because he was married to a Native American," Errol suggested.

"No," Imogene said with disappointment. "Of course no one liked it that he married an Indian, but Sara minded her own business, so they more or less just tolerated her."

"Then why?" Lily asked.

"I thought you were smart enough to figure that out, Lily, dear." She sighed like a parent dealing with a slow child. "The way it works is every member of the coven—there're eight, by the way—can ask for a death favor. If the reason is sound, it's almost always granted. I mean, one couldn't ask for a death favor just because someone didn't yield at a stop sign."

"But if a patient ended up paralyzed because of an operation, that would be reason enough to kill him," Lily said flatly.

"Very good. That deserves an A."

"But you were just a little girl, Genie," Sash said. "You couldn't have ordered Alison's death."

"Right again. Grandma Daisy was the grand oligarch then. But she handed the mantle to me before she passed away."

"You must have been so proud," Lily said bitterly.

"Tsk tsk, cousin. Sarcasm suits me much better than you. But yes, I was very proud." She leaned forward, resting her gun arm across her knee. She swung her leg and the others could tell she was getting agitated.

"What about my mother? Did your group or whatever the hell you called yourselves kill her, too?" Sash asked.

"Yes," Imogene said without further explanation.

"Because Eudora asked a death favor?"

Imogene applauded. "You're all getting very good at this."

"And you came to me, pretending to help us find out the truth about all these murders so you could keep tabs on what we uncovered," Sash said, disgust heavy in his tone.

"That one's too obvious."

"They killed our mother, too, because she overheard something?" Rusty asked.

"Well, yes and no. They didn't kill her for what she overheard. It was because of what she found." Imogene said. "If I remember right—I was just a little girl eavesdropping on adults, so I'm not exactly sure of all the facts—the three people who Grandma sent to kill Alison and Sara Hutton hid in Lily's playhouse until they were sure the coast was clear, to borrow a trite phrase. When Dr. Two Moons told Helen Star he was taking Lily to Oklahoma to live, she went to the playhouse to gather her toys. She found blood on the floor and a diamond that had been knocked loose from its setting. She made the mistake of mentioning it to Mother when she came by that evening." Genie laughed. "Which reminds me, you want to know the greatest irony of all, Sash?"

He hunched his shoulders. "Not really, but it's your show."

"None of them ever saw you in that house. I told them you were there. Mama went back to the Hutton's looking for you. If she hadn't, Helen probably would have told the police what she found, and Sara would have been free as a bird."

"Did she get her diamond back?" Errol asked.

Genie chuckled appreciatively. "Funny man."

Silence settled over the room as everyone tried to digest the horrible truths they were hearing.

"What? No more questions? Then I guess the party's over—"

"Wait! I have one," Lily said. "Why was Sander so adamant about living in my house all these years?"

"That's so pathetically obvious, any fool would see the answer. Belinda and Davis had their own house. They inherited Grandma Daisy's. Marla and Sander wanted your house for Caroline."

"Genie! I still don't understand about this . . . this coven or whatever the hell it is you were involved in," Sash said, desperately stalling for time.

Genie gave her head an impatient shake, but her audience could see the pleasure and pride that danced in her eyes. "*I* was the grand oligarch, chosen by Grandma Daisy to be the supreme ruler. Of course only my two high priests knew. The others, they did my bidding with blind obedience just as others have for centuries."

"But why?" Lily asked, her incredulity at such mindless allegiance evident in her tone.

"No, Lily, dear, the question isn't why? The question is why not. They had power, money, influence. Again, why not?"

No one spoke, but Imogene seemed not to notice. A smile spread across her face, as she let her gaze move slowly over the face of each of her captives. "It was brilliant, the oligarchy set up in a pyramid of rank and responsibility with a woman always at the pinnacle. And do you know why for more than two centuries we never once erred? Because Grandma Rose understood that men are not equipped to govern with the heart. Only women can hand down decisions that might seem harsh but are based on fairness and justice."

"You murdered innocent men and women!" Lily screamed.

Genie ignored the outburst, continuing on as if no one had spoken. "We needed the men, of course. Brawn has always been useful, but in the heart of a woman's breast, that's where it must always begin."

"And was it this noble and gentle heart that directed you to murder your husband, and cousin and aunts and uncles today?" Sash asked quietly.

"You always were a fool, Sash," his sister answered quietly . . . deadly. "You don't understand anything I've been saying. I've been wasting my breath."

She brushed her hair away from her face with the back of the hand still holding the gun, then looked at the others.

"Well, if that's it, I think it's time to get the show on the road." She reached inside her bag, coming out with a plastic bag of white powder and a roll of duct tape. She held up each item, one at a time, explaining their significance though it was understood what she intended. "Cocaine. Everyone knows that you people from New York are into drugs. Such a rotten shame you brought it with you to our beautiful city." She laughed and looked at the Star sisters and Sash. " 'Course you three didn't have to be such willing players.

"Duct tape, all the better to tie you up with, my dears.

"And, of course, big brother dear, I want to thank you for selecting a house that is so far out on its own. It certainly is going to make life easier for me. No witnesses, no—"

The bedroom door opened behind Imogene's prisoners. Startled by the unexpected creak of rusty hinges, Imogene almost dropped her gun. She recovered quickly, raising it and aiming it at the intruder. "Daddy! What are you . . . ?"

"I was listening to your confession, Genie. Along with the state police. They wired the house before you arrived and they've surrounded the grounds."

"Why, Daddy?" she asked in a puzzled, childish whine.

Lily saw Jason Rivers flinch.

"You're a cold-blooded murderer," he said in a quaking voice. "My God, you killed six people today alone and all because you *thought* one of them had betrayed you. Last year, you ordered a woman's death because she refused to sell you her oceanfront property, for God's sake."

"How do you know about that?" Imogene asked.

Jason hung his head, shaking it from side to side. "I didn't know any of it until a couple nights ago." He looked up again, and tears stood in his pale blue eyes. "Do you realize I was so unimportant to you and your mother, that when you followed us home after Marla's dinner party, you sat at our kitchen table discussing who would get rid of Abe Joseph, and if necessary, who would win the call to kill Lily if she didn't get the message and back off. Neither one of you even noticed me standing in the doorway listening.

"After you left to come over here, your mother went upstairs to take a shower. But guess what she left behind on the table? The book you record all your misdeeds in, Genie. I read it all."

"Then you know just *who* you're talking to, you idiot!" Genie yelled, standing up and pointing the gun at her father's head.

Lily turned into Sash's arms, and he spun her around

so that it was his back that faced the barrel of Imogene's gun.

Errol covered his head and folded himself over in his chair as best he could.

Kitty and Rusty fell to the floor.

Only father and daughter stood facing one another.

"Yes, I know who you are," Jason said, his voice thready with emotion and fatigue. "You're the greedy, selfish, evil product of eight generations of insanity from Rose Price all the way to your mother."

Imogene lowered the gun, cocking her head as if struggling to understand his inability to recognize her stature and importance. "I'm the grand oligarch, Daddy. Don't you see? Everything you have is because of the women who have protected your rights and guarded the future for your progeny. Now *I* am that woman."

Slowly, the others in the room relaxed a bit. Tension had ebbed. As long as there was a dialogue going, there was the chance that a peaceful resolution could be achieved.

"You are a murderer, Imogene, just as your grandmother was and all those other power-hungry women who preceded her. You kill the same way normal people buy a new car or choose a restaurant. Impulsively, on a whim, because it feels right. My God, are you entirely without moral conscience?"

"But that's the problem, isn't it? We are *not* normal people. We are the exceptional; the chosen. Neither are we as cavalier as you're crediting us with being. We are jurisprudence at its finest, because we aren't blind. We see exactly who our enemies are and we hand out justice swiftly and harshly. That's why we are the single most prosperous small city per capita in the country today."

"You see exactly who your enemies are," Jason repeated wearily. "Is that right? Well, what about Abraham Joseph? What was his terrible crime?

"You ordered your mother to kill him, but what was he guilty of, Genie? Helping his grandfather?" Tears ran along Jason's cheeks now as he spoke. "I couldn't believe she would really do it. I stood there in the attic listening to her bait him out there on the widow's watch, watching her lure him to the railing, and I knew I was wrong. Not only was she capable of murder, she would enjoy it. She would push a man to his death simply because there was the remote possibility his grandfather—a feeble old man—*might* remember something damaging from fifteen years ago." He shook his head with disgust. "You make me sick."

"*I* make *you* sick? You pathetic excuse for a man. So high and mighty. Such lofty morals! What about Sash? Did you go to the police and suggest that your son might know something about Alison Hutton's murder? No," she said, shaking her head. "Yet you knew. Mother told you Sash was in the Hutton house that day. I heard her taunting you, telling you how she'd persuaded me not to mention to the police that I'd seen him go in."

"There was no reason to tell them. He'd left Rosehill. I didn't know where he was," Jason argued.

"He's been back for five years," she countered. "Come on, tell the truth, Daddy. You discouraged him from coming around because you were afraid my mother would hurt the precious son of that gypsy whore—"

"You're damn right! Your mother was vile, but she can't hurt anyone anymore, can she? And do you know something?" He held up his hands as he posed the question to everyone in the room. "When I threw that knife and watched her fall off that roof, I didn't feel a single iota of guilt. She repulsed me and all I felt was relief that she was dead."

Genie's answering scream belonged to a demented animal. She raised the gun again, but it never fired. A marksman with the South Carolina State Police shot her through the back of her head.

The nightmare was ended.

Chapter Thirty-nine

The first day of spring, 1995

"Wow," Errol said as Lily pushed his chair out of the hospital where he'd been confined for a week. "Spring's really here, isn't it?"

"Pretty day," Lily agreed without heart.

"Hey," he said, reaching behind his head to cover her hand. "You gotta snap out of it. I know this week has been a pisser. Hell, you went to how many funerals? That's enough to stall the Eveready Bunny. But it's over now. You did what you set out to do. You cleared your mother's name."

"And a lot of people died."

"Fucking A, but they were all the bad guys. What you gotta think on is what that state trooper said. We'll never know how many more innocent people would have been murdered if the truth hadn't been uncovered."

Lily laughed softly. "Okay, get down off the soapbox, you're beginning to sound a little too philosophical to suit me."

"You're a hard lady to please," he complained. "So where's our taxi?"

"Rusty said she was bringing the car around. She'll be here in a few minutes."

"And then we're going straight to the airport? No stopping to say good-bye to a certain tall, dark, and handsome Ruskie?"

Though Errol wasn't facing her, Lily shook her head. "No, we said our good-byes last night."

"Yeah," he said softly, giving her hand a tight squeeze. "I thought it might be something like that when I saw how puny you looked when you came in to my room." His voice brightened. "Listen, kiddo, don't give up on him yet. He had a hell of a load of shit dumped on him. His sister's betrayal. His father's collapse after watching his daughter shot down by the police. And his dad was the head honcho over a major empire. Sash is going to have to keep the sharks at bay until Jason's back at the helm or they divest their holdings."

Rusty arrived with the van to drive them to Charleston. Both women helped Errol into the front seat, then Lily climbed in the back.

"You sure you don't want to sit up here?" he asked.

Lily shook her head. "No, you talk to Rusty. I think I'm going to doze until we get to the airport."

She closed her eyes and leaned her head on the window. She wouldn't sleep. She hadn't been able to sleep more than an hour or two at a time since the past Sunday.

As she had for seven straight days, Lily went over the events again and again and again. Listing the names of the dead who had been buried this week.

Eudora Rivers.

Dixon Price.

Stuart St. Charles.

Marla and Sander Hutton.

Belinda and Davis Hutton.

Imogene Rivers.

A tear slipped from the corner of her eye. Would she ever be done crying?

Not if you think of Sash, a cruel voice whispered in her mind.

Lily's heart twisted. How could she not think of him? How could she not remember the thrill of being in his arms? Of hearing him tell her he loved her? Of seeing the agony on his face when he realized that it was his sister who had been betraying him all those years? And how could she not remember what had happened after the coroner had removed Imogene's body, and the state police had taken Jason to the temporary facility they'd set up on the outskirts of town.

Errol's color had paled to sickly gray, and Kitty being the first to notice, offered to drive him to the hospital.

Rusty had taken one look at Lily and Sash, and grabbed her coat. "I'll go with you, Kit."

Sash helped them get Errol to the car downstairs. When he returned, Lily was on her hands and knees washing the blood from the hardwood floor.

"You don't have to do that," Sash said, reaching for her arm and almost jerking her to her feet.

Lily pulled away from him. "I don't mind. We can't just leave it here. It'll stain the wood."

"So let it," he said angrily, but she'd heard the catch that betrayed his anguish, too.

"Sash—" she began, dropping the sponge she'd been using in the pail of water.

"Don't, Lily," he said. "Don't feed me any damn platitudes."

"But, honey—"

"I've got to be alone," he said, almost running for the stairs to the second-story attic studio.

Lily was stung by his rejection. She thought she understood his suffering and his anger, but she couldn't help if he wouldn't let her. Still, it was his pain to work through. She vowed to leave him alone, let him find his way through all the rubble left in the wake of the day's destruction.

For the next two hours, she scrubbed blood and gore from the floors, the walls, and the furniture. She swept up shards of window glass overlooked by the police cleanup team, and straightened all the furniture that had been disturbed and upset in the siege.

Hardly a siege, she amended, remembering the choice of words used by one of the state troopers. But maybe she'd merely lost sight of how serious Imogene had been about killing them. If Jason hadn't convinced the state police to . . .

Lily shuddered, pushing the thought away.

Two troopers had been left behind to ward off curiosity seekers and reporters, and Lily could hear them ordering someone to get back in his car and drive away.

And that was just the beginning.

She returned the broom and dustpan to the pantry, emptied the pale of filthy water in the sink, and rinsed out the sponge and rags she'd used.

She was exhausted and sat down on a chair as far away as possible from where Imogene's body had lain, drawing her knees up to her chest and huddling there as she waited for Sash to rejoin her.

He'd mentioned earlier that they still had to pick up her rental car from the pier and take Abe's car back to him at the motel. She hoped he would come soon before she was too tired to care.

She turned her head toward the stairs that led to an attic. What was up there? she wondered, and what was Sash doing?

The house was as quiet as a tomb, and she grimaced

with the analogy, glad she hadn't made the observation aloud to anyone.

She blew out a tired breath. "Enough's enough, Rivers," she said, climbing from the chair at the same time. "You can feel sorry for yourself all you want, but not alone. You're just gonna have to unload some of it with me. We're a team, and I'm not going to let you forget it."

She marched up the steps, prepared to do battle, but the fight went out of her as soon as she opened the attic door.

He sat there on the floor, a little boy lost amid a sea of paintings.

Lily pivoted in a small, tight circle as she took in the brilliance of portraits, landscapes, seascapes, and still lifes executed in oils, watercolors, and pencil. These were Sash's creations. She wasn't sure how she knew that. After all, his mother had been an artist. These could have been hers, but Lily knew different. Sash was the genius behind these, and then she saw the full-length portrait of Sara against the far wall. Without speaking, she stepped past Sash, stopping before the lifelike image of her mother. Like a child first experiencing the magic of the theater, she stood there too awed to move, yet grinning from ear to ear.

She glanced to her right and there was a picture of herself. This one was rougher, not as polished or well thought out, and yet Lily was touched by the beautiful aura Sash had found in her and transferred to canvas.

"Oh, Sash, these are so—"

A portrait of Imogene lay on the floor beside him. She recognized the blond hair and the cornflower-blue eyes, and the full, impish lips. Otherwise she might not have known who the subject had been, for Sash had sliced long gashes across her face.

Lily fell down on her knees beside him, and tried to

wrap her arms around him, but Sash held her away. "Take Abe's car, Lily. Go on home. You can call him, give him the all clear. Tomorrow ... well, tomorrow we'll just see what happens."

Lily shook her head. "No, I want you to come home with me. You're exhausted and upset—"

"*Upset?*" Is that what you think I am? Upset?" He shook his head, laughing at the understatement. "Baby, I'm not upset. I'm furious. Devastated. And blown away. You can color me crazy, but don't say I'm upset because that doesn't even come close to cutting it."

"I'm sorry, Sash. I know how horrible this has been for you. I was here, remember? But I can help. We can share the pain and the anger, and we can heal together."

"Why should we share it? Your family are victims, and you can put it all behind you. I'm the one who's guilty here. I let my crazy sister almost get you killed. My old man had to kill his wife because I was so stupid I set Abe up."

"You did not!" Lily protested. "You went along to protect him, and you did."

Sash was holding the knife he'd used to destroy Imogene's portrait. With a loud growl, he threw it, burying it in the wall. "Go away!" he cried. "Go back to New York. Go back to your friends and your dance. Just go away from me!"

Lily had tried again and again after that to reach him, to pull him out of the black hole of despair and guilt into which he'd climbed, but he refused to hear her, and by Saturday, she'd given up.

"Hey, sleepyhead, wake up," Rusty said, reaching around the front seat to shake Lily's leg.

She sat straight up, blinking rapidly, then sagging back against the seat with a sheepish grin as she realized where she was and what had happened. "I can't believe I fell asleep like that."

"It's allowed," Rusty said with a laugh. "You were done in. But wake up, now. Your flight takes off in an hour, and you can sleep all the way to New York."

Lily reached over the front passenger seat to tap Errol on the shoulder. "How you doing?"

"Would you believe I feel like I got run over?"

"Cute," Lily said finding a laugh that she'd thought was gone forever. To Rusty, she said, "Why don't you go get a skycap while I wait with the invalid?"

"Hey, give a guy a little sympathy here. All you had to go through was a night in the swamp. I was pushed off a fucking—"

Lily's eyes darkened at the reminder of what she had suffered which led naturally to what she had lost, and Errol could have gladly kicked himself for his stupidity. "I'm sorry, babe. Just remember how stupid I am, and you'll be able to forgive me."

In spite of her heartbreak, Lily smiled. "How could I ever forget how stupid you are when you're so good at reminding me?"

Rusty arrived with the skycap and Lily climbed out of the van, ready to help Errol into the wheelchair. For the next thirty minutes she was so busy checking baggage, finding their gate, and getting boarding passes for the two of them she hardly had a moment to think about Sash. But when she finally stopped to get a sweater from one of her carry-on bags, she was caught up short by the conversation going on between Rusty and Errol. She'd parked the cart behind them while she went to the ticket counter, and neither of them saw her return.

"I still don't understand what Eudora thought she was going to accomplish by having that Davis guy run me down. If anything, she should have known that would make Lily even more determined to get to the truth."

Rusty nodded. "I know. That's why Sash told Genie and Kitty to make it look like you'd gone back to New York. He didn't want her finding out, 'cause he knew exactly what she'd do."

"Yeah, good thing, too. Those people were out there, you know? We're talkin' bleeping Twilight Zone, baby. I'll tell you what fuckin' blew me away."

"Don't tell me," Rusty said, getting into it. "Those weird journals they kept. Like they were proud and wanted to make sure people knew what they'd done if their society ever died out."

"You got it, but in a way I guess we should be glad they left a record. I think Lily needed to know exactly what happened the day her father was killed."

"Mmm," Rusty said with a doubtful shake of her head. "I don't know. I'm not sure it helped her to know that it was her father's brother who actually killed him."

"Gotta disagree. She said she needed the closure she got from reading the account. And just think, you were able to locate your mother's body and have it buried in a proper plot in the cemetery."

"I know. I'm grateful for that."

Lily walked away. Closure. Yep, she'd gotten that. All the way around. Her parents could rest in peace now, and she could let go of Sash.

"Princess?"

Lily spun around on her heel at the tentative question. "Oh, God, I was just thinking about you. I can't believe you're here, that you came."

He smiled, but it did little to erase the profound sadness in his eyes. "I couldn't let you leave without telling you good-bye."

Lily choked on a sob she wouldn't let him hear. "Oh. That was nice of you. But silly. Two hours just to say good-bye. You could have sent me a postcard in New York. You have my address, don't you?" She was talking too fast, but it was the only way she knew to hold back the tears that were burning behind her eyes.

"No, but—"

"Oh, well, wait. I'll write it down for you. You can drop me a note sometime, or have your secretary do it now that you're a big wheel in your dad's . . ." She pulled a notepad from her purse and quickly scratched her address and phone number. She pressed it into his hand and busied herself with putting pen and paper back in her purse. *Now go away, please, before I make a fool of myself right here in front of you and God and everyone.*

"Lil," he began, then stopped when he saw Errol and Rusty glaring at him from their seats only a couple of feet away. He turned so that he stood with his back to her bullying squad. "I wanted to talk to you this week. Every day I almost called you."

"Why didn't you?"

"Because I didn't know what to say. Because I didn't want you in the middle of so much ugliness anymore. Because how can I judge what you and I had when I couldn't even see through my own sister."

"Bullshit!" Lily said. Several people turned their way at her outburst. She didn't care. "That is a crock and you know it. You're a coward, Sasha Rivers. You got hurt, and now you're afraid to feel 'cause you might get wounded again. Well, guess what, buddy, life has a lot to offer. Only one of them isn't a guarantee."

He looked at the floor for a long moment before meeting her gaze again. "You've got a brilliant career ahead of you. Starring on Broadway. It was your mother's dream for you even when you could hardly reach the exercise bar in the studio your dad built for you. I've got a lot of rubble to clear away down here. I can't leave, and I wouldn't ask you to stay. It's that simple. We belong to different worlds."

"Coward," she said, though she barely made a sound as she choked on her tears.

He released the catch on the chain he wore on his wrist. "Take this, princess."

"I don't want it," she said, pushing his hand away. "And I'll tell you something else. I was my father's princess. I'm not yours, so don't call me that again."

"Okay, but take the bracelet, Lil. Please. My mother would have loved you. And it'll bring you luck on opening night when you dance the part of Maria Tallchief."

Her eyes widened. "How did you—"

"Errol told me."

"American Airlines, Flight 399 is boarding at gate 11. Please . . ."

Sash hooked her neck with his hand and drew her to him, covering her mouth with his. He kissed her hard and this time there was no doubt what it meant.

"Be happy, prin—Lil." He flashed a grin. "And break a leg up there on that stage. I want to read about your success in the paper."

Lily didn't answer him. She couldn't. It wasn't possible to speak when her heart was breaking.

Rusty and Errol were embracing, and Lily turned away, unable to watch the happy pair. Their parting was different. Temporary. Errol was returning to New York only long enough to pack up his things and have them shipped to California. Then Rusty was driving to Manhattan to pick him up and the pair were heading west. Errol had decided his fame and glory might lie in the world of movies rather than the New York stage. Somehow, Lily didn't think it mattered much to Rusty whether he succeeded or not. As Errol had confided that morning in the hospital room, "The girl's in love with my pretty face. She thinks I'm glamorous."

Five minutes later, seated in first class, Errol placed his order for a Bloody Mary. "What about you, babe?" he asked Lily.

"Nothing, thanks," she said, leaning her head against the window and closing her eyes.

"Ah, parting is such sweet sorrow," he quoted.

"Put a sock in it, Mills," she said without looking at him.

"You're missing my point, and it's important."

Lily knew from experience there was only one way to shut Errol up. She had to let him have his say. She pulled her sunglasses from her purse, put them on, and turned to face him. "Okay. What's your point?"

"You weren't the only one hurting back there."

"Damn it, Mills—"

"Wait one more sec, here. I was watching him. He was bustin' up big time. He won't be able to let you just walk out of his life forever. He'll come looking for you soon as he starts getting over everything that went down here."

Lily shook her head. "You know, when we get home to Manhattan, I'm going to get you an appointment with a neurologist. I think you suffered some brain injury and now you think you're Aristotle or Plato or some other long-winded philosopher."

"That's the second time you've accused me of that," Errol said, wagging a finger in her face. "I'm going to get my feelings hurt if you don't let up."

"Okay, but you're way off base about Sash."

"Yeah? Tell you what. I'll bet you two hundred dollars he shows up in New York before . . . when? Christmas! Yeah, two hundred big ones says you don't trim your tree by yourself."

"You don't have two hundred dollars," she pointed out.

Errol shrugged. "So what, I will when Rivers arrives in New York."

Chapter Forty

The week before Christmas, 1995

Sash had never been to a Broadway show before, but he knew magic when it happened, and he was watching it now.

Tears had filled his eyes when he arrived at the theater and saw Lily's name in lights on the marquee. But that emotion didn't come close to what he was feeling as he watched her dance. Hers was the starring role as Maria Tallchief, the great ballerina from the same Osage Indian tribe. He knew what an honor it was for her name even to be mentioned in the same breath as the legendary ballerina. But he thought Miss Tallchief would be proud to have Lily portraying her.

He'd never seen anything as graceful or as elegant as she, and he thought of Sara and Alison and wondered if they knew how beautiful and accomplished their daughter had become.

The last dance, the pièce de résistance, inspired a hush over the entire theater. All the lights were brought down except the single spotlight that shone on the star. Lily performed on pointe to music written especially for the finale. It was a haunting melody and her graceful interpretation enthralled the audience.

She brought down the house and Sash, sitting front-row center, shouted "brava!" and applauded the loudest.

Sash hadn't gone backstage or even waited for her at the stage door. He'd taken a taxi to her apartment.

Lily arrived home almost two hours later.

Up close, she was even more beautiful than she'd appeared on stage. That had been a star. This was his Lily.

She stopped as soon as she stepped from the car that picked her up every morning and returned her home every night.

"For you," he said, holding out a bouquet of roses that had long since frozen. "The super wouldn't let me in," he went on through chattering teeth.

"Your skin is almost as blue as your eyes," she said. "How long have you been waiting?"

"Since the show ended. I was there."

"Come on in. We can talk while you thaw."

"You were magnificent, Lil," he said as he followed her into the warmth of the building, then into her apartment. She led him over to a heating register. "Stand here for a little while. I'll go make some coffee." She started around the corner to the kitchen, then backed up a couple of steps. "You're crazy."

"Yep, you got that right," he called to the other room. "And speaking of crazy, how's Errol?"

Lily laughed. "He's fine. He and Rusty split up. She's engaged to some other wannabe actor. But Errol's got a major part in a pilot for a sitcom. He met a hot-looking reporter on a flight last week. Jane Talbut. Writes for one of the Chicago rags."

"Busy man," Sash muttered under his breath.

She returned a few minutes later with two cups of coffee. "You warming up any?"

"Much better," he said, rubbing his hands together and crossing the room to join her in the living room.

She sat on the sofa, placing his cup on the far side of the table in front of one of the chairs.

"Nice place," he said, sipping his coffee and looking around. "Big, roomy. Not bad for New York."

Lily nodded.

"How's Jesse and his wife and their kid?"

"Great. Really super. I swear Uncle Jesse shoots a roll of film every other day on that boy," she answered, loosening up because of the pleasant subject. "They'll be here for Christmas. Arriving day after tomorrow, as a matter of fact."

Sash stared at his hands for a long moment. Then he laughed. "I miss you," he blurted.

"Sash—"

"I know, I don't have any right to miss you or to feel anything at all for that matter. I've told myself that over and over, and my head listened. That's why I never wrote or called. But my heart isn't as smart."

Lily couldn't believe she was letting him do this to her. It had taken her months to get over the terrible hurt. No, scratch that. She still wasn't over it. So why the hell was she listening to him now? She posed that question aloud.

"Just give me one good reason for listening to you."

"I don't have one," he admitted, "except I'm prepared to beg if I have to. I've never stopped—"

"Don't! I'm too worn out for this," she told him on a long weary sigh as she arched her back and rubbed the nape of her tired neck.

He sat there on the end of her sofa looking devastatingly handsome in his tuxedo, but it wasn't the attraction that she'd always felt for him that persuaded her to relent. It was the light she saw go out of his eyes when she cut him off.

"Okay, if you'll give me five minutes to get out of these clothes and into my sweats, I'll listen," she offered quickly when it looked as if he were about to accept defeat and leave.

"Thanks," he said.

When she returned, she kept her word, curling up on the sofa, feet tucked beneath her and head lying on the arm rest as Sash talked.

He told her about the rage that had consumed him for so many months. And the guilt for the heartache and anguish his sister and stepmother had caused so many people. But mostly, he'd been ashamed of falling in love with her.

"Ashamed?" she cried. "Why?"

"Because I thought I was scum. Not worthy to shine your shoes much less love you."

"You're not scum, Sash Rivers, but you are probably the stupidest man I've ever known," Lily said. "None of what they did had anything to do with you."

"I know," he said quietly.

"But—"

"I know *now*, Lil. I didn't then."

"So, what changed the way you saw yourself?"

He shrugged. "The people in Rosehill. All the townspeople. They've been great. Rallying around us instead of condemning us as they could have. Working for my dad's company and seeing pride come back into his eyes and replace the same shame I'd felt." He smiled. "The grand jury handed down a verdict of justifiable homicide, so at least he didn't have to go through a long drawn-out trial."

"I know," she said. "I followed the news reports. But I never thought they'd do anything else, did you? Jason saved Abe's life, after all."

"Hey, there's one you'll want to hear about. The man was just elected district attorney. How's that for poetic justice?"

Lily laughed and clapped her hands. "That's terrific. And how about Joe Joe? Still healthy, I hope."

"Yeah, seems to do okay from what Abe's told me."

"Give them my love when you see him."

"Well, that might be a problem. I've left Rosehill."

"For good?"

"Well, except for visits to see my dad."

"Is that good?" Lily asked.

Sash grinned. "Yeah, that's excellent. I've got a major art gallery interested in a private showing."

"Oh, Sash," she said, forgetting herself for a minute and jumping from her seat to hug him. "I'm so thrilled for you," she said after an embarrassed moment.

"Thanks," Sash muttered when she stepped away from him.

"Well, anything else?"

Sash sighed. Obviously, she didn't want the same thing from him that she had nine months before. *Stupid!* he cursed himself silently. "No, I guess not." He stood up and she rose with him. He was picking up his coat when he changed his mind. He dropped it again, and grabbed her by the arms. "Damn it, that's not true. There's a hell of a lot more.

"First of all, I want you to know I had a mighty serious crush on your mother."

Lily rolled her eyes. "Now, that's an earth-shaking revelation—"

"Let me finish," he snapped. Then more quietly and reasonably, "I had a crush but I didn't love her. I envied what she and Doc Alison had, but hell, I envied you for being their kid, too.

"When I was visiting her in the hospital, I thought it was small repayment for all she'd ever done for me, and when she came out of that trance, I thought I was some sort of fucking hero. And then she had that heart attack." He let go of her, and walked away, keeping his back to her as he continued. "That night—"

"Don't, Sash. It doesn't matter. My mother loved

you, and she will thank you forever for setting her free of that nightmare she was locked away in."

He turned around, and he was smiling though the pain was still in his eyes. "Yeah, I finally came to realize that myself. And that's when I knew I had to start living for me again. I told my dad I was going to try my hand at painting full time for a while, and he told me to go for it."

"I'm glad," she said. "I'm really, really glad."

"So, now I'm almost whole again," he said.

Lily held her breath. "Almost?"

He nodded. "This half"—he indicated himself with a circling wave of his hand—"is well and good, but my other half isn't with me anymore." He met her gaze with his, and held it until he asked, "Is it?"

Lily laughed and stepped into him, wrapping her arms around his neck. "You talk too much, you know it, Rivers?"

"You're a hard sell."

"No, I'm not. I just wanted to hear you beg."

"How did I do?"

"If your art doesn't take off, we'll give you a cup and put you out on the street. You're a natural."

"Funny girl."

"Mmhm, but there are other things I do better."

"I remember. But before we get to that, do you think you could kiss me?"

"Sure, if you'll stop talking so much. You haven't shut up since you got here."

"Well, I had—"

"Okay," she said, plying his ear and throat with kisses, "if you're going to keep talking, say something in Russian."

"But I only know how to say one thing."

Lily giggled. "I know."

Epilogue

The woman sat at the kitchen table in her two-story West Hill Road house. A book that was yellowed and brittle with time, yet well preserved, lay open in front of her.

She leaned heavily on fisted hands as she pondered the greatest question she'd ever faced.

What to do?

She remembered well what Grandma Daisy had told her more than a decade before. She was to be the guardian of the original journal printed in Rose Price's own hand.

"Our predecessor was a woman with incredible understanding of the human animus," Grandma Daisy had told her solemnly though she hadn't understood exactly what that meant. But before she could ask, her grandma had continued. "Rose recognized the inalienable truth that women are the superior gender just as she realized that often the most childlike among us are sometimes the only ones we can trust to see through all the hubris that has been responsible for the fall of entire empires."

Jenny Lynn Afton hadn't understood any of that, but she'd known what Grandma wanted her to do with the book. And she'd kept it hidden all these long years. But how did she go about selecting another quorum of eight worthy of wearing the cloak of Rose and ruling Rosehill?

She squared her shoulders. She'd find the way. The ghosts of her ancestors and the unborn of future generations were depending on her. Rosehill had always been theirs. It would be again.